"Dorothea Benton Frank is the bad girl of southern fiction—
the bad, bad girl. Her books are funny, sexy,
and usually damp with seawater."
—Pat Conroy

Praise for Dorothea Benton Frank's
Isle of Palms

"*Isle of Palms* is as light and gratifying as a sand dollar just washed to
shore . . . The author and Anna like to remind folks of the things that
matter most: finding inner peace, learning to forgive, and cherishing
friends who become family." —*The Atlanta Journal-Constitution*

"Entertaining . . . Garrulous, engaging Anna's a treat, talking up a
storm about life in the South Carolina Lowcountry as she makes her
second coming of age. Really, it's best just to take Anna's initial
advice—sit back, relax, sip some sweet tea, and listen up. She's got a
story to tell." —*Orlando Sentinel*

"[A] page-turner." —*St. Petersburg Times*

"Frank uses the same sweet southern charms that enticed readers to
her previous novels, *Sullivan's Island* and *Plantation* . . . A fun summer
read, and its scenery entices the reader to take a trip to the beach."
—*The Daily Oklahoman*

"Beneath the Fannie Flagg–style jocularity and small-town anecdotes
lies a more serious subject: loneliness. Credit this unlikely cast of
characters with having the strength to form unconventional loving
relationships, an ad hoc family of sorts, to fill the void left by their
less-than-perfect biological ones. Upbeat and uplifting, Anna's song is
one of hope in the face of modern realities for all those whose dreams
have been derailed by circumstance." —*The Fort Myers News-Press*

continued . . .

Sullivan's Island

Isle of Palms

A Lowcountry Tale

Dorothea Benton Frank

BERKLEY BOOKS, NEW YORK

THE BERKLEY PUBLISHING GROUP
Published by the Penguin Group
Penguin Group (USA) Inc.
375 Hudson Street, New York, New York 10014, USA
Penguin Group (Canada), 10 Alcorn Avenue, Toronto, Ontario M4V 3B2, Canada
(a division of Pearson Penguin Canada Inc.)
Penguin Books Ltd., 80 Strand, London WC2R 0RL, England
Penguin Group Ireland, 25 St. Stephen's Green, Dublin 2, Ireland (a division of Penguin Books Ltd.)
Penguin Group (Australia), 250 Camberwell Road, Camberwell, Victoria 3124, Australia
(a division of Pearson Australia Group Pty. Ltd.)
Penguin Books India Pvt. Ltd., 11 Community Centre, Panchsheel Park, New Delhi—110 017, India
Penguin Group (NZ), Cnr. Airborne and Rosedale Roads, Albany, Auckland 1310, New Zealand
(a division of Pearson New Zealand Ltd.)
Penguin Books (South Africa) (Pty.) Ltd., 24 Sturdee Avenue, Rosebank, Johannesburg 2196,
South Africa

Penguin Books Ltd., Registered Offices: 80 Strand, London WC2R 0RL, England

PRINTING HISTORY
Berkley hardcover edition / July 2003
Berkley mass-market edition / July 2004
Berkley trade paperback edition / January 2005

Berkley trade paperback ISBN: 0-425-20010-8

The Library of Congress has cataloged the Berkley hardcover edition as follows:

Frank, Dorothea Benton.
    Isle of palms: a lowcountry tale / Dorothea Benton Frank.
        p. cm.
    ISBN 0-425-19136-2
    1. Women—South Carolina—Fiction.   2. Isle of Palms (S.C.)—Fiction.   3. South Carolina—
Fiction.   4. Islands—Fiction.   I. Title.

PS3556.R3338185 2003
813'.6—dc21
                                                                    2003044442

PRINTED IN THE UNITED STATES OF AMERICA

10 9 8 7 6 5 4 3 2 1

For my wonderful children,
Victoria and William

Barrier Island

Where nothing is certain, we awaken
to another night of delicate rain
falling as if it didn't want to
disturb anyone. On and off
foghorns groan. The lighthouse beacon
circles the island. For hours, melancholy
waves tear whatever land we're standing on.
Listen to sea—rain dripping
Through fog, suspended at the edge of the earth
on a circle of sand where we are always
moving slowly toward land.

—MARJORY WENTWORTH,
poet laureate of South Carolina

Contents

Acknowledgments

THIS story is the result of the friendship and support of many people. First, I want to thank my family—Peter, Victoria, and William—for their unwavering support and great ideas on certain scenes and dialogue. It can't be easy to live with someone who lives behind a closed door half the time. I love y'all more than I could ever say. And I want to offer some seriously bended knee thanks to my beautiful daughter, Victoria, who helped me plot many chapters in this book involving Emily and made sure her language and slang rang true. You mean a teenager in the year 2002 wouldn't say *neato*, *groovy*, or *golly gee whiz?* Thanks, sweetheart, for putting this old poop on the right track.

Here comes the disclaimer: the grandmother in this book bears no resemblance to my actual mother-in-law. Hanna Frank of Dearborn, Michigan, is a saintly woman, a gentle woman, who did indeed immigrate to the United States after World War II. She was very generous to allow me to use some of her experiences, but the personality of Violet Lutz in this story is a raving paranoid. Hanna Frank is perfectly sane, extremely intelligent, and thank God, she possesses a healthy sense of humor.

And naturally, I want to thank Shannon Gibbons, my best girl-friend, for proofing this and for listening to me moan when the going got tough. Rar rar rar! That's an inside joke about talking dogs, but she'll know what I mean.

I thought it would be fun to use a lot of real people as characters in this book so I want to thank the following warm, wonderful and trusting people for the use of their names: Big Al from Shem Creek Bar & Grill and of course John and Angie Avinger, who own the place, for their generosity. Next, Mary Meehan, Mrs. Helen Clarkin, and Miss Marguerite Stith, who live in these pages as clients of the Palms Salon. Marilyn and Billy Davey, Betty Hudson, Larry Dodds, Patty Grisillo, Brigitte Miklaszewski, Bill the Butcher, Tommy Proctor, Dominique Simon, Ed Williams, Sparky Witte, and Miss Vicki, formerly of Dunleavy's fame, and of course Patty and Bill Dunleavy, who own it and serve up the best hamburgers to be found. And special kudos to the Mayor of Sullivan's Island, Marshall Stith, who owns the Station Twenty-two Restaurant. I asked him why his shrimp and grits were so good and he said probably it's the butter and the half-and-half. Great. Good-bye, belt. Hello, sweatpants.

Special thanks to one of my oldest and dearest childhood friends, Francesca Jean Gianaris. Hey, Fran! Aren't we due for a *Big Chill* weekend on the island? Don't forget, okay? To Charlie Moore for his extraordinary goodwill and the use of *so good it'd make a bulldog break his chain!* And huge thanks and love to my brother, Michael Benton, of Irving, Texas, a.k.a. the Reverend Ben Michaels, for performing the wedding! Lord, honey! We all thought those two would never tie the knot! You done good!

Gargantuan thanks to all the salon community, who perform miracles every day and who gave me great advice and stories to tell—Francis DuBose of London Hair in Mount Pleasant, the entire cast of characters from Salon and Company on the Isle of Palms, and last but not least, that fabulously talented and wickedly funny magician William Howe of the John Barrett Salon in New York.

Thanks to Bruce and all the guys at the Wine Connection in Pound Ridge, New York, for the correct vino to go with Anna and Jim's dinner at High Cotton in Charleston, South Carolina. Think it's easy to plan dinner, do you? Yeah, well, I hadda bring in some high-tone talent for that one!

Many thanks also to Marjory Wentworth for her friendship and support. Madge! Love you, girl! When are you coming up? Special thanks to Michael Uslan, my Hollywood producer friend of *Batman* and *Swamp Thing* fame, who believes my crazy books should be movies and keeps trying to move that along with ideas while he's busy with ninety-two projects of his own. Michael, if a serious offer ever shows up, you know who I'm calling, don't you? Good. Okay. That's settled then. And thanks to Mary Jo McInerny for her love, vigilance, humor, and everything—she's the greatest cousin and friend a girl could have. And we have to discuss my other cousin, Charles "Comar" Blanchard Jr. Thank you, thank you, thank you! Without this handsome, young, talented fellow, my family could never enjoy the inner coastal waterway or sleep as well as we do when we are there. And Dennis Craver of Beaufort—what a great friend you are too! Honey, this man can flat steam some oysters! Also thanks to Alex and Zoe Sanders. To Jonathan Green, for lifting us up to a higher place. Love you, man!

To Cassandra King, who is my writer buddy (and who wrote *The Sunday Wife*—go buy it!), for her friendship, advice, humor, support, and just for being such an inspiration to us all. And, okay, Pat Conroy, the Franks love you to pieces always and forever. You among all men we know have paid their lifetime dues with us. We will split the check where others go into comas. Come on back, anytime. Did y'all read his new book—*My Losing Season*? Everything he writes is fabulous. Gotcha, bubba!

To Robert and Susan Rosen of Charleston for their decades of amazing friendship and generous support of my new career—I can't think of a soul who wouldn't be thrilled and honored to call y'all their friends.

Special thanks to the township offices of the Isle of Palms and Mount Pleasant for providing me with statistical information and good humor.

And now for the big kahunas at Berkley Publishing. Gee whiz. Where do I start? For Norman Lidofsky and his crew of Houdinis, I offer my services to polish your shoes. Okay, maybe I didn't mean that literally, but my gratitude isn't fiction. But you know how indebted I am to all of you. As always to Joni Friedman, my art director, for her unsurpassed visions of great beauty and to Rich Hasselberger, for your extraordinary efforts on my behalf, please accept my most sincere thanks.

Obviously, I kiss the ground my magnificent and fearless publisher, Leslie Gelbman, walks on and thank her in all my prayers for her extreme patience, excellent guidance, and generous support. For Liz Perl and Hillary Schupf? Man! I love y'all so big time! Not only are you both brilliant but you make the hard parts of selling books such a breeze. Thank you, thank you. And so do you, Matthew Rich. Mr. Planet PR, I've got a place in my heart for you forever. And Buzzy Porter? Okay. Insider information: All southern writers, no, all writers on book tour should try to schedule a signing with Buzzy at B&N in Mount Pleasant, South Carolina. It will blow your mind at how this man can organize an event. Needless to say, you'll sell a whole lot of books. Besides all that, Buzzy is a doll baby to work with. Little Debbies and cappuccinos! Love you, Buzzy! Crazy name but a very sane and very wonderful man.

And I know she's sick to death of plays on her name, but who wouldn't want their editor to have Fortune for a last name? Gail Fortune is the extraordinary talent behind anything worth a rip that comes out of my work. Not only does she have the capacity to see from day one what I'm trying to accomplish with a story, but she's got the tool chest to help me get the job done. Never unkind, never anxious, always available. Gail, it's you and me, baby. Forever! And, thank you for everything over and over.

For my agent, Amy Berkower? Well, Amy? I never talk to you that I don't learn something new about this crazy world. Thanks for understanding me and for all of your excellent help. Tell Al I still owe it all to his book—*Writing the Blockbuster Novel.*

Finally, I'd like to say thank you to all the readers and booksellers. I've loved all the emails. I've loved being in your stores. Most of all I've loved connecting with you, especially when my stories inspire you to tell me yours. In a few short years you've shown me a truth that I suspected was there all along—that storytelling allows people to find common ground and better understand each other. In this very imperfect and uncertain world, a little more understanding and tolerance can only be a very good thing. Thank you and love you from the bottom of my heart, 'eah?

Isle of Palms

Prologue

OKAY. I had a dream about my mother last night and I always seem to dream of her when she has had a beyond-the-veil itch to scratch my back. She was waltzing with my father at an enormous celebration of some kind. They were smiling and having a wonderful time. I couldn't remember ever seeing Doc so happy or Momma so beautiful. She never said a word. She just smiled at me. I had so many questions I wanted to ask her but for some reason, I couldn't speak.

The next thing I knew, I could sense the light of morning growing all around me. I must have been born with the thinnest eyelids in the world. You know how that is? Well, I realized I was awake. But for a few moments I hung on to the fringes of sleep, trying to retain the details of everything I had seen. I wondered, like I always did, if there was a larger meaning to the dream. Half of my DNA is German, but it was the all-American Lowcountry remainder that wore itself out to a frazzle searching for cosmic explanations.

Maybe something *was* going to happen. Had we all been at a wedding? The old salts said that when you dreamed about weddings it meant the opposite, that something was coming to an end. More change? No, thanks.

That was when my feet hit the floor. There was no way another blessed change *could* happen without me pitching a hissy fit. Big time. We'd had enough change around here to choke a goat. We had made it through Thanksgiving and were now trying to focus on Christmas. Thanksgiving had been enough to make anybody's head burst like an overripe melon. Like Bettina says all the time, *it's enough already.* Bettina's from New York. She's our manicurist and you'll love her when you meet her.

There's so much to tell you about.

Anyway, next I got myself a cup of coffee—ground Colombian beans with a piece of split vanilla bean thrown in the filter—and went outside to get the paper and look at the sky. The first thing I noticed was that my blasted garden still continued to climb all over my trees and my house. Every night it took over a little more. Not that it wasn't pretty. Hell, no! It was nothing less than a horticultural miracle. Jack's beanstalk.

The sky looked fine, no storms coming or anything like that. In fact, it was going to be a beautiful day. I stood there watching the sun rise on the Isle of Palms. Right then and there, I decided that my dream had been a message that it was way past time to tell my story. So, here I am.

Now, you don't know me yet, but by the time I'm all done working my jaw, you're gonna see that I'm not one to blab. Even though I've heard more tales than every bartender in Ireland, I've always tried to keep my distance from trouble. Gossip was trouble and I gave it a wide berth. At least I had tried to. Not that I hadn't had my share of tight spots. Lord! Jeesch! Man! There were days when I thought the devil himself was out to get me. Maybe he had been, but lately, I had been feeling like he thought he'd given me his pitchfork enough. Not that I'm suspicious, but don't repeat that, okay? Saying things were going great might get his attention.

Here's the thing that had landed me in trouble in the first place.

Most of my years had been spent careening through life, keeping my plans on a back burner. I kept waiting to live. But wasn't that what women did? Didn't we always put duty to others before our own ambitions? Were we not the caretakers, the peacemakers, the homemakers, the ones who told our men and our children that we would always be behind them, no matter what? We told them that everything would be alright and that life was worth living.

Well, most of us tried to do these things. Not all women. Some women were so mean if you looked at them funny your hair could turn into snakes. But all they ever got themselves by being mean was older and more bitter. Ooh! I'd tolerated a few women like that for too long. Somebody better tell them to run and hide because Anna's talking now. That's me. Anna Lutz Abbot.

My professional life has earned me nothing but beat-up eardrums and a grossly underexercised tongue, mainly because I own a salon. I've been working in the salon world for getting on to twenty years. See, when my clients bared their souls, what I thought and what I said were very often two different things. Who in this world has the privilege to really speak their minds? The lunatics, honey, that's who. Naked truth from my lips would have put me in the poorhouse long ago. Besides, isn't it better to try to deal with people and all their problems with some little bit of sympathy? Of course it is. But, bottom line? I have heard it ALL!

Have I got a story to tell? Yeah, honey, let's get you a glass of sweet tea and then plop yourself right down in my chair. I'm gonna tell you a lot of secrets, but if I hear them told, I'll come after your tongue with my shears. Or worse, my hammer! Yes, I will. This entire tale is true to the very last word and all the names and places are real to expose the guilty.

I was telling Arthur the other day—Arthur is the man who drives me crazy with the shivers—that I had been thinking that maybe it was time to tell some people about how my whole world had changed in just a few months. If it could happen to me it could happen to anybody, right? He laughed so hard I thought he might up and die on me, so I said, Just what the hell is so funny, and he said, Since when *don't* you talk? I was not amused. Not at all. No.

Besides my own discoveries, it had occurred to me that it would be très cool if people knew about another side of life in the Lowcountry and baby, there's plenty to talk about. Every possible thing you needed to know about southern living was discussed under the roof of Anna's Cabana—and don't tell me, I know: Anna's Cabana sounds like the name of a seedy juke joint on the back beaches of the Virgin Islands. It does! But, when you come to understand how it was given that name, you'll see why I let it happen.

In any case, my crazy little salon is a gold mine in human behavior studies. When you take one part old salts, mix it up with gentrification and garnish it with tourists, you got yourself one mighty cocktail, 'eah? What happened here a few months ago literally turned the tide. It did. In any case, if I charged the same for listening as I charge for fixing hair, I would own the biggest house on this beach. No joke.

And this whole drama isn't just about what I hear at work. No, no. There's a whole universe here on this island. We say we are from Charleston, but we are really from East of the Cooper—Cooper River, that is. Around here you're either from Charleston, East of the Cooper, West of the Ashley (that's the other big river), or out by Awendaw. Maybe you lived in one of these weird developments that keep cropping up that look like a movie set of downtown or one of the islands you could only get to by boat. The point is that in this neck of the woods, you can better believe that where you hang your hat makes all the difference in how you tick. I am and have always been an island girl and there was nothing to be done about it.

My family hasn't been in Charleston for a thousand years. We don't have some grand family home, plantation or any silver we rescued from the Yankees by hiding it in the bricks of our chimney. In fact, I don't own a lick of silver and it suits me fine. Polishing silver would not be the best use of my time. But we do love the history of the Lowcountry with a wild passion and we romanticize it all, telling ourselves we are anything except ordinary just because we can call this place home.

My momma and her people were from Beaufort and I guess the only thing unusual about my background is that my daddy immigrated here with his parents after World War II. They wound up in Estill and were peach farmers. That means my daddy and his daddy worked like coolies to get to where they got and what they got was a comfortable but unspectacular life with no frills.

I can tell you right now that I was never indulged, coddled, or overly nurtured. But that was probably because my daddy's family had to fight for their very survival. Things were tough in the early days for them and for me too. For the longest time it seemed like my life would be an endless exercise of pushing big rocks up a hill. Take money. My daddy was the one who taught me the value of a dollar. Okay, he's got a reputation for being a massive tightwad but he can't help it. And, sometimes when I least expected it, his wallet would open, the moths would escape, and then the buckolas would start to flow. He's full of contradictions, just like everybody else. Anyway, I learned from him that saving money and perseverance could get you something you wanted if you wanted it badly enough. And the only thing I ever really wanted was to get back to the Isle of Palms and live my life.

That took longer than it should have, to say the very least. But you see, nothing in my life ever happened quite the same way it did for the other people I knew. Everything happened in wild extremes, which made for a whole lot of hullabaloo and lessons in life. Frankly, I could do without more learning experiences for a while. (Lord, I hope You heard that.) The most important thing I learned is that to be truly happy, you've got to pay attention to that stupid little inner voice we all have. It knows what you need and will drive you shit crazy until you listen to it. Guaranteed. My New Age clients—and I know them on sight because they wear crystals to which they have attached human names—call it *connecting with the universe*. Like my daughter says, whatever. I'll just stick with my own name for it, thanks. Now, that inner voice thing sounds simple but you wouldn't believe how many people I know who are stuck in the rut they dug for themselves. And the good Lord didn't mean for so many people to be so unbelievably dissatisfied with their lives. I'm pretty sure about that.

Think about it. If you spend ten years thinking you wish you could go to China, then there's a good chance the experience would give your soul something it really needs. I'm not talking about people who say, Damn, I wish I could run away to China this minute. Running away never solved a daggum thing. In fact, real happiness is hidden in facing yourself, asking yourself what it is you really want out of this life and then being honest about it. By the way, you couldn't pay me money to go to China.

I'm lucky because I *always* knew what I wanted. It just took one helluva long time to get it, that's all. For me to be content and happy, I had to be on this particular island. I mean, I couldn't breathe right anyplace else. I'm serious. I've asked other people who live here what they think about that and they actually agree with me. They don't feel like they belong anyplace else either. And, my whole spirit is stronger here.

Naturally, I have a little theory about why that's so. Islanders are their own species. We have to live near the ocean to stay in touch with our souls. Everything is amplified. The breeze is sweeter, the air is thicker, the sun is relentless, and the nights are more mysterious. God's fingerprints are all over it and, before y'all go get your knickers in a knot, I know that you should go to church but I also believe you can talk to God anywhere. Especially on the Isle of Palms.

We're not a bunch of shiftless pansies either. We're actually a pretty courageous bunch, usually unafraid of anything that Mother Nature slings our way. Hurricanes? Big deal. This may sound crazy but for some peculiar reason we need to, no, we *have* to stand in front of the angry ocean right before a storm hits. When I was little my daddy, Doc, would say, Anna?—let's go have a look at what the Atlantic is up to before the eye hits. We would stand on a sand dune and inhale enough salt to actually elevate our blood pressure. It was good for us.

Evacuations? We usually stayed at home. Until Hugo. Then everybody threw up their arms and said, just why did we pay these hefty insurance premiums in the first place? If the hurricane was a real monster, we just packed up our precious belongings and the family photographs and got out of town. We'd let the old storm have her way for a day or two and then we cleaned up her mess. Afterward, we'd rock away the nights on each other's porches, laughing and telling stories about hurricanes for a million years.

Islanders recognize something kindred in each other. Shoot, if I get a tourist in my chair and she says she's from North Carolina I handle her one way . . . like a Yankee, but don't let's go around telling that, okay? But if she tells me that she lives in Wrightsville Beach, well, then she gets treated like an old friend.

Beach people love life harder than anybody else. We do! We have a tendency to be, well, slightly excessive in our behavior. You usually won't see us eat one boiled peanut, drink one beer, tell one joke or get just a little bit of sun. So if you tell me you're from a beach, I *know* who you are. Except if you're from California where everything wiggles. See what I mean? Hurricanes don't ruffle me, but earthquakes? Not me, sugar.

People who live on islands are generally unpretentious too. This is a quality that is greatly overlooked and undervalued by others. Look at all those people who live in New York. They have outfits for everything! They have jogging clothes, which aren't the same as their workout clothes, which aren't the same as their weekend clothes and, Lord have mercy on us, every stitch they own is black! Shoot! They probably blow out their hair to go around the corner to buy a newspaper!

I just couldn't live like that. I mean, God bless them, they've had their trials for sure. It's just that I don't think life is supposed to take that much effort. Down here in the Lowcountry, we just prefer to take things a little slower and savor each moment.

Arthur says that in New York City dinner for two in a fancy restaurant can cost hundreds and hundreds of dollars. You could spend a right good bit of money down here on dinner too. That is, if you wanted to drive to Charleston. Out here on this island, you'd probably have to wait twenty minutes for a table, if you went to a restaurant that took reservations (which they don't), because we don't like to rush people when they're trying to have supper and enjoy each other's company. Actually, most of us would rather stay home and eat what somebody caught that day along with a salad or something. Maybe it's because of the heat, but our big meal is in the middle of the day, if we can manage that much time for dinner. But supper (which is called dinner elsewhere) is usually a smaller meal.

Island people aren't like other people out there across the cause-way and we don't want to be either. We have our own style of every-thing and our own point of view. Living here makes you practical. I knew all along that my business would be recession proof. Go ask any woman you know. If it's a toss-up between doing her roots and buying a dress, she's getting her hair done before you can blink. And I knew, or at least I hoped, that my old clients wouldn't mind coming over here from Charleston. Every last one came because when women find a hairdresser they like, they stick with them like white on rice.

And then there are the transplants. These days it seems like every-one I meet is from Ohio. All these folks moved here to live. I tell them, Look, sugar, you might not be able to become a Charlestonian until you've been dead for a bazillion generations. But! I say, you can become an islander and they seem plenty happy with that.

Attitude is everything in life, isn't it? We are all capable of change. Even me. In the last six months, I found myself believing in the basic goodness of people again, and in the power of love and in miracles. You don't believe in miracles? Well, when we're all done here, come on by my house and see my yard.

I had somebody from a magazine stop by my house the other day. This fellow was a horticulturalist and a photographer for some maga-zine in Vermont or someplace like that. He wanted to know what kind of fertilizer I used. I laughed so hard I had to reapply my mascara. I said, Honey, I don't use a thing except Lowcountry air and island magic! He shook his head and left, thinking I was playing with his head. But I had told him the truth. I never lie. Okay, I might leave out some facts but that's different.

I'm sure you've heard all these stories about the South being haunted and people here talking to the dead and seeing ghosts. Bad news. They are all true. Every last one of them is true. Things happen here all the time that you can't explain. That's just the Lowcountry. When you get out to the islands, the weird factor accelerates. We don't mind. We adore the bizarre and inexplicable as much as we treasure our eccentrics.

Every life has its share of trouble. Like Miss Angel says, every dog has his day but every cat has his afternoon. Miss Angel is my next-door neighbor and the neighborhood philosopher. She's also a regular Edgar Cayce. I dream, but not like her. But don't worry, we'll get to her. There are a lot of people I want you to meet.

I wasn't always content, you know. I went through some hellish suffering to finally love my life. But I never gave up hope. Like I said, it was my early years that were the worst. I had to go through them to understand what was worth fighting for and what wasn't and I needed to learn how to just get along in the world. I guess the best place to start would be with Momma.

Do you need some more tea? Well, let's get it now because I've been holding back the tide for a long time. I think all the failures and victories of my life have come together pretty nice—like a string of graduated pearls. I can talk about Momma now without being upset but, when I was ten? Honey, I would rather have taken a stick in my eye than hear her name so much as whispered.

One

Hearts of Fire

~~~~~~~

1975

THIS is what I remember. That day, all I could think about was getting home and riding my bicycle. In my ten-year-old opinion, I had wasted the best hours of my day as a prisoner of the Sullivan's Island Elementary School, in a hot stuffy classroom, on the receiving end of an education that I was absolutely sure was entirely unnecessary. It was late May and the temperature was already up there in the stratosphere.

Teenagers with surfboards and suntans crossed every intersection of the islands coming to and from the beach. Summer residents were already arriving in hordes and my vacation was overdue. I could barely concentrate on anything except going barefoot.

I climbed up on the school bus at two forty-five and rushed for a seat by a window, that is, a window that would open. It's funny what the mind remembers and what it forgets. Like most girls would, I remember exactly what I wore. It was my pale yellow sundress, hand-smocked with green thread. I had on green sandals that matched. I was a major hot tamale in that dress. It was true. In the pecking order of my peers, I had the best clothes. Not the best hair (blond and thin) and not the best face (too pale—invisible eyebrows and lashes), but definitely the best clothes. I remember thinking that even though I had on my favorite dress that day, the humid weather and the proximity of summer vacation were making me cranky.

As I struggled to push the window open, I began to perspire. It just annoyed me that the adults in charge of our lives gave so little consideration to the comfort of children. Our desks were so hard on our bony little backsides, it was no wonder we squirmed around like our britches were spray-starched with itching powder. Weighted down by books, we were positive we would grow up with warped bones. The steaming cafeteria could clean your pores. Everything about life seemed worrisome and inconvenient. Even the paper towels in the girls' bathroom had a chemical smell and were so stiff that you were better off just to dry your hands on your clothes, if you washed your hands at all, which, of course, I always did. Germs.

Worst of all, by May, the voices of our teachers were like unending white noise—just some droning yammer in the background. I'd had enough of the fifth grade and I knew one thing for sure. When I grew up, I was determined to change a few things about the slipshod way children were treated by the authorities.

That day, I was just all a-twitter recounting my juvenile list of complaints as I boarded the ancient yellow rattletrap to go home. The only good thing about the bus ride was Lovely Leon, the driver. He was so cute and he flirted with all of us girls. His longish straight brown hair was always in his eyes, which I found irresistible. We loved him and our little hearts danced when he winked at us. Leon was a senior in high school, but he finished classes at two o'clock and was hired to drive us home. Because I lived at the end of the Isle of Palms, I got to ride with him longer, as most of the others got off the bus sooner. Sometimes he would start with the furthest stop and work his way back. And that was what he did that day.

In the back of the bus, Eddie Williams (the first stop on his route) was giving Patty Grisillo (the third stop on his route) an Indian burn of Olympic quality. She was biting him on the arm. Hard. They were both screaming. Patty's friends were whacking Eddie with their backpacks and Eddie's friends were laughing and telling him to cut it out.

"Y'all are acting like a bunch of idiots!" Leon said. "Eddie? Get your butt up here and work the door! I'm going to the Isle of Palms first!"

The bus lumbered up Middle Street toward Breach Inlet at twenty-five miles an hour, moaning and complaining with every shift of the gears. Restless drivers passed us and we swore they would get tickets for passing a school bus. We made faces through the windows and hollered at the top of our little lungs at the disrespectful criminals who zoomed around us. They were merely further proof of the overall disregard adults had for children.

We crossed the bridge and headed for Forty-first Avenue, way up at the end of the island. Everybody was carrying on, despite Leon's pleas to *Please y'all! Shut the hell up!*

Somebody, Sparky Witte, I think, said, "Look at all the police cars!"

All at once, the bus became quiet. There was a huge commotion where I lived. Fire engines appeared behind us and Leon pulled over to let them roar past. They were from the Sullivan's Island Fire and Rescue Squad. Must be huge, I thought. We followed them, going a little faster than before.

When we got to Forty-first Avenue, the police had blocked off the road. People were all over the streets. Leon didn't know what to do, so he stopped and waited for a moment. I started to shake, afraid that whatever the trouble was, that it was happening at my house.

Leon got off and told us to stay put and be quiet. He walked over to a police officer and must have explained his predicament. He had a kid on the bus who lived on that street and what should he do? The police officer walked over to the bus with Leon, boarded the bus, and called my name.

"Anna Lutz?"

"Yes, sir?" I felt numb.

"Come with me, honey."

I looked at this uniformed stranger with the gun on his hip and knew something terrible had happened. Lillian, my best friend, wanted to come with me, but he said, *No, just Anna.* It wasn't a good idea, he said. Lillian started to cry and so did I. I still remember her crying and everyone saying, *Oh, no! What happened? Call us, Anna, okay? You okay?*

I wasn't okay. Not one bit. How could I be anything *but* scared to death? I walked with the policeman who introduced himself as Beau. He held my sweaty hand and carried my backpack for me. I knew something horrific was waiting for me. As we rounded the corner, I saw it all.

My house was surrounded by police cars. It frightened me so badly I wanted to run. I just stood there with this Beau person, waiting for someone to explain this to me. *What did it all mean? Had my house been robbed? Did they get away? Did they steal all our stuff? Were there a bunch of bad guys still inside—was that why so many police cars were there?*

Our neighbors were like statues in their yards, rooted by the spectacle before them. The Emergency Medical Service ambulances and attendants waited with a stretcher. When I saw Daddy's car, I panicked. *Was he in there? Oh! My God! What about Momma? Where was she? Where were they? Where were they?*

Out of nowhere my daddy appeared by my side and lifted me up. He was breathing so hard I started getting hysterical. I couldn't understand what was happening but I knew it was a catastrophe.

"Momma is . . . Momma's had a terrible heart attack," he said. "I'm so sorry, Anna." Did that mean she was dead? He shook and gulped while he held on to me. Then he coughed, pulled out his handkerchief and blew his nose, hard. "Oh! Dear God! Why? How could I let this happen?"

I couldn't talk; I could scarcely breathe. Did he have something to do with it? I could only watch. *Momma was dead?* It just didn't seem possible to me. The rescue workers had disappeared inside the house. Shortly, they came back out with a body on a stretcher. It was

Momma. She was covered in a sheet. The ambulance attendants zipped a bag around her. A few minutes later, the police reappeared with a man. His shirt was unbuttoned. From where I stood he seemed to be in handcuffs. Was he? I started screaming. *What did he do to my momma?*

"Hush!"

The *hush* came from our neighbor, Miss Mavis, who broke through the crowd and grabbed me by the arm. It seemed she wanted to take me to her house on the next block.

"This child doesn't need to see all of this, Douglas! Have you lost your mind? Someone should have brought her to me right away. Come on, baby!"

She started to lead me away with Daddy bringing up the rear. My mother had not spoken to Miss Mavis for a long time. They'd had an argument about something so I thought it was a little peculiar for her to jump into the middle of this. Momma said she had a tongue as long as a telephone wire and that she was going to hell for gossiping. But since Daddy was coming along with me and Miss Mavis, I went without arguing. It was no time to resist adult decisions.

Miss Mavis had a house worthy of a full-scale investigation, but I would not have wanted to live there. I think because she had multitudinous cats, she thought it was necessary to stick one of those deodorant frogs or shells on every table and potpourri in bowls all over the place. It smelled seriously sickening to me. On the occasions I would stop by for a cookie with some kids from the neighborhood, we would always hold our noses. The minute we got out of there we hollered *Phew!* and laughed about it, making gagging noises for the rest of the afternoon.

Her house was divided in two, upstairs and downstairs. She lived on top and could see the ocean, and Miss Angel, who worked for her, lived downstairs. Miss Angel was much more interesting than Miss Mavis. She could trace her ancestors back to slavery. She was also a master basket weaver. She had so many stories, her stories had stories.

We would always see Miss Angel sitting in the backyard, weaving sweetgrass, sewing it around and around with a strip of palmetto, or on other days shucking corn or stringing beans. If we were too tired or hot to run around anymore, we would wander into her shadow, asking her what she was doing.

"Ain' you chillrun have nothing better to do than come around 'eah bothering Angel?"

She would stare us up and down, one by one.

"No, ma'am," we would say.

"Well, then I expect y'all want something to drink?"

"Yes, ma'am."

She would sigh, put down whatever she was doing, and, like ducks, we would follow her into her kitchen. Then the storytelling would start.

"When I was a girl, we had to *pump* our water . . ."

When she got warmed up she would go on and on.

"Tha's right! My daddy, he say to me, 'Angel?—be my angel and go fill this 'eah bucket like a good girl. Lawd! That girl is strong like two bull ox!' Tha's fuh true, 'eah? You chillrun don't know what hard times is! I hope y'all helps your momma when she call. Do you?"

"Oh! Yes, ma'am!" we would all say, lying through our teeth.

"All right, then. Angel gone give y'all fresh lemonade she make this morning. Just this morning I say, Angel?—gone be hot like de Debbil's breath today! Better have something fuh dem bad chillrun when they come 'round, and come 'round y'all surely did. Drink up and gwine leave me be!"

Homemade lemonade! Wonderful! She thrilled us all the time.

Miss Mavis was the exact opposite of Miss Angel. Momma said she was always *putting on airs*, whatever that meant. Miss Mavis had a daughter who was away at college and a son who was married, living way off in California trying to be a movie star. She would show me his publicity pictures and tell me that he was up for a commercial or a part in a movie. Daddy always said her son was a damn fool because he had changed his name from Thurmond to Fritz. I didn't know which name was more stupid.

Miss Mavis and Miss Angel were the neighborhood's official but revered old biddies. They had taught us plenty, and contrary to what Miss Angel thought about us being just a bunch of spoiled Geechee brats, I was to learn what *hard times* were.

We climbed the steps up to Miss Mavis's part of the house and the minute we stepped inside you couldn't smell anything except dried flowers and pine. I sat on the couch, crying and hiccuping. Miss Mavis handed me a box of Kleenex, covered in needlepoint with magnolia flowers on a red background. She was one of those craft people.

"I don't understand," I said. "Who was that man? Was Momma murdered? Was he a robber?"

"No, baby, I'm sure he didn't murder her. Good gracious! Too much television!"

I started to wail. What a mean thing to say! I wasn't crying because of some television program! My momma was dead! Daddy was rubbing a hole in my back. He was in shock himself and I guess he couldn't begin to think of what to do with me.

"Come on now, Anna," Miss Mavis said, "let's blow our nose, all right? I'm gonna go over to your house with your daddy and see what we can find out. You just stay put and we'll be right back, okay?"

"Okay," I said, and thought for a second about why grown-ups said stupid things like let's blow *our* nose. Miss Mavis was nice, but she was making me mad.

When they closed the door behind them I felt very alone, confused and out of place. I didn't know what I was supposed to be doing while they were gone. I mean, watching television seemed inappropriate. Calling Lillian didn't seem right either. I guess I was sort of stupefied because the only thing I seemed capable of doing was looking around the room and wondering how something so awful could happen to me. I could feel a terrible weariness in my chest and for a moment I worried that there was something wrong with my heart too. What if Momma and I died on the same day? I didn't want to die. I tried to relax.

Miss Mavis's coffee table was covered with magazines and her end tables were jammed with framed photographs. I wasn't interested in any of it, but then my eye caught a picture of her in her wedding dress that must have been a million years old. She looked pretty in that picture and really young. Momma always said that her husband ran around on her like his pants were in flames, and he turned his liver into a rock. When he died, Miss Mavis went around telling the immediate world that he was a saint. He wasn't any saint. Even I knew that.

Daddy, who had as many stories as Angel, used to tell me a story about this pirate named Major Stede Bonnet. People said he became a pirate to get away from his nagging wife. Well, he wound up with his neck in a rope. I never understood how somebody could do something so mean to his family and his liver and then get to be a saint. I wasn't absolutely positive what *running around* meant, but I figured it had to do with other women. Stede Bonnet would've told him he'd be better off to just stay home and behave himself. Anyway, this slew of happy family pictures was pitiful because Momma told me Miss Mavis and all her people were all a bunch of screwballs.

Momma. I was so tired then that I just wished I could lie down and sleep. I hadn't realized I wasn't alone until Miss Angel appeared to see what I was doing.

"Come on, honey," she said, "Angel fixed you something to eat."

Angel hardly ever said *I*. Maybe she thought I couldn't remember her name. I followed her to the kitchen to find a slice of homemade peach pie on a flowered plate and a glass of milk. Angel was the only person I knew who could really cook. The pie was so delicious I ate it in huge bites and then threw it up all over the floor and all down the front of my favorite dress.

"I'm so sorry," I said and began to cry again. "I have allergies."

"Poor baby," she said, "don't you worry about a thing. The pollen is terrible this year and pollen can sure make a body sick."

It wasn't allergies. Being a natural born liar, I didn't want to tell her that it was that I had felt sick ever since I got off the school bus, that the smell of all those cats was disgusting, and that trying to swallow food had pushed my stomach over the edge. Didn't she smell the cats? Apparently not. She wiped my face with a damp paper towel, I tried to stop crying, and she said, "Come on now. Come with Angel."

She took me to Miss Mavis's daughter, Merilee's, room.

"All right, let's see now." She dug in Merilee's drawers and pulled out a big Citadel T-shirt. "Take off that dress, put this on and I'll throw she in the wash. Be good as new in two shakes."

She was so nice it was hard to feel embarrassed, but I wasn't taking off my clothes in front of her, so I waited. She waited. I waited some more.

"You want me to turn my back? I don't mind but Angel can tell you that you ain't got nothing Angel ain't seen."

"Sorry," I said, "it's just that . . ."

I must have looked like I was going to start crying again so she said, "That's all right, baby. Angel understands. You just go on and do it and she'll be right outside the door."

She left the room; I quickly changed and handed my ruined dress to her.

"Okay, now you lie down on that bed and get a good nap. This has been a terrible day, 'eah? I'll call you when your daddy gets back. But you shut your eyes like a good girl."

She closed the door behind her. For the second time that day, I was going to do as I was told without giving anybody any lip.

I remember that Merilee's room was filled with the standard array of girlhood memorabilia. Her walls were covered in posters of Audrey Hepburn and other old movie stars. Audrey Hepburn was the only one I recognized because I had always watched her movies with Momma. It was one of the few things we did together that she seemed to really enjoy, but then, Momma had a weakness for all things glamorous. She loved to go shopping too and would take me to Evelyn Rubin's on King Street in Charleston for my clothes. I'd miss those afternoons an awful lot, I thought. Would Daddy take me shopping? What would he say? It would be awkward and embarrassing and the thought of it made me feel heavy with sadness.

Merilee's bed was covered in stuffed rabbits, probably from Easter baskets, and Teddy bears from who knew where. There were books, old dolls, cheerleader pom-poms, class pictures, and about a hundred ribbons from swim meets were hung across a cord over her dresser mirror.

Under different circumstances, I would have snooped through everything. Not then. My legs weighed about a thousand pounds each and my eyes just wanted to slam shut. I crawled up on her high bed, pushing everything aside, and put my heavy head down on a soft cool pillow.

As soon as I closed my eyes, the image of my house and all the police cars came back. *My momma was dead. My beautiful momma had a heart attack.* Damn, I said to myself and I marked the occasion as the first time I had ever used a curse word and really meant it, although it wasn't said aloud. So I said, *"Damn everything!"* out loud to Merilee's room. I was entitled to say it, too. I felt clammy and woozy, like I was going to throw up again, so I held very still and said my favorite prayers over and over again. I heard a soft voice in the twilight calling me. *"I'm sorry, Anna. I'm so sorry."*

I thought it was my momma talking to me, telling me it was a mistake and everything was going to be exactly like it was, but it was just Miss Mavis. She was sitting on the side of the bed. It was night and I had slept after all—a black sleep with no dreams.

"It's eight o'clock, honey," she said, and wiped my hair back from my face. "Do you want some supper?"

"No," I said, and forced myself to add, "thanks." I was suddenly very angry.

"I made Campbell's Chicken Noodle soup for you with some saltines and a Coca-Cola on shaved ice," she said. "I always made shaved ice for my children when they felt bad."

Her voice was so sympathetic and heartfelt that I nodded my head and sat up. She turned the bedside lamp on and left the room assuming I would follow. What I really felt like doing was throwing every rabbit and bear of Merilee's life right out of the window and smashing the faces of all her dolls. I wanted to scream. Where was my daddy? Why wasn't *he* here?

I pulled down Merilee's T-shirt to cover myself and wandered out to the kitchen. Miss Mavis plopped me on a kitchen stool and left to answer the doorbell. I sat in front of the steaming soup watching Miss Angel wipe the counters to a polished sparkle. My dress, starched and ready to dance on its own, hung on a hanger from a cabinet knob. I said nothing. She said nothing. Nothing was going to make me happy. I just sipped the Coke and eyeballed Miss Angel.

Miss Angel was as tall as a woman could be without hitting the ceiling, I thought. She stood straight as a ramrod, not that I knew what a ramrod was, either. It was just something people said. When all the neighborhood kids, including me, pulled plums from Miss Mavis's cherished trees, Miss Angel would threaten to call the police and we would scatter like mercury. (I know about mercury because once when I was trying to fake sick to get out of school, I held the thermometer next to the lightbulb and it burst.) On other, brighter days when she liked us, she'd call us away from our street games to test her famous chocolate chip coconut cookies.

"I want to be sure they're okay to send to Miss Mavis's chillrun," she would say with a wink. "If y'all bad apples get sick, tell me quick so I can throw them out, 'eah?"

We would snicker and gobble them up like a pack of starving beagles, knowing she had really made them for us. She was a force to be reckoned with.

She wore her hair as she always had, pulled back tight in a neat bun. Her perfectly white shirt was a sharp contrast to her smooth complexion that had always reminded me of the color of light pecans. I figured her to be around forty, which was decrepit in my book. I was fascinated by the fact that she never wore and didn't need a stitch of makeup. Probably because my mother wore so much. But Angel didn't need a thing to improve her appearance. Her thick curly eyelashes framed her light hazel eyes like awnings and those crazy light eyes of hers held the wisdom of a thousand ages. I was about to get an unsolicited dose of it.

"Gone be all right," she said, finally breaking the silence, "by and by. You'll see. Now eat up."

"I wish," I said, "but it won't."

"'Cause the good Lawd take care of His own and you're one of Gawd's chillrun, ain't you?"

"No offense, Miss Angel, but God ain't sending my momma back. She's dead, you know. Dead is dead."

"Your momma was a beautiful woman, Miss Anna, and she was the finest gardener I ever knew. She's up in heaven now, tending the Lawd's flowers. Eat up that soup. Ain't no good cold."

"Ain't no good hot," I said and waited for her reaction to that one. She looked hard at me and I thought she was going to tell me how ungrateful I was, but she changed her mind and sat down beside me instead.

She exhaled a long breath and slapped her hands on her thighs. "You know what?" she said.

"What."

"This ain't no good," she said with another sigh, "it ain't no good."

"What? This soup?"

"No, chile, this day. It's plain awful and that's all she wrote."

"Yeah, it sure is," I said and let my spoon rest on the side of the bowl.

She looked at me for a few minutes and then she looked straight through me before she spoke, as though she saw something on the wall behind me.

"I'm a Gawd-loving Christian woman, Miss Anna, and I never miss Sunday church. My preacher, he say all kind of things about Gawd and how He got His plan and His mysteries and such. But I gone tell you this, and let the lightning strike me down righ' chea in this kitchen, things happen in this world that ain't the hand of Gawd. People do all kind of crazy things, the innocent get hurt. These thing just don't make no sense. No sense, no how. This whole business never should have come to pass."

"Yeah," I said. My tears were streaming again and I wiped them away with the back of my hand. What was she saying? I couldn't hold a thought in my head. I could barely sit. I felt faint but Angel just continued to talk as though I wanted to listen.

"Never should have come to pass," she said again, handing me a tissue from her pocket. "I'm so, so sorry to see this day. You go on cry, baby. It's okay."

I put my head down on my arms on the counter and sobbed. What did she mean that it never should have happened? Did anybody know what *had* really happened? I wanted to get out of there and run. If I could just run and run, I would feel better. I wanted it to be day, not night. The dark seemed scary for some reason. It had never bothered me before. Now everything seemed wrong. I wanted to go home to my room, slam the door and lock it. I wanted my daddy. And, I wanted my momma.

Daddy was probably at our house. I suddenly realized I couldn't go there, not even to get clothes. I had been told to stay put. On an ordinary day, I would have ignored that and taken the consequences. I realized I was afraid to move.

"I can't go home," I said. I looked at her and knew my face was all twisted because I could feel a hard pull in my jaw. I started to shake and burst out into tears one more time. "What am I supposed to do? Just sit here? Just sit here?"

My bewilderment must have sobered her, made her realize that what she took for granted that night had only begun to dawn on me. I was a sassy island brat, but I was still a little girl. And now I was a sassy island brat, little girl, with no mother, refused even the comfort of her own bed for some inexplicable reason, and with a daddy whose grieving would come with a price to pay.

"You're not going to worry about that just now," she said. "You listen to me good, Miss Anna. Your daddy is a good man and you are a good girl. Dr. Douglas needs for you to hang on to yourself. Neither one of you deserve this kind of terrible thing, but here it comes anyhow. So now what? If you go off all half-cocked and crazy it's just gone make a bad situation worse. So you need to tell yourself that you gone be the smart young woman Angel knows. Ain't that right? And don't you know your daddy's gone need you to be strong? I'll bet he feels pretty bad too."

"Yeah."

To tell you the truth, I didn't care how anyone felt. I was so stunned that I couldn't think about anything or anybody. I quit crying and, switching gears from that short blast of deep sorrow, I felt my fury grow. I couldn't do anything with or about my anger, so I clenched my jaw and quit talking to her.

There were people out in the living room. The door had been opening and closing every ten minutes. Daddy was probably back, but why hadn't he told me if he was? A car horn honked loudly, outside in the backyard.

Angel looked annoyed and opened the back door, calling out, "Hush! I'll be along directly!" She took her purse from the closet, went back to the door and turned to me. "That's my nephew. I promise to him I go see his new baby tonight. Shuh! Got him a man-child now and he ain't got the brains Gawd give a garden pea, 'eah? There's your dress all done up."

She pointed to it hanging there on the wall. I had forgotten all about it.

"Thanks." I looked at it and tried to control myself. "It looks great."

"Glad I could do *something*. You all right now?"

"Yeah, I'm okay."

"All right then. Miss Mavis and I gone help you and your daddy. Don't you worry. You just ask Gawd to send you strength and He will. All right?"

"All right, Miss Angel, I will."

She paused for a moment, gave me one of her loving half-smiles, and said, "All right." Then she was gone.

I poured the cold soup down the drain and went into the living room, where there was a growing crowd of our neighbors. I went to

Daddy's side and he smoothed my hair, squeezed my shoulder and proceeded to ignore me. Nobody was acting normal. Miss Mavis and Daddy were talking all around my head, never once asking what I thought, so I wandered away from them. Daddy was in a corner chair, sometimes talking but sometimes with his head in his hands and his elbows dug into his knees. He was listening, nodding, and occasionally standing to shake someone's hand. I saw that his eyes were all red and swollen, even behind his wire-rimmed glasses. It was very obvious that he had been crying. I had never seen my daddy cry and even now on this night when we should have been able to console each other, he had hidden his tears from me. It broke my heart to think about my daddy crying all alone. My mother had done this to him and to me. Why? What would happen to us now?

People were coming and going. My best friend, Lillian, and her momma came with a bunch of flowers for me. It made me feel worse instead of better. They handed me a bag from Belk's. I opened it to find a new nightgown and some underpants. They must have known I wasn't going home that night. They knew more than I did, which made me even angrier.

Everyone who came that night brought something for us—a bouquet of flowers, some Coca-Colas, a pie. I looked at all the things before me and it began to dawn on me that my life was changed forever. My breathing changed to something deep and rushing, as though I were going to hyperventilate. It scared Lillian. She hugged me hard, thinking she could calm me down. I jerked away, gasping and struggling to get a grip on myself.

"Quit!" I said.

"Come on, honey," her momma said to her, moving her away from me. "Anna's had an awful thing happen." She turned to me, bending down and putting her hands on my shoulders, and said, "Sweetheart, we are so, so sorry for you and your daddy. But don't you worry. The grown-ups will have this all figured out in no time at all."

"Thanks," I said.

At least I thought I had said thanks. I was working as hard as I could to control myself in front of everybody and I was about to lose it.

What Lillian's mother had said was now the undisputed most stupid thing I had ever heard an adult utter in my whole life. The *grown-ups* would figure this out? Weren't the *grown-ups* the ones who caused this in the first place? Didn't they always start the trouble?

I might have still been a kid but I wasn't a daughter of the South for nothing. The Civil War and Civil Rights had been hammered into my brain from the day I was born. War and suffering followed by more war and suffering. Even with all the great minds and hundreds of years, the world still had war and suffering. What adult was going to solve this? I had no mother. And, it was obvious, even to me, that this wasn't an ordinary death or else the police wouldn't have taken that man away to jail. My house was probably still crawling with the police. I didn't know because nobody was telling me anything. I was afraid to ask.

No. This couldn't be fixed. Was there anyone on this earth who could possibly have the nerve to believe they could make things right for me and for my daddy? As a matter of fact, it seemed that yes, there was. Daddy's mother, that's who. Just when I thought they were shutting me out completely, Daddy said, "My mother is coming tomorrow."

Grandmother Violet, who preferred to be called Grandmother—not Nana, not Grandmomma or Mama or Grandma, but Grandmother—had been called in Estill and given the news. She was coming in the morning. Great, I thought, just when it didn't seem possible that my situation could get worse.

My grandmother was the most unpleasant woman I ever knew. She found fault with everyone and everything. She had never liked my mother either, calling her a *gold-digging nobody* whenever she was out of earshot. Adults thought kids didn't know what was going on, but they did. I heard every single thing she said in our house because she had this unbelievable haunted house voice. When she got upset or laughed too loud, the dogs outside would howl. I'm not kidding either.

They did. It wasn't that I wanted to eavesdrop, it was that the noise she made was near impossible to avoid. Maybe my momma wasn't from some stuck-up self-made American Dream family like *Grandmother's*, but she was a former beauty queen and spoke like a normal person. Besides, if there was any gold around to dig for, I never saw it.

Maybe, just maybe, Momma being dead would be big and horrible enough to make Grandmother be nice. Inside, I doubted it. I really did.

All night long, I heard the grown-ups talking about funeral plans. I was brushing my teeth in the hall bathroom with a new toothbrush that was too big for my mouth. I had decided the best thing for me to do was stay out of the crowd, but the door was ajar and I could hear them.

Our pastor's wife said our church was going to put together a reception for us. Somebody else was going to make phone calls for Daddy. Daddy's best friend, another doctor, came in with a brown bag of booze for him and a Barbie for me. He didn't know what to do for me, he said, but he figured a Barbie might be welcomed by a little girl. Eventually they got around to talking about me and who would take care of me in the afternoons after school.

A voice drifted from the living room, saying, "Well, you could send her to boarding school."

I couldn't believe my ears. I was standing there wearing my new nightgown and all at once, ranting and raving gushed out of my mouth like I was the Hoover Dam with a drastic leak. I screamed at all of them.

"Just what's going on here? What's going on? Don't y'all know I'm sick? I threw up tonight! I don't *want* to go to boarding school! I *have* a school and I have to go tomorrow! I didn't even do my homework!"

They all stopped and stared down at me, realizing the disaster was too much for me to absorb. I would never forget their faces— embarrassed that they had overlooked me that horrible night. And it was all made worse by the fact that they knew I had seen my momma dead, being carried out from my house. Miss Mavis had been right. I had not needed to be a witness to my mother's body being put in a bag. I wanted all those people gone from the house that minute.

There I stood, barefoot, with my toothbrush dripping and hair shot in every which way, looking up at them, them looking down at me. I was as mad as every demon in all of hell. They were pushing Daddy into all kinds of decisions. I wanted to wait and discuss these things with my daddy by myself, the same way we always had. Then, as though someone said *Action!*, they all began talking again, to each other and to me.

Honey, as a practical matter, certain things have to be done at once. Plans have to be made, right, Doc? Sweetie, we know you love this island. All the children love this island. Don't worry. You won't go off to a boarding school. Oh! Look at you! Of course, you've had a terrible, terrible loss! This is too much for her, Doc! She needs to be in bed, Doc. It's past ten o'clock, Doc.

Daddy moved through the crowd, picking me up.

"Come on, my beautiful string bean," he said in a weary voice, "Daddy's gonna tuck in your bony bahunkus and tell you a story. No school tomorrow."

I let him tell me one of the same old well-worn yarns to make him feel better, but that night I knew I was too old for any more bedtime tuck-ins. I felt tiny and weak but for all the world, I didn't want him to know it. He rubbed my back and finally said a few things to me that I needed to hear.

"We'll go home in the morning. I love you, baby, and I don't want you to worry."

"I'll help you, Daddy," I said. "I'm almost eleven and there's a lot of stuff I can do. I can cook scrambled eggs, you know."

I could see him smiling in the dim light of Merilee's bedroom.

"I know, honey. You're growing up fast but you'll always, always, always be my baby. Don't ever forget that." He got up and walked to the window.

"Daddy?" He didn't answer. "Daddy?"

"What, sweetheart?"

He turned to face me. Maybe it was the blue light and shadows of night that cast his face in such a way that he looked completely spent. And old.

"What happened? I mean, how did all this happen?"

"I don't know." After a moment or two he said, "I really *don't* know. Try to get some sleep, okay?"

He kissed me on my forehead and left the room, without closing the door all the way. If I needed him, I would call him, the same way I had when I was really little and had nightmares. It was always Daddy who came to make my world right. After all, Daddy was a pediatrician and he understood children. Most people, except me, called him Doc. The nickname alone implied that he was the one who could make things better.

But no sleep would come to me that night. And Daddy never came to check on me. I called for him a couple of times, but he never came. Despite the late hour, the front door of Miss Mavis's house continued to open and close with people offering sympathy and help. While it was really nice of Miss Mavis to let us stay with her, I wished all the loud voices would be quiet. And why wasn't Daddy at least looking in on me?

Then I heard Officer Jackson, the Chief of Police, say, *"I'm sorry, Dr. Lutz. They were in bed. We're holding the fellow over in Charleston. Apparently he was giving her a controlled substance—amyl nitrite—and her heart just stopped. He's going to lose his pharmacist's license and . . ."*

They had been in bed? My momma had been in *bed* with that man! The man drugged her? Even though I was a kid, just a Geechee brat from the Isle of Palms, I knew what that meant my momma was. My momma was a whore. From that moment, and for the rest of my life, I was sure I would despise her. I was so ashamed I wanted to die. And, worst of all, where was my daddy to tell me that everything would be all right?

Two

Split Ends

May 2002

BETWEEN the time Momma died in 1975 and now, enough stuff happened to me to make your hair stand up just like it would if you stuck your tongue in a football stadium light socket. I ain't lying. I got married, had a baby, got divorced, moved back in with Daddy, went to beauty school, became a stylist, raised my daughter, Emily, and learned so much it makes my head spin like a globe in the hands of a third grade boy.

I pride myself on the fact that I can garden like nobody's business and, honey chile, I can cook, doing my voodoo on chicken and pork chops in a most excellent and reasonable, down-home fashion. Now, I have no intention of dragging you through every blessed detail of my life. I just want to give you some highlights. Highlights? Get it? Salon humor. God, I just crack myself up sometimes. Sorry. Occupational hazard.

Where were we? Ah, yes. The present situation. Here's something nobody knows except me and the South Carolina Federal Bank. I have seventy-four thousand eight hundred and eighty-three dollars in my interest-bearing account, not that interest is anything to brag about these days. But, I have no debt. I never thought I'd see the day, but here it is. But there was this monumental problem blocking the path of my beach house spending adventure.

Daddy.

I knew it was time for me to leave because he had been completely driving me out of my cotton-picking mind. But I was afraid to go because, somewhere along the line, I had forgotten to get a life for myself.

I love when people say that. Get a life. What is that stupid cliché anyway? (I think, if one wants to be taken seriously, one should avoid clichés like the plague.) Some guy cuts some other guy off in traffic. *Get a life!* the guy in the other car yells. Well, my father spends years in front of a television. So, *get a life!* I think to myself. Wouldn't you know, this stupid *get a life* business finally got around to me. Thank you so much. Took long enough! My eyes got yoinked open in a most unceremonious and insensitive blast delivered by Jim and Frannie.

Jim lives in San Francisco and Frannie lives in D.C. They're my best friends in the world since forever. We were doing our monthly conference call last week and they gave me the freaking, red-suited devil. I made the foolish, self-indulgent, tiny mistake of complaining once too often about Daddy's moodiness.

"Anna? Girl?" Jim said. "You know, Frannie and I are so not ready for you to start your rag on Doc. I think it's a little tired, you know? Like a lavender, glen plaid polyester pant suit."

"With a safari jacket," Frannie said. "And shoulder pads. With epaulets."

"Oh!" I said. "O-kaaay." I started feeling largely and understand-ably defensive. I mean, if I couldn't take my troubles to my dearest friends, who could I tell?

"Give it up! It's worn out!"

"Anna, Jim's right," Frannie said. "Look, you haven't had a date in two years, that I know of. You haven't been to the movies since when? I mean, do you even know who Cameron Diaz is?"

"Yes, I do. But who cares?"

"Look, hon," she said, "and I mean this in the nicest possible way, it seems to us that when you come home from work, you piddle around in the yard, fix dinner, and go to bed, only to start the whole thing over again the next day! You're acting like you're sixty years old! Like me dear old granny from Waterford was fond to say, you need to dry your arse. Go have more fun, excuse me, *any* fun in your life and then your daddy wouldn't bother you so much. Or us!"

"Anna? You need to rise from your rut and never go back."

I exhaled my disgust at myself and my frustration with them. Dammit all to hell. I hated it when I was wrong. "Well, you're right, all right? You both are. I know that." I was chewing on the ends of my hair, a disgusting habit of mine, I suppose, but one I had found comforting since I was a kid.

"Well, that's a start. It's just that I hate to see you like this, you know? We both do. Hell, Anna, Frannie and I love you!"

"Listen to Jim. You need to move out of your *daddy's* house, Anna, and you know it. It just ain't natural for our generation to go through menopause under our daddy's roof. It just ain't becoming for a Magnolia to pale on the branch in daddy's shadow."

"Ouch! Jeesch! Menopause! Of all the despicable and totally disgusting thoughts!" That would have been the old proverbial cold water sloshed in my direction. God. Reality truly sucks. Sometimes. "Frannie? Okay. You're right. Listen, I know y'all won't believe this but I've actually been looking for a house on the Isle of Palms. Sort of."

"What?"

"Finally! Great God, woman!" Jim said. "Great God!"

I could hear Jim sit up straight and Frannie's gasp was powerful enough to blow any earwax I had right to the core of my brain.

"Just be sure you're having a guest r-r-room," Frannie said, trilling her r's. "Ocean view would be good."

"Dream on, but yeah, I'm looking. Maybe something will turn up."

"Sugar Pants, if ever there was a woman who deserved a beach house on that island, it's you!"

I giggled at Jim calling me Sugar Pants. I told them about how I had been combing the ads and how I had a real estate broker working on it. We all agreed that a house was essential for my relationship with Emily and for my own sanity.

"God's good, Anna, but now you're tap dancing in a small boat! What if you actually find something? Old Doc will howl like a wild animal on a full moon!"

"Well, he's gonna have to howl. I also know that eventually I *will* find something and then what will I tell him?"

"Girlie, listen to your ex-husband. You're gonna tell him that *I* said you should do this and that Frannie said so, too."

"Oh, *that* will solve the whole issue!"

I wished it would but we all knew it wouldn't. Yes, Jim was my ex-husband and we will get to him soon. Suffice it to say that Jim was my closest and dearest love, despite the fact that his hormones had other plans for our marriage. Frannie was my most important girlfriend of my entire life. If it hadn't been for her, my Emily would have been at some loser school instead of Georgetown University. Frannie was an alumna and a recruiter and one of the most powerful lobbyists in Washington. She had spearheaded and won Emily's acceptance. Frannie and Jim were devoted and vocal feminists, believing that every woman should be able to stand on her own two feet. I had adored both of them since Momma died. They had saved me then, but I guessed they were a little weary of propping me up. I couldn't really blame them.

"I'm gonna do it," I said. "I have a lot of money in the bank, enough for a deposit and I know I can get a mortgage. Hell, I've been working for Harriet for a billion years."

"If you need help, let me know," Jim said.

"Thanks, sweetheart, but I gotta do this on my own."

"However?" Frannie said, laughing.

"Okay, I'll holler if I can't manage it, but I swear to God, y'all, I'm gonna do it."

"Just make sure it has a room for me. I wanna tell everybody in San Francisco that I have a house on the infamous Isle of Palms!"

"Ocean view, please."

"I'm taking notes," I said.

That was it. I knew my days of assassinating Daddy's reputation had ceased or else their respect for me would be compromised. That innocent monthly chat with Jim and Frannie lit the final and long overdue draggling string of my bloomer's fuse. I emerged as a woman on a pyrotechnic mission.

I was like an IRS agent, sifting and scrolling the ads and minding the obituaries every day—with the proper respect, to be sure. It was a known fact that this was how the "classic houses" on the Isle of Palms came onto the market. Sadly, somebody had to keel over and drop dead.

If the deceased was over eighty, the odds were that the departed's offspring already had their own brand-new beach houses with Anderson windows and Pella doors and were anxious to settle the estate by selling the well-worn family home. That was how I house shopped and I told myself that it wasn't morbid or callous.

My real estate agent, Marilyn Davey, kept me on the go. She called me every time she thought there was something in my price range. We would race out to see it and sure enough we would be greeted by the sellers shaking hands with the buyers. Every single time.

"Damn it!" I could see her mouth the words from behind the steering wheel of her navy blue BMW. She would get out of her car and apologize. "I swear, Anna! We just got the listing this morning!"

"It's okay," I'd say, "the right house will find me when the time's right."

Apparently, there were a lot of people with the same plan I had, but I was still hopeful. Counting up my chits, I figured I was next in line for an intergalactic, multidimensional, karmic act of Divine justice to reclaim, at the very least, my rightful spot on the planet. Just gimme my damn house, okay? While I'd never been someone to believe in entitlements, I had come to believe that this time, I was *entitled*. I got gypped out of living on the Isle of Palms as a child, my daughter got railroaded into living with her grandfather because of my problems, and we had all endured enough.

I didn't want a big splendid house on the ocean, mainly because I knew I couldn't *afford* a big splendid house on the ocean. Maybe fate would throw in splendor at a later date. Just a reasonable house would have sent me to heaven.

At last, excellent news! Mr. Randolph Simmons, of the Isle of Palms, eighty-eight years old, choked and died last week on a hunk of mustard pork barbecue at a family picnic. His children were playing touch football and thought he had a heart attack. When they realized later the Heimlich maneuver could have saved his life, they were aghast with shame and consumed with regret. Guilt worked for me. Mr. Simmons's tiny house would suit me fine. I considered it a sign from God that I heard it in the salon at the same time Marilyn heard it from one of Mr. Simmons's children. Affordable houses stayed on the market for about two seconds, because that kind of news traveled faster than Palmetto bugs in the kitchen when you turned on the lights. And, in a bizarre twist of fate, Mr. Simmons's house was only a few houses away from where I had lived as a child. I made an offer and shook hands. Marilyn and I hugged and screamed like schoolgirls.

Now I had to tell Daddy. I sweated it all the way home.

First, I called my gurus for courage. I squirreled myself away in my room and dialed their numbers.

"Jim? Hang on. Let me flash in Frannie."

"Hey!"

"Hey, Frannie!" Jim said, "Okay, Angel Heart, spit it out! I'm out here tasting Merlots and we all know California grapes don't hold forever!"

"Yeah," Frannie said, "I'm on the way out. Got a dinner at the Capitol for some jokers from Merrill Lynch."

"Okay. I have major news," I said.

"Doc find himself a bride?"

"No such luck," Frannie said, "that would undermine his chances for martyrdom."

I giggled. "No, Daddy ain't found no babe, but I found a house!"

Much screaming ensued.

"That's wonderful!"

"Tell it and be quick! I got two seconds and then I'll call you tomorrow for details."

"Well, I told y'all I was looking, 'eah? It ain't no palace and it's little, but I can afford it. And y'all can please help me figure out how to make it look like something?"

"No problem. I've got so much stuff in storage, you wouldn't believe it," Jim said. "Is it on the water?"

"Are you insane? But it's two houses from the path to the beach, across from Wild Dunes. And it's got a big yard, so I could add on at some point. But then there's the kicker part." Jim's wallet lived in another world than mine and no doubt what he had in storage would be better than anything I could ever afford.

"Lemme guess," Frannie said, "Doc is gonna kill himself?"

"Basically, yeah."

"Shit," Jim said.

"How should I break the news?"

They were both quiet for a moment and then Frannie spoke.

"He'll understand, Anna, I'm sure of it."

"Anna, just tell him straight out and be sweet about it. Old Douglas adores you. We know that. Christ, it's not like you wanna move to Patagonia or something!"

"You're right. Okay. I'll do it. I'll call y'all tomorrow."

"You'd die without us, you know," Jim said.

Frannie said, "If he gives you a hard time, I'll be home tonight around ten."

"Thanks, y'all. Love you madly!"

It was still light outside so I decided to weed the beds and deadhead the flowers until Daddy came home. Gardening was a kind of meditation for me. I would have my conversation with nature and the answers to my problems would always come. Now I needed to find words. First, I checked the chicken stew I had started that morning in the Crock-Pot and it smelled wonderful. It was thick and rich. When

I lifted the lid the whole room was filled with the fragrance of onions and celery. That would put old Douglas in a good mood for sure. I picked out a mushroom, blew on it, and popped it in my mouth.

"Damn, honey," I said out loud to myself, "you ain't fancy, but you sure 'nough know how to put the hurt on a bird!"

I was relishing my extraordinary good humor and suppressing my nerves. Eventually I got myself outdoors and began yanking some grass intruders from the azaleas. Daddy's car pulled up. My heart sank, knowing *the moment of truth was nigh*, like Daddy always said when my report card came. I had cut a handful of basil I was going to chop with tomatoes for a salad, and some parsley to garnish the stew. I walked over to greet him, forcing myself to smile.

"Hey! How was your day?"

"Hey, sweetheart! Let's see," he said, pulling his well-worn black leather doctor's bag from the floor of the backseat of his sensible Buick. "Three cases of stomach bug, four ear infections, lots of DPT shots, and one appendicitis. All in all, an average day, I'd say."

He hadn't noticed anything different. Good.

I followed him into the house and began setting the table while he went through his mail. I watched as he began to reenact his daily routine, saying the same things for the millionth time. Odd. His words that had grown to a stockpile of irritants now seemed to spark some melancholy in me. I realized the day might arrive when I would miss hearing him say, *I wish I had the money it costs to produce all the junk mail I throw out every day. We got any beer?*

"I wish I had the money it costs to produce all the junk mail I throw out every day. We got any beer?"

I reached into the refrigerator and, after some digging around, produced a Corona Light. I drank Corona. He drank Beck's. Corona was going to make him say *Humph, sissy beer.*

"I need to go to the store," I said. Next, he would ask about supper time.

"Humph," he said, "this is sissy beer. When's supper?"

What did I just say? See what I mean? Sweet but annoying. Maybe

ISLE OF PALMS　　　　　　　37

it *would* be a while before I missed the dazzling repartee we shared every night.

I served the chicken stew over biscuits and we began to eat. Now he would ask about my day.

"So how was your day? This is delicious, Anna."

"Thanks," I said. "My day was the usual baloney with Harriet and the normal gossip with my clients. Did you know that Alex Sanders resigned from the College of Charleston? I heard he's running for the U.S. Senate for Thurmond's seat."

"Well, personally, I like Alex Sanders very much. However, if Thurmond can still frost a mirror, that's his seat."

Strom Thurmond had been a U.S. senator since before we were all born, was a hundred, and it seemed like he would live forever. People would vote for him even though he fell asleep during Senate sessions. Tradition. It's how Charlestonians were wired. No one cared if the rest of the country snickered. What the hell did they know? Not diddly about what mattered to us, let me assure you.

"I think Sanders can win if he runs." I wasn't too sure about that but said it for a couple of reasons. One, I thought Alex Sanders was brilliant—not only as the college's president, but he had shown himself to be a man of grace and integrity, something in short supply around Washington. Second, I was in the mood for change of any sort. Last but by no means least, I was using this little politico discussion to figure out how I was going to break the larger news to Daddy. "At least I'd *like* to see him win."

"Who knows? Personally, I think the guy who raises the most money wins, which is very sick to consider."

We fell silent for a while and then Daddy spoke again.

"What's on your mind?" he said.

"Why?"

"Anna, since you were a tiny girl, whenever you had something on your mind, you chew your hair."

I knew the longer I delayed the news, the more difficult it would be to tell him, so I just blurted it out.

"Okay. I have something to tell you. I've found a house on the Isle of Palms and I think I'm going to buy it."

He sat up and looked at me as though I had just announced peace between the Israelis and the Palestinians. I didn't think he believed me; in fact, I was certain of it.

"Tell me this again," he said and gave me his full and rapt attention.

"I found a house on the Isle of Palms and—"

"I thought that was what I heard." He wiped his mouth with his napkin and sat back in his chair, still staring at me. "Why, Anna? You don't need to leave here. I mean, I thought that we had a pretty good arrangement, you and me. You were able to save money, buy yourself a nice car . . ."

"That's not it, Daddy. You know that."

"How would you manage? I mean, who's gonna take care of all the insurance forms and all those kinds of things? You hate that stuff! And, who's going to cut your grass and paint your window trims every year and unplug the garbage disposal and . . ." He stopped and got up from the table, putting his napkin down by the spoon of his place setting. "Fine," he said. "Do what you want."

"I'm sorry, Daddy."

"Don't be sorry. You're a grown woman. I knew this would happen one day, I suppose."

He went outside to the backyard to stare at the water of Charleston Harbor. That was what he always did when he was upset. He'd go out there for a while and think through whatever was bothering him. This was different, though. Daddy was sixty-seven, near retirement. He might be worrying about getting old, getting sick, being alone. I knew these were terrible and dark thoughts for him. But the thought of growing old under Daddy's roof was just as frightening for me. Was I wrong to want this for myself and for Emily?

We had no other family on his side and I had produced only one daughter. College meant she was gone, really she was, and there was no promise that she would ever return to settle here. But I wanted so badly for her to have her own home to come home to and to see that I could accomplish this.

I wanted to say to him that he could have a room in my new house for himself, but I knew that would only perpetuate the troubles that made me want to leave in the first place. I felt I had the right to live measuring up to my standards without a daily review of my shortcomings from another single person. Daddy couldn't help himself. I knew that. The scars of immigration to this country and his marriage to my mother had made him exacting, overprotective, meddling, patriarchal, and unforgiving.

I began to clear the table and rinse the dishes, putting them in the dishwasher. I wiped the table and the counters of crumbs and thought about all the times I had cleaned up meals in that house. There were so many memories that sprang just from the table. Thanksgivings, Daddy carving the bird, saving me the wishbone. The early days with Grandmother Violet and her Polish specialties she produced, attempting to fatten up Daddy and me. If I stopped and held my breath I could almost see our ghosts in the room with me then, moving, breathing, and talking. How many years had been spent around Daddy's table? Emily's birthday dinners of spaghetti . . .

Blow out the candles, Emily! I can't believe you're six years old! Emily in her best dress, her baby-fine hair slipping from the barrette and falling in her face, squinting her eyes as she made a wish, Daddy with his camera, both of us delighting in her squeals of excitement . . .

Want to know what I wished for, Momma? She always asked me that. *No, baby, if you tell, it won't come true.* I always made her cake myself— a yellow cake, chocolate pudding and bananas for filling, chocolate icing. She would lick the icing bowl and ask a million questions. *Did Doc buy me something? Yes, baby. Did he take my training wheels off? Go look in the garage! Did Daddy call? He's calling tonight. Did he send me something? There's a big box under my bed. . . .*

All the ways we had measured our lives around that table were about to end. Daddy would be alone when I left.

I walked over to the picture window and looked at him. His hands were shoved down hard in his pockets.

He stood by the old dock, watching the sun set. Somehow, his shoulders seemed slumped and everything about his posture told me he was feeling bad. Seeing him that low over the thing that thrilled me made me feel terrible. I didn't want Daddy to be lonely. Even though he was persnickety and had to have everything just so, I loved him to death. I told myself that I would have him over for dinner all the time and that I would bring dinner to him or that we would cook together. I knew my daddy's heart and could almost read his mind. If I left, what would he do with himself?

I tied the garbage bag and took it outside to put in the big can. The Mount Pleasant sanitation engineers would collect it tomorrow. I remembered for a flash chasing the "salad wagon" on my bicycle when I was a kid and my grandmother had thrown out my Barbies to punish me for something. Sass, probably. The garbage man had given them back to me and told me to hide them. She was so harsh and so cold. I hated remembering her.

When I returned, Daddy was inside, standing in front of the television, surfing through the channels.

"Three hundred and sixty channels and nothing but junk."

At least he was talking to me. "Yeah, nothing but junk."

He clicked off the television and turned to me. "Listen, I know you want to go back to the island. I've always known that. I mean, it's pretty hard to live with you and *not* know what you want."

His remark gave me a small signal that I could start relaxing and he continued.

"I just hate to think about you not being here, I guess. But it's only natural for you to want to live on your own, and not just because of the island flag you've been waving since your mother died. I mean, I'll help you, if you want. That's the decent thing to do. If you *need* help, that is."

"Before I run to the Bi-Lo to get you a *case* of Beck's, I *need* to hug your neck!" I threw my arms around him and squeezed. "Thanks, Daddy. I do need your help. Desperately! And, I always will!"

He smiled and there was immense relief between us. He was putting up a brave front. I knew he worried that time would reveal whether or not he had outlived his usefulness. Outliving your own usefulness might be worse than death.

"Okay, enough said. Go get my beer. You need money?"

"Nope. It's on me."

Before poor old Mr. Simmons's funeral flowers wilted, the ink was dry on my mortgage. Larry Dodds, Marilyn's cousin, did the closing and afterward they took a petulant Daddy and near-levitating me to Station Twenty-two Restaurant for the best shrimp and grits to ever pass my lips. I was one very happy woman. Marshall Stith, the mayor of Sullivan's Island and owner of the restaurant, stopped by our table.

"How are y'all doing? Everything all right?"

"Fabulous!" I said. "I just bought a house on the Isle of Palms today and I'm celebrating!"

"I always said, the Isle of Palms is the best next thing to Sullivan's Island!"

"Just ignore him," Marilyn said, laughing, "he is the mayor, after all!"

When I was a young girl, before Momma died and before the disaster occurred of my grandmother coming to live with us and ruining the rest of my childhood and making me long for a terminal illness (mine or hers) . . . well, believe it or not, there were some beautiful memories of my childhood.

Before the developers arrived, the Isle of Palms was where all the mysteries were hidden. It was untouched, virgin beach, dunes larger than houses that went on, seemingly forever, in a kind of twisting maze. I could stand on the empty beach and scream clear across the Atlantic to London. It was the kind of beach where you might find a genie in a bottle, or at least a message. Some days, the only footprints in the sand were mine.

In those days, Momma was young and beautiful. Daddy was deeply in love with her and I really was the apple of his eye. Momma was Daddy's grand prize and, with us at his side, all the nightmares of World War II and immigration were behind him. And even though Momma wasn't always happy in her role, I was able to live around it. Until the day my grandmother came to stay.

Then all the scars of the war and their quest for safety came screaming back like Hitler's Panzers rolling up Palm Boulevard toward my house.

Three

Violet

THE day after my mother died, good old Grandmother Violet arrived as threatened, with a bushel of peaches and the energy of a hundred men, prepared to take control of the entire situation, me included.

There are certain events burned into your memories like streaming video; for example, the day men landed on the moon and the landing of Grandmother Violet. I would never forget the precise moment she touched down. I was on the front porch lollygagging away the day in our ancient creaking swing. My intellectual occupation at the time was chipping away layers of paint with my fingernail. I was very involved in my own funk.

Young as I was at the time, I recognized and hated the much secreted and heavily denied fact that Momma had only the most minimal affection for me and Daddy. You wouldn't call it love. Worse, she couldn't have helped it. I had arrived at the conclusion that she just plain hated being married and having a child. She *must* have felt that way, because she never showed much enthusiasm for anything we ever did. It wasn't like I was so horrible that I failed to make her love me.

Or Daddy either. There just wasn't any love to get. Like Daddy used to say about oranges in July, "no juice." Momma had no juice.

So when Grandmother arrived, I was busy trying to figure out how my life could turn so horribly upside down in one day and I was wishing with all my heart that Angel worked for us instead of Miss Mavis.

Grandmother's car, a huge white Cadillac, swung into our driveway, kicking up a cloud of dust and coming to an abrupt halt. The dark cloud hung in midair for a few minutes, which I would have recognized as a sign if I had possessed a peanut of intuition. As the haze drifted and settled, I could see her backseat was packed to the hilt. She stepped out, arching her back with her hands at the bottom of her waist, and squinted toward the house with a resolute expression of *I will finally assume my rightful position as Head Executioner.*

Every hair on my body stood on end. I wasn't sure why, but I knew I was in deep shit, and that was the first time I had ever thought that word. Frankly, the language does not possess a more correct term.

The enemy approached and barked, "Don't just be sitting like a daggum bump on logs! Come! Give me my sugar and help unload this car!"

Giving her sugar did not entail passing a bowl. I was meant to deliver a kiss to her hollow cheek and then be her pack mule until the task was completed. Worse, despite over twenty years in the United States, she still saw little to no use for articles in speech. The order of verbs and her eastern European accent reminded me of those awful German war sitcoms that run at two in the morning. *I'd like to introduce my grandmother, Colonel Klink.* Having no escape and no alternative, I jumped from the swing and feigned willingness for my own sake.

"Hey! Grandmother! Can I help you?"

I was experienced enough to know that obstinate behavior would result in anything ranging from sharp words to a switching from her across the back of my legs.

"Certainly you can, young lady."

The woman must have been descended from crows with that horrible voice of hers.

I struggled under the weight of a cardboard box she placed in my skinny arms and made it up the steps to the porch. She passed me with a suitcase in each hand, opened the screen door, holding it open with her foot for me to enter, and called my father's name. No wonder my grandfather had died before her. A wise choice. A wise choice, indeed.

"Dougggg-lassssss! Wheeeerrrree arrrreee youuuuuu?"

"He's *trying* to take a nap," I said, dropped the box on the floor and ran back outside, down the steps, to get another load of her freight. I was rude and didn't care one bit either.

I heard her hiss something like *The impertinence!* but I just kept moving. I really thought she should leave Daddy alone. But Violet had no intention of leaving *anybody* alone.

I came back with another box. Daddy had come down the stairs; he gave the old crone her obligatory peck, and then, Lord save us all, she burst out into tears, hugging Daddy's neck. I didn't think the shriveled-up old battle-ax had any water in her.

"It's okay, Mother," Daddy said, "we're fine, Anna and I. It's just the shock of it all. We're really fine."

"Fine? How can this be? Mary Beth, her body is not even cold yet. Let me look! Oh! My poor boy!"

Ignoring me and my mental state, I guess she decided Daddy was okay, because then she composed herself and said, "Where I am supposed to put my things? Let's go."

Daddy led and I followed behind them, my trap shut tight for once in my life.

Our house was no castle but it was passable looking and sensibly designed. It was standard beach issue—up on stilts with a front porch built for breezes. There were at least a hundred houses like ours. When you entered through the main door, you came into a hall with a staircase, but if you went straight you'd wind up in the dining room. On the right side of the house was the living room, behind it the kitchen and the den, which continued around the back of the house. The left side of the first floor had two bedrooms and an adjoining bathroom. Upstairs were two more bedrooms and another bathroom. That was about it.

Daddy mumbled that his mother would probably settle into those two rooms downstairs.

"How long is she staying, Daddy?"

"As long as she wants, honey."

Holy hell, I thought, my life is over. Over and ruined.

"I need lamps, son," Grandmother said. "Overhead lights give me migraine."

"Okay. We can do that," Daddy said.

She harrumphed at the wallpaper in her room, which was faded from sun and pretty ugly, even I'd have to agree. She sniffed and sniffed at the mildewed closets and frowned at the scuffed condition of the floors. Momma had never been the world's greatest homemaker. My grandmother continued to sniffle from room to room, nearly to the point of an allergic fit.

"You want a Kleenex?" I asked, rolling my eyes. She saw me.

"Douglas? Are you going to tell Anna not to sass her grandmother?"

Daddy looked at me in a way I'd never seen. His face was cold and in that one glance I saw that he had given all power to his mother. She had become the Berlin Wall, dividing father and daughter.

"Anna? Why don't you go and get a cold Coca-Cola for your grandmomma," Daddy said.

"Oh, I'm fine, son," she said with the smallest of all smug smiles. "I think with effort, we can make this place very presentable. I will work on it. People will be coming here from funeral, of course. What plans are made?"

The funeral! Gee, God! I hadn't wanted to even *think* about that. *Don't bring it up, please! Don't talk about it in front of me!*

I took off and ran upstairs to my room. I wanted life to be normal as fast as it could and listening to funeral plans wasn't normal. I didn't want to hear about it and I didn't want to go to it either. I had lost my mother. Wasn't that enough?

It wasn't long before Grandmother stuck her head in my room.

"What you are doing? Why you don't clean this room?"

"I hate my room," I said, "it's ugly."

She looked around at my single bed, turquoise walls, and flowered curtains and didn't disagree. She said, "Be glad you have a bed for sleeping, missy. Plenty of children in this world sleep on hard cold ground with raw turnips for supper. Your daddy slept in box for keeping apples, you know."

"A crate," I said. I didn't really mean to correct her English. It just came out of my mouth.

"Yes," she said, "crate."

I just looked at her. She was on the verge of another story of her personal suffering. My angry jaw dared her to tell it. Didn't she know how I felt? No, Grandmother Violet was not a geyser of healing warm waters for me, her only granddaughter. Or anybody else. She skipped the lecture but for the rest of the day, at every chance, she would remark in a whisper how frightened she was that I looked like my momma. Her thoughts hung in every room like a dreary dampness brewed with dangerous herbs.

"Before God, I tell you, she is looking just like Mary Beth, Douglas," she said. "You better do something or she is winding up just like her!"

In her mind I was guilty of some genetic sin, like Eve's child. I knew from the start that I would be well advised to stay out of her way. However, may I just say that despite my anxiety over her arrival, I was completely surprised that she thought I looked like my mother. I had never been told that and thought it was a wonderful revelation. To her it was anything but a compliment.

My mother's looks were how she had met and snagged my daddy. They were introduced at the Water Festival in Beaufort and started dating. She was the Assistant Queen or something and Daddy had been invited to some party for the Queen's Court. Even though he was a lot older than she was, they fell in love. If I would ever remind Daddy of my momma it was okay with me. He loved her like mad, even if she didn't love him back. You see, I was born in the Land of

Beauty Queens. There was a Peach Festival, a Watermelon Festival, and a festival to celebrate everything we grew, including azaleas. All these festivals had parades, parties, Queens, and Queen's Courts. Beauty was highly valued by most adults I knew, whether it had to do with their yards, their dogs, or their daughters. When it came to daughters, they were expected to be, at the very least, well groomed and without vanity. That was one difference between Momma and me. I was groomed; she was vain. Early on I had made a vow to never become vain because in my young mind I had somehow linked it to self-centeredness, which led to loving yourself too much and not having any left over for others. I wasn't stupid; I was dejected.

Unfortunately, I had to face it; there *was* still the matter of my momma's funeral the next day. All I remember is that I went and that the church was very hot and crowded. And that I was wearing my yellow dress, which I would never wear again.

I just couldn't get it through my thick head that Momma was really dead, even though there was a brass-handled, mahogany coffin right in front of me. I didn't cry one single tear, until we got to the cemetery. Then I wailed like a baby. The minute I saw that box go into the ground, I started screaming.

"Momma! Momma! No! Momma, please, no!"

I was terrorized and out of control. I wanted my momma back. How could she ever become the mother I wanted and needed her to become if she was dead? For the first time in my life, I was hopeless.

Daddy, and even Grandmother, put their arms around me and hugged me so hard I thought I would faint. It was like it finally hit me and there was nothing I could do to stop the panic I felt. People said, *We are so sorry. If there's anything we can do . . . We'll keep y'all in our prayers.*

I just sobbed and sobbed.

"Is terrible," Grandmother Violet said, angry tears rolling down the pleats of her wizened face. "Terrible. Terrible."

She handed me a handkerchief and I had two fleeting thoughts as she did. One, her hand was reptilian, and two, the handkerchief smelled like lavender. It was the only time I ever felt my heart move in her direction.

I looked at my daddy. He was completely miserable and his grief was more than I could stand. He had loved her, she was gone, and that was all. Love was dangerous. I understood at that very moment that passion could be fatal. If I ever made the mistake of marrying the wrong person I could wind up dead. If I let myself feel passionate I could be like Daddy, hanging over a fresh grave. Love could wreck your life.

At some point, we wandered back to the limo and went to the reception. Momma was buried, and I felt like kicking the crap out of somebody. (Crap. Bad word number four. So what?) But I couldn't do that. My throat was all scratchy and dry and I just wanted to go back to before all this hell happened to Daddy and me. I would rather have had a mother who didn't love me than not have one at all. I wanted to crawl into my bed and stay there. Maybe I was just having a long nightmare. If I went to sleep and woke up maybe it all would be gone.

There was no peace and quiet in our house. Even though there had been a crowded reception at the church hall, it seemed like everyone who was there had followed us home. It wasn't often that a young mother died. We were getting a rush of diversion from every friend we knew, plus the families of Daddy's patients. They meant to sustain us through the most horrible day of our lives.

Cars were parked up and down the street and all over the yard. The house was bursting with people who had brought enough food for a month. Egg salad, tuna salad, chicken salad, all seasoned but without the mayonnaise, in plastic containers for sandwiches on another day. Glazed hams, macaroni and cheese, and chicken divan in Pyrex dishes to freeze, chocolate pound cakes, cases of Coca-Cola, and a whole turkey with stuffing and gravy. There were cheese balls and eggs rolled in crushed pecans, and chocolates from Russell Stover. I felt like I was going to throw up just looking at it. Someone set up a bar and started serving drinks. The adults seemed to be having a party, a seriously depressing party, but to my mind, the atmosphere was too much like there was something to celebrate.

The neighborhood kids I knew so well barely talked to me and were unusually awkward, not knowing quite what to say. I didn't know what to say to them either. I had an overwhelming urge to pretend, to run and play and pretend nothing had happened. I couldn't manage it because I knew it would be wrong. But wasn't everything wrong? We were all standing around in our church clothes, humidity and heat having its way with shirttails and hair. Sparky Witte finally said, "You okay?" I said, "Yeah, I guess." That was about it. It seemed to me that they all knew about the circumstances of my mother's death and what she had been doing. I mean, it was bad enough to lose a parent, but were they supposed to be sympathetic in this case? So everyone acted uncomfortable, except Lillian, who knew I was deeply upset and tried to make me see the world wasn't coming to an end.

"That was the worst part, Anna. The funeral, I mean."

"No, that wasn't the worst part. This is awful. Don't you understand? My whole life has been stolen away from me."

"Yeah, but it's not gone and you'll be okay. I swear you will. My mom says time heals everything. Man! I've never been to a funeral before."

"I hope your mom's right and I hope we don't have to go to another funeral for a billion years," I said. I wasn't so sure about her mom's wisdom. In addition, who was going to dispense advice to me? My grandmother? "Funerals suck." My language was deteriorating.

"You're right. They sure do."

"My grandmother's staying."

"Oh, no! Forever?"

"Forever."

Lillian and I looked at each other and sighed like two old ladies.

Grandmother Violet was in the kitchen the whole afternoon with Miss Angel and Miss Mavis, trying to record what had come from who and to keep the platters on the table full, so that as much food as possible would disappear.

Making things disappear and go away seemed like a good idea even to a child of my age. I wanted to disappear too, but I was trapped. All afternoon the adults would stop talking whenever I approached and their intense whispering would immediately become overt condolences. I knew they were talking about Momma and what a big whore she was. I couldn't have labeled it then, but I saw the pattern of their thinking. Momma was gone because she was bad. If I looked like Momma, that was bad. Something might be wrong with me because I was her child. Something bad would happen to me one day because I was bad.

I wandered into the kitchen and found Angel. She was slicing a pot roast and wrapping it up in packages to freeze. I stood there for a little while before she noticed me.

"You okay, sugar?"

"Yeah, I guess so."

She ran her hand down the side of my face, smiling at me with the most loving and knowing expression I have ever encountered.

"Grandmother's staying," I whispered to her.

"That's all right, baby. Let her love you."

"She doesn't love anybody or anything."

Angel nodded and then shook her head. "This ain't right. I said it before and I gwine say it again. This ain't right."

Sometimes, when I would think of Angel, it was as though that moment and her simple gesture of touching my face coincided with my first acceptance of how things were. My life wasn't over; Momma's was. Mine had changed in unimaginable ways, but it wasn't over.

EVENTUALLY we began to inch along. Life was measured by test grades and a year-end report card—of which I was sternly reminded by old Violet that good grades were my duty and ineligible for reward. I had saved it for dinner, wanting Daddy to see it first. I was starving for some praise.

"Anna, this is wonderful," he said. "I'm very proud of you, honey."

"Douglas! You must never let Anna think you expect less! Let me see."

The way she stuck her raptor claw across the table, it was obvious she expected Daddy to turn it over to her without a word. He did.

I had made an A in English, History, and Science, a B in Art, and a B– in Math.

"What's so wonderful about this? It's average and believe me, your father knows average to be the same as mediocre. If you want live a life of mediocrity, that's your business. But it's nothing for celebration, believe you me. If your father was bringing a report card like this to his father, he would be getting a horse whipping. The whole problem with American childrens is that they don't know what it takes for surviving. They're weak."

"Maybe we should give up television until you've finished your summer reading," Daddy said. "Your grandmother is right, actually."

Silence from me. Silence all around as a small but undeniable smile crossed my grandmother's face. Another victory for the enemy.

Between my grandmother's negative thoughts and the blistering weather, I couldn't find comfort or peace. That June and July were hot enough to make you swear the world was going to burst into flames, coming to an end. I tried to let my grandmother love me; God knows, I needed some affection. But her meager affection took the shape of worry.

"You must not swim alone, Anna! It's dangerous!"

"Okay, don't worry. I won't go without my friends."

"How deep will you go? The ocean changes with every tide! Please be careful! Your father couldn't stand it if anything happened to you!"

For the first time I became cautious—about the ocean, where I went to play, how high I climbed, how much sun exposure I got—and I called if I would be late. She always knew where I was. These small concessions were the respect I tried to give, and her concerns were the only love she could show. It wasn't wonderful, but it was tolerable.

I was extra sweet to an all but unresponsive Daddy and prayed he would cheer up. I wondered if I had lost him too. I became less raucous and Daddy became more distant, probably hoping his mother would fill in the gaps. He was mourning Momma and I understood that but I didn't like it. I would find him sleeping in the hammock or on the couch. He slept all the time. Dinner conversations were punctuated with periods of silence and deep sighs from Daddy and then from Grandmother. Part of me played their drama but my childish side was hungry for action.

For the hell of it, I would run through my neighbor's sprinklers, getting my clothes wet. After all, it was so hot, the dew in the early morning yard would rise like steam. My grandmother would make me stay on the porch until I dried, which suited me fine.

One day when the temperature climbed over a hundred, Lillian and I fried eggs on the sidewalk, making a mess, not fried eggs, which put us on the receiving end of a lecture about the sins of the wastrel, from you know who. I finally figured out the way to get along with Violet was to just do what she wanted. When she barked an order I moved as fast as I could; otherwise, I tried to avoid her. That was how the new order and a semblance of peace were established. Grandmother Violet was a one-woman police department. Daddy was all but a zombie. I was reasonably well behaved.

Life was almost acceptable until she announced that she felt very strongly that we should move to Mount Pleasant, which was to say that the decision had already been made. She felt slighted by the neighbors because of my scandalous mother. She didn't like me running all over creation with so little supervision, even though I had attempted to comply with her demands for information about everything I was doing. She was very upset that my mother had never become a Catholic even though she had agreed to raise me as one and had not even come close to attending any church, except on Christmas and Easter.

I was lying in bed one night in early August, holding my breath and listening to her dictate our future to my father.

"I'm telling you, Douglas, I won't be standing by and watching you raise this child to be a heathen! She's going to be turning into a wanton I don't know what unless we are doing something. She needs structure, discipline, a religious tradition, and a chance to leave this dirty, sordid past."

"Come on, now. I don't know if it's all that bad," I heard Daddy say.

"Well, fine then. If you don't feel you need my advice, then . . ."

"All right, Mother. Whatever you want to do is fine."

There was no soul in his voice. In just days, Grandmother Violet had sold our house, moved us to Mount Pleasant, and, by the six-teenth of August, I was a new student, at Christ Our King–Stella Maris School.

All I wanted to do that first day was to spit. I began, instead, that long infamous road of self-preservation through denial. I became the near-perfect child in the presence of all figures of authority, having learned over the summer by living with Grandmother that it just didn't pay to be yourself.

First, I willingly embraced Roman Catholicism. The Sisters of Charity were entranced by the dark and mortal details of my back-ground, which slid from the wagging tongues of every uncharitable housewife East of the Cooper. Maybe I was wrong, but I thought that everyone tried to use our trouble for entertainment.

Heaven knows, there was nothing the Sisters coveted more dearly than to snatch a compromised child from the clutches of Satan, save her immortal soul, and earn their rightful throne in heaven within proximity of the Blessed Virgin Mary herself. Their work began with a fevered pitch.

"You look so nice in your new uniform," Sister Rosaire said to me my first day.

"Thanks," I said, feeling like an alien.

"Anna? The children of Stella Maris say, 'Thank you, Sister.'"

Desperate to make a good impression, I replied, "Thank you, Sister."

In my mind I silently added, *Where the hell am I?* And, *You sure do look weird in that getup.* Almost immediately I knew that the goal should be minimal trouble with the Sisters of Propriety. That, coupled with a running internal dialogue, would keep my true spirit safely in hibernation. Someday, I would escape the madness. The only place I could think of that could have been worse than Christ Our King–Stella Maris School would have been a Jesuit military boarding school.

Being a smart-ass in the environs of Stella Maris wasn't worth the torrents of hell that rained on the morons who tripped the visceral alarm system of the NUN IN CHARGE (the "NIC") at any given moment. On my third day, I got a sample of the efficiency and style with which smart-asses were handled.

"May I have your attention, please?"

The voice of Sister Whoever crackled through the static of the public address system. We stopped work, placed our pencils in the groove at the top of our desks, and stared at the speaker above the large blackboard as though she could see us right through the dust-encrusted brown linen cover.

"Everyone please stand."

Everyone stood and I fumbled to my feet as well.

"Proceed quietly and in order to the halls. Do not block the doors of other classrooms. Stand in silence by the walls."

My history teacher, Sister Immaculata, took a breath and said in a whisper, "Let's go, children. Let's go." Her arms scooped the air like a conductor directing her orchestra, bringing the symphony to a crescendo. In turn, we hustled our little plaid jumpers out into the hall to bear witness to the actual deliverance of corporal punishment.

The dumb-ass of the day was Sally Denofrio, who was nicknamed from Salvatore, no doubt the reason for his trouble. In Bubba Territory, if you are stupid enough to name a boy Sally, that child will pave his childhood with bricks of sweaty mortification, bloody noses, and the paddle of the NIC—in this case, Sister Gonna Show You Where the Bear Went in the Buckwheat—a.k.a. Sister St. Pious.

Sally Denofrio, a transfer student from Albany, New York (Yankee—making him all the more hopelessly clueless about what was acceptable), stood trembling in the center of our cross-shaped hallways while a fifteen-year-old eighth grade boy—massive jock, not brain, bound for Clemson's football team—brought out Sister St. Pious's heavy wooden chair and placed it at a particular vantage point for the reluctant audience.

The late August air was thick with the odor of perspiration and the egg salad breath of one hundred and fifty-seven uniformed sympathizers. We waited, anxious for it to start and end. I knew at this point that a) I was about to see something I had heard about and never believed to be true and b) No one would have ratted on Sally except Theodore McGee, the school's aspiring cleric, who was widely ostracized because he was a suck-up of long-standing repute. I had heard about Theodore McGee the minute I enrolled.

"I saw old Pious take McGee in her office and close the door," Frannie said on my first day.

We were sharing brown bag lunches with Penny Wilkins and some boy named Tommy Proctor under the persimmon trees in the schoolyard. A cool breeze saved us from the sweltering heat, but the news was so interesting I didn't care about the weather. I had already heard from my new friend, Frannie Gianaris, that Sally had emptied all the soap in the boys' bathroom and stuffed the toilets with paper towels, causing a flood.

"Who's Theodore McGee?" I said, dying to know everything.

"He's a huge hairy asshole," Tommy said.

"Euuuuuuuu!" we girls said in unison.

"Tommy!" Penny said, horrified. "Anna's gonna think we're just like public school kids! He's the skinny little nasty geek with the big glasses, a runny nose, and he wears elastic-back pants."

I had, indeed, spied the traitor earlier that morning. But before I could defend my prior life in public school, Frannie jumped in.

"I don't know about the hair on the butt of Theodore McGee, but he'd sell his mother to get any one of us in trouble. Everyone hates his guts. He *is* an asshole. Tommy is right."

Asshole was a useful and popular pejorative in the vocabulary of my new friends at Christ Our King–Stella Maris School. I, being the perfect child, had never uttered it aloud on school property; I merely thought it. But by not chastising them for saying it, I was on the road to becoming a benign confidante.

In any case, at two-thirty that afternoon, right before dismissal, we lined up for the public paddling of Sally Denofrio. Sister St. Pious appeared from the bowels of her office, paddle in hand and spoke to Sally to be sure he understood why he was the object of this assembly and punishment.

"Salvatore? Do you understand that destroying public property is a crime and a sin?"

"Yes, Sister. I'm so sorry. I don't know what made me do it." He was crying and frightened.

"Perhaps the paddle will help you remember not to do it again. Lean over my lap."

When he failed to do so in the time she deemed appropriate, she grabbed him by the arm. I felt like I was going to barf. *Whack!* I opened my eyes to see if Sally was alive. *Whack!*

"Jesus Christ! You're killing me!" Sally screamed.

We all bit our lips and then Frannie whispered to me, "Think he's stupid? He's breaking the Commandments in the middle of a whipping!"

"You take the Lord's name in vain?" Sister St. Pious said. She was incredulous. Sally scrambled away from her and ran out of the door and down the street toward Highway 17, where he lived. He was screaming at the top of his lungs.

"Police! Help! Police!"

Sister St. Pious did not flinch despite the echoing lament of Salvatore Denofrio. She rose from her chair and looked up and down our lines to see if anyone had giggled.

"I'm calling the Bishop," she said and turned, her jaw squared to the front door. Then, she gave us the once over again with her sparrow eyes and then said, "Go back to your classrooms and get your things. School is dismissed."

That was my orientation to Catholic school education. Sally Denofrio was expelled and transferred to public school. I knew right then that it was best to buy into the politics of the ruling class and double-bolt my big mouth.

I refused to let anyone taunt me. *I heard how your momma died, Anna.* That came from the intermural basketball team's head cheerleader. *Yeah, my dad and I would appreciate your prayers,* I said. Shoot, I could play this game, I thought.

But sometimes, I got caught off guard in the girls' bathroom.

"My momma said your daddy is screwing his nurse," Denise McAffrey said to me while we washed our hands in the same sink.

I was stunned, believing for the moment that she knew something I didn't. Then a stall door opened and out came Frannie.

"Go to hell, zit face, and leave Anna alone. Your momma doesn't know shit."

Frannie was very helpful in my adjustment period.

When spring came, I made May altars in my room at home to honor the Blessed Mother and prayed the rosary on my knees at night with my grandmother's supervision.

"Now ask God for your special intention," Grandmother Violet would say.

Please make my grandmother drop dead, God. God, if you love me at all, please, if you won't kill her at least send her back to Estill.

I said enough rosaries and novenas that first year to liberate the entire citizenry of Purgatory, Limbo, and the outer fringes of Hell's gates. But not to rid my life of my grandmother.

God was either busy with another call or not interested in my problems. He was probably trying to unravel a bigger disaster than mine.

Then there was still the problem of Daddy. As if having a wife who died in the arms of another man wasn't enough to reconcile, my daddy was still emotionally detached. I knew we would never be the same again. All the while, Grandmother blustered about every single thing.

Did you make your bed, Anna? No television if your room isn't clean, Anna. Did you clean bathroom? That means toilet too! Did you rake up the yard? Do you think I am this family's slave? Before God, you are looking more like Mary Beth every day!

I developed new ways to get her goat. *Did you eat the pecan pie I made for your daddy's supper? You selfish girl!* Of course, Frannie, Jim—a new friend—and I had woofed it with a half gallon of two percent milk. *Well, that's just fine! The next time you are wanting something, don't ask me, young lady!* Fine, I don't need anything from you anyway, I would think.

I could never win with Grandmother Violet. I had come to accept that some people just didn't like kids. There wasn't anything to be done about that. How was it that with all the nice women out there in the world, the two I'd lived with were both so difficult? No matter how hard I tried, my slightest infraction of any of her rules was met with a heavy-handed derision. I'd talk to Lillian about it, but she had a new best friend and all she talked about was her. Eventually, we stopped calling each other. Once I even called Miss Angel, but Miss Mavis said she wasn't there. I never called back. I don't know why. I just felt funny about it. I just knew if my grandmother found out I was talking to Miss Angel, she'd be mad as hell.

As time went on, I got used to her being there, in the same way I guess you got used to a leash if you were a dog. I was in the middle of the eighth grade, I had evolved to the status of an A student with an occasional B—partly from desire and partly from the unending efforts of the stalwart Sisters of Charity. They gave me books to read—Jane Austen, the Brontës—I loved them all and escaped through them to a nicer world. I was never flippant with them because even their most stringent demands paled next to my grandmother's. In fact, I sort of liked the nuns and was curious about them. And I knew their *happy quotas* were limited by what one old bat was willing to do to help the other old bat. So sometimes I would even stick around after school and give them a hand. It was better than rushing home.

I closed classroom windows, helped them load their cars, put away books in the library and cut flowers from the schoolyard for the chapel's altar. I think they grew to sort of love me and I was glad of it too. My exemplary behavior caused no end of speculation among them as to whether or not I would make a good postulate for the convent. I just let them think it was possible, because why not?

When parent/teacher conference time came, it was my grandmother who would come on behalf of Daddy. When the nuns told her how wonderful I was she informed them that they were being manipulated by a child. *What about her grades, Mrs. Lutz? They're very good! She's won every spelling bee for the past two years!* How are you knowing she's not cheating? *Come now, she's a dear girl!* You were not knowing her mother.

You didn't know her mother. This was her standard reply to anything which muddied her built-in poor opinion of me.

The good Sisters, renowned tough nuts, were horrified by Granny's polar chill, which only served to increase their concern for me. Granny's spew made spandex of the arterial steel that pumped their sanctified blood. They clucked over me like a flock of Rhode Island reds. My friends—Frannie, Jim, Tommy, and Penny at the core—were never jealous of that attention. There was a sense of justice among us and from what they had learned about my domestic tyranny, they all figured I was entitled to something out of life. They would have preferred the streets of Calcutta to *Life With Violet.* Besides, the last thing they wanted was an old goat with Communion breath hugging on them. That was how it was. And at least I had learned that not *all* adult women were cold-hearted Nazis.

As soon as I was old enough to get in a car with somebody's sibling who had the Holy Grail—a driver's license—I'd beg to go to the Isle of Palms. It became a joke. *You got a boyfriend over there waiting for you in the sand dunes?* Sure. Every guy in town was dying to date a bag of bones with glasses and bad skin. *What'd you lose over there?* The awful truth was that I had lost everything on the Isle of Palms.

We would jam ourselves into somebody's mother's sedan and ride, windows down, radio blaring. In fact, riding around in someone's car all but completely defined my teenage years, as it was a popular Low-country pastime.

As soon as we would cross Breach Inlet, I'd hang my head out the window like a dog and cure myself with beach air. My friends wanted to cruise Burger King to see who was there. Not me. Just keep me out of Violet's reach, long enough to allow me a dose of island breeze.

As the years passed, my single obsession was to go back to the Isle of Palms and make things clear in my mind. I had suppressed too many things for too long. Maybe I thought that if I could begin again on the Isle of Palms, I could wipe away the pain of my childhood and teenage years.

I finally arrived at the moment to face my past. There we were on moving day, Daddy and I, unloading the truck together. I was sure he was thinking about Momma, the day she had died and how we had left this place. I was thinking about her too. I had many things on my mind.

I sat down on the truck's back bumper for a moment. Retracing the events leading up to our move to Mount Pleasant and my return here, I couldn't help but think of all the years I had worked and saved to make this purchase of poor Mr. Simmons's house become reality. It was a huge coincidence that my new house was next door to where Miss Mavis and Miss Angel had lived when I was a kid. I wondered if they were still kicking. If they remembered me . . .

Four

Miss Mavis Says,
There Goes the Neighborhood

2002

"ANGEL? Angel? Where are you? Come quick!"

She was ignoring me and I knew it. It made me plenty hopping mad when she did that, I can tell you. Whoever on God's earth named her Angel didn't know what the hell they were doing too, 'eah? I pay her *good* money. She should at least have the decency to answer me.

There I was, just like any other Thursday. I was just going about my business, as I normally do, fixing to get ready to go on and water my African violets. They're my babies—besides Blanche and Stanley, my kitties.

I heard the hullabaloo outside and peeked through my living room curtains. Some wiggling tart was moving in that awful little house with a man old enough to be her father. I nearly sucked in my tonsils and had a stroke of paralysis from the sight. If I hadn't realized that a fall could damage my hand-painted watering can that I created myself in craft class last February, I might have just let myself collapse.

"Angel? Answer me!" I passed through my living room and dining area and swung open the kitchen door so hard it hit the wall and I did not care one iota. "Well?"

There she stood right in front of the sink, polishing my copper pots as though the world wasn't coming to a complete standstill.

"Well, what?" she said, just as sassy as she could. "Just look at this pot! You can see your pretty self in it clear as day!"

I poured myself a glass of water, scooting her big old lanky self over a little. "You want to see something, you come with me! Why didn't you answer me?"

" 'Cause I didn't hear you. Did you call me?"

She was lying like I don't know what. She always did.

"Just dry your hands and come with me this instant. You know you hate to miss anything."

She came behind me muttering about Lincoln freeing her people and Dr. King and all kinds of liberation speeches but her jaw flopped like a crocodile's when she looked down at the yard next door. There was Exhibit A—young woman in shorts with old goat in long trousers.

"Um-um," she said, staring right out the window so the entire planet could see her. "I had a dream last night about flowers blooming all over that house."

"What?"

"I said, *Last night I dream that house was covered in flowers!* You are so deaf!"

"I am not! And there's nothing in that yard except stickers and dollar weed! Move back, you old buzzard, they're gonna see you!"

She stopped and turned to me with that look of hers, that laser of ice only Angel can deliver. It gave me the chills.

"Who you calling old? If I is an old buzzard then you is one too! Tell me, what got you all rattled up? That woman down there ain't no floozy! She's a schoolteacher or something!"

"And just how do you know *that*?" I leaned over her shoulder to have another look. There wasn't a single indication for my money that she was a teacher.

"Her shoes. She's wearing them awful Birkenstocks that my granddaughter wears. All her friends too." Then she narrowed her eyes at the scene below and added, "She's a little long in the tooth for 'em, too, 'eah?"

"Humph! Even so! It's because of women like *her* that I never remarried."

It had always been a particular point of sadness for me that another man never came along for my comfort after my Percy died and went to hell. Angel and I had discussed it many times.

"Iffin you say so," she said and went back toward the kitchen.

Now what was that supposed to mean? I just shook my head and followed her, deciding to ignore her double entendre for the moment.

"Where are you *going?*" I said.

"Gone make our new neighbors a pound cake, that's what."

"What?"

"I said, *I gwine make a cake!* Catch more flies with sugar? Where are your manners, Miss Mavis?"

Now. You may tell me all manner of things and I won't get upset, but don't anyone tell me I have lost my manners or I'd send them from here to Kalamazoo! However, when it came to Angel, I just let her run her mouth. We'd been sharing a roof for so long, I had already heard every thought of hers a thousand times anyway.

When my Percy was alive, he bought me this house thinking it would only be temporary. We had a nice couple living downstairs and we lived upstairs. Both apartments were very acceptable. Our apartment had three bedrooms and two bathrooms and a lovely view of the Atlantic Ocean. The downstairs had two small bedrooms, a living room combination dining room and a tiny kitchen. It was smaller, to make room for our carport and utility room, and it was a little dark, but still could be very cozy in the right hands.

When our little Thurmond was born, Angel came in to help me. She helped me raise Merilee too. Then when Percy drank himself to death and when the couple downstairs got divorced and moved out, Angel moved in. I imagine she has been here almost a hundred years. Now my Thurmond's changed his name to Fritz and he's off in California with his third wife, Karyn with a *y*, thank you. Merilee is still married to that banker in Atlanta. I never saw either one of them unless I was at death's door. It's just *Life With Angel*, and an orchestrated visit to death's door every five years.

All right, I'd admit it. I liked a little drama now and then. Kept my blood sugar down and my spirits up. Still. My new neighbor? I knew her type, all right. Home-wrecking man chasers! Humph!

It made me sad, it truly did. I picked up my watering can and began to give the babies a drink, watching through the windows, sighing all the while that Blanche walked in between and around my legs. Stanley just laid up there, happy in the front window as though a fish was going to fly through the air and land in his mouth.

Cats are nasty things, licking everything and then licking you too, but they were company for a single lady like me. If I found a nice man for me but he was allergic to cats, I'd throw them right out the door and they knew it too. As a result of their ESP, they were extremely well behaved.

I sat down in my pink La-Z-Boy recliner and turned on *Oprah*. I wondered what she would have to say about this May–December nonsense next door. Maybe I would write her a letter. I must have dozed off because the next thing I remembered was Angel turning down the air conditioner and putting my afghan over my legs. Bless her heart, I thought, and drifted back to sleep. I was dreaming about something . . . what was it? Ah, yes, Anthony Hopkins was asking me to dance. *Why, I'd love to . . .*

Five

Loose Screws

~~~

I CONTINUED to unload the van while Daddy was inside with his toolbox fixing a stubborn sliding door. I could hear him cussing up a blue streak. The thermometer was over ninety and his mood was foul. It was perfectly understandable that he was out of sorts. We had become used to each other, in the same way you sprain an ankle and wonder what you'd do without crutches. We did so many small things for each other and now there would be no one to anticipate his needs. My leaving cut a hole right in the middle of his daily routines and meant that he'd have to clip his own coupons and grocery shop, take in his dry cleaning and pick it up, and all the rest of my share of chores.

To make it worse, ever since I had announced my move, he had second-guessed every decision I made, leaving me with some serious insecurity over my abilities to handle a house on my own. Perhaps the day would arrive when I would decide to live in a condominium at Wild Dunes, where maintenance crews took care of everything. Until that day arrived, I was determined to have my own yard, my own property, and real land.

"Who are you going to call if the roof leaks?"

"You."

"Where are you going to go if there's a hurricane?"

"You."

"Then what's the point of moving? Wouldn't you rather travel every year for the same money? See the world? Stay in nice hotels? A mortgage isn't anything but a rope around your neck!"

"No, that's not true, Daddy. This house is an investment. If I spend the money on travel, it's gone. Poof! I have nothing for my future!"

"If you traveled, maybe you'd meet a nice man for your future."

"That's a cheap shot, Daddy. I'd rather be responsible for myself than marry somebody for financial security." This made him mad because that was what he thought my mother had done. "Why don't *you* travel? Maybe you'd meet a nice *woman.*"

"Don't tell me what to do, okay? All you feminists! You're all crazy as hell! You ruined it for the nice girls who just want families!"

"Sure. The feminists ruined it for the *nice* girls. That's what you always say when you know I'm right."

"Go ahead! You're gonna do what you want anyway! You always have!"

"So do you and I'm your daughter! Where in the hell do you think I learned to be such a mule?"

The quiet would swallow us until we'd come to the same realization again—that it just wasn't mentally healthy for either of us to lean on each other like we did. It caused stagnation. Although parents and children we had known forever lived out their days together unless one or the other married—and sometimes you just moved the spouse in and life went on—we knew it wasn't an optimum situation.

We had traded those same remarks one hundred times in the past weeks. If it wasn't travel he suggested, he would bring up furthering my education. He was completely riled over the purchase of my house. I ignored him to the extent it was possible. Despite my nightmares over Daddy's doubts and general unhappiness and my nerves over my *great leap forward*, I was still irrepressible.

He finally came around last night with a new angle to justify my leaving to himself. I was hanging clothes in a wardrobe box when he came into my room.

"You know, Anna, I've been thinking."

Was he going to try again to change my mind?

"Yeah? About what?" I turned and smiled at him, thinking that if he could see my happiness, it would deter the appeal.

"Well, it's about your mother. You want a glass of tea?"

"Sure," I said and stopped, followed him to the kitchen and stood by the counter as he poured me a glass. "Thanks. What's bothering you?"

"Your mother's parents were closer to my age than I was to her age when I married her, you know."

I squeezed a wedge of lemon into my glass and let him continue.

"I realize now, looking back, that she married me because I offered her a way to get away from living at poverty level."

"That's not the worst thing, Daddy. Her parents were ancient and she was working as a checkout girl at the grocery store. I mean, it wasn't such a grand life for a beautiful young woman. People marry for a lot of reasons."

"Yeah, they do. You want a sandwich?"

"No, thanks," I said. "Open the new salami—the other package is past the expiration date."

We had a little issue about throwing away food and I knew he would eat anything without fur. I made a mental note to come over and clean out the refrigerator every so often.

"Right," he said, and pulled out the cutting board. "People do marry for a lot of reasons and even though you and Jim couldn't make it last forever, that boy always loved you and Emily."

"I think he always will too."

"Yeah, but your mother's motive wasn't exactly pure. She jumped at the first chance for a respectable life that came along, you know?"

"Look, Daddy, I love you to death. You know that. I'm tired of pee-peeing on Momma's grave. I think she was young and stupid. That's all."

"Baby, listen to me. That's not what I'm saying here. I'm saying that she didn't give herself the chance to be on her own for a while and then marry. She never gave herself a chance to find out what she wanted. So this is a good thing for you to do, in that way. Just don't jump at some foolish guy who promises you the world. If it's not working out, for whatever reason, talk to me, okay?"

"First of all, I'm not leaving you to find a husband. And, there isn't a landslide of men around here to date anyway, Daddy. They're all married or screwed up or losers. And marriage isn't for everyone, you know. I mean, this is about me living where I have always wanted to live and having a place for Emily and me that's ours. I'm not exactly the romantic type anyway. And the last thing I'd do is dive into a marriage without considering your opinion and Jim's and Frannie's and Emily's. Right? Come on! You know me better."

"I do know you better, but I also remember how easy it was for me to convince myself that Mary Beth really loved me. That's all."

"Don't worry. I'll keep you posted, okay? Now, finish your sandwich and help me unpack!"

I had hardly slept last night, I was so excited. For good reason. All I had to do was look outside. The afternoon sky was filled with so much blue it made me feel like flying. Great pillows and sheer tears of clouds invited the hide-and-seek of angelic creatures. Gorgeous!

I had opened every window in the house and the stuffiness of the rooms was immediately sucked out by the pull of the ocean. The air was as warm and tasty as any I could recollect—a fat-free gumbo of heavy saline, wrapped in the sounds of frond rustle and bird song. It was a perfect summer day. You know it had to be if I was talking *frond rustle*.

"Come tell me if this is the way you want it!" Daddy called out. There was defeat in his voice. I hated the mood he was in, but I wasn't going to let him ruin mine.

"Coming!" I said.

"Hey!" someone called out from above. "Y'all moving in?"

The greeting and raspy voice, unmistakably feminine, came from the house next door. I looked up to see a very blond woman, somewhere in the zone of my age, maybe older, leaning over her porch railing.

"Hey! Yeah," I said, calling back to her, "just moving in!"

"Good! This neighborhood could use some life! I'm Lucy. What's your name?"

I smiled up to her and called out, "Anna! Anna Abbot!"

Okay. Maybe it's impolite to bring this up, but she wasn't wearing any underwear under her gauze sundress. I am *not* kidding. Normally, I do not care what people wear or don't wear under their sundress. I thought for a moment that she probably didn't realize the afternoon sun made her smart little frock all but transparent and so I pretended not to notice. Or maybe she had just taken a shower and was in the process of getting dressed or something.

"Be back in a moment," I said. The box I was holding wasn't getting any lighter and then I couldn't resist the tap of the Devil himself. "Daddy?" I said, all innocence waltzing through my new front door. "Would you mind bringing in the box in the back of the van next to the wardrobe box? It's too heavy for me."

He adored helpless females. He came to my aid immediately, grumbling a little. I witnessed a complete mood swing as he stepped out into the front yard and got an eyeful of my neighbor, who was a living mood elevator—a double dose. I was right behind him.

"Hi!" Lucy said, waving and parading full feathers up and down her upstairs porch in the breeze. "Are you Mr. Anna Abbot?"

Daddy looked up. His gasp could have inhaled the entire square footage of Lowe's in the Towne Centre in Mount Pleasant, including part of the parking lot.

"I'm Dougle Lutz," he said. "Douglas, I mean, but my friends call me Doc. I'm Anna's father, Miss . . . ?"

"Ah!" She took a long pause. "I see! I'm Lucy, Dougle," she said and giggled. "Gimme ten minutes to organize something and I'll be *rat* over!"

She turned and went inside her house, the screen door slamming behind her. Poor Daddy. He was just blithering spittle every which way and I had to bite the insides of my mouth not to fall over with laughter.

"Great God," Daddy said under his breath. His face was a parfait of horror, piqued testosterone, and questions of decency. "Did you see that she had no . . . what was her name?"

"Lucy," I said, groping for an explanation, at the same time asking myself why I thought it was my responsibility to make sense of this cockeyed world for him. "Well? What can I say, Dad? At least the natives seem friendly."

"Very," he said.

I slapped him lightly on the shoulder to bring him back to earth. His eyes burned a hole in the space where she had stood moments before. It had probably been quite some time since old Douglas, now and forever *Dougle* in my mind, had witnessed something so provocative in broad daylight—or the dead of night for that matter. The same held true for me, but I wasn't about to admit it to him or anyone else.

We returned to the piles of boxes all over my house and Daddy was still muttering about her.

"Who was that woman? Where do you want the stereo?"

"I don't know. Delilah?" Poor Daddy. "I guess the stereo should go here in the living room?"

I had one of those reasonably priced mini stereo units from Wal-Mart that could be tucked neatly into bookshelves. The only major splurge for decorating my new home was a Scandinavian blond wood wall unit for my living room. I had bought it from Katie at Danco in Mount Pleasant. It was beautiful—light but sturdy, clean lines and modern. After years of boards and bricks I decided my books deserved a more dignified resting place. Not a soul on this earth would ever have called me materialistic, but I sure did have an overgrown bed of gardening books, a ton of cookbooks, and a small collection of leather-bound classics that were precious to me. Now I had this wonderful piece of furniture to hold them and I was thrilled by it. Collecting books and preserving them for another generation was a worthy pursuit. If there was one thing Charlestonians understood, it was saving things they loved.

I was so deep in my thoughts that I didn't hear my new neighbor rapping on the screen door. Daddy must have, because I looked up to see him talking to Lucy, who held a blender filled with something to drink. She had changed into another outfit—very short overalls and a tight T-shirt. Daddy stood there with his hands deep in his pockets, completely agog, staring at her from head to toe while she drew circles around him with her sweet words of welcome.

"So I said to myself, Lucy?—you need to go on over there and help your new neighbors! Can I pour y'all a drink? I even brought us some paper cups!"

"Sure, thanks a lot," Daddy said. "This was very thoughtful of you."

"Hey! Thanks, Lucy," I said.

She leaned over to pour out the drinks on top of a low box. What appeared to be a frozen fruit drink flowed into the cups. If she leaned over another inch Daddy and I would have more facts about her than we needed to know. I must admit, however, with certain authority, that the moment soon passed when we inadvertently learned that her sofa did not match her curtains, not that I thought they would.

She handed us a cup, lifted hers, and said, "Well, honey? Welcome to the neighborhood and if you ever need a play date, you know where to find me. Cheers!" As she spoke, the sun coming through my living room window bounced around her thick lip gloss to such an extent that her large and expressive mouth became a moving light show. In all my years, I had never encountered someone quite like Lucy. Flamboyant didn't begin to cover it.

I took a big gulp and struggled to swallow. "What *is* this?" I said, coughing.

"Oh, it's a sort of frozen Planter's Punch," she said, "but it's my secret recipe! Good, huh?"

"It's delicious," Daddy said. "May I fill your cup, Miss Lucy?"

"Honey, you can fill my cup anytime!" she said and burst out laughing with the silliest laugh I had ever heard.

In fact, her remark, followed by that laugh, was so outrageous that I decided she was only kidding. She *must* have been.

Daddy blushed a deep red. He was beside himself, staring at her shoes, which for the record were espadrilles with three-inch platforms and black strings tied all around her ankles. The overall effect of this getup was a kind of construction worker—gladiator—centerfold. Maybe she didn't have a full-length mirror?

She turned to my new wall unit, ran her hand over its smooth wood and said, "Golly, this is so pretty. Is it new?"

Okay. What can I say? She had an appreciation for the wall unit of my dreams so she wasn't without some merit. Besides, even as my mind ran through the faces of all the most conspicuous clients I had ever had, she was most definitely a mutant species, far too interesting to shut out.

"Yes," I said, "it is and I have to admit that I'm insane over the thing. Isn't that ridiculous?"

"Not one little bit! Since when is it a sin to appreciate something beautiful?"

That's when I decided that I liked her, slut or no slut.

Daddy handed her drink to her and said, "Miss Lucy?"

She smiled at him and said as bold as can be, "Thanks, Dougle, darlin'!"

Dougle. We cracked up—all of us—partners in a growing haze of unaccustomed alcohol. Well, for us anyway. Daddy and I *never* touched a drop of alcohol in the daytime! I don't think, however, that we could have said the same for Miss Lucy.

Daddy's reserve dissolved sip by sip. The ice was officially broken, no, melting and it was clear Lucy wasn't going home anytime soon. I was happy to have her company because Daddy was completely entertained. I guess it was impossible for him to be crabby when this odd little sexpot flirted shamelessly with him. I was having the time of my life watching it. Best of all, I was getting unpacked. Lucy decided to take over the linen closet while we asked her a million questions about herself.

We learned by our second pitcher of this tropical concoction of hers that she was divorced from her husband, who was an extremely successful residential contractor.

"Hugo was the best thing that ever happened to old Danny," she said, remarking on the horrible hurricane of 1989 that nearly blew Charleston and all its barrier islands off the map. "He made a killing."

"So where is he now?" I said, unprepared for what was to follow.

Her eyes filled with tears and she said, "He left me and went off to Key West to fish. He was the love of my life! One day, out of nowhere, he was gone! Kazam! I came home from aerobics and there was a bag of Zoloft samples, an empty bottle of Absolut Citron, his favorite, and a note on the kitchen counter." She stopped, cleared her throat and read an imaginary paper in her hand. " *Dear Lucy, I cannot stand you for another minute. You drive me shit-house crazy. I took the boat and fifty thousand dollars out of the savings account and you can have everything else. Good-bye. Don't try to find me. I quit.'* Is that the most insulting thing you have ever heard?" Bulbous tears rolled down her augmented cheekbones to her augmented breasts and Daddy all but pounced to her side with his handkerchief. Like his mother, Daddy used handkerchiefs, not tissues.

"Jeesch!" I said. "That's awful!"

"He was the love of my life," she said, repeating herself.

"He was a damn fool, Miss Lucy," Daddy said, in all sincerity, "a damn fool."

"I did everything he wanted. I mean *everything!*"

Daddy cleared his throat and God only knew what he was thinking about *that* statement, but Lucy continued.

"I made his favorite casserole, his momma's recipe, every Wednesday and, oh, hellfire! Why do I always cry when I start talking about him? Y'all must think I'm as crazy as a bedbug!"

"We think no such thing, do we, Anna?"

"No, absolutely not," I said. *Yes, absolutely yes,* I thought. If my husband had left me a note like that, I'd have followed him to the bottom floor of Hades and stuffed it in his ears with a pencil.

"I ironed his shirts and folded his stupid underwear . . ."

She began to wail and all I could do was wonder why underwear was so problematic for her.

Daddy put his arm around her shoulder and she turned into his chest and boo-hooed for all she was worth. Turned out that what she was worth was a lot. Danny the house builder turned fisherman had bought Microsoft and America Online stocks in the eighties and they had split about a bazillion times. He also never spent a dime of what he had earned in the boom years. Danny left Lucy in Fat City. Lucy had turned her portfolio into cash early last year.

"I wasn't comfortable having my whole future in the stock market," she said. "Turns out I made a lucky guess."

To say the least. The injustice of her windfall versus my unending battle with bills wasn't lost on me, but this was not my first brush with an unfair world. By the time she had calmed herself down, she and Daddy went next door for a few minutes to get a casserole from her freezer for our dinner.

I was busy organizing cassette tapes and CDs and I had the feeling someone was watching me, you know, that creepy feeling when the hair on the back of your neck bristles? I looked up to see a little old lady at my door.

"Anybody home?" she said, knowing perfectly well that I *was* there, since she had been spying for who knew how long.

I went to the door and stood inside the screen, sizing up my visitor, a tiny woman of perhaps eighty. Was it Miss Mavis?

"Hi," I said, knowing I reeked of booze and not giving a damn either. Bottom line, don't stare in my door. Second bottom line, I was cruising the River Rum.

"I live next door and I brought you a cake!" she said. "Aren't you going to invite me to come in?"

She was so cantankerous that it gave me a start.

"Oh! Of course, where are my manners? Thank you," I said, holding the screen wide for her to pass. "Welcome to my mess!"

She stood in the middle of the living room and looked all around her at the stacks of boxes and wads of packing paper and then gave her unsolicited opinion.

"Well, it's gonna be a million years before you get *this* disaster straight! Do you have a dog?"

"No, ma'am, just me and my daughter—that is, when she's home from school."

"Who? What?"

She was obviously losing her hearing, so I raised my voice a little. "No, ma'am. Just me and my daughter, who's in college."

"Well, that's good. I have two cats and I don't want some dog bothering them. Are you a party person? Here, take this from me, for heaven's sake."

"Thank you," I said and put the cake on the one bare spot on my dining table. "If you want to know if I make much noise, the answer is no, I don't make noise."

"Good. I need my sleep and I like to leave my windows open when there's a nice breeze."

"So do I, Miss . . . ? I'm sorry, I don't think we ever told each other our names! I'm Anna."

"Well, I'm Miss Mavis. I've been living on the Isle of Palms all my life and my mother and daddy before me. Used to come here for summers." She looked me up and down with her hands on her boxy hips. "There's not a grain of sand on this island I haven't seen and a story about this place that I don't know. *Ask Mavis!*—that's what they say."

"Well, it's awfully nice meeting you and I surely do appreciate the cake, Miss Mavis."

She obviously didn't remember me and I really didn't know what to do with her at that point. I couldn't invite her to sit and have a cup of coffee. I hadn't unpacked the coffee machine yet, I hadn't bought tea or any groceries at all, and every seat held a box or a pile. Besides,

I was a little looped and that wasn't the best time for reacquainting myself with her or anybody.

She smiled then for the first time and I saw the face that I remembered from years ago, the one that had been so kind to me the day my momma died. Yes, I remembered her. I wasn't ready to revisit my past quite yet. But, how wonderful! Wonderful to find her alive and the same, really. She still liked being called Miss Mavis. She had remained an old-fashioned island girl all these years—sassy, opinionated. I would be smart to treat her with the same deference. Her years and history had earned it. I'd tell her who I was some other day.

"Well, it's Angel's cake, really. I just came over to have a look and say hello."

"That's fine. I appreciate it. I love angel cake." *Rolling down the river* . . .

"How's that? No, girl, Angel's cake! Angel made it!"

"Well, please tell her I said thanks so much." So! Angel was still around too!

"I'll do that. Now. Where's the man?"

"What man?"

"I distinctly saw a man helping you. Are you one of those fast women living in sin?"

I burst out laughing. "Are you kidding? That was my father!"

"Well? Where is he? Isn't he going to come out and say hello?"

"Oh! I'm sorry! No, he's next door getting a casserole."

"What? Lucy's already been here? Already sunk her claws into your daddy?"

"No, ma'am, I don't think she . . ."

"Humph! You mark my word, young lady, that woman is . . . she's . . . well, you just watch out, 'eah?"

Miss Mavis was more aggravated than I thought she should have been that Daddy wasn't there to greet her, but I let it pass. Besides, I didn't need her to tell me what Lucy was.

She started to the door, taking a deep breath to compose herself.

"The world has changed around me, Anna, but I'm too old now to change myself. If you need anything just come on over."

I watched her walk across the yard back to her house. There was more spit and vinegar in her than I'd seen in anybody in a long time. She was still just a little old Carolina blue crab and I knew I was going to like, no, adore living next door to her. She could tell me stories about what I had missed over the years on the Isle of Palms. I'd be a grateful listener. She could help me patch up the wounded part of me. If she wanted to.

I started to wonder what had happened to Daddy and Lucy but I kept working, unpacking the kitchen boxes, and putting things away, plugging in the Mr. Coffee.

When they returned an hour later, Lucy had changed clothes again and Daddy couldn't look at me in the eye.

This behavior was very unlike him. I decided it was probably best not to mention that the back of his hair stood up like Alfalfa's cowlick. Old one-spike Dougle. I mean, Daddy surely realized that women like Lucy were emotional train wrecks—self-serving, self-promoting, opportunistic . . . Whoa!

What was the matter with me? So my daddy scored a little hands-on in her kitchen? Was that a big deal? God! I mean, when was the last time Daddy did anything to be embarrassed about? Hell, it might improve his mood and his health! Please understand. I also never thought about my father having a sexual urge in my entire life. Ever since Momma died, Daddy had all but given up on women who put out. But here he was, caught like an unsuspecting flounder on the lampoon of a pro. He probably didn't even put up a fight, and good for him. God knows, if there was one thing my daddy and I needed, it was, well, you know . . .

So, there was Lucy with her casserole, which in case they find me dead tomorrow, was the most awful thing to ever kick its way down the old gullet. It was chicken—a seemingly naïve enough main ingredient—drowned in cheddar cheese, refried beans, and taco chips. Vile. But Lucy was so proud and Daddy was so smitten, how could I not be gracious? Our first meal in my new home and the Health Department had not been notified to rescue us. Daddy was chomping away, while I picked through the taco chips and Lucy drank (with a gusto I found remarkable) the martinis she had brought.

"Lucy, this was really thoughtful of you," I said.

"Oh, honey," she said, "it was nothing at all!"

"Oh, no, Miss Lucy," Daddy said, "this is a night to remember! Isn't that so, Anna?"

"Yes, it is," I said. It definitely was. "We have cake for dessert, if anyone would care for a slice?"

"Cake?" Daddy said. "From where?"

"Miss Mavis next door," I said.

"Mavis? You're kidding! She's still around?" Daddy said.

"Yep," I said, "didn't recognize me."

"Oh, God!" Lucy said. "Oh, God! Y'all better brace yourselves!" No surprise that Lucy had missed the comment that we knew Miss Mavis. I was surprised she could still sit up.

"Why?" I said.

"'Cause, honey, she's like the Snoop Sisters and Detective Columbo rolled into one! She watches the comings and goings of my life like the FBI! I ain't lying, y'all! It's true! Got these nasty cats and this old Gullah woman who does God knows what kind of hexing over there! Oh, listen to me, y'all, just rambling on?" Lucy stood up and stretched, revealing her belly button. "Must be time for Miss Lucy to get to her boudoir, 'eah? Gosh, Anna, I'm so glad to have you as a neighbor!"

"Me too, Lucy. Thanks for all your help."

"We'll have such fun," she said.

Once we sober up, I thought.

All the while she had been talking, Daddy and I had just listened and nodded our heads. Now we had been given the signal that she had to go and it was apparently up to us to make a move.

Daddy stood up. "May I walk you home, Miss Lucy?"

"It would be my greatest pleasure!" Lucy said.

I followed them outside and watched them walk across the lawn and up her steps to her porch, the moonlight all over them like the stadium blanket of a naughty Cupid. When I looked up at my daddy talking to her on her porch, for all the world he looked like a young man falling in love.

I couldn't watch to see if they kissed. Too gross. Besides, Daddy was entitled to his privacy—privacy was one small part of why I had moved. He would tell me they kissed if he wanted to, but I would not ask.

He returned in the phoniest bad mood I had ever seen, a defense mechanism dredged up at the last moment to avoid the anticipated daughterly Q & A session. He never should have worried about that. I just kissed him on the head and said, "Thanks, Daddy, I never could have done all this today without you."

"Get some sleep," he said. "I'll be back tomorrow."

I watched him back out from my yard in the rental van. The Isle of Palms was quiet. The Misses Mavis and Angel to my left, the alleged Snoop Sisters, appeared to be gone off to sleep for the evening. Lucy's house was almost dark. I walked to the edge of my yard and headed for the beach.

That night was all important. With one turn of the tide and one night's sleep, my biggest dream would be coming true. I walked down the damp path to the ocean. The dark beach was measurably cooler in just the hundred yards from my yard. The breezes were stronger and the sky was a deeper hue. Every aspect of the landscape was amplified and slightly haunted. I began to walk a little toward Sullivan's Island, thinking about all the mechanics of moving, the list of chores remaining to be done.

Emily was coming home from school soon. For the first time since Jim had left us, I had a home. I couldn't wait to tell him about moving day and Lucy. Our little house would remind him of the carriage house we had shared when Emily was born. I made a mental note to call him in the morning and bring him up-to-date. I was excited about the possibilities of everything.

Unlike some women who lived through men, I had figured that I didn't really need a husband. I had dated plenty of great guys, but just never fell in love. That was probably more my fault than anyone's. I had been too busy working, saving for a house, taking care of Daddy, and raising Emily to focus on much else.

At this point I only needed to prove to myself that I could do what single parents all over the world could do—make a home for Emily and for me. Maybe when I got my life the way I wanted it, maybe then I would allow myself to think about a wild love affair and a possible husband.

I wanted my new life to begin with a white-hot fever. I had just three weeks until Emily would arrive. I directed my attention full force to pulling together something that looked and felt like a home.

I couldn't help wondering what Momma would have thought to see me now. She would probably have been amazed. And Violet? Thinking about Grandmother Violet caused convulsive laughter. She'd have a freaking cow, no, a whole barnyard, if she could see me moving into my own house on the island, especially given her convictions. If she was still around I could have laid the bulk of my problems at her feet. And the remaining problems? Well, I caused them or allowed them to happen, to be sure. There was a long list of names of women who had given me pain. First it was Momma, then Grandmother Violet, and later on there was Trixie. Trixie is Jim's mother. If there was a stadium in hell, it would have been named for her.

Six

Light of Day

WHEN the first hint of daylight seeped in, I jumped out of bed. It was five-thirty, a lot earlier than I usually woke up. I stumbled through the boxes and piles into my new kitchen to get the coffee started that I had set up the night before. A trace in the air of the rich ground beans stopped me for a moment. It was my first pot of coffee. My first morning here had arrived.

I pulled on baggy khakis, a white T-shirt, gave my teeth a preliminary brushing, and splashed my face with water. In minutes the asphalt was under my feet.

The island around me still slept, porch lights glowing amber through the morning haze. Maybe they had been left on for someone who never came home or maybe someone who came home simply forgot to turn them off. I liked to muse about the lives of others and what they were thinking when they closed their doors against the night. Take Lucy for example. Did she drink herself to sleep every night? Was she really unhappy or just an actress? Manipulative? Had Daddy gone to sleep thinking about her? I had always thought the unseen comings and goings of others were more interesting than what people showed of themselves to the world. And, I loved the masks people wore. The masks we wore were proof of the strength of southerners. I mean, hadn't the South resurrected herself with enough frequency to impress the planet? Everybody knew it was near impossible to figure out what we thought by just looking at us. We had smiling poker faces. Lots of teeth. Polite to a fault. It was probably the sin of pride that we assumed the world acknowledged and coveted our excellent dispositions.

True southerners were pickled from birth in our ancestral marinades of charm and grace. Money and possessions had little to do with personal conduct. Southerners of every race and creed held each other to a higher standard of behavior. And we understood the nuances that separated good old boys, bubbas, and rednecks.

Good old boys were the most traditional. They polished their Weejuns, monogrammed their shirts, smelled good, and held your door open. They were more worldly, could mix cocktails, and may have gone to graduate school. Bubbas might have a truck for no particular reason, but they were nice guys who didn't get a lot of exercise, might get caught drinking beer for breakfast, and never walked away from a manly challenge. Rednecks never ate pork chops or chicken with anything but their hands, trained their Heinz 57 dogs to bite, occasionally hit their wives, used their trucks like a minivan to haul the kids around to tractor pulls, and provoked the manly challenges.

That's not to say we didn't honor all kinds of people. We had more than a few bugs among our Magnolias, like my other neighbor, old Miss Mavis. She was anything but concerned about how the world perceived her. I grinned just thinking about her. What an incredible old fussbudget! It must have been nice to act any way you wanted to and have the world accept it. It certainly had never been my fortune to have that freedom. Maybe when I told her who I really was she would remember the past and congratulate me and be a grandmotherly friend or something.

I walked on. At first, the air was so thick with fog and dew that I could almost grab it. I could barely see ten yards ahead. Then, it was as if someone said, *Okay, it's time for a little sun!* The curtains of wet air began to lift and all the sights I had hoped to see were there. Everything was alive and in living color.

In the distance two dogs were chasing seagulls, running back and forth to their owner. He appeared to be cheerful enough, swinging their leashes around and giving an occasional whistle for his dogs to fall back in line with him. And they, two gorgeous Irish setters, would do just that. That is, until they spotted another flock of seagulls at the water's edge. They were off again, barking and running after the birds, who, at the last possible second of safety, took off across the water, squawking and screeching. It was a pleasant sight and I didn't mind sharing the beach with the other fellow in the least. I even gave a few seconds of thought to getting a dog of my own. I'd never had one and didn't know the first thing about them, but a dog might be good company, even though Miss Mavis would most likely complain.

I was in excellent humor and I wondered if I should feel obliged to greet this stranger if he passed by me, but it was a decision I didn't have to worry about. He crossed the dunes with his dogs and vanished. Once again the beach was mine.

I looked at my watch. Six-thirty. It was still early and my first appointment was booked for ten. Something was going to have to be done about old Harriet's House of Hair. I had been there since I was barely twenty years old. I didn't mind the work; in fact I enjoyed it. The money was good and most of the clients were very nice. It was Harriet. Like Lucy's ex-husband would say, she drove me shit-house crazy.

Walking home, I stopped to knock the sand out of my running shoes and briefly considered taking up running since I already owned the shoes. Had I unconsciously outfitted myself to become athletic? Not a chance. Anything but a jock, I laughed at myself that I had spent years with my hands in the hair of strangers, in a climate-controlled salon, unaware of changing seasons (not that Charleston had them).

I realized how happy I was. Maybe for the first time, certainly for the first time in many years, I was happy.

I reached my little cottage and stopped for a minute to look at it, nestled between the two much more imposing houses on either side. Miss Mavis and Loosey Lucy. The differences between Miss Mavis's and Lucy's houses reminded me what Daddy had always said, *islands are filled with characters.* Maybe with a little luck, I could become one myself.

My yard needs major work. I was continuing my mental list of miracles to accomplish when the phone rang. I assumed it was Daddy, calling to make sure some lunatic hadn't carried me off in the night. It wasn't. It was Jim's mother, Trixie, my ex-mother-in-law.

"Ah just wanted to call and see how it's going, dear! Ah just spoke to your father. He told me everything. Ah can't believe you bought a house and moved in and Ah haven't even seen it!"

"Yes, well . . ."

"You didn't tell me a thing! But then, isn't that how you've always been?"

As always, her hee-haw accent set me on edge as though I had done something wrong, breached some protocol, by not clearing everything with her. Trixie defined repressed anger. I was trying to be nice anyway.

"Well, you'll just have to come and visit! I just need a few days to unpack and get organized," I said. "It's little, I mean, it's just two bedrooms."

"Merciful heavens! Two bedrooms? Well, Ah'm sure that's all you need."

God forbid I ever have one helping more than you think I need. "Actually, it's more like an apartment with a yard," I said, "but I can see the water, sort of, and that's kind of special."

"Well, if you're satisfied, Ah'm sure Ah will be too. Why don't Ah bring luuunch over this Sunday?"

Lunch is not supposed to be a three-syllable word, Trixie. "Sure, that would be nice!" I knew her visit was inevitable so I figured get it over with as soon as possible. And, golly gee whiz, I thought, the malcontent in me rising, I hope she's *satisfied!*

I could hear her flipping paper. "Oh, dear, no, Sunday's out. Regatta! Goodness! Ah almost forgot! Can you imagine whut . . ."

"No, that would be *terrible* if you missed that," I said, and hoped I hadn't sounded too disingenuous.

"Well, Ah'll have to let you know, Anna. And, how is *our* Emily?"

"Great! Coming home in three weeks! I can't wait to see her. It's been almost six months—the longest we have ever been apart!" *Our Emily, indeed.*

"Isn't that grand? If you speak to her, give her my looove and tell her Ah want to hug her neck so bad I could *just* die!"

We hung up and I had a nearly uncontrollable urge to pin her picture up in the bathroom. I'm going to tell you something no one knows and I just hope you won't go taking this around town. This is the abridged version of why you should never take something from anyone except your own flesh and blood, and even then, beware.

First of all, the person who had the *money* usually thought they had the power. Worse, money puts price tags on relationships. Sometimes that was so true it tore families apart. In my case, even though I didn't sign up for the class, my education began with my infamous date rape that resulted in Emily's birth.

It may be hard to believe that there was such a thing as a date rape drug in 1983, but there was. I bear the dubious distinction of being the only person I know to ever have ingested Rohypnol, the original date rape drug. It was very effective.

My grandmother had fixed me up with a fellow she decided was an appropriate escort for my senior prom. It is important to note that this was my first date, as my grandmother thought that going to the movies with a boy meant you had sex. She also thought that lip gloss led to sex. I did not, just for the record, even do anything about those kinds of pronouncements except snicker. Not that it would have mattered to her what I thought. When I was a junior and senior in high school, I still didn't date but it was because I didn't know anybody I wanted to go out with. I was happy with my friends.

Anyway, this major loser date she found for me, who was the next step in the drama of my life, was Everett Fairchild, the son of a minister from Atlanta. I guess old Grandma figured a minister's son was a safe bet, but she hadn't mixed the college part into the equation. In the crazy days of the eighties, college students were as renowned as in the sixties for their wild antics. As hostess to many colleges, Charleston society in general turned her head to the bad boy fistfights and the insane alcohol consumption, justifying the students' rowdy behavior as being a result of too many rules or homesickness or any of a thousand excuses. Well, Everett had a South American roommate who was in the import business—importing medication for recreational purposes.

Everett, prepared with a pocketful of "roofies," took me to the prom and then to a beach house out on Folly Beach where a lot of my friends were planning to spend the weekend. We had changed into shorts and sandals and the night was going swimmingly well. This all could have happened yesterday, my memory is so clear, but then this would also easily qualify as a memory which would become emblazoned in the mind of a blue-bottomed baboon.

Everett, a platinum blond with perfect teeth, sea foam green eyes, and deep dimples, was a nice enough fellow until he started drinking PJ—which stands for Purple Jesus, a terrible punch of fruit juices and any available alcohol—and started putting the moves on me. I was so stupid I was flattered by it. I'd never touched a drop of alcohol. My best friends, Jim and Frannie, were there at the party with each other, which was nice since Jim was assumed to be gay and Frannie was too fat at that point in her life to get a date, so Jim took her. But they rolled their eyes every time Everett put his lips on my neck. I just smiled. What a dope I was.

We were all drinking whatever anyone gave us and the next thing I knew, sweet Everett was leading me to a bedroom. I still remember thinking that a nap was a good idea, because I wasn't in any shape to do anything else at that point. My vision was blurred and I was feeling wobbly in the extreme.

The next thing I remember is that Jim and Frannie were standing over me. Frannie was crying and I was bleeding. Jim had a T-shirt wrapped around his fist. Apparently, he had punched Everett all around his pretty head and abdominal area. Everett stumbled out the door and took off in his car, leaving me stranded. Somehow Jim and Frannie got me into their car and took me to the emergency room at St. Francis Hospital. My nose was broken, gushing blood, and I was feeling pretty green.

"Oh, my God!" Frannie said over and over, "what are we gonna tell your grandmother?"

"Fell down the steps," I said, through my blur of what I assumed was only alcohol.

"Yeah, that's good," Jim said, "that's what we'll say."

"Just drive," Frannie said and continued fretting over me, "hang on, Anna, we're almost there."

It was after one o'clock in the morning by then. Jim and Frannie stayed with me while some poor sleep-deprived resident cleaned me up and gently attempted to set my nose, after icing it, covering it with surgical tape, and handing me a prescription for an antibiotic. He suggested that I see a plastic surgeon in the next few days, which, of course, I never did, hence the bump in the middle of my nose. No one ever thought to check for sexual assault. Including me. I mean, it simply didn't occur to me.

Jim and Frannie never mentioned my state of dress. When I finally gathered enough nerve to ask them about it, I think they had been so traumatized by the whole scene—Everett drunk on the bed beside me, cursing when they came in the room, and me bloody, moaning and disheveled—that they had only wanted to help me get out of there. That is, after Jim beat the crap out of Everett. Jim might have been gay but he was no sissy stereotype, all right? He loved me to death. We would have done anything for each other.

Daddy accepted the story of me falling down stairs and wrote it off to teenage carelessness. I think I can recall him sort of chuckling about it, teasing me, probably glad that I had done something a little reckless for once in my otherwise boring life. It made both of us seem more normal, less starched. He filled my prescription, wagging his finger, and told me I was lucky I hadn't broken my neck.

Six weeks later I thought I had the flu. It was the middle of July, hot as the tar on the roof of Hell, and I thought I was dying for sure. I ached all over and was so tired I could hardly raise my head or keep my eyes open. I slept all the time. Finally, Daddy became suspicious. At first he thought I had mononucleosis, then anemia. Exasperated after a few weeks more, he sent me to an internist, an old pal of his, who ordered a battery of tests for me that included blood work and a urinalysis. It took Dr. Goodman about one minute to assess the situation and give a diagnosis. I was sitting across from him at his desk in his office after my examination.

"You're about ten weeks pregnant," he said.

"That's not funny," I said and jumped up from my seat as though I had been sitting on a wet electrified fence.

"No, I don't imagine that it is, Anna," he said. "How old are you?" He was perfectly serious, assuming that I was some kind of teenage tramp to have deceived my long-suffering father in this unspeakable manner.

"It's impossible," I said, the words flying out of my mouth. "It is."

Thank God and all of His angels and saints that Dr. Goodman had the presence of mind to search my face because he saw then, and most importantly he believed, that if I was telling the truth, then something else had gone terribly wrong. Indeed, something had.

One patient waited to see him in his waiting room as it was the end of his day.

"Anna," he said quietly, getting up and coming around to my side of his desk. He took my icy hands in his and sighed heavily, looking at me for the longest time. "I have to leave you for a few minutes. There's an elderly lady in my waiting room with an ear infection. I want you to sit here and try to reconstruct how this may have happened. Then

you and I are going to figure this out, without anyone getting hysterical. It's my job to worry, not yours, okay?"

He patted the back of my hands and as soon as he left the office, I
began to shake all over. He may as well have plunged a dagger through
the wall of my chest.

I tried to concentrate. The only time in my entire life that I had
been unaware of a passage of time was after my prom. I knew then
that I was carrying Everett Fairchild's baby. Everett Fairchild had sex
with me and I didn't even know it had happened. What in the world
was I going to do? Had I told him it was okay?

I asked myself the same question over and over—how could this
have happened? And, why me? How horrible and unfair! I was supposed to go to the University of South Carolina in August! I had
earned my escape! Now this? I paced his floor.

My anxiety skyrocketed as my whole future began to melt away
right before my eyes. What would Daddy do? Would he get a gun and
shoot Everett Fairchild dead? Would he force us into some kind of a
marriage? Worst of all, I didn't have the least desire to be a mother!
Not at all! Abortion? No way! I was too terrified to even think of such
a thing! What if it really was murder? I didn't want to go to hell forever. But if God loved me, how could this have happened in the first
place? Guardian angels? What good were they?

My fear escalated while my religious convictions waffled. I became
more and more afraid and I had never felt more alone. I heard the
nurse tell Dr. Goodman good night and that he should lock the doors.

By the time the next few minutes passed and Dr. Goodman
returned, I was spiraling in quite a state, cold and shaking from head
to toe and crying as hard as I ever had. I was loath to say that I had
been raped, because I had no memory of it. I had never felt so hopeless and so helpless. Who would believe me? No one.

He offered me a box of tissues and a cup of water.

"You wouldn't . . ." I said, stammering, "I can't remember . . . oh,
God!"

"Anna," he said, in the most gentle of all voices I had ever heard from an adult, "look. I have an idea what went on here and I want to help you."

"How can anybody help me? I'm finished! Ruined!"

"No, you're not," he said. "Someone has taken advantage of you and I want you to tell me what you can."

I don't know if he thought I was some nincompoop who had been sleeping with her chemistry teacher without understanding the birds and the bees, or what. Or maybe he thought I was deranged. I didn't know, but the story came tumbling out, broken nose and all. He listened carefully to every word and by the time I was finished recounting the night, he sat back in his leather chair, took off his reading glasses and rubbed his eyes. He seemed as old as Methuselah. In the same moment, I knew I had crossed a threshold, leaving my girlhood behind me forever. I was so filled with the injustice of it all that I wanted to die. I was just so incredibly sad.

"If we can establish paternity, Anna, we can send this fellow up the river, you know. Rape is a serious felony."

"What good would that do?" I twisted the tissue in my hand and then took another, getting angry then.

"The son of a bitch broke your nose, Anna, pardon my French. He raped you and left you pregnant. Think what he might do to the next girl."

It was too much to think about. "I don't know," I said. "How am I ever going to tell my dad? This will kill him!"

"I'll help you, Anna, and I think you're going to want someone impartial to help your dad keep a cool head. Listen, I've known Douglas Lutz for years and he is an entirely reasonable man."

"You don't understand! You don't know how he is with me! Ever since Momma . . . and the war . . . and my *grandmother,* oh, my God! What am I going to *do?*"

"They aren't stupid, Anna; they know what goes on in the world. Both of them will absolutely realize at once that this is not your fault. Come on, I'll follow you home."

All the way home, I crawled into my head, cocooning myself

against every possible scenario. What was the worst that could happen? That my father and grandmother would throw me out on the streets? I doubted that. My grandmother maybe, but not Daddy. He loved me and I was sure of it. He would be shocked and angry like I was, but then he would . . . would what? I didn't want to think about it.

I was grateful to God that Dr. Goodman was behind me. Since there was cause for legal action, it would give Daddy someone calm to think it through with before calling anyone, like the police or a lawyer. Oh, my God, I thought, what if they *did* that? What if it was in all the papers? What if there was a trial?

Wasn't it enough that a baby was growing inside of me who I didn't even know was there? Wasn't that enough for God to give me to deal with for one night?

Apparently not.

Daddy was on the front steps and saw us arrive. Dr. Goodman turned in the driveway behind me and we got out at almost the same time. Daddy mistook the horror on my face to be news of a terrible disease and his face turned white.

"Hey, Douglas, you got a beer for an old friend?" Dr. Goodman's words were an attempt to put Daddy at ease and amazingly, Daddy regained his color and composure.

"Of course," he said. "Come on in."

We convened at the kitchen table and the silence in the room hung heavy. Daddy popped open two bottles of Beck's, handing one to Dr. Goodman.

"So what's the word?" Daddy said.

I started to cry again, putting my face in my hands.

"Anna's pregnant, Douglas," Dr. Goodman said, "drugged and raped at her prom by her date."

There was not a sound to be heard for what seemed to be forever. Then came the questions.

"How far?"

"Ten weeks."

"Anna's okay?"

"As far as I can tell."

They went on and on for a few minutes and then Daddy turned to me.

"I'll murder the son of a bitch with my bare hands," he said, as though he had said instead *Pass the butter.*

"You'll murder who?"

It was Grandmother Violet coming in the room and the demons in her started to dance. She started screaming, ranting and raving like a madwoman, calling me every name in the book. Daddy and Dr. Goodman tried to calm her by explaining it was rape. Rape only drove her insanity to new heights and made her even crazier. *The disgrace! How could you? You whore! Why didn't you fight? What's wrong with you?* They told her I had been drugged, which ratcheted up her volume somewhere near a sound that only dogs can hear. *Drugs? Drugs?*

At first I thought she was faking it, but she held her head, then both sides of her face, her eyes went up in her head, and she collapsed on the floor. In delayed reaction, Daddy just stood there, catatonic as he usually was when his mother went crazy, but Dr. Goodman rushed to her, held her pulse, and lifted her eyelid.

"Call an ambulance, Douglas; I think she's had a stroke."

Holy Mary, Mother of God, I thought, *this is my fault.* I didn't know what to do. I walked out the kitchen door and sat on the back steps in the growing darkness, watching the water of Charleston Harbor. I was wishing for the first time in all those years that my mother was alive. I don't know what she would have said, but she would have known and thought better of me than to call me a whore. I was not a whore.

Sirens came closer. I went back in the house, looked at my grandmother's ugly twisted face, and I was so angry that I wanted to slap her. When my father and Dr. Goodman left the room to bring the ambulance attendants to her side, I did the most terrible thing I had ever even thought of doing in my entire life. I leaned over her and said in a whisper, "I am not a whore and this is your fault not mine. I hope you die, you mean, old, nasty, nasty bitch."

She died peacefully a week later. I never felt one shred of guilt. I never knew that I could feel that much resentment toward another human being and it surprised me. Moreover, I had been robbed of my chance for repentance from her. Dead women seldom apologized.

If the nuns were right, my tongue had probably earned about twenty million Frequent Flyer miles to rush my immortal impudent soul to a special torture chamber in Purgatory. It was a great selling point of Catholicism that you could work off sin in this kind of halfway house for the wayward. Even I knew that it would take more than one trip to the confessional to redeem myself with the Lord. It didn't matter. I would gladly face whatever consequences my Maker had for me. At least I had defended myself.

Her funeral was small and mercifully swift and we hauled her remains in a small procession out to Magnolia Cemetery and buried her with more consideration than she had ever shown me for one minute. Oddly enough, even Daddy seemed relieved by her departure. Once it was clear that she could never make a reasonable recovery I guess he thought death would be preferable to life as her stroke had left her.

Needless to say, I was still pregnant and flipping out. The irony of it all was that the woman who disliked me the most intensely had inadvertently chosen my rapist. This detail wasn't lost on me or on Daddy. Grandmother Violet had never uttered a word of regret about what she had said about me from the day she had her stroke until she closed her eyes for the last time. Unbelievable. Anyone else's grandmother would have wept with regret for days; not mine. She blamed me for my pregnancy and for her stroke. My heart hardened stronger than ever toward her because I knew how wrong and dangerous it was for her to blame me. Blaming someone was a serious issue.

The fault was Everett Fairchild's unconscionable act of violence and my grandmother's stroke was brought on by her own stupidity. Miss Bible-Thumper didn't know the first thing about compassion and forgiveness. And, with the lid on her—so to speak—it was time to talk about Everett.

It was the afternoon of the burial. Daddy and I were in the

kitchen. Jim and Frannie were helping me put food away. I had told them that morning that I was pregnant and they were understandably stunned. Frannie cried and ranted and Jim was just as upset as we were. They knew everything about me there was to know, especially that I didn't deserve this.

We were flooded by company that day. As always, to mark the passing of a neighbor or the arrival of one, the whole neighborhood had appeared at our door with cakes, turkeys, hams and casseroles of every description. I couldn't believe people came with meals to honor Violet, but they did. We wouldn't have to cook for a very long while. When our friends had dwindled down to just Dr. Goodman, Frannie, and Jim, we all sat down at the table for another piece of cake.

"Do you want some milk?" Frannie asked me.

"Sure," I said. "I should probably give up Cokes, huh?"

"She knows?" Daddy said. He looked worn out, his face a mixture of sadness and resignation.

"They both do. Jim and Frannie are my best friends, Daddy. They were *there*, remember?"

"Yes, of course." Daddy paused, cleared his throat, and said, "We haven't ever had the opportunity to talk about this, but I want both of you to know how deeply grateful I am for how you helped Anna that night."

"Sure, Dr. Lutz," Frannie said. "We had no idea . . ."

"No," Daddy said, "I'm sure you didn't."

"I'm gonna marry her, Dr. Lutz, that is, if you'll let me," Jim said.

You could have pushed me off my chair with the flick of a finger, I was so shocked. My face must have turned blood red, because it suddenly felt much warmer. Frannie's jaw dropped, as did Daddy's and Dr. Goodman's.

"I said, sir, that I'd like to marry Anna," Jim repeated. "This child needs a name and a father. She can't possibly marry Everett Fairchild and I wouldn't let her. I've loved Anna since we were children and I think I am the best man applying for the job."

"Jim!" I said. "You *know* I love you to pieces, but I can't marry you!"

"Why not?" he said, and stood up.

"Because I don't *want* to get married! Besides, you're my friend! People don't marry their best friends!"

Daddy cleared his throat and said, "Well, they *should*."

Daddy's remark unleashed a pack of wild dogs in my mind. Was Daddy saying that marrying for love was for fools, that he had been a fool to love Momma, and that I should marry Jim, when he knew perfectly well that Jim was, in all likelihood, a gay man? It wasn't enough that I was raped and now pregnant, that I couldn't go to USC, pledge Tri Delt, have boyfriends, and go to dances and football games. Now he wanted me to sign away my life to a man who would never be a traditional husband. Was it because parents couldn't stand to think about their children having a sex life? All of this so that this baby would have a name? Even at my young age it seemed too much to ask of me. I gathered up my courage to speak.

"Jim? You are so unbelievably generous to make this offer or proposal or whatever it is, but I can't accept. I just can't."

I got up and went to Jim to give him a hug. He hugged me back, took my hand, and led me to the back door, turning to speak to the jury. "Would y'all excuse us for a moment?"

They were still in a stun gun state and nodded their heads in the same way corks bob on water.

Jim walked me out to the yard and said, "Sit."

I sat on one of the three Adirondack chairs that had been on the lawn since we moved there.

"Okay. Have you considered an abortion?"

"*Jesus*, Jim! Listen, in the first place, I'm almost three months' pregnant. Maybe if I had known six weeks ago, I might have thought about that. But I am so stupid, I didn't even think in my wildest dreams that I *could be* pregnant! Besides, I can't go through with something like that. I just can't. I'm too chicken."

"Well, I needed to ask that."

"Jim! Do you realize I didn't even know I had sex with that bastard? He drugged me, for God's sake."

"Good Lord. Somebody needs to beat the shit out of that no-good son of a bitch."

"You already did. Remember?"

"Yeah, well, if I ever have the chance I'll bust his head wide open like a watermelon."

"That would be why I have always loved you."

"And, I will always love you too. Look," he said, "I'm doing us both a favor. This might be the only chance I'll ever have in my whole life to call a kid mine. My brother, Paul, is graduating from college next spring and marrying this girl he's practically living with. She's got big damn hips like an old brood mare and will probably get pregnant before they cut the cake! Honey, she's gone go and start spitting out grandchildren for old Miss Trixie and Mr. Jimbo like I don't know what!" He was snapping his fingers all around himself.

I smiled. Jim was so wonderful and even in a moment of that intensity, he was funny.

He took a deep breath and kneeled down in front of me. His face was very serious and he spoke quietly. "I would love to have a child, Anna. I would also love not to be disinherited from my father's will, okay?"

I picked my cuticles and looked at the ground. "Jim, you know this isn't right. People don't get married so they can inherit money."

"Since when? Are you kidding me? Read your history! People marry for every reason in the world! Don't you see? If my father knew I sang Judy Garland songs in the shower, he'd kick my pretty ass all over downtown Charleston and then some!"

"What if it doesn't work?"

"What if *what* doesn't work? Listen, we can go to the College of Charleston. My parents will help us. My mother will adore you and the baby! Jesus, girl, you'd think I was asking you to lie down in front of a speeding Mack truck! Come on, say yes."

I got up and walked to the water's edge knowing I was looking at my best offer and my only offer. If I didn't take it, my baby would be illegitimate. I thought about that and knew this baby didn't ask to come into the world this way. I had three choices. Adoption. I knew I couldn't do that. Two, I could raise an illegitimate baby with Daddy, or three, a legitimate baby with Jim.

"Look, Jim, let's be blunt here. You're gay. Right?"

Silence. He just stared at me as though I had slapped him. But I had some difficult things to say and it wasn't easy to hear or say them.

"You're my best friend, Jim, and I'm gonna love you for this until the day I die. But I don't want to throw away whatever chances I have for a marriage to a man I fall in love with because I'm married to my best friend who is also gay. And, I don't want you to be stuck! You know what I mean, don't you?"

"Anna, I know what you mean. But that could happen when? Ten years from now? Look, here's what I propose. Marry me and we'll live together and give this baby a name. I will be discreet. You be discreet. You don't embarrass me and I won't embarrass you."

"You mean *what*? That if we want to fool around with someone it's okay as long as we don't announce it?"

"Yeah, I mean, I know that sounds kind of crummy, but yeah."

"How much money is your father supposed to leave you?"

"Buckets," he said and smiled.

"Jeesch! Okay, okay. I'll marry you but only if your family approves."

"Are you kidding? If we're crazy enough to do something like this, we're not asking their permission. We're going to Georgetown this weekend and that's it!"

"Can we take Frannie?"

"Come here!" Jim put his arms around me and hugged me good and tight. "Anna, I want you to not worry, okay? I'm about to become a family man, God help me!"

That was the beginning of Jim's mother, good old moneybags Trixie, wedging herself into my life.

Seven

How's Trix?

OKAY, you're shocked. I married a gay man. Well, let me tell you this: being married to Jim wasn't bad at all. In fact, he was a sweetheart pussycat every single day during the four years we were together. As for sex? Listen, I wasn't ready for one-half of what was happening to me, much less sex.

Just imagine this. You are barely eighteen years old. Your rock-hard abdomen is growing with the speed of light. There's talk that there's a baby in there who is going to fight his or her way out. Then, your husband comes in from school, fixes you a cold drink, rubs your feet, and makes you laugh your head off with endless crazy shenanigans. He tells you that you're beautiful, is thrilled to place his hand on your tummy and feel the baby kick, and brings home stuffed animals and little outfits every time he can find some extra cash. He is entranced by your metamorphosis. He can't wait to start Lamaze classes. He, honey chile, is the perfect man. To this day, I kiss the ground he walks on.

Now, about Trixie. Okay, I know she meant well and I truly believe she did. From the minute we announced our marriage, his mother was delighted. His befuddled father, who had suspected something all along about Jim's sexuality, went into a dither. He was joined by Daddy, who we didn't tell where we went on that Saturday. The three of them scrambled like wildcats until Trixie emerged as victor.

She announced she would take charge, find an apartment for us, and take care of everything. She did—she found a perfectly adorable carriage house, tucked away in a private alley right off of South Battery. It was owned by a widow, Mrs. Augustine Bennett, who declared she was pleased to have a young married couple on her property. Miss August, as she liked to be called because it implied she was a centerfold, was a darling octogenarian who rarely left her house.

Trixie negotiated the lease, since we were too young to sign one anyway, and insisted on paying for it, saying that she didn't want Jim or me to work. It was a small thing to ensure that Jim had ample study time, and she said that I should rest. Besides the fact that I couldn't think of anyone who would hire a pregnant person, I couldn't work because I didn't feel very well. I intended to start classes and work as soon as the baby came and I could arrange for day care.

Filled with determination to create marital bliss, Trixie proceeded to decorate for us. Although the two-bedroom cottage was furnished, she had everything moved into storage while every square inch was scoured and repainted. Trixie then refurnished it as she thought it should be done, mostly with cast-off Depression relics from her attic. Jim's childhood furniture—a single bed, bookcase, chest of drawers and a bedside table—was repainted with white enamel for the baby's room. Our bedroom had a queen-size mattress and box spring on a frame, pushed against the wall and covered to look like a daybed with every pillow in Christendom. We had two end tables and a sofa in the living room and a rectangular table for our dining area, which quickly became Jim's study space. The kitchen had a two-burner stove and a tiny refrigerator. Trixie wanted to change them but Jim and I insisted they were fine. I figured we'd live on what I knew how to make, as neither one of us had learned to seriously cook.

Once Trixie had covered the windows with remade curtains from some dead relative and once the bathroom was hung with new towels, she finally began to slow down. Somewhat. Her last gift was a copy of *The Joy of Cooking.*

"Ah just want to be sure you feed mah boy *properly.*"

Nice shot to the head, I thought. "Thanks."

"Ah hope you don't think Ah'm intruuuding?" she would say.

Nothing to be done about her accent. "No, ma'am," I'd answer, "I don't know what we'd do without you!"

Now, in all fairness to everyone, I was a motherless, grandmotherless, pregnant teenager who did not possess one clue of what was normal in the arena of maternal parental involvement. But I can tell you this without a degree in psychology: Trixie was a well-meaning but overbearing mother who probably knew in her heart that this baby was no more her son's child than the man in the moon's. Still, she drove me up the wall.

Meanwhile, she made all attempts possible to take me into her family and supported the charade with all the heart she had. I think she always knew that Jim was gay. Maybe she thought if she loved me really hard that Jim would become straight. Maybe she thought if she tried to micromanage our marriage, it would last. Poor thing. She even tried to turn me into Julia Child, that is, when they could get me to rise from the couch.

I spent the next six months inspecting the bathroom and the ceilings of our apartment.

"Ah've never seen someone so nauseated from pregnancy in all mah days!" she would say. "Why don't you eat some saltine crackers, dear?"

The mere mention of saltines sent me waddling at my top speed for the relief of release and then back to the couch to recover. Jim was always standing by with a cold cloth for my head and a Coke with the bubbles stirred out.

"Don't talk to her about f-o-o-d, Mother," Jim would say and turn on *I Love Lucy* reruns to divert me. "The doctor says she's fine and the baby's fine. This just happens sometimes."

"Well, you're a regular Terry Brazelton," she said over and over. "Ah never got sick like this! Ah blossomed with mah boys!"

So, go blossom in hell, I would think but never say. She tried. She really did. I had a lousy sense of humor then.

And, Jim began to take an interest in our home, doing lots of things to make it ours. He brought in plants and rearranged the furniture. It was clear he had an eye for interior design, because with a natural ease and almost no money, he made our carriage house something worthy of a layout in a magazine. He was a marvel.

But show house or no show house, when Emily was born with platinum blond hair and the spooky green eyes of Everett Fairchild, Trixie never said a word. Maybe because I was blond. But those eyes of Emily's had obviously come from somewhere else. It was at that point that we both realized a lot was going unsaid but we let the silence be what it was and went on with living.

From the time Emily was six weeks old, I would roll her up and down South Battery in her enormous English pram, another gift from Trixie. There I was, dressed in old Gap jeans and a faded T-shirt, pushing a thousand-dollar carriage. It was absurd.

Money was tight even though Jim had an allowance from his parents. Jim gave me what he could but I didn't have much gumption when it came to asking for anything for myself. I started to cut his hair to save money and did a pretty good job at it too. This grew to a part-time thing of me cutting the hair of other students for five or ten dollars. Word spread that I was pretty good with scissors.

Daddy would sometimes slip me twenty or fifty dollars when I saw him, but he had taken the position that if I was married, I should pay my own bills. I hardly ever disagreed with Daddy, though it seemed the circumstances I was in should have made a difference. It didn't. As much as I loved my father, I knew it was futile to ask him for help. Violet's legacy was a strange one. Daddy had become cheaper than ever and as petulant as a child. Or so it seemed to me. Besides, he was occupied with all the spaghetti dinners and pound cakes being delivered by various widows since the news of my departure had traveled the circles of Mount Pleasant society. That, I thought, was probably a good thing. Nonetheless, there was a growing uncomfortable distance between us.

I racked my brains trying to figure out how he could justify his stingy behavior with me. Maybe he just wanted me to grow up. Maybe he was jealous of Trixie's support because he had suffered so much deprivation when he was a kid.

I was living dangerously in a depressed lull. Instead of enjoying my motherhood, I worried and sulked. I hated that I wasn't qualified to do anything. I didn't have money for school. Daddy wasn't willing to lend it to me. I was afraid to take a loan. How would I pay it back? Ask Trixie? No way! I ticked days from the calendar with growing impatience. Was this my life? Changing diapers and waiting for Jim to graduate and leave me with a child? I needed to figure my way out of my dark hole, dug by everyone around me and by my own complacency.

Walking Emily up and down the streets of Charleston fast became a screaming bore. I decided I needed a hobby and turned to my first attempt at gardening. I remembered watching my mother work in the yard when I was little. I had always enjoyed helping her dig little holes with my own spade and refilling the watering can, especially on hot days. Maybe I would enjoy it now too.

Our little carriage house had a garden plot on either side of the front door and a long narrow plot that ran down the side of the house facing east. The other side faced a brick wall and had no sunlight. I decided to start with the front door area.

With Emily napping in her carriage, I began to weed and then to dig the tiny courtyard, sifting out old roots, bulbs, and stones. On my meager budget I was only able to afford to plant a few flats of flowers and herbs. Once they were in the ground, I thought it cheered the front of our cottage up tremendously. And me too.

Not long after my petunias began spreading and blooming, I was outside deadheading the flowers to encourage new blooms and Miss August surprised me by appearing right behind me it seemed from nowhere.

"Your flowers look very nice, Anna," she said.

I jumped at the sound of her voice. "Thanks. I thought they would add something, you know, and give me something to do."

"Yes, well, when I was your age, this entire garden was filled with blooms of one sort or another all year long. But now I can't worry about all of that. Arthritis, you know. Kills the knees and you have to have obliging knees to garden."

"Yes, ma'am," I said, unsure of what to say.

"I used to be an officer of the Charleston Garden Club," she said. "I knew Mrs. Whaley."

"Wow. Well, that must have been fun," I said, deciding she was probably just a little lonely and anyway, old people loved to reminisce.

"Your garden is only as good as your dirt, you know," she said.

"Yes, ma'am, I've heard that said."

"Every three feet is a new garden, you know," she said.

"Yes, ma'am," I said and giggled. She was absolutely working herself into a lecturing lather saying *you know* with every statement, as though I knew anything, which I didn't.

"I assume you like to garden?" she said.

"Well, I guess it's something about me that I never knew," I said. "Turns out that I like it a lot."

"Hands in the dirt and a new baby in a carriage. What could make you closer to God than that?"

"Yes, ma'am," I said.

Long after she was gone I was still thinking about what she had said. I had neglected my religious duties since marrying Jim. Emily had yet to be baptized. Maybe it was because Catholicism had belonged to my grandmother and had been shoved down my throat. I had not taken the time to think about it. Everything had been too confusing and I was still angry that I was in this situation anyway—married and a mother instead of being in college like Frannie. Frannie had gone off to Georgetown University and was studying political science. She would probably become a professional rabble-rouser. There was no question that I felt cheated, but I decided that I needed to stop complaining for a while. I was even getting sick of my own thoughts.

But, my life wasn't a complete bummer. Every time I looked at Emily—her perfect fingernails, her innocent expressions—I felt blessed and grateful. Yes, grateful to God to have a healthy child and ashamed of my dissatisfaction over not getting exactly what I wanted. I told myself what the nuns had drilled into my hard head—that God had a plan for me. I wondered when the last time was He had reviewed it and, thinking He might have taken His eye off the ball, I began again to worry about a plan for myself. I began reading the want ads in the paper, hoping I would find something where I could work from home. Even something part-time.

The following week, Miss August knocked on my door.

"You busy?" she said. There was bounce in her question.

"No, not at all," I said, wondering what in the world she wanted with me.

I stepped out to the curb to see a truck with twenty yards of topsoil and huge bags of manure and vermiculite. They dumped the soil on a tarp in the driveway and two huge men stood by waiting for instructions.

"It's a little gift from me to you to me," Miss August announced, pleased with her cleverness.

"Well, then, let's have us a garden!" I said.

She produced a pitcher of iced tea from her kitchen and then supervised the men while they removed her shrubs and mixed the dirt into her beds and the ones in front and on the side of my cottage. I had carefully removed my plants from the ground to the side and would replant them later.

We were just sitting on her porch like two old friends, sipping sweet tea and watching the men dig and mix the ground.

"I've instructed the manager of Abide-A-While Nursery over in Mount Pleasant that you are coming to choose planting materials for us. Get anything you want. Does that suit you?"

"Oh! Yes, ma'am!"

Well, I was as happy as a wannabe gardener could be. Besides, it was the first time in my whole life that anyone had said, *Get anything you want!* I was so excited at the possibilities of it all. I was still nursing Miss Emily With the Voracious Appetite and this would be the perfect pastime to occupy me. Then Miss August surprised me by adding, "I thought I might be able to offer you a little stipend if you'd weed my part of the yard too. You know, just keep it tidy? How is seventy-five dollars a week? I mean, I think every girl should have her own pin money, don't you?"

I didn't know what to say so I just sat there in her wicker rocker trying to think of some way to say thank you. Jim didn't have that many friends with hair for me to cut!

"All right, we'll make it one hundred fifty dollars a week, but if you tell your husband, the deal's off! And your mother-in-law! Busybodies! This is between us; is that clear?"

"Miss August! This is wonderful! Thanks, and believe me, I'm not telling a soul!"

"Fine! You can't do any worse than that last fool I had working this yard. Irish drunkard he was! Had a black thumb and a hollow leg, I tell you!"

"Well, Miss August, I'll do my best."

And I did. The new gardens took root and grew into a kaleidoscope of color and fragrance. Trixie thought it was astounding, that Miss August had found a magician. She had no idea her magician was me until she caught me working in the yard.

"Ah didn't know you liked to garden, Anna!"

She made the statement the same way you'd say, *I didn't know you could read, dear!*

"Yeah," I said, "I love it."

"Well, if you can do this for Augustine, maybe you would do it for me?"

"Sure, well, we'll see."

I thought that was noncommittal enough, but the message was

clear that since she paid all our bills, I owed her something. But that wasn't how I felt. Maybe Jim owed his mother something, but I didn't think that her paying our rent entitled her to my manual labor. Motherhood and marriage without the conjugal fulfillment had made me slightly bitter.

I told Jim that Trixie wanted me to take care of her yard and he said to ignore her and she would forget she had ever said it. I should have known better.

The gardens continued to grow—great mounds of Blue Danube asters, hollyhocks and picta ribbon grass sprang up against the spillage of blue, white and pink flowers of Lamium and the gray-blue velvet texture of lamb's ears. I had adopted the determination of my advisor from Abide-A-While to plant the entire yard without impatiens or begonias. Her name was Libby Hawkins. Libby had this hard-core philosophy that impatiens and begonias made your yard look the same as a gas station. I didn't quite agree with that, but I decided to give her advice a shot and see how it looked. She was right about one thing. The absence of impatiens certainly gave the garden distinction.

It seemed that all I had to do was put something in the ground and it took off heading for the sun. I found a stack of old trellises in Miss August's shed and cleaned and set them up, then planted small mandevillas, with Confederate jasmine sprigs at their bases. In no time at all, they crawled all over the trees and everywhere they could travel. I bought a book on pruning and went to work on her ancient boxwoods. In four weeks they were filled with fresh sprigs and looked as vital as new shrubs.

By the summer's end, I had money in the bank and Miss August was thrilled. I cleaned up the old wrought-iron table and chairs in the garden and on occasion I'd spot her there from my window just looking around, smiling and enjoying a cool drink.

As Emily became more blond and her eyes more green and passed from infant to baby, Trixie was butting into our lives full force, undaunted by the clear evidence of questionable paternal identity.

My father-in-law, Jimbo, who just shrugged his shoulders the first

time he saw my tiny infant daughter, knew better. After being driven
to the outer edges of sanity by Trixie's bossy personality for nearly
three decades, he took up tournament bridge with a vengeance and
traveled the world competing. He was in London when he died of an
aneurysm at the Connaught Hotel. He was only fifty-seven years old
and holding enough spades to trump the planet. Trixie made a swift
recovery and Jim took a turn.

Jim's father's death was the beginning of the end for my marriage.
He began staying out late and coming in sweaty reeking of cigarettes
and beer from dancing all night in Charleston's private gay bars. I
would find him in the morning, sleeping in his clothes on the couch.
When I woke him he would say, "Oh, my God, Anna! I can't believe
you let me sleep like this! I'm late for class!" He'd hardly finish brushing his teeth before he was out the door, returning home to sleep until
ten or eleven and go out again until all hours. I mean, he didn't do
this every single night and when he was around he still gave generous
time and attention to Emily. He loved her to pieces. But by her third
birthday, his behavior had become a resolute pattern. And it was
obvious from the phone calls and the way he responded to them that
he was seeing someone.

With his father dead and his inheritance secured, his end of the
bargain was technically fulfilled. He wasn't asking me to leave or anything like that. No, there was a tremendous bond of affection between
us but I was really uneasy. I knew he wanted to get on with his life and
I couldn't blame him.

I mean, I had always known in my heart that our marriage would
eventually come to some kind of watershed, but I wasn't prepared for
it. And, I didn't want Trixie to know the truth. It's true what the old
people said, that when families started keeping secrets, trouble came
in the door.

Trixie pretended to be oblivious. She was as attentive to Emily as a
grandmother should be, which is to say she never missed a birthday
party or a Christmas morning. When Emily had the chicken pox, it
was Grandmomma Trixie who put the calamine lotion on her blisters

with a Q-Tip, while singing her Broadway show tunes. Under her tutelage, Emily learned all the words to the theme songs of *Beauty and the Beast*, *The Lion King* and *Les Miserables*. Emily also sang the title song to *Cabaret* like a miniature Ethel Merman, which was not necessarily the best thing in the world, but never mind.

Trixie's attention to Emily was not the problem. The trouble started when Trixie began to recognize Jim's general discomfort. Jim was her son and, as they say, blood has always been thicker than water. No mother wanted to see her son unhappy. She also suspected that I was sitting on a pot of money from Miss August, which she intimated all the time and I ignored all the time.

Trixie began to give me the chill while she investigated our lives. At first, it was subtle. She would call late in the evening and ask for Jim. He wasn't home, of course, and I would tell her some fib, like he was at the library. These excuses were met with prolonged silences and deep sighs.

The phone calls led to seemingly innocent I-was-just-in-the-neighborhood unannounced visits. Trixie would arrive with a little something for Emily and sniff around for evidence like a bloodhound. She would take note of the crumpled state of the couch or the single bed in Emily's room, where Jim usually slept. She knew *exactly* what was going on and what *wasn't*. There was no marital bed and therefore, no marriage.

Finally she said something, breaking the wall of dishonesty between us. Emily was in her stroller and we were walking her down King Street, stopping to look in the windows of all the antique stores. We paused in front of Birlant's Antiques and she said, "You know, Anna, this can't go on *fuh-evah*. Ah mean, it isn't right for *me* to be supporting *you and Jim* while *you garden* and he goes *catting around*."

Was my life about to be dismantled again and would I have no say in it? She had caught me very off guard. Of course, I had given massive thought to my *marriage*.

"It's a problem," I said, but that was all I had intended to say.

"It's more than a problem," she said, "it's a *terrible* sham."

I felt the heat then, rising in me like a furnace. I had to get away from her. I began to push Emily's stroller faster and faster and Trixie had to almost jog to keep up with us.

"Slow down, Anna," she said, almost breathless, "let's *talk* about this."

"No," I said. "I don't want to talk about this with you. I'm going home."

I rushed down the streets and away from her until I was safe, back at our house. Emily's eyes were wide when I reached down to pick her up. She sensed that something was wrong and began to cry.

"Momma!"

"Hush, baby. Everything's all right. You need a nap, honey, come on. Momma's gonna put you in your bed."

"What's wrong, Momma?"

"Nothing, sweetheart."

Sometimes Emily and I napped together on her single bed in her room. I would put her between me and the wall and she would snuggle next to me like a baby cub. But that day, she needed to stretch out and sleep and I needed to think. I tucked her in under her favorite quilt, closed her blinds and put on her favorite cassette tape of lullabies. There was something extra reassuring to her when she slept with her music. Maybe I was giving her an extension of permission to be a baby.

"You go to sleep like a good girl," I said, handing her Lulu, her favorite baby doll.

She struggled to keep her eyes open, and I left her room, leaving the door ajar. I didn't know what to do so I called Daddy. His receptionist, Naomi, put me on hold. It wasn't often that I called Daddy at his office but he never failed to speak to me when I did.

"What's up, Anna? Emily all right?"

"Emily's fine. I'm not."

"What's the matter, Sugar?"

"I need advice, big time."

"Shoot."

"Not on the phone. Can you come over?"

"As soon as I vaccinate the Salerni triplets and take a throat culture of the McGinnis child, I'll be on my way."

While I waited for him, I paced the floor. Emily was sleeping like a stone. There was no point in lying to Daddy. I would just tell him the truth about everything. I imagined that he already knew anyway. True to his word, he was in my living room within the hour.

I gave him a kiss on the cheek and said, "You want a glass of tea?"

"Sure. What's this all about?"

"Me and Jim and Trixie," I said.

"You got any beer?"

"Sure." I opened one for him and one for myself. We clinked bottles and he braced himself for what I was sure he didn't want to know.

"Daddy, I have to leave Jim," I began. "I can't live like this anymore."

"What has he done?" He put his bottle on the coffee table and sat on the edge of my sofa. "What's happened?"

"It's not really his fault or mine . . ." I said.

I told him the whole story and by the end of it he was standing by the window, staring out at the yard. Silence so penetrated the space between us that I could hear my own pulse beat in my ears. When he turned to face me I could feel his sadness and disappointment.

"I never should have let you marry him," he said, holding his hands up in surrender. "I'm sorry. I should have been, I don't know, stronger-willed or something."

"Daddy," I said and put my arms around his waist and my head into his chest, "it's not your fault."

"But Mother had just died . . ."

"It's not anybody's fault."

He patted me on the back and moved away from me. "Let's consider all the alternatives," he said, picking up his bottle and finishing its contents with one long drink. "You could get an apartment, put Emily in day care, exposing her to God-knows-what kind of diseases and pedophile abuse, and get some kind of menial job flipping burgers and super-sizing people's fat rumps. Or, you can come home with

Emily until you get on your feet. You can go to school. I can probably find someone to watch Emily for you. Then you can move out and support yourself."

"That second one sounds good. Great, in fact. Thanks, Daddy."

The tears started to flow and like a river rising over its banks, I wept until my shirt was wet. We sat on the couch and he rubbed my back, around and around on my shoulder blade, the same way he had when I was a child. Around and around, until I had cried myself out.

"I never should have allowed you to marry him," he said again. "I should have stepped in. It was a terrible time, with Momma dropping dead and all."

"She hated me," I said, "blamed me."

"So what? Listen, it doesn't matter and, believe me, I've given this a lot of thought. She was as mean as a Chihuahua and a Bible-beating, judgmental, heartless old witch who's probably shoveling coal in hell, God rest her soul." Daddy faced me then with his lop-sided grin and the same sentiments I held about her.

"Yeah, bless her heart, the old bitch."

"You said it!"

It didn't matter if he really believed that about his mother. He was trying to make me see that everything was going to be all right and that it was the two of us, no, the three of us that were a family. Daddy brought me a glass of water and I drank it, hiccuping and gulping. Even though I was still crying I began to laugh at the same time. The vision of her shoveling coal in hell was too heavenly to continue weeping. If she could have seen me and the fix I was in, she probably would have burst another vein.

"God, I love it. Thanks, Daddy, I needed that."

"Well, her self-righteous nonsense may have sent her to the devil, but you are still my little girl." He put his arm around my shoulder again and gave me a firm squeeze. "Emily too. Always will be."

I could hear Emily playing and knew I had to pull myself together and be Mommy. And what would I say to Jim?

I turned to Daddy, hugged him around the waist and said, "I need to figure this out. Thanks, Dad. I love you so much!"

"Call me later," he said. "Now, can I see my granddaughter?"

Emily came walking out. "Doc! Doc! Pick me up!"

Over the following hours, after Daddy had played with Emily and left, and until Jim came sailing through the door, I made a makeshift plan. Daddy had never said anything unkind about Trixie. He had never said, "I told you so." He had simply, and with love, offered shelter. Thank God! I had thought he wouldn't, but when he came to understand the depth of my problem and when I admitted it was my own doing, he came through. I would talk to Jim. If not that night, then the next.

I wanted to hate Trixie and say it was all about money. That wasn't true. She *did* always make me feel like I was a blood-sucking leech, but I don't think to this day that she could help herself. I wasn't a blood-sucking leech. I was too stupid and lazy and preferred painting myself as a victim. Was I going to be that kind of person forever? A coward? I had to face it that it—my marriage, the entire arrangement—was about deceiving others. What was honest and true was my father's generosity and the innocence of Emily. I took an oath that I would never be a liar or play a game with my life again. Or anyone else's.

Eight

Changing Tide

2002

*M*Y first week on the Isle of Palms was comprised of working at the salon during the day and, when I came home, still unpacking, daydreaming, organizing, and sunset cocktails with Lucy, and that almost always included Daddy. Sometimes it seemed that he was there because of me and sometimes because of his fascination with Lucy. Whatever the reason was, he became animated with a shot of Lucy's attention. And, he was obviously assured that he was still relevant in my life with all the little tasks I had for him to do. It was a good thing he had a cordless drill.

Naturally, I was indulging myself in a lot of looking back. It was so easy to be swayed into delicious sentimentality when the hours slipped by on the rise and fall of sunlight and tides. During the mornings I was surrounded by glittering water and brilliant blue skies. The night was sensual, damp, salted and insistent on its deepest urges being fed. I found myself not wanting to ever leave the island.

I went to work every day at Harriet's House of Hair, but my mind was elsewhere. It was time to stop dwaddling in my dreams, get serious and pull everything together before Emily arrived from D.C.

I was walking on the beach and stopped to fold my newspaper and weight it against any sudden breezes with my coffee container on the bottom step of a walkway. I began to jog a little. It had been so long since I had run anywhere (except away) I wondered if I could even run without tripping. I probably looked like an ass, but my only audience was feathered. So, who cared? I figured I would jog a while and then walk a little, see how my pulse was doing. I had read about doing that in a magazine in the checkout line at Harris Teeter. All those magazines were designed by pathetically young men and women and aimed at letting people like me know we were on the way to a sagging, clogging imminent death unless we signed on to pump and sweat. I knew I was out of shape and I wasn't fond of the idea of reckless running until my heart exploded. So I checked my pulse, walked a ways, and then jogged some more, figuring I wasn't going to turn into a jock in one day.

The tide was going out and the wet sand was packed hard, glistening in the morning sun. In minutes, the same two Irish setters from the other day were running at my side, in front of me, around me and seemingly involved in a canine conspiracy to make me land headlong in the sand. It wouldn't have taken much. I stopped and looked at them.

"Listen, you silly dogs, do you want to break my neck?"

One went down on her front paws, fanny poised high in the air, tail wagging, ready to play. The other yelped, stood on his hind legs, and then took off running toward something behind me.

"I'm sorry." I turned to see the owner standing there behind me, clamping a leash on the collar of one dog. "Crazy dogs! Come here, Nikki!"

Nikki, the friskier dog, had a cute name. She began to run in circles while I stood there with this guy, waiting for him to take control of his animals. But, instead, he waited too. Apparently he thought Nikki would wear herself out and come to him. It was certain that her energy could outdistance his patience, so he held out the leash for her to see and said, "Hey! Let's go!" Nikki slowed to a halt and then came to his feet, lowering her head for him to attach the leash to her collar as well.

"They really are good dogs; just full of the devil, that's all," he said. "I'm Arthur, by the way, Arthur Fisher."

"Hey, Arthur, I'm Anna Abbot."

We shook hands and he said, "Well, an abbot is better than a monk." Then he chuckled, proud of his precious wit.

"And I'll bet you think that's the first time anyone's said that, right?"

"Sorry, couldn't resist."

He had dancing eyes, nice, deep brown eyes with thick lashes. Brown hair cut short, sort of spiky. A few gray hairs here and there. About five ten or so, I guessed. Old jeans. Chambray shirt. He looked trustworthy. Not gorgeous, but nice looking. A little rugged. Harrison Ford type. No wedding ring.

"It's okay, you're a riot," I said. "So, do you live around here?" Boy, was that an inane remark or what? Think I was going to be single forever?

"Uh, yeah. I'm actually keeping a friend's house for him while he's in Alaska. These are his dogs. He's doing research for *National Geographic* on the mating habits of puffins."

"Good Lord!"

"They're birds."

"Thank God. For all I know, that could've been a tribe."

He smiled wide and I could see his dimples. "I've been working in Charleston and thinking of staying. You?"

"I grew up here, first on this island and then in Mount Pleasant, the city, for a while and now I'm back here."

"Why do I get the feeling you're leaving out something?"

"What?" Off guard again. God, couldn't I talk to a man without sounding like a living brain donor?

We were walking along at that point, watching the Atlantic suck out the surf and sand. The sound of it was music, raw and demanding then quiet and satisfied. Pardon me, but the racket made you think about sex. It even made *me* think about sex.

"Your life?" he said. "Lots of geography, not much else?"

I bristled. Who in the hell was this guy, this stranger, a possible pervert, asking me personal questions about my life? But I decided to be charming, thinking he might *not* be a pervert, but an available man with a mind and some assets and a hankering for a gal like me. You never knew.

"So," I said, mustering all available poise, given the hour and the fact that the beach now had other joggers who might possibly come to my rescue if necessary, "you're kinda nosy, aren't you?" I laughed a little and looked to see if he had taken this in good spirits. If he didn't have a sense of humor, I wasn't interested anyway.

"Let me guess. You buy cottage cheese premixed with pineapple and eat it on Ritz crackers?"

"Jeezaree!" Okay, he was weird. "What a thing to say! Why in the world . . . ?" And how could he have *known that*? Was he spying on my refrigerator?

"Because, madam, I am the Cheese Whiz of Charleston."

I burst out laughing. *Nerd alert.* But a funny nerd.

"The Cheese Whiz of Charleston. Well, that's nice. That's great! Really! It is! It's great! I'm, um, honored."

"No, no. It's quite serious, this position."

"No, of course it is, I mean, every city needs one, right?"

"But af coss!" he said, with a terrible French accent. But he sensed, correctly, that obscure was only interesting up to a point and then sane people rightly expected explanations. "No, I mean, you know how restaurants have sommeliers to help you pick wine?"

"You mean like at Dunleavy's?"

Dunleavy's Pub had a billion kinds of beer, but wine came in white, red, and blush.

"No, wise guy, like at High Cotton or Cypress, where the wine list is leather bound and it takes two people to lift it."

"Ah! Well, I haven't been there, so I wouldn't know."

I narrowed my eyes at him in silent warning not to do the gentri-fied *walleto* thing with me. People who threw money around gave me the creeps. But the longer I walked along talking to him, the more engaging he became.

We chatted about the current status of restaurants around Charleston. New ones opened all the time and people were always in search of the ones hidden by a dock, like The Wreck in Mount Pleas-ant on Shem Creek or the legendary restaurant at Bowen's Island off Folly Road. Of course, Shem Creek itself held the record for the most complete choices. There was the Trawler, California Dreaming, The Water's Edge, and my all-time great favorite, The Shem Creek Bar and Grill.

The Shem Creek Bar and Grill had a main attraction, besides the views, the excellent food, and the warm service. It was Albert, the man at the back oyster bar. Al was a shucking machine. He could shuck faster than any man on the planet. Oh, my God, the oysters they had were so smooth and delicious, it was like taking a drink of life and finding out what made it tick. Watching Al, and being the recipient of his talent, was my preference for a night out. I mean, everyone has their own list.

In Charleston's population, swollen with tourists all year long, we had several kinds of restaurantgoers. There were those who thought the only way to eat anything was fried and refused to go anywhere if they had to dress up, which in the city meant long pants or a sundress that covered your tan line. These mainstream folks could be found, happy as the day was long, in any one of a dozen waterside establish-ments sharing baskets of batter-dipped everything. Those were the places where I went on the rare occasions I went anywhere.

Then, there were those who coveted a particular table at a partic-ular chic spot to maximize their visibility, usually to show off their dinner companion, be it business or bimbo or both.

Last, there were the hordes of tourists who were happy to spend the price of a Mercedes-Benz for dinner, giving our local chefs the opportunity to explore and hone their skills. Now, it seemed, we had ascended or descended to the realm of Fromage Sommeliers—Fromagiers?

"Are you married?"

"What?"

"You know, husband?"

Oh, my God! Was a man going to ask me out on a date?

"Who wants to know?" I could feel perspiration growing and spreading.

"I just thought y'all could come by some night when I am working and I could show you what this cheese business is all about."

"Yeah, well, thanks, but my husband is sort of permanently out of town. And I work at the House of Hair in the city."

I could have just said I was divorced, but hell no, I couldn't do that. I had to make a big stupid autobiography out of it. His dogs were pulling on him and I knew we were about to say good-bye.

"Oh."

"Divorced. You know, supporting myself."

"Oh. Okay, well, if you ever want to know about the world of cheese . . ."

Here was the most appealing man I had met in ages, even if he did call himself the Cheese Whiz, and he was about to take off and disappear. Admittedly, his eyes did cloud over a bit when I mentioned divorce. Well, maybe he was married. Just because he was talking to me didn't mean he wanted to go out with me, I told myself. Why did I get so carried away?

"Hey! Arthur?"

"Hang on!" he said to his dogs. "Yeah?"

"If you ever need a haircut or something . . ." Boy, that was about the dumbest thing I could've said. "Just one question. How did you know about the cottage cheese and pineapples?"

"Your plastic coffee container over there is from Dunkin' Donuts, not Starbucks, and you're jogging in regular shorts and a T-shirt, not some coordinated outfit with logos all over it. You're not concerned with status stuff and you eat on the run."

"Dead giveaway, huh?"

"Whatever."

He shrugged his shoulders, smiled, and began following the yank-ing lead of his rambunctious dogs, waving at me over his shoulder. *Nice meeting you,* I thought. *Go screw yourself.*

By seven that night, I had cut ten heads of hair, given three perms, and I was pretty darn tired. When my work didn't require my full attention, I spent my time burning fuel over my encounter with Arthur, thinking that I hadn't handled it right. I should have offered him a cup of coffee. But I didn't. Not very astute. I didn't believe you should just walk down the beach picking up men and looking for a lit-tle action either. So I convinced myself that I had done the right thing and if he wanted to find me, it wasn't that hard. I drove to work hoping that he would.

It wasn't until Miss Harriet of the House of Hair asked to see my book for the eighteenth time that I decided that maybe our days together were coming near an end. After all the time I had worked for her I couldn't believe she thought I might be doing someone's hair and pocketing the fee. But as the years had passed, she had become more and more peculiar. I couldn't stand her another day. When it had come to the point where I wanted to give her the finger behind her back or some other vulgar juvenile thing, then it was time to leave.

When I came home, I called Marilyn Davey, my real estate broker. "Marilyn? Hey! It's Anna Abbot. Um, what do you know of on the market in commercial space?"

"On the Isle of Palms?" she said.

"I don't know. Charleston or Mount Pleasant would be fine too."

We talked for a few minutes and when I thought she understood what I was after, we hung up. She promised to call as soon as she had done the research. There was no rush and I was merely considering it. I reasoned that if I could take the jump and leave Daddy's house, why not go have a look at the high dive? I was daydreaming, trying to fig-

ure out whether it was even a possibility, when I heard a rap on my
screen door. It was Lucy.

She was attired unusually conservatively, in black capri pants and
a modest, loose black top. Her sandals were flat slides. Okay, the shoes
had silk fruit and flowers on the front, but remember, this was, after
all, Lucy.

"Hey! Anna! You home?"

"Come on in!"

"Come with me for five minutes. Your daddy's at my house and he
wanted to say hello. I told him I would come to get you. Honey, girl!
Look at you! You need a little glass of O Be Joyful."

"I need *something!* What's going on?"

"Sunset, sugar plum, and you don't want to miss it."

I followed her over to her house, up the stairs around the porch,
and up another spiral flight of steps to her widow's walk. Daddy was up
there, looking out over the ocean.

"Hey, Daddy!" I gave him a kiss on the cheek and wondered who
had called who. Were they dating? Did this make me their chaperone?
Lucy handed me a goblet of white wine. There was a bowl of shrimp
and cocktail sauce on the small table next to the wine bucket. Given
Lucy's culinary skills, this was one high-tone party.

"Hey, sweetheart," he said, smiling.

He was wearing cologne! What did *that* mean? *Ignore it*, I told
myself, and I did.

No one spoke; we simply watched. The heavens were streaked
with deep purple and fuchsia and the blue of day deepened with the
passing of each minute. The sun had become a great red pulsating
mass and was slowly and with a sure reluctance slipping into a slit torn
across the lower sky.

Soon the sky would be heavy with the white shimmer of countless
stars, the breeze would pick up, and another day would give way to
history. It was a time for waking dreams. We stood together, each of us
keeping them our own. Every thought was not meant to be given in

speech. It was good to feel my heart's muscle pump through the thought of a man in my life, a salon of my own someday, my daughter's imminent arrival.

I watched Lucy's hand travel the rail to rest on Daddy's. He smiled at her, putting his other hand on hers and giving her a few reassuring pats of affection. I didn't mind seeing it. We were all just people with our aches and desires, and even if those desires were never fulfilled, it was okay to have them. It was important to take the time to recognize them, examine them, and consider their possibilities, their probabilities. What would this world be if we never dreamed?

"I called your daddy," Lucy said, "and then I came over to . . ."

"Lucy? It's okay. Don't stress. I'm just so happy to be here right now."

"Oh, thanks, Anna, I just thought you and your daddy would . . ."

"I've met a man," I said.

"Who? How wonderful!" Lucy said.

Daddy just looked at me, dumbfounded.

"I've met a man and I am seriously considering opening my own salon. Maybe."

"What?" Lucy said. "How? Why?"

"Good question, Lucy. These are very good questions. But I will figure it out."

"You don't need your own salon! You just bought a house!" Daddy said. "I mean, have you lost your goddamn mind, if you will excuse my language, Miss Lucy."

"I'm not opening a salon today, Daddy. Don't get all torched!" God! I had just thought about it and made one stupid phone call.

"Watch your mouth, Anna," Daddy said.

"She hasn't lost her mind, Dougle. She's just dreaming out loud."

"I apologize, Anna."

He deferred to her and I began to see that it wasn't the first time he had done it, either, remembering how he had treated her when they first met, their long absences, and the state of my father's hair. All signs read that Daddy had big heat for Lucy.

"It's okay. Look, y'all, nothing could be a bigger pain than Harriet."

"She's got a reputation for being a little crazy," Lucy said.

"I didn't know," Daddy said. "I mean, you always seemed happy enough to be working there."

"Daddy? In all my life, I have had to be resigned to too many things. If I ever want my life to change, I have finally decided it is me who will have to do the changing. I'm in my thirties! It's way past time."

"I never knew you were that unhappy, Anna," Daddy said, and the exhale of his voice wrapped itself around me, squeezing my heart. Did he think this was his fault too?

"Douglas? I think what Anna means is that she wants her life to be *hers*. I mean, wasn't it Gloria Steinem who said that thing about history being *his story* and what we needed was *her story?*"

Daddy and I stopped and looked at Lucy. She could not have been more succinct if she'd spent her whole life studying psychology. This was Lucy? Quoting Gloria Steinem?

"What? Did I say something wrong? I didn't mean to . . ."

Even in the twilight, I could see her bottom lip quiver. She was going to cry any second if I didn't say something. Or Daddy.

"You don't know how right you are," I said. "Gee, God, Lucy! You are so, so right!"

Daddy, beside her, stretched his arm around her and gave her a squeeze and Lucy's fear dissolved into a crooked grin of relief. I imagined that Lucy was unaccustomed to any accolades for her intelligence. Probably because she had her dim but well-meaning light completely buried six feet under her bushel.

"I told you she was a smart cookie," Daddy said.

He had said no such thing to me, but Lucy threw her arms around him and old Douglas was rewarded for his remark with a full frontal encounter starring the swell of her saline implants.

I was sure Daddy's face was scarlet, but fortunately I didn't have to see it in the fading light.

It was growing darker by the instant now, and soon we would be leaving Lucy's skybox to find our dinner. I would suggest that they go out and bring something back for us. I would make a pot of decaffeinated coffee and set the table.

"Anna?" Daddy said an hour later, putting a large paper bag on my table. "Who is the man?"

Took him long enough to ask.

"What man?" I opened the brown bag and peeked inside, then lifted out the box of chicken lo mein and the plastic container of soup carefully. "Let me just throw this in the microwave. Be right back. Where's Lucy?" I had temporarily forgotten about Arthur Fisher and was fully focused on dinner.

"She'll be over in a minute. She said she wanted to check something. Probably her email. Now. You say you've met a man?" He poured himself a beer.

I stirred my noodles and threw them back in for thirty seconds. "Unfortunately, there's really not much to report in the man department."

"He wasn't much?"

Lucy had reemerged, bedecked in a new ensemble of red linen with a bare abdomen, featuring sufficient cleavage to provide flotation for a fleet, and enough lip gloss to slide over the Cooper River Bridge.

"No, I just met him this morning. If he calls, I'll make a cake and invite you over."

"You gotta prepare yourself," Lucy said. "I'm gonna give you a book to read called *The Relationship Book*. Find out his birthday."

"What do you mean?"

"This book is amazing. And I mean that if you want a man to call you, you have to be ready when he does!" she said. "Y'all might think I'm a screwball sometimes . . ."

"We think no such thing!" Daddy said.

"Never!" I said. *Always*, I thought.

"Just hang on and listen to me. I'm taking you shopping, Anna.

Okay? And, you're gonna find out his birthday. Is that okay? And I'm gonna put some makeup on your face."

I started laughing. Lucy started laughing.

I might read the book but there was no way Lucy was coming near my closet or my face. No way.

Nine

Miss Mavis Says, Check Your Roots

*T was another Sunday. Some days it seemed to me that all I do is go from my bed to my kitchen and then to my pink recliner. At least I had Sunday Mass to break things up. Oh, I played with my kitties and watered my violets, but it was pretty dull. I can promise you that! Yes, it was, dull as dirt. Speaking of dirt, I was standing by my curtains, looking down on my neighbor digging up flower beds, and I thought to myself that there was something odd and familiar about her. How could that be? I knew I was getting on in years and that the mind plays tricks on old people, but before I let myself go and turned into some crazy old lady people talk about, I decided to investigate. I took off my cardigan and went outside.

Moses! It was hot! Well, Angel would say that I was feeling the heat so bad because I kept my air conditioner so low during the day. So what? That's my business! I paid the bill! In fact, I paid all the bills! What a nuisance!

The oleanders between our properties were another nuisance, I'll tell you. No matter how careful I always was walking through them, they always seemed to snag my hair. The stems were like long fingers, just waiting to annoy me. I got my hair washed and set every Tuesday and it had to last me a week. I'd admit that I wasn't very good with my hair. When a disrespectful branch of some overgrown bush would grab me and a big lock would shoot out from the side of my head, well, there was a good chance it would stay that way until the following Tuesday. That day, I didn't care. I was determined to find out what it was that bothered me so about that girl next door.

"Anna?"

"Hey, Miss Mavis!" She stopped digging her hole and stood around to face me. "How are you this fine day?"

"Thinking about fixing to go on and get ready for church. Do you go to church?" Now, don't tell me it's none of my business what this young woman did with her Sundays. *I know that!* However, I feel that I am entitled to an inkling of the morality of at least my direct neighbors.

"No, ma'am. Not in a long time. But I should. Where do you go?"

I knew it! "Oh, it depends on my mood," I said, just as sweet as pie, hoping she would understand that decent people kept the Lord's day holy. "Mostly, I go to Stella Maris on Sullivan's Island. That Father Michaels is a handsome devil. Smart too. Gets to the point and doesn't fool around. I like that. But if Angel is in the mood to drive, she'll drop me off at Blessed Sacrament across the Ashley. I haven't missed a Sunday in over thirty years!" *Think about that, missy!*

Do you think a shred of guilt crossed her face? No!

"Blessed Sacrament? That's a long way, isn't it?"

"Yes, it is. But then I can get her to go with me to the S&S Cafeteria over there on Highway 7. That way we don't have to cook. And, they have bread pudding and I can have as much as I want."

"I like bread pudding," she said. "Fattening, but good."

"Humph! I don't worry about that nonsense at my age. My doctor, that old fool, says I should watch what I eat. But I figure, I'm already past eighty, so what if I don't live to one hundred! I'll live to ninety-nine instead."

"Yes, ma'am."

She was just standing there, shifting her weight from one hip to the other. I kept staring at her and I knew she was waiting for me to say my piece. So, before she thought I had lost my marbles, I just came out with it. Besides, the gnats were out and I hate them! Nasty things, trying to get in my eyes.

"I know you!" I said. There. It was done.

"Yes'm, and I know you too."

"You do?" Lawsa mercy! Who was this woman?

"You took me in the day my mother died, Miss Mavis. Don't you remember? I'm Anna Lutz."

"Great God in heaven!" I thought I would collapse! Collapse and die right on the spot! "I had better sit down." The shock was too much for my delicate nature.

"Oh! Please," she said and took my arm. "Come inside!"

I let her lead me in to her couch and allowed myself to fall back against the pillows. It was a pretty couch, slipcovered in ivory linen, but not very practical. "Thank you," I said.

"I'll get you a glass of water," she said.

Well, this gave me a moment to look around her living room. Not that I approved of snooping, but you can tell a lot about a person by their possessions. She had a very nice bookcase that looked foreign, but very nice all the same. And she had one ton of books. Maybe she was a teacher after all. Well, I would find out. Anna Lutz! She had been a nice little girl, high-spirited, but nice.

She returned and handed me the glass of water, which I was very glad to have. I took a long drink and laid back against her sofa again.

"This is a shock!" I said. "Why didn't you tell me who you were?" Suddenly, I was provoked with her for playing this game with me.

"Miss Mavis? I wasn't sure it was you either, and when I realized who you were, you were already halfway out the door. I figured we'd get around to this conversation sooner or later. Do you remember when I used to steal your plums?"

"Do I? Humph! All you sassy little children running around here, making noise and driving me crazy! Oh! Those were wonderful days!"

I took another drink and put the glass on the coffee table, feeling much, much better.

"Yeah," she said, "they really were."

"Little Anna Lutz! Where do the years go?"

"I don't know, Miss Mavis, I surely don't know."

Well, she sat down opposite me on the edge of her coffee table and we just started to talk. Glory! It felt so good! Everything was going along so nicely until she brought up her mother. She started to get upset.

"I never got over it, the horrible embarrassment she was to all of us. Poor Daddy. Then my grandmother Violet all but wrecked my life . . ."

"Now wait just a minute, young lady," I said. "See here! I think you're old enough to consider both sides, aren't you? I *knew* your mother. She was a beautiful woman! And a good woman too! She tried and tried to please your father, but let me tell you this, and if you repeat one word, I'll say you're lying . . ."

"Promise," she said. She had a funny look on her face.

"In those days, your father was a difficult man, Anna. He probably still is."

"Aren't all men difficult?"

I had to agree on that. "I imagine they are, but your daddy had a way about him that, I swanny, well, it wouldn't have made even *me* cut up the fool, 'eah?"

"What do you mean?"

Here sat this nice young woman, years after she had gotten over her mother's death. Was it my business to tell her what I knew? Yes, I decided, it was. Somebody needed to set her straight. Why was I *always* the one who had to do this?

"Anna, there was a time when your momma and daddy first moved over to the island. We were great friends—Percy and I along with Mary Beth and Douglas. We were all young and gay, going up to the Seaside for a drink together or sometimes we would play canasta. When your daddy was at work, your momma would come sit in my kitchen and tell me stories about your daddy and the war and all the hell he went through along with *his* parents. They only wanted to get here, become Americans, work hard and be somebody."

"Daddy never talks very much about his parents or immigrating, and when he came here he was just a kid."

"Well, that may be, but your momma had plenty to say. Someday I'll scratch my head good and try to remember some of the stories. You just need to know this much today. First, you take a young, beautiful, high-strung woman and marry her off to somebody a lot older, who's never home. Then you stick her in a drafty old beach house at the end of this island. And, finally, you let your mother run your marriage and never give your wife any spending money. You think that's a pretty picture? Now, it's ten o'clock. I gotta get myself to eleven o'clock Mass by ten-thirty or I won't get my seat."

I stood up to leave then turned around and had another look at her. Her jaw was hanging open and her confusion was as plain as day.

"Don't go," she said, "wait. Please. Talk to me."

What was I supposed to do then? Leave this child all upset? Heavens to Betsy! What a predicament! I just couldn't forsake my religious obligation. I was too close to death to take any chances on earning more time in Purgatory.

"I'll tell you what, dear. You come over for dinner and I'll talk to you all you want. Angel always makes fried chicken and red rice for Sundays. We eat at three. All right?"

"Yes, thanks. I will."

"Now, let's have a smile, okay?"

Finally, Long Tall Sally smiled and I let myself out the door. Walking across the yard, I hollered back to her. "Three o'clock!"

"I'll be there!" she called out.

Do you want to know something? Knowing too much about people can be a terrible burden. It's unfortunately true.

Ten

The Chicken Was Committed

~~~

THREE o'clock had almost rolled around but not before Lucy had the chance to look in on me. I was starting to wonder heavily what these people did with their time before I bought this house.

"Hey! Anybody home?" Lucy said, calling through the screen.

"Come on in!" I said, calling back.

"Wow! What's that smell? Lord, chile! Gimme a bite!"

I was in the kitchen, which as you know was so small you could stir a pot on the stove and empty the dishwasher at the same time. A one-fanny kitchen by anyone's definition. I was pulling a sheet of chocolate chip cookies from the oven. My chocolate chip cookies were pretty darn good, if I said so myself. I figured after the tonnage of Miss Angel's cookies I had eaten years ago at Miss Mavis's the least I could do was to show up with something.

"I made cookies for the Snoop Sisters," I said, lifting one with a spatula and offering it to Lucy. "I'm going over for dinner in a few minutes."

"You must be crazy as hell, 'eah? Gonna be cat hair in the soup. You wanna get a hair ball?"

"Ain't no cat gonna get between me and my dinner. Don't worry."

"Damn, gir'! Thith id tho goot!"

"Hot?"

Lucy shook her head up and down, whooshing air through her teeth trying to cool her mouth. I poured her a glass of water and handed it to her.

"Got milk?"

"You sound like an ad campaign."

I poured her a glass of milk and she took it and another cookie, blowing on it first.

"Thanks," she said. "So what's the occasion? I mean, is there any reason for the invitation besides their usual nosiness?"

"You're not gonna believe this," I said, "because I can hardly believe it myself."

"That one's broken. Can I eat it?"

I looked at my watch and saw that it was almost three, quickly deciding to tell Lucy about the Mother of all Mother Discoveries later.

"Of course," I said. "Oh! I'm almost late! I'll tell you what." I began gathering up the cookies and stacked them on a plate. "I'll come knock on your door after dinner and I'll tell you all about it."

"I'll make you supper. Should I call Dougle?"

"Sure, call him. Ask him to make pierogis. Kielbasa. Golabki. Tell him I think we might have the beginnings of an interesting conversation coming up."

"O-kaaay! This sounds mysterious. Fun! We could use it!"

"No doubt about it."

I left Lucy and with my plate of cookies covered in aluminum foil, I crossed the yard between the oleanders, almost pulling my hair out of my head.

"Ow! Damn! That hurt!" I would definitely take a machete to the oleanders at some point. Damn things were dangerous.

But I forged on, yanking my hair out of the branch. What could Miss Mavis tell me that I didn't know? I couldn't imagine that she knew much. In fact, I was very, very annoyed that she thought my mother was worthy of *anything*. How *dare* she? My mother was a huge and horrible part of my life. Okay. Maybe that wasn't the most loving way to describe my feelings but I hadn't had much time to prepare. Tongues of fire were waiting to throw flames, mine included.

Wait! Was I going next door to fight with a couple of old ladies? What was the matter with me? Why shouldn't I listen to them and then think about it?

Hellfire, Anna, all they want to do is feed you and tell you how they saw things. Calm down! Isn't anybody entitled to a point of view besides you? You claim to be such a good listener—then be one!

This dialogue with my little internal voice was about to save my ass for the billionth time.

Composed, repressed and in hospitable humor, I knocked on their door. Miss Mavis answered it and the minute I stepped inside her living room a thousand years came sliding back. I could smell the frying chicken. Delicious! And the same damn pine-scented frogs from Glade that she used to mask the cat box smell of her nasty cats. All at once I was ten years old. But if that was true, how did Miss Mavis get so old? I caught myself mid-daydream.

"I made some cookies for you," I said.

"Oh!" she said and choked up a little. "Thank you, Anna. Come on in."

I could have sworn she was crying or had been crying or at the very least was emotional about something. I would find out, I told myself, but wasn't sure I really wanted to. I followed her to the kitchen, where Miss Angel was turning out chicken onto paper towels spread across the counter.

"Well, well! Look who's 'eah! Miss Anna! Let me look at you!"

She put down her tongs, wiped her hands on the skirt of her apron, and came to stand right in front of me.

"Miss Angel," I said. "Isn't life strange?"

"No, life is *wonderful*, 'eah?" She stood back from me with her hands on my upper arms and her eyes went from my head to my toes. "This does me so much good to lay my old eyes on you." She sighed deeply and shook her head.

Miss Mavis, watching Miss Angel's lips said, "Mine too, mine too."

"It's *good* to see you, Anna."

"It's so good to see y'all too," I said. I meant it.

"I mean to say that it's so good to see you on this 'eah island, because this is where you *belong*."

"Thanks." I stopped for a moment and, looking at her dead on, I said, "I think so too. It's like coming full circle or something."

"What?"

"She say she glad to be home!"

"Don't holler so, Angel! Well, you poor thing, you probably have a mortgage that could kill you," Miss Mavis said.

"It's not too bad. But things have changed around here a lot. What do y'all think about the new shopping center in Mount Pleasant?"

"What? What was that? I missed it," Miss Mavis said.

"She say, How do you like the new shopping center in Mount Pleasant!"

"Oh. Well, I'm too old for some of those crazy stores, but it's nice to have a Belk's."

"I had actually looked at a house over there before I saw this one."

"What? Are you crazy, girl? You're an old island Geechee, just like us. And that traffic! Mercy! Drive you right out of your mind, 'eah?"

"Let's get this 'eah meal going, girls," Miss Angel said. "This chicken gave up he ghost for y'all."

"And, you too!" Miss Mavis said, turning to me, whispering. "She can be so *bossy* sometimes!"

"I hear you!" Miss Angel said from the kitchen.

Miss Mavis's expression was like the skipping line of a heart monitor before it went flat—the disease had been diagnosed but there was still some fight in the patient, and without an end in sight.

Their little bickering act improved my mood and I helped them take the food to the table.

The platter of fried chicken was the centerpiece, and I'd like to take a moment to discuss its attributes. It was golden brown and not in the least bit greasy. Miss Angel had a batter recipe that would send the Colonel off a tall building in shame. It was the kind of magazine photograph chicken that made you want to pick off chunks of crunchy batter when no one was looking.

There was also a covered dish of red rice, another one of string beans boiled with onions and ham, a plate of deviled eggs, and finally, a basket of steaming hot biscuits, and no doubt the basket had been woven by Miss Angel. Miss Mavis had set the table with her best china and silver and I knew that this was something of an occasion for them. I was very pleased that I'd brightened up my attitude. They may not have had tons of company to help them pass their Sunday afternoons, but I'll tell you this. If anyone knew how Miss Angel's chicken melted in your mouth, they'd have a single-file line from their front door to Shem Creek every single weekend.

"Let's say the blessing," Miss Mavis said, and we bowed our heads. "Dear Lord, please bless this food, forgive my mouth for what I am about to tell this young woman, and thank you for teaching Angel how to fry chicken that doesn't make us too fat. Amen." She raised her head and looked at me. "I forgot something."

"That's alright, Mavis, you just go on and say it."

She cut her eye at Miss Angel and bowed her head again. "Lord? You still there? Well, today is very special for us because one of our own has come home. I hope that when the time comes for me and Angel to come home that somebody in heaven might be half as excited as we are. Thank you, Lord. Amen." She opened her eyes and looked at Miss Angel, adding, "If the Lord lets you in, that is."

"Humph," Miss Angel said.

Well, that was it. I felt the pain of my entire life coming up my throat.

One of our own has come home.

My eyes burned and I felt ashamed for having dragged Daddy's story through the years, never once thinking or asking if there had been another side. Worse, I had forgotten about the sense of belong-ing the island had always given me. Loving it was one thing but it was marvelous to actually belong someplace. How many years had I spent feeling that I didn't belong anywhere that I was? How many people never felt that they belonged in the space they inhabited?

Taking some chicken, a large breast and a hefty second joint, I cleared my throat so that I wouldn't get weepy, already knowing that I *would* eventually cry like a pig. I wanted Miss Mavis and Miss Angel to hurry up with the story. Impatience and anxiety were eating me alive.

Miss Mavis heaped a mound of red rice on my plate and two spoonfuls of snap beans. I took three deviled eggs. Miss Angel offered me a biscuit; I grabbed two and slathered them with butter. I couldn't wait to get the hot dripping things in my mouth.

"Angel can fry some chicken, 'eah?"

"She always could! I can't wait to taste it! See if she lost her touch."

"Humph. Lost my touch? When's the last time you *ate*, girl?" Miss Angel said.

"Miss Angel? You are *still* so, so bad!"

We laughed and Miss Mavis said, "What'd she say?"

"Deaf as a doornail," Miss Angel said to me under her breath and then loudly to Miss Mavis, "I said, *She seems mighty hungry!*"

"Don't pay her any mind," Miss Mavis said, "she's just an old woman. Would you care for tea? And you! Quit yelling at me, you old coot."

We began to eat and the standard pleasantries were exchanged. I told them that Daddy had never remarried, that I worked at a salon in Charleston, and that I was divorced. I told them all about Emily and how wonderful she was. Miss Mavis bragged on Miss Angel and how her baskets had won a grant from the National Endowment for the Arts. Miss Mavis went on to say that Fritz (a.k.a. Thurmond) was up for a part in *The West Wing* and that he was doing well, determined not to ever need rehab again. I didn't ask what had taken him to rehab to begin with and, cross-checking all my mental gauges, I decided that I was acting well enough.

We all admitted that the men in our lives were scarce but that had been all right since we were always too busy to worry about it anyway. But mostly, we talked about how much I had wanted to come back to the Isle of Palms and that's when Miss Mavis took a deep breath and began to talk.

"It's important and right that you came back, Anna."

"Yeah, I dreamed about it for years."

"There's very little more important in this world than knowing where you belong."

"Why is that? I mean, coming back to the Isle of Palms has always mattered to me so much. I'm just not sure why."

"Anna," Miss Angel said, "you know you're in the right place when you can feel it under your feet. Now maybe that sounds crazy, but when I stand on this island, it ain't even close to how I feel when I stand on the sidewalks of Charleston."

"Not weird at all," I said. "On top of that I think my heart rate lowers here. I mean, I really feel different. Relaxed. You know?"

"We've always thought so," Miss Mavis said, looking at her fork of rice and then putting it back on her plate. "Did your daddy ever tell you about his brother?"

"Daddy doesn't have a brother," I said, thinking that she was a little addled with age.

"Well, he did. His name was John. Johnny. He died when he was two years old. Terrible. But those were terrible times for your grandparents and for your father too."

"I had an uncle? Why have I never heard this story?"

Miss Angel pushed back from the table. "I'm gonna get us some more ice for the tea. Anybody want lemon?"

No one answered her and she went to the kitchen without another word. Maybe she didn't condone all that Miss Mavis had planned to tell me.

"Probably because it was so horrible to talk about. He caught the measles and there was no medicine. Well, there was, but they weren't handing it out to displaced persons working in an underground airplane factory. That's for sure. He died in your grandmother's arms. The poor woman! Lord, have mercy!"

"Oh, my God! That's horrible! And, it might explain why she was so heartless."

"She wasn't really, Anna. I think there's only so much a person can take and then something in them can't feel anything anymore. You know? I can tell you that if I lost one of mine, I'd lose my mind! But, you ask your daddy. He'll tell you if you ask him."

"Are you kidding? Daddy has always avoided talking about those years other than to say they were awful. Life began for him when Grandfather bought the peach farm in Estill. I knew they had lived in Warsaw and Grandmother's family was from there. But I could never figure out how they wound up in Germany."

"What?"

"I said, *How did they wind up in Germany anyway?*"

"I'm sorry, Anna, I don't hear so well anymore."

"Humph," Miss Angel said, dropping cubes of ice in our glasses, "You can say that again."

Miss Mavis narrowed her eyes at Miss Angel, I smiled at both of them, and Miss Mavis said, "To work to get money to live, for heaven's sake. Besides, Warsaw was all blown up and there wasn't even electricity all the time. Food was scarce. There was no work and they never knew when a Russian soldier might put a bullet through their heads."

"It must have been terrible."

"Yes, I imagine so. After the Russians occupied Warsaw during the war, and the Germans were forced out, your grandparents went to Augsburg, where they lived in housing for displaced persons. They were crammed on a train with all kinds of people for one week, in a cattle car. Your grandfather's socks dissolved in his shoes! I can't even fathom such a thing! When they finally arrived, your grandfather worked in the munitions plant and your grandmother had a small job

as a bookkeeper. Would you believe she used an abacus? She showed it
to me once and she told me all sorts of things."

"That's why she kept it! My God! Wait! Were they, could they
have been Nazis?"

"Great God! No! They were Prussian! Didn't anyone ever tell you
about your family's history?"

"No, I guess not. I mean, I know they immigrated and all that.
What—I mean, how do you know all this?"

"Your mother told me, of course. And your grandmother. How else
would I know? Did you know that your father and his family can trace
their roots back to the time of Charlemagne? Their ancestors were
buried in full armor! Warriors for centuries!"

I shook my head.

"Well, they can. I can see you don't know your European history
very well."

"Probably not."

"You see, Poland has belonged to everybody under the sun at one
time or another. The Germans, Austrians, and Russians haggled over
it for centuries. But, hell's bells, they're all crazy anyhow. I don't know
what's the matter with people, always fighting."

"You want some tea, Mavis?"

"What?"

"*Tea?*"

Miss Angel, annoyed each time she had to repeat herself but
resigned to it also, passed the biscuits around again.

"Your grandparents worked for their government the same way all
these people in Charleston worked at our Navy Yard for years. War or
no war. Some people were civilians but they were employed by the
government. When the front of the war got pushed back from Warsaw by the Russians, they wound up in Germany. Let me tell you
something, Anna. Your grandparents didn't give one fig about politics.
It was war! They were just trying to stay alive."

"Good grief," I said, "I can't imagine . . ."

"Well, think about this. They were young, had just been married, and the war broke out. One day in September, I think she said September. Wait! Yes, September 1939. Well, your grandmother was a young girl still and she walked outside her house and there was a huge blasting noise. Sirens started to wail and, oh, Lord! She said she was almost frightened to death. I would have been, I can tell you that."

Miss Mavis seemed to drift away. She began eating again as though she had said everything there was to say. Miss Angel looked at me, tightened up the side of her mouth, and shook her head.

"Mavis!" she said. "Go on and finish up your story!"

"Oh!" Miss Mavis said. "Where was I?"

"You were telling us about the bombs in Warsaw, Miss Mavis," I said, "and how my grandparents went on the train to Germany."

"Do you want some more red rice?" Miss Angel said, holding the covered dish. "Or another biscuit?"

"No, thanks, but it's delicious," I said. "Miss Mavis? Were they terrified of the Nazis?"

"Of course! I mean, I'm sure they *must* have been! Your grandmother never said that directly that I remember, but gracious! Who wouldn't be?"

"Daddy would know."

"Yes, and you should ask him about all the war business. You know, the point, Anna, of me telling you all of this is that war changes people. It really does. Sometimes it's for the better and sometimes you are wounded so badly in your mind that you stay afraid for the rest of your life. Every little thing is a potential catastrophe."

"And you think that's why my grandmother was such a witch?"

She just stared at me.

"She all but drove your mother out of her mind. And whatever was left of her got chewed up by Douglas. Let me tell you, anyone who really, really knew your mother and father never blamed your mother for what happened. Let's help Angel clear the table. I want some ice cream. And one of your cookies. You know, I always have one cookie with my ice cream." She pushed back from the table and followed Miss Angel to the kitchen with her plate.

Just like that. I sat there with all the wind knocked out of me. I needed a fuller picture and to understand a lot more before I was willing to even consider forgiving my mother. What did she mean? How could she say what she said? I could believe that my grandmother made my mother a wreck, but Daddy? Never! I remembered! Daddy loved Momma completely! She was wrong and that was all there was to it!

I made myself get up and join them. I felt weak all over and my hands were clammy. I picked up my dinner plate, the biscuit basket, and the butter plate and went to the kitchen. They were bickering again and suddenly stopped when they saw me.

"What did I miss?" I said to them.

"Miss Anna?" Miss Angel said. "I just say to Mavis that she don't have all the facts straight. I can see why you never understood. You was just a little girl, knee high to a grasshopper, when your momma pass. And, your grandmother? She didn't have a single thing in common with your momma. Not one little speck of nothing."

"Anna," Miss Mavis said, "honey, your daddy was their only child after losing their other son. Can't you imagine how that must have been? They worked so hard and suffered so much to get here. Then they had to learn a new language. They had almost no money, no friends, no family. It took *years* for them to grow roots here. When your daddy upped and married a beauty queen with no education, they liked to have just died!"

I put the dishes on the counter and leaned on it to listen. "I want to know everything. Please. Tell me."

"I can do the dishes later," Miss Angel said. "Let's have us some dessert."

"What?"

"I said, *I will do the dishes later, Mavis!*" She brushed by me to reach the freezer. "Some days I want to strangle her."

"Hush!" Miss Mavis said to Miss Angel under her breath. "And I could throttle you!"

"Hears what she likes and nothing else," Miss Angel said.

"Oh, fine!" Miss Mavis took the plate of cookies I had brought and passed us on her way back out to the living room. "Let's sit on the porch. There's a nice breeze out there and too much hot air in here!"

We settled ourselves in rockers and Miss Mavis began to talk.

"Your mother was a head turner, Anna. You are more like her than you think."

"Yeah, she was beautiful, but I think she was a little overdone, you know? Too much makeup."

"Hmmm. But you be the one in the beauty business. Ain't it so?"

My face flushed red, the heat traveling down my back, and I didn't know what to say.

"I hate it when she's right too," Miss Mavis said. "Such a prickly thing she is!"

"I only say what's fuh true, Mavis, and you know it! Lawd! She had a pretty garden, just like you. Your momma could have been a lot of things."

"If your daddy would've let her! Wouldn't even let her drive a car until Percy and I pleaded with him."

"Spend a nickel? Humph. He make her write it all down and show it to him on Friday. Yes, he did."

"And he called her every five minutes. If she went out, she had to call him and report in. She cried in my kitchen on many a day. Yes, she did. That poor child cried a river."

Miss Mavis's watery and red-rimmed eyes, faded with age, met mine. I knew what they had said was true.

I'd had an uncle I'd never heard of, a grandmother whose behavior could *almost* be understood—some of it anyway—and a father who was a paranoid zookeeper for my misunderstood dead mother.

I was drowning in the connections, the story I had heard and the prospects of the truth yet to come. It was absolutely horrible how truth could be rearranged to justify one's own behavior.

Eleven

I've Had Sufficient, Thank You

⌐⌐⌐

F I'd made the mistake of banging my way through the oleanders to Miss Mavis and Miss Angel's house like a moody
teenager, I knew I shouldn't charge across to Lucy's yard for
dinner like Cardinal Fang of the Spanish Inquisition either. It was
one of those days where nothing was turning out as I expected it
would. Something was telling me to pull in my claws. Yes, it was that
freaking little inner voice again.

After I came home from the Snoop Sisters, I took a long shower
and stared at the television for a while like someone in a mental hospital. The words and implications of Miss Mavis and Miss Angel were
running around in my head. I was so deeply upset and so utterly per-
plexed that I didn't know where to start with Daddy. It was inevitable
that it would surface at Lucy's. Or was it? I needed to think about
everything. After all, it was highly possible that Miss Mavis's recollec-
tions of my mother were skewed by an elderly lady's romantic vision
of the past. But Miss Angel had agreed with her and she wasn't given
to drama. How could I ask my father if he and Grandmother had

painted a counterfeit childhood for me? All the lies! All those years of saying how bad Momma was!

I would just ask him and that was all there was to it.

No. No, I couldn't. I was a weak and sniveling coward.

What lousy timing to be carrying the worst scars of your childhood heart over to your friend's house to serve up to your father as an hors d'oeuvre. For the first time ever, I had seen my daddy not merely enjoying, but reveling in the company of another woman. Crazy Lucy, no less. Daddy had dated scores of age-appropriate, well-meaning widows and divorcées over the years. They were a flesh trail of conservative, Talbots-attired, sensible ladies who blushed. Here he was with good old Lucy. The only blush she knew about came in a compact with a brush.

But what could you say? The fact was that Lucy, discombobulated as she was, had been nothing but a pussycat to me and a bracelet of shining silver charms to Daddy. I had no right to blow away their evening with my anger.

Still! *What the hell had really happened in those years?* Was my mother the flighty, insincere, unloving, total and complete whore I had always been led to believe she was? Or was my father some overbearing, second-guessing lover of a younger woman he had no business marrying in the first place? Had he really driven her to the arms of other men with a legitimate cause? *Was* there a legitimate cause for infidelity?

I was wildly fearful of knowing this truth. I loved my father more than anyone except my daughter. Was the reason I never had a healthy or affectionate relationship with my mother because Daddy worked her into such a knot that she had to somehow punish him by withholding her love from us?

I waited until Daddy's car was in Lucy's driveway for at least thirty minutes. The time passed so slowly I could hardly bear it. I wanted to know! I was *entitled* to know but I realized the truth may be the kind that stung deep and ached forever.

I tried to calm down and think and at last came to a temporary conclusion that I would find a truth I could live with somewhere in the middle space of Miss Mavis's version of the past and what Daddy believed had truly happened.

I needed to be polite and show up with something in my hands to add to the dinner table in the same way I had brought something to Miss Mavis. What did I have? I dug around my kitchen and a quick inventory revealed a choice between a cheap bottle of wine and a half pound of undistinguished cheese. I decided on the block of sharp cheddar.

I sliced it and added crackers down the sides of the platter, with a tiny bunch of frilly multicolored toothpicks stuck in half an apple, and decided it looked pretty much like a Mardi Gras porcupine positioned to tromp over an orange rubber road. It would do. At least I was composed.

I would be civil and look for an opening after Daddy had had a few drinks. I would strike Daddy with the tiniest of all blow darts to the neck when Lucy wasn't watching. Okay, it wasn't fair. I knew that. And to think I had almost told Lucy about what Miss Mavis had said! I didn't care. It was so far beyond the time for setting the record straight that it wasn't funny.

There was more to consider. What about my grandmother? I wanted to know *why* my father had allowed my grandmother to perpetuate that kind of horrible history about my mother, if it was indeed a lie. And why he'd never made any attempt to change the record after my grandmother died. And why had he let her run my life the way she did? It was all pretty miserable.

"Hey! Come on in! We were just about to go watch the sun set."

"Here," I said, unconsciously pushing the platter toward Lucy, "I brought this for cocktails."

"Cwanky? Do we need a dwinky?"

Lucy tottered away on her hypodermic-heeled mules, which, for my fashionista diary of all things notable, were black patent leather, painted with stylized hot pink flamingos wearing sunglasses. *Where did this woman shop?* A catalog monster. Had to be.

Daddy and I greeted each other as we always did—a slight hug and the requisite peck on my cheek. I listened to him describe how Lucy had brilliantly marinated chicken and tuna in teriyaki sauce with garlic and scallions and his only lowly contribution had been to flip the Ziploc bag and to preheat the oven for the frozen garlic bread. He was bragging on Lucy's commandeering of the meal. It was ridiculous to see him behave that way; at least at that moment it seemed so to me. I was scowling at them.

Daddy and Lucy knew right away that I was out of sorts and made the kind of dance-around-you small talk that doesn't invite you in, but is hopeful that their good humor will change yours. I took the glass of white wine Lucy offered and drank most of it while I listened to them jabber on. Jabber. Jabber. For the love of God, why didn't one of them just ask me what was wrong?

It was because they didn't want to know. Sure. I was in the mood for World War III and all they wanted to do was have a nice evening. I hadn't felt more like a third wheel in a long time. The stink around my mood was probably unbearable. But they were so happy they did everything except to whistle Dixie.

It wasn't until we climbed up to the widow's walk to see the night sky present herself that my disposition began to shift. The blue light turned rose and then purple, giving me the time I needed to quiet my mind.

I looked over at them. Daddy's eyes, deeply lined, shouting from their dusty, spent riverbeds, the decades of self-inflicted denial of all but the smallest pleasures, those eyes followed Lucy's every gesture with a kind of gratitude for her appreciation of him. No, it was less— her very notice of him was sufficient.

To be only seen as *viable* by a woman of such vigor was an all-powerful youth serum. And, moreover, whatever affection she had for him was enough to elevate his endorphins, spray his pheromones with abandon and needless to say, pump the stash of testosterone that had so long ached to be called to task.

Who could blame him? Not me. No, I couldn't. Not for this, any-

way. I couldn't recall ever having seen my father this excited. For all
his conservatism, he may as well have said his name was Tarzan and
that he would now take over the navigation of the jungle for this little lost Miss. Daddy had effectively, and with certain glee, fallen off
the cliff.

Can I refill your glass, Miss Lucy?

Oh, Douglas! Why, honey, you are such a gentleman! Isn't your daddy a
gentleman, Anna?

"He's the best."

And I saw Lucy differently too. She wasn't nearly as young as I had
thought. There were surgical lines in the crease above her eyes. As the
breeze took her hair back in a blast, I saw them behind her ears as
well. Well, if Lucy had lifted her face, so what? That explained her
lips. Collagen. The first day I met her, I had recognized her breasts as
implausible and her cheekbones as suspect. You had to wonder. How
much of her was authentic? But! What did it matter anyway? She was
the kind of woman who needed something to feel better. My daddy
was her drug of choice.

The cruel side of me, the one that had brought an angry woman to
Lucy's house with the platter of second-rate cheese, would have said
that Daddy appeared to be Lucy's dog. *Fetch!* All she had to do was
toss the stick and he would bring it back to her, dropping it at her feet,
happy with a mere scratch behind his ears, ready to leap and run for
the stick all night long. *Get it, boy! Good dog!* But the irony was that
Lucy was Daddy's dog just as well. These two middle-aged orphaned
dogs, transformed by the sight of each other into Blue Ribbon cham-
pions, were strutting their stuff for me, the judge.

This was not the right moment to take Daddy into the boxing
ring. There was something of great value here to be learned. Something, maybe some small something, was in evidence that would
eventually be worthy of clinking glasses and offering a toast. And why
eventually? Why not let them just be happy now?

I decided, then and there on crazy Lucy's widow's walk, watching
the sun slide into the grand ruby stretch of horizon, that I would not

pick Daddy apart. I would not interrogate Daddy in front of her. I would probably not interrogate him anywhere unless I found myself in an easy circumstance.

If watching the signs around me told me anything then, it was that everybody was entitled to some happiness. They weren't hurting anyone and the only risk was their own pride.

"What a gorgeous sunset," I said, exhaling my change of heart.

Their posture relaxed; their faces softened. Whatever storm they had anticipated from me had passed out to sea on the turn of day to night.

"Yes," Daddy said, putting his arm around Lucy on one side and me on the other.

"I'm so happy I could just cry," Lucy said.

"Please! Why don't I help you incinerate that chicken instead?" I said. Even I, the plain food chef, thought that the chicken could be salvaged under a watchful eye at the grill but the poor tuna had been overmarinated beyond hope. If I ate that tuna, I'd never get my rings on again.

With the gas grill finally at the right temperature, I placed the chicken over the coals, alternating basting the bird with cursing and swatting mosquitoes—the unofficial state bird of South Carolina. Daddy and Lucy were inside making salad and, I suspected, whoopee. This was confirmed when I slipped through the screen door to get the soggy fish without making enough noise. His back to the door, Daddy was standing at the counter and Lucy was behind him with her hand up the back of Daddy's shirt.

"Okay, tell me what *this* says." She traced a word on his skin with her fingernails.

"Nunk?"

"Nunk? No, you silly! Hunk!"

I cleared my throat. "Okay, you two, there are children in the room."

Lucy giggled and Daddy said, his face turning crimson, "She was just . . ."

"Oh, forget it," I said, "I was young once too, you know."

"Golly, Anna, we need to find you a man, honey. What's up with your love life?"

"You know what? That's a darn good question. I met this guy and then . . ." And then, nothing happened, I thought.

We picked our way through the chicken, bagged salad and garlic bread in addition to two bottles of Fat Bastard white wine. Lucy, true to habit, had managed to squeeze in a pitcher of frozen Margaritas and some vodka shots, which only she and Daddy drank.

After all, I had to negotiate the yard to get home to nobody. They gave me the blues.

When it was time for me to slip out, leaving them the lion's share of the evening alone, I stood up from the couch.

"You leaving?"

"Yeah, I gotta get up early. Hey, Lucy! Thanks for dinner."

"Oh, honey, wasn't nothing at all!"

"Lucy? I'll be back in a few minutes. I want to take a look at the lock on Anna's back door."

"Sure, baby boy! I'll be right here waiting!" Lucy gave me a hug and Daddy a kiss on the cheek. "See you later, Miss Anna! Sleep tight!"

Daddy and I walked down her stairs and across the yards to my back door.

"My lock is fine, Daddy."

"I know, I just wanted to talk to you for a minute."

I unlocked my door and we went in the kitchen.

"You want a glass of water?"

"Yeah, thanks," he said and leaned against my counter, waiting for one of us to speak. "What's bothering you, Anna?"

He did not speak with an accusatory tone nor was there any trace of anything that would have allowed me to put up my guard and fight. It was just my father asking his daughter what was wrong and could he help.

I was not a woman who cried easily or often. There were two occasions in my life that I recall really losing it and weeping like a child. One was my mother's death when I realized she was really dead forever. Those tears sprang from a deep well of profound sadness. The other was when I knew I couldn't live with Jim anymore. That major crying jag was brought on by my guilt and fear of standing on my own feet. This was entirely different. It was about digging up the bones.

As my hot tears, the kind you dare to start up with you but they defy everything and come anyway, those steaming, streaming traitors, started running down my cheeks I lost all my words. I didn't know what to say to him. He came to my side and his hands held my shoulders. My hands shook, trying to fill the filter with coffee for the next morning. I put it on the counter and the coffee grinds went everywhere. I turned around and put my head on my daddy's shoulder, my arms around his waist, and ugly gulping sobs began to roll. I didn't care.

"Whatever in the world has happened, Anna?"

"Oh, shit. Nothing."

"Yeah, sure. Come on, baby. Tell me. God knows, this old man of yours has heard it all."

"I don't, oh, God, Daddy, I mean, I just don't know where to start. I guess I just don't know what's true anymore."

He pulled his pressed handkerchief from his pocket, shook it open, and handed it to me. "I hate the way the laundry is doing my handkerchiefs. Too stiff. Blow."

"I don't have the heart to ruin it," I said, and pulled a tissue from the box next to the microwave, blowing my nose with a frightening racket.

"That's you, Anna. Practical. Thoughtful."

"It's the thoughtful part that gets me into trouble," I said.

"Well, if you don't talk to me, I can't tell you if what you're thinking is right or not."

"Okay. I have to ask you a question. How come you never told me you had a brother who died during the war?"

Daddy took a deep breath and stared first at the ceiling and then at the floor.

"I don't know. Because there was no reason to."

"And is it true that you made Momma call you if she left the house for, say, a trip to the grocery store?"

"She was a terrible driver and I worried about her being on the road."

I could see him getting mad. And, I could see him trying to control his anger. We stood there for what seemed like years until he finally said, "What's this really about, Anna? Those two old busybodies got your motor going? *God Almighty!*" He began to circle the living room. "*People should mind their own business! I can't stand it when people talk. It's vicious and it's wrong to try and reinvent the past. What's done is done!*"

I was exhausted enough to go to sleep right there on my kitchen floor. I had forgotten about the power of release brought on by tears. My muscles ached; I felt heavy all over. I hardly had the strength to talk anymore about something so serious at the end of a long day.

"It's getting late, Daddy, and Lucy is waiting for you." I chewed on my bottom lip, waiting for him to respond. His anger was white-hot.

"Is this all?"

"No. It isn't all. I guess I'm just trying to look at Momma differently."

"You can do that *all you want* but it won't change a single thing. Your mother was the biggest disappointment of my life, Anna. She was a *disgrace*. Her death nearly killed me too."

"It nearly killed *all* of us, Daddy. I just think that maybe she wasn't as bad as I've always thought. You know? I mean, when children want something they can't have, they stomp their feet and carry on."

"And what she wanted was *another man*, Anna. Remember she died doing drugs and having sex with *another man*."

Now I was getting angry. "Like you or Grandmother ever let me forget. But I don't think that's what she *wanted*, Daddy."

"Oh? *You're* an expert on marriage now?"

He was pissed off to the gills. I didn't have the strength to have a knock-down, drag-out fight with Daddy, I just wanted him to help me understand. Maybe if I could understand, we could have some healing in both of our screwed-up minds.

"I think she was *suffocating*, Daddy. I think she felt *trapped*."

"That's ridiculous."

"No, it's not!"

"You're jealous of my affection for Lucy, aren't you?"

"Good Lord, no!"

"Yes, you are. I could see you tonight, brooding around. You're jealous!"

"I was brooding because I was trying to think of a way to talk to you about *Momma!* Jealous of you and Lucy? No way!"

"Oh."

A few seconds passed and then I threw in the towel for the night. "Lucy's a fruitcake, but I love her to death. She's probably exactly what we both need. I mean, we're too serious. She's a ball of fire."

The smallest of smiles crept across his face, dissolving his anger. When I saw it, I put aside my anger too.

"Well, she sure puts the pepper in my pot."

Good Lord. Pepper in his pot? I hadn't heard that since I used to watch reruns of reruns of *Donna Reed* or some such show from television antiquity.

"Oh, Lord, Daddy! Pepper in your pot? Let's talk tomorrow, okay?"

"Well, take some Motrin. I'll call you in the morning. Maybe you're getting a cold or something."

He kissed me on my forehead and left. I stepped outside and called after him.

"Night, Daddy."

"Night." Then he stopped and turned to come back.

"What?"

"Anna. About your mother. There were reasons . . . well, I was a very foolish man. And possessive. Prideful."

"I've been a fool before too, Daddy. And prideful."

"The human condition."

"Yeah."

That half admission that all the fault may not have been my mother's was the closest to an agreement on the facts that I would ever get from him.

I waited until he was halfway up Lucy's steps before I even thought of turning away from the sight of him. Daddy was getting older. I could see it in his walk. Where he had once possessed a kind of deliberate gait, there was now a sort of rhythmic shift to one side. He seemed to be relying more on his left side than his right. I wondered if his hip hurt, or maybe his knee.

At least he had a love life.

For a moment I thought of Arthur, the Cheese Whiz. Indeed. But Lucy was right. I needed someone in my life besides her, Daddy, and the ever shrinking circle of people I knew who lived on the anorexic pages of my social calendar.

And hadn't I made some sweeping stupid remark to Daddy and Lucy only nights before that I had met a man and that I had been dreaming about opening my own salon? There you had it in a nutshell—none of us was perfect or logical or totally honest, even about the big issues. Maybe we were more likely to fool ourselves about the big issues than the small ones.

I was relieved that I hadn't confronted Daddy at Lucy's. My father's relationship with my mother wasn't Lucy's business.

Maybe it wasn't mine, either.

What would my obsessing change? Rehashing the past would make my father feel worse and there was no guarantee that I would feel better. Did it matter anyway if my mother was a saint or a sinner at this point? Was there a way we could look at her indiscretion and make our own lives better?

I washed my face, brushed my teeth and dressed for bed. I was so tired. I settled under my covers and closed my eyes and began to try and see my mother with my mind. For the first time in years, I decided to pray for her.

Momma? Momma? I need to know. Was everybody wrong about you? I'm looking for you. I want you to know that I'm thinking of you. I hope you're at peace. I really do and I'm asking God to give you peace. I miss you. I've always missed you.

I needed you then and I don't know why you couldn't help me, but it's okay now. I forgive you. I do. Please help me understand. . . . I am so lonely. I didn't even know that until now, but I am tired and I am so alone. I'm sending you my heart; please send me yours.

Twelve

Getting Hairy

I DREAMED about my mother again last night. I was little and she was pushing me on a swing. What did it mean? Maybe she was just trying to tell me to lighten up. At least that was all I could come up with as I walked on the beach, looking for sand dollars and answers. There were few of either to be found.

I had so many things on my mind. I was still bothered by last night's argument with Daddy. No one would ever completely change Daddy's opinion of Momma but I could change my own. In the end he had admitted some guilt over how he had handled their marriage, but Daddy's pride was just about as thick as a stone wall. Was mine? Well, if it was, I wouldn't let it be that way any longer. Having been cornered once or twice myself, I could understand how Momma would have rebelled. Obviously, she chose badly when she took it up with the pharmacist. Maybe she was afraid of divorce. Maybe she just got caught being stupid. I felt sympathetic toward her. Hell, who was I to judge anybody? I was only a few years younger than she was when she married Daddy and I had gotten drunk at my senior prom and wound up with a baby. Nobody poured the alcohol down my throat and nobody pushed her down the aisle. Both of us had our eyes open when we made our poor choices. The difference was that giving in to her frustration came with a price tag of her life. Mine had given me Emily. *Marry in haste, repent at leisure.* If old Violet had done needlepoint, she would've had that on a pillow for sure!

And last night I had cried my eyes out like a baby. When the tide turned on the island, and most especially on the edge of day, your heart would swell with all sorts of longing. Who wouldn't have wept? Anybody who holds back the truth for over twenty years and then has to face it? I'd had an uncle? And, although I'd never admit this out loud, I've always wondered what I could've done about Momma. If I had loved Momma harder, if I had just let her know that I needed her more, would that have made her more devoted to us? It had simply never occurred to me when I was a little girl that I had a responsibility of that magnitude. Now, as an adult, I could see that it was slightly abnormal to think that I was partially to blame, but I always would.

If dealing with the past wasn't enough, I was getting more desperate for freedom from Harriet with each passing day. The accumulation of her nit-picking, spying, and accusations had driven me to the limit of what I could tolerate and still hang on to any kind of good humor around her. Unfortunately, this really wasn't the right time to quit. Not that my mortgage was so horrible, it was that I'd never had one before, and I wasn't accustomed to having long-term bills to pay. I just wanted to get used to the new commitment in my life before I took another risk.

I saw Arthur from a distance and he waved. I threw my arm around, waving back with more enthusiasm than cool dictated, but I was wishing he would come over, be a pal, listen to my woes, and give me some advice. He was through with his morning walk and he turned and crossed the dunes.

If there was one column in which I was sorely lacking, it was friends in whom I could confide. Since Frannie had stayed on in D.C. after college and Jim left, sure, we talked all the time, but talking on the phone all the time wasn't really enough. I needed friends to go out to dinner with or to the movies, you know, people I could hang out with. I had been so busy I'd never found the time to cultivate new friends. This had an unmistakable downside.

Truth be told, Daddy and I had stepped into each other's lives in ways that were probably unhealthy. I don't mean there was anything weird going on. Jeez! No. It's just that when I moved back in with him I think it was probably normal for me to have assumed certain roles—grocery shopping, housekeeping, cooking, and gardening. He was the handyman, confidante, even though he was a grump, and he covered the mortgage. I was his shield against another marriage and any poor son of a gun I brought home would undergo the *interview process from hell*. For years, we went safely nowhere on the road of personal relationships. That was what laziness and fear could do to a life.

And another good case to illustrate my laziness was that about the same minute I signed my mortgage, as I was still slinging hair for crazy Harriet, I realized that my days with her did have a number. Great, Anna, just great. I just hoped I would have the presence of mind to recognize which actual day would be most auspicious to tell her to take my pillared position at the House of Hair and insert it in the region of the Great Never Tanned.

Dragging myself back home to dress for work, I decided that I should probably give my career much more thought. There had to be a solution.

I wrestled with the choices before me while driving to Charleston—stay with Harriet and go slowly insane or go slowly insane in another salon. Given the choice of lunatics, Harriet almost seemed preferable. At least I knew what caliber of nut she was. There was an old Gullah saying I remembered about changing partners—*keep the evil that you know*. I had escaped Daddy's house by the skin of my teeth. The thought of another uprooting change made my stomach ache.

Working for any other salon would have been worse than a lateral move. Crazy though she may have been, Harriet had the best salon in Charleston. We had more walk-in traffic, more stylists and a larger product and accessory selection. Most importantly, just because I had a robust dislike for her, it didn't mean I wanted to disengage at any cost. I absolutely needed to know where my next paycheck was coming from. Still, what was the answer?

If I were to go out and buy a new car (which I wouldn't be doing for at least five years), I'd probably visit several dealers and see what kind of deal I could get. But as long as I was ever so gently kicking around a career change, I decided to take a discreet poll of my trusted clients to see if they would follow me to a new salon. Maybe that would satisfy my urge to bolt for a while so that I could stand Harriet a little longer. Yes, that was what I would do.

I walked in the door and picked up my appointment list from Carla, our receptionist of almost six months—a longevity of mind-boggling proportion in House of Hair history. She ran the front desk and the scheduling, and was a wizard.

Carla Egbert was tall and lanky like a runway model, had a flawless face, and operated the front of our salon like the head of strategic planning for the armed forces. All with good humor and ribald wit. To say she was loved and feared was an understatement. If you crossed her, she overbooked you with new clients and you could be frazzled to death. If you gave her the correct regard, she was your secret weapon against Harriet and the hairy hordes desperate for a holiday makeover or prom night teens with acne-pocked T-zones who wanted to look like Jennifer Aniston. If you *really* aggravated her, she stuck you with wedding parties.

"Hey, Carla," I said, taking the paper from her, "how was your weekend?"

"Good, good," she said, smiling, "you've got a new victim on your hit parade."

"Yeah? Who's that?"

"Somebody named Lucy. I tried to give her to Nicole, but she said, no, it had to be you. I booked her in for an hour. Sorry."

"No sweat," I said, "she's my new neighbor. At least I think that's probably her."

"Oh! Right! You moved! How did it go?"

"Well, I got me a little noose, that's all. Not a big one, but I was a virgin in the noose department until I signed my mortgage. You need to book me up the wazoo, okay? It's only been two weeks and I'm still jittering."

"No problem."

"Thanks."

I walked to the back and poured a cup of coffee into "my mug," the one with an endorsement for the Piggly Wiggly on the side. GOTTA LOVE THE PIG it read, with a smiling porker on the other side. While I loved a comfortable gutter as much as the next person, I didn't want to spend the rest of my life drinking watered-down coffee from a chipped five-dollar mug.

I earned a decent living because I'd outlasted Harriet's psycho explosions and because Harriet would grudgingly mumble the fact that I was her most reliable employee. She knew I would open the salon early or close it up tight if she was going out of town or didn't feel well.

That's not to say that I had keys. No. If Harriet was ill, I had to stop by her house on Beaufain Street and pick them up. Periodically, she would change the salon locks, probably thinking I had copied them. That made me laugh because what did she think? That I would sneak in during the night and rip off the frigging shelf of shampoo and conditioner and then sell them on the street? She was crazy as hell.

We managed to get along by staying out of each other's path. She paid me one-half of all my service charges when most of the other stylists were on low salaries or receiving a lesser percentage. So although she was a certifiable nut job, she would be difficult to replace. Maybe.

I saw my first client of the day waiting in my chair and hurried over to greet her. Susan Hayes, one of my regulars and favorites. My assistant was combing out her freshly shampooed hair and offering her coffee.

"No cream, just black. Thanks," she said. "Well, hello there, Miss Abbot. How have you been?"

"Oh, I'm fine, thanks. You?"

"I imagine I'm holding together all right, all things considered."

"Well, that's good to hear. You married to that Simon yet?"

"No, but we're thinking we should probably go ahead and get it over with. Now that my ex-husband is married to his concubine and living happily ever after in Vermont, following the teachings of his new guru, taking coffee colonics, and representing a co-op of organic farmers, maybe it's time. I dunno. What do you think? Serial spouse? Should I do this?"

Smiling, I stood behind her and ran a comb through her hair, checking the condition of her ends and roots. "Marry him," I said, "before he gets picked off by some little nurse."

Her eyebrows narrowed and she looked at herself in the mirror. "Think I need to lipo my chin? The thing's sagging like a baggie of yogurt!"

"No way. You look great. Little color, little trim?" I said. "Little freshen-up?"

"Please! I have that Medical University dinner party this weekend. The annual gathering of cadavers and donors. I don't need to look like my own mother! How are my roots?"

"What roots? And, honey, nobody wants to look like their mother, with the possible exception of Catherine Deneuve's daughter."

"You said it! Oh! Does she have a daughter?"

"I couldn't tell you!" We laughed and then I said, "I'll just go mix up some magic in a bowl and I'll be back in a flash. You ain't gonna look like yo momma when I'm finished with you!"

Within the hour she was planting a folded twenty-dollar bill in my hand and about to sail out the door feeling like a new woman.

"God, Anna, you're the best! Thanks."

"Susan?" I drew her back, looking around to see if anyone else was listening. "If I left here would you still be my client?"

"Are you crazy?" She whispered, "I've been with you since Kim left

Charleston! Shoot, I'd follow you to Columbia! Maybe even Greenville! You're my ultimate secret weapon! Thinking of leaving old Harriet the Hellhound? Good! Never liked her anyhow."

"I'll let you know."

"It would cripple that mean old bitch but good." She laughed and said, "Sweet justice!"

"You're terrible," I said in a whisper, tightening my lips around my teeth so I wouldn't burst out laughing.

Score! One client in my pocket. I only needed about another two hundred or so and I'd be fine. I went up front to check my schedule again with Carla. Lucy was coming in the door. She was wearing tight cropped jeans, mules, and a big cotton shirt with about two tons of papier-mâché jewelry. I had never been to Coney Island but I imagined that she looked like a refugee from such a place.

"I wanted to see how your salon was, so I . . ."

"Lucy! What a wonderful surprise! I heard you were coming!" I took her by the arm.

"Oh, my God! This place is fabulous!"

"Thanks. Come on back!" I led her as far as my chair and said, "You want a Coke or some coffee?"

"No, but ice water? Y'all have that?"

I handed her a folded smock and told her to put it on. My assistant, Ivy (who indeed had all the talent and intellectual horsepower of a houseplant), moved away in a slow glide to get her drink. If that child pierced one more place she would look like a chain-link fence. I quietly thanked the Lord that my Emily wasn't into self-mutilation.

I had actually been thinking about Lucy's hair ever since I had met her. Other people's hair was a fixation of mine. Hers was particularly disturbing. I was about to launch a rescue mission on her fried fluff.

"Okay, Lucy, I'm gonna take ten years off your face."

"Be my guest," she said.

Hot oil treatment, clear glaze on top of highlights and lowlights, and three inches minimum of her downy ends all over the floor later, Lucy's head was looking remarkably promising. Her hair moved and was as shiny as though I had paste waxed and buffed every strand. She actually looked, if you can believe this, classy.

"Damn, Anna. You're good. I mean, damn." She grinned from ear to ear and was about to reapply that Whorehouse Red lip gloss when I stopped her.

"Thanks. Wait. I have something else besides that. It's newer." I went over to the makeup counter and selected a beige lip liner, pale pink lipstick, and a rosy sheer gloss. "Let me show you."

She was fidgeting but she humored me. After all, all she had to do was wipe it all off if she hated it. When she looked in the mirror, she was very surprised and apparently pleased.

"Light lips make my eyes look bigger," she said.

"Exactly," I said.

"I always thought my lips were my best feature."

"They're good, but always make up from the eyes out. Come on, I'll walk you to the door."

"Can you sell me the liner and the lipstick?"

"Absolutely!"

She picked up her things, checked herself again in the mirror, and we started toward the front counter.

Not that it was unusual, but Harriet had been milling around the salon all morning wearing a sour face. Now she was stalking us for some unfathomable reason. This woman needed hormone replacement therapy in the worst way.

At the same moment we all converged at the reception desk, a man came in the front door, not that that was odd, because we had lots of male clients. It was in his eyes, darting from the back of the salon to the front and all around the faces of our other clients, taking inventory of their jewelry, as though he was about to pull out a gun and rob the place. I told myself to get over it. Suddenly I could pick out a criminal walking in the door? The Miss Marple of the hair world?

Well, I should've listened to my instincts. I looked at him from the side and his forehead was covered with perspiration. He *was* going to rob the salon, *and* our clients, and I knew it as sure as I knew my name. I didn't want Lucy to open her purse. Carla was on the phone taking an appointment and didn't take notice of him. Frau Harriet stepped behind the counter and with great storm-trooping flourish, began to review the total charges for Lucy's visit.

"You had a glaze application too, didn't you? It's not on here. Why isn't . . ."

Her voice was an accusation more than a question. For once, I wasn't going to subject myself and my client to another of Harriet's episodes.

"Lucy?" I interrupted Harriet, the urgency of personal safety eclipsing normal protocol. "Why don't you pay this later? Come on, I'll just walk you to your car."

"But I didn't get my lipstick and—"

"Move it, Lucy!"

I had grabbed Lucy's arm and started moving around toward the door, past the strange man, trying to send a signal to Harriet that this fellow was risky and to watch out.

"What do you think you're *doing*? Your client *cannot* leave without paying," Harriet said, calling out and looking up into the man's face at the same time.

I saw him pull a pistol from his jacket.

"Open the cash register and then get on the floor," I heard him say. "Gimme your wallet, lady."

God in heaven! I pushed Lucy out the door and we started running. There was a patrol car on King Street about two blocks from us and we flagged him down, screaming and frantic.

"Our salon's being robbed! He's got a gun! Harriet's House of Hair!"

"Stay here!" one police officer said to us while the other one stomped on the gas. They raced down the street and double-parked in front. Both officers jumped out, pulled out their guns and hurried inside.

"Great God!" Lucy said. "You saved my life, Anna!"

"No, but maybe your watch. God, what's going on? Come on!"

I started moving back toward the salon just to see if I could see something, even from across the street. That was when I heard the gunshot. A single shot. Pop! Then another. My heart was in my throat and I was frozen to the glass windows of the Olde Colony Bakery. Lucy grabbed my arm.

"Damn it, Anna! Move!"

She yanked me from my stupor and pulled me inside the storefront. I felt like I was going to faint. A gun! Somebody put me in a chair and handed me a glass of water. Maybe ten minutes passed, each one dragging with anticipation. I heard the police cars, first a loud kind of horn blast and then a trail of sirens.

"I've got to go back," I said. "God, what if Harriet got shot?"

"Don't even think it! I've got to pay my bill," Lucy said.

Shaking, we ran back down the street. When we pushed the glass door open, the salon was in chaos. Clients were crowded around Harriet, who was lying on the reception couch wailing, holding ice on her jaw. Carla was fanning her with a magazine. Others were on their cell phones, calling their husbands to report the incident.

"She tried to take his gun," Carla said, "and he socked her one in the jaw."

"Jesus!" I said. It wasn't a curse and it wasn't exactly a prayer. It was more relief that she hadn't been killed.

I looked around. The mirror behind the reception counter was shattered from gunfire. Hair gel, mousse, sprays and brushes were all over the floor. There were huge holes in the plaster ceiling and dust was falling in a storm, covering every surface.

Harriet looked up at me.

"Hey, are you all right?" I said.

"No, I'm not, and you're fired," she said.

"What?" I was stunned.

"You heard me! *Get out!* You tried to help your friend here run out on her bill and then I was nearly killed because of you! Get out!"

The whole place fell silent to listen. I was so shocked I didn't know what to say, but I tried to explain anyway.

"Harriet! You couldn't be more *wrong!* I was the one who *spotted* the man! I *tried* to signal you! I was the one who got the *police!*"

"I've been *watching* you," she said with the nastiest guttural voice I had ever heard used by a real person. "Now get out before I have you *thrown* out!"

Carla looked at me and rolled her eyes in silent agreement that Harriet was a raving madwoman. The customers began to move away, embarrassed for me, mumbling to themselves. *I can't imagine . . . How could she say . . . I have known Anna since . . . It can't be . . . What's the matter with her? Harriet's gone off the deep end this time. . . . Do you remember when she . . .*

I didn't know what to do next. It was clearly a waste of time to try and explain anything to her in her state. She needed twenty milligrams of something I didn't have and wouldn't share with her if I did. I decided to just leave.

"Carla, if my clients want to know where I am, tell them I went home sick, okay?"

For the second time that day, Lucy yanked my arm, and said as loud as she could, "Don't you know a sign from God when you see one? Damn, girl! You're as thick as a brick! Go get your stuff and let's go get us a salon of our own." She looked at Harriet lying on the couch and said, "Not only are you dead wrong, you're lucky you ain't dead! And you're mean and stupid too!"

Carla giggled but I couldn't. I was still flabbergasted. I hurried back to my chair as fast as I could and took my tote bag from the small closet, threw in my scissors, straightening iron, brushes, and the all-important address book with clients' names and color references. I yanked Emily's pictures from the mirror and several books I had there for clients to browse. On the way out, passing everyone, they offered condolences. *Let us know where you go. . . . I don't blame you a bit, honey. . . . It's not your fault, Anna . . . not in a million years!*

Lucy and I walked out of the front door into the light of a perfect South Carolina afternoon. She followed me back to the beach in her car. I cried and cursed Harriet the whole way home. It was amazing that all those years of my life could fit into one tote bag. When I got out of my car, Lucy came walking across the yard toward me.

"What on earth is the matter with you?" she said.

"Are you serious?" I said. How could she be so insensitive?

"Listen, honey, that woman ain't worth the sweat offa hog's behind, much less your tears. And that job ain't shit compared to how much money you're gonna make on your own!"

"Lucy! Are you nuts? I can't think about anything like that now," I said.

"Who's your broker?"

I pushed my front door open and she followed me inside.

"Marilyn Davey. Her card's on the bulletin board in the kitchen closet on the door. But don't call her. Wait for me to think this through. I gotta wash my face."

I rinsed my face over and over with cold water. I was so depressed I wanted to go to bed and not get up for a week. I pulled my hair up in a rubber band and took two aspirins, thinking they couldn't hurt and they might help.

Lucy was on my phone making arrangements to push me into bankruptcy. I decided to change my clothes so I put on shorts and sneakers, thinking it would be therapeutic to walk the beach and wondering at the same time how I had lived without a beach for so long. I'd take Lucy with me and tell her to back off. I'd had enough shit for one day.

You didn't need a beach because you had your daddy to run to—maybe it's time you seriously grew the hell up for once and for all!

That little voice inside my head was becoming a major pain in the rear.

"Get in the car," Lucy said.

"What?"

She was writing something on the back of an envelope.

"I said, Get in the car. Marilyn Davey, who is a sweet pea if I ever talked to one, says she has a space to show us for a salon. So, move it! She's squeezing us in her day."

"I'm not ready to do this, Lucy. This is insanity. I can't afford it. I just bought this house."

"Yes, you can afford it. We're gonna figure it all out."

Where did Lucy get her nerve?

I went along with her because I was too numb to resist.

The place we saw was just raw space in a relatively new shopping center and, unfortunately for my nerves, it was full of possibilities. With any luck at all, it could be a great salon. Where would I find the money to do it?

Against my own better judgment, that night I talked to Daddy and Jim and Frannie. Everyone wanted to help. I couldn't think straight. Even though I hadn't deserved it, getting fired had blown me out of the water. Lucy and I drank two entire bottles of wine and I fell asleep on my couch.

I heard the phone ringing and realized it was morning. I should've taken more aspirin. It was Harriet, semiapologetic, testing the waters of forgiveness. I told her I was tinkering with opening a salon on the Isle of Palms. She went so crazy that her yelling probably shook the foundations of the Customs House in Charleston. *If you take one single customer away from me I will see you in court! I'll sue you from here to hell and back!*

So much for a going-away party.

"Come on, Harriet, why don't you just wish me well?"

She had slammed her phone down in my ear so hard that I jumped. Clearly, I wouldn't miss *her*. In a way, I felt sorry for her. For years I had apologized to the faithful for her temper and suspicions. No more. Who would protect her now?

Who cared?

Over many cups of coffee, I made a budget. Every time I thought about Harriet, I said, *Screw you, baby.* I figured out that I needed some-where around fifty thousand dollars for starters, to get the space fitted out and to stay alive for six months. Lucy wandered in with sausage biscuits from Burger King and announced she was writing the check. I broke out in a cold sweat.

"Here's the deal, Anna: I get a job. I'm gonna be the receptionist. I make ten dollars an hour, okay? I gotta get out of the chat rooms, you know what I mean?"

"Lucy!"

"And I wanna buy gifts and things to sell, like those things that go on ponytails and pretty little baby barrettes and . . ."

"Lucy!"

"What?"

"I can't take that kind of money from you!"

"And just why not? Shit, if I'd left my money in the stock market, I sure woulda lost that much in a week! I figure you're a better investment than a company I can't watch and don't know what the hell they do anyway. What the hell is Enron anyhow?"

"Beats me."

"Is that a yes?"

Do it! the little voice said.

I took the plunge from the top of Mount Everest.

"Yes. It is a yes. But only as a loan." *I'm gonna throw up, pass out, and die.*

"Deal!"

I was a trembling and shaking sack of anxiety as I signed the lease. Lucy was perfectly collected, walking through the new space like a foreman, chatting away with Marilyn about the layout.

"I should have brought a darn pad of paper," she said. "Next time."

"Take mine," Marilyn said.

All I could think was, What have I done? What the *hell* have I done? *Get a grip, Anna.*

Screw you, spook, I said silently to my inner compulsive gambler.

Getting a grip meant that I had to start whipping the new space into shape. How long would it take? To my complete amazement,

Lucy seemed to have that all under control. She might have looked like a cone of cotton candy, but let us not forget, O Danny Boy was a contractor. Still, it was surprising to listen to her spit out recommendations on amps and socket placement and on and on.

I was about to open a salon of my own? Was I completely off the wall? No. I wasn't. Only partially. And I'd like to know since when a tough little nut like me started getting so sentimental, but I couldn't help watching the movie in my head, the one from seventeen years ago. It could have been yesterday that I opened the door at the infamous House of Hair for the first time.

It was in the mid eighties. With my beauty school diploma in one hand and a want ad from the *Post & Courier* in the other, I pushed open the glass door to the House of Hair on King Street in Charleston. The blow dryers were deafening. "I Will Survive" was blaring full tilt through the stereo speakers. Another warning on my life unrecognized. I just wasn't that smart. I was so insecure I could hardly keep my shoes on my feet.

I looked around. In the salon area, there were about a dozen stylists in black pants and white shirts. Their arms and round brushes seemed to be everywhere at once. In the reception space there were two couches, some chairs, and a coffee table stacked with well-worn current magazines and women flipping their pages, not reading a word.

I tried to stand straight against the counter and appear poised. First impressions lasted forever and I wanted mine to be good. I waited for the harried receptionist to hang up the phone. She looked exactly like the front office person at a hip salon should. Great haircut, short and blunt, so gelled you could see your face in it. Well, almost. Dramatic makeup, tight clothes, great body. Too much jewelry. No gum. Very cool.

"Nope, sorry, nothing until next Thursday, Mrs. Akers. I know, I know. It's *terrible*. No, it's been *wild* here! Yes, I know! You're *right!*"

She looked at me and rolled her eyes. "How about Stacy? No, I promise, she's very gentle." *Just a minute,* she mouthed to me. "Okay, I have you booked for a manicure with Stacy at four o'clock this afternoon. Sure. I will. Bye-bye!" She hung up the telephone and took a deep breath.

"Jeesch! You'd think her cuticles were like the queen mother's or something! Okay! Sorry for the wait. Do you have an appointment?" she said, as though she asked that all night long in her sleep.

"No, I'm here for an interview?" I said.

"What are you—desperate?" She looked at me as though I was the one with the eighteen coats of blue mascara cemented to my lashes. "I'm *just* kidding!"

"With Harriet? For the assistant's position?"

"She's probably in the back sharpening her teeth."

While I wanted to giggle I thought it better to keep my place. I just nodded my head and started to go to the rear of the salon to look for Harriet.

"Hold on a second! Come back here."

I thought I had done something wrong, like maybe she had to announce me or something. I was instantly washed with embarrassment.

"What?" I said.

"What's your name?"

"Anna," I said.

"I'm Kelly. Listen to me, I'm gonna tell you something. Harriet's gonna hire you on the spot. Don't worry about that. I know her. She goes through assistants faster than I go through boyfriends. Know why?"

"Because she's demanding?"

"Because she's got a worse personality than anybody I ever met. Don't say I didn't warn you."

"Thanks," I said, and meant it.

That interview and career path came after Jim and I filed separation papers and I'd finally moved back to Daddy's house. Trixie had closed the wallet when Jim told her we were breaking up. I mean, if shortly after the death of your husband, your son announced he was gay and his marriage was over, would you pay all the bills for his wife?

But there weren't a million options for me. Bartender? Hostess? Waitress? Salesperson? When I found out that it only took six months to complete the required course of study in South Carolina, there wasn't another alternative that made sense to me. Cutting hair was something I actually liked. Daddy wasn't thrilled about me becoming a hair stylist. I think he thought I should go to a liberal arts college and maybe teach school or something. But I was stubborn about it, deciding that I was going to do something I enjoyed. Gardening had taught me that you shouldn't spend too many hours a day doing something that would make you miserable.

That's how and why I eventually found myself standing in Harriet's House of Hair looking for Harriet the Beast. Great. Have a nice life.

After asking two people who gave me sorrowful faces in sympathy, I remember I saw Harriet for the first time sorting permanent rods in a rolling cart. She was about forty, rail thin, dyed red hair, no fingernails to brag about. I remember thinking that her heels were too high for a woman her age. Frankly, she was slightly tacky.

"Harriet? I'm Anna Abbot and I was hoping I could talk to you about the assistant's job?"

She looked me up and down and without a trace of any sort of pleasantry she said, "The broom's over there. Sweep up this hair and we can talk while you work."

"Sure," I said.

"You ever been arrested?"

"Heavens, no!"

"You're hired. Minimum wage, don't hustle tips, hours are ten to six, Tuesday through Saturday. You gotta work late before all holidays, understood?"

I nodded my head.

"If I catch you stealing products, you go to jail. Got it?"

"Good grief! Do you have a problem with that sort of thing?"

"I got trouble you can't imagine, girl. What's your name again?"

That was the end of her personal interest in me and the beginning of my career as a stylist in Harriet's Kremlin. Tough interview.

I got trouble you can't imagine, girl. Seventeen years later, those words were still ringing in my ears. Everything had all happened so fast.

Freaking Lucy. There I was with this wild woman Lucy planning my new life. We stayed there until eight that night, drawing and redrawing the space until we were happy with it. She went home to call Daddy and I went home, unplugged my phone, and slept like the dead.

The next morning, I decided to call Emily, Jim, Frannie, and of course Daddy and tell them what I had done. First, I dialed Emily's dorm room. She was there and sound asleep. It was only six-thirty in the morning. I was so excited I had forgotten to check!

"*. . . Hello?*"

"Emily? Baby? It's Momma."

"Whaddayawant? Whatimeisit?"

My darling child didn't sleep, she went unconscious. Rousing her wouldn't be easy, but since I had her on the phone, I decided to go through with the conversation.

"I'm sorry, baby. I know it's early, but I'm so excited I had to call you!"

"'Kay. 'Sup?" (Translation: Okay, what's up?)

"I just signed a lease on my own salon! Can you believe it?"

"Ma! You're losing it! You can't!"

Ma? When did I become *Ma?*

"I certainly can and I did!"

"'Ja rob a bank or sumpin'?"

Something had undermined her ability to enunciate.

"Yeah, I won the lottery. I can't wait for you to see it! What's the date you're coming home?"

"Oh, fuck!" There was a moment's delay and then she said, "Okay, I'm back. I dropped the phone."

"What did you say?" I couldn't believe my ears. She had never used that sort of language.

"What? I said, *Okay, I'm back. I dropped the phone*, okay? No big deal, Mom. God!"

Well, at least she said *Mom.*

Over the last two weeks, when I couldn't sleep, I would roam Emily's tiny new room as though it were a wing of the Metropolitan Museum of Art, huge and endless, touching her new white wicker headboard, the tiny flowered pillowcases and quilt I had chosen for her, the mountain of choices I had made.

What if she didn't recognize it as a new beginning? What if she didn't care at all? And down deep inside I worried, in a dark place I kept behind a locked door, that it was too late. Not by much, but too late nonetheless. Too late for her and for me together.

Thirteen

Tangled Liberation

*J*IM and Frannie cheered when I told them the news about the salon and cracked jokes about the robbery.

"You are some big operator, Anna Abbot, I am so proud of you!" Jim said. "What can I do to help?"

"I'm good right now, thanks."

"Too bad the guy didn't shoot Harriet in the tongue," Frannie said.

"No kidding! Know what she did? Listen to this . . ."

I told them how she had called me back and how she went crazy when I told her what I was doing. I could see them shaking their heads.

"God bless the child that's got his own," Jim said.

"Sing it to me, Jimmy!" Frannie said and started singing in our ears.

"I'll call y'all later!" I said and we hung up.

Then I called Daddy and told him about everything. You would think that signing a lease on a salon would've been the main thrust of our conversation, but it was that I had done it without his consent that seriously irked him.

First, we talked about the robbery at Harriet's. As he listened to the details, he was blowing air like Old Man Winter. You see, Daddy didn't sigh. He blustered, puffed up his cheeks, and blew a northeast wind. As we talked, Channel 5 was probably issuing emergency small-craft warnings.

"Merciful God," he said, "you're lucky you didn't get killed! What's become of this world?"

"You're right," I said. "The guy was probably looking for money for drugs. I mean, it wasn't a very smartly planned robbery. Just a lone villain."

"I mean, what kind of a man wanders into a women's salon, pulls a gun, and scares the daylights out of everyone?"

"A creep who knows how much cash goes over the counter on any given day. Daddy, we had over a thousand dollars in the drawer. We always do. Harriet does business like crazy. Hell, a bottle of shampoo alone could cost twenty dollars."

"Gee-nimminy," he said and let out another gust. "I don't think I have spent twenty dollars on all my shampoo in five years! And, I expect you'll be selling this kind of thing as well?"

"Actually, what lines I can sell remains to be seen. There are all sorts of rules about how many salons a vendor can sell in the same area and I won't be the only salon on the Isle of Palms."

"So much the pity. Well, I'll see you around dinnertime—Lucy's invited me over."

"Okay, good, maybe y'all can help me figure some of this out."

"Sounds like you don't need my advice."

"Don't say that."

Great, I thought, here comes a mood.

"By the way, did you take the money Lucy offered?"

"Daddy, I'm not sure what to do about this. She wrote a check to the broker for two months' rent for the salon without me even realizing or thinking about what she was doing. Does this make her my partner or what?"

"If you really want my opinion . . ."

"I do!"

"Yes, but you had no problem signing a lease without even running it by me. . . ."

"Daddy? I'll admit it was unusual. . . ."

"Yes, and a terrible gamble that could backfire in your face. . . ."

"Look. I don't want to sound disrespectful to you, but since I've been in this business for my entire adult life, maybe I know something about it that you don't. I mean, I need support here, not criticism."

"You know it all, don't you? You don't need my advice. Go find yourself a lawyer."

"Come on, Daddy. Talk to me."

He was such a child.

Dead silence.

"Come on."

"All right, if it was me, I'd set up a separate account for your business. You know what I mean?"

"Yeah. I do."

"Then you should probably incorporate your business and use Lucy's money as a loan to the business, not a personal loan. Keep it simple, legal and clean."

"Right. Then if there's a problem the business is liable, not me personally."

"Well, any half-witted lawyer on Broad Street would sue the dickens out of you too, but it helps to keep your personal life and the business separate in case of an audit. The IRS loves to find stuff like that."

"Right."

We hung up and I thought about what he had said. My stomach had been very uneasy for the past forty-eight hours. Between the shock of the robbery, Harriet's fury, and most of all the lease, I didn't know what to do first or next. I had a terrible amount of work in front of me and it seemed I took one brave step forward and then one whimpering step backward.

Finding out what kind of merchandise I could manage to sell was

only one detail of a thousand. My immediate future would mean haul-
ing around a very irritating long list. And I did need a lawyer.

I scratched my head and looked around my living room. I still had
a few moving boxes to unpack, but most things had been put away in
a somewhat organized fashion, which is to say that at least I knew
where everything was. In a small house there were only so many
places to hide.

I decided to walk over to Lucy's house and see what she was doing.
Maybe she would invite me to dinner too and I could help her cook or
something. I wasn't interested in cooking alone and I was more than a
little overwhelmed.

I saw her working at her computer on the kitchen counter so I
rapped on her screen door.

"Stick 'em up, doll, and nobody gets hurt," I called out in a manly
voice.

"Lord! I didn't even hear you coming up the steps! Come on in!
Look at this!"

I imagine that what I expected to see was a website for used salon
fixtures but what she showed me was something quite different. She
was online at a site called Love@AOL.com. I had heard about these
places on the Internet where you could advertise for a boyfriend or a
long-lasting relationship, but I had never seen any of them. There it
was. A guy named Antonio, in his bathing suit, leaning on a Harley,
wearing sunglasses, smiling wide, trying to look casually irresistible.
He was so pumped up macho you could almost smell the coconut in
his suntan oil.

"Look at his bio!"

"Sorry," I said, "I was staring at his biceps."

" '*Likes dogs, opera, walking in the rain . . .* ' " she said, clutching her
bosom and letting loose a breath of carnal longing.

"If he doesn't have the sense to come in out of the rain, why would
you . . . ?" Suddenly I was a little annoyed with her. Wasn't she seeing
my father?

"He's just trying to show how sensitive he is! God, Anna! When's the last time you dated anybody?"

She had me there. "I had a date last year, I think." I knew my voice had a trace of defensiveness.

"Well, honey, this is how you meet people in this techno age. Nobody goes to singles bars anymore. That's so sleazy! This gives you a chance to email back and forth and see what you think about someone at a safe distance. Email tells you a lot about someone, you know."

There was a dish of celery sticks on the counter and I helped myself to one. I'd still take a singles bar any day of the week.

"I don't know," I said. "Seems like a good way to meet a whack with a chain saw."

"Oh, Anna," she said with another sigh, this one a sigh of despair for the state of my non-affairs. She brightened and said, "Here, I'll show you my ad!"

"You have an ad on this thing?" I hoped my eyes weren't bulging.

"Yeah," she said, "look!"

Click. Click. Exhibit A—there was Lucy, in a hat and sunglasses, leaning on a Porsche (she did not own a Porsche), wearing a tell-all tank top, grinning like a hyena, right there on the Internet, for all the world to see. The description below her picture read: *Everybody Loves Lucy! Single, tall, with curves in all the right places, loves to cook, slow dance, and laugh. Thirty-ish, M.S. in social work, never married. No more jerks, please. If you are a mature, professional, successful male, interested in a long-term relationship and maybe someday marriage, then I'd love to hear from you!*

I gaped at the monitor. "Lucy! Good Lord!" I said a silent prayer that my eyeballs wouldn't fall out of their sockets onto her granite counter.

"What?"

"You're *divorced* . . . "

"So what?" This remark was followed by a silent scream toward the ceiling.

"You have an M.S. *in social work?*"

"Hell no!" More eye-rolling and snicking sounds followed.

"Then why in the world . . . I mean, why do this in the first place, I mean, I don't know, it just seems so, I don't know . . ."

"Anna. Girlfriend. Calm down, okay? Sure, it ain't exactly accurate, but I guarantee you that all the others are filled with some bodacious bull too! This is mostly a place to flirt, you know, see what's out there. It's about fantasy." I was about to witness Lucy's version of self-righteous indignation. "I've met some very nice men in chat rooms, I'll have you know."

I didn't want to offend her social sensibilities but I thought the whole idea was a kind of gross exhibitionism. Let's face it: putting a suggestive picture of yourself on the Internet with a bunch of lies to describe yourself, with the end goal of finding a decent man who would respect you, was, to say the very least, problematic.

But in the spirit of nonjudgmentalism I said, "I'm sure you're right." To show how open-minded I could be, I threw out, "Hell, it's probably fun?"

"Yeah, that's all it is, really. I mean, most of the guys who email me are most likely old married coots. I don't usually follow up unless I'm pretty sure the guy's okay and, even then, I would only meet them in a public place. You should try it! Hell, honey, what are you saving it for? It could dry rot!"

This was a small indicator of the possible trouble I could have with Lucy as a partner. Relationships were not a joke. Lying was just not okay with me. I was glad I'd had even a brief but cranky discussion about the loan/partnership with Daddy. What would Daddy think if he knew Lucy was strutting her stuff on the Internet like a blooming mail-order playmate? Not good.

"I'm not saving anything. I guess I just don't think about it too much."

I opened her refrigerator door and looked inside like I was in my own house. I needed to change the topic. The whole business made me uncomfortable.

"You want something to drink? God! I should've bought champagne! We have some big time celebrating to do!"

Champagne? Celebrating was the furthest thing from my mind. But, once again, the screwball was right.

"I'll go get it," I said, "that is, whatever they have at the Red and White that looks drinkable. Should I get some munchy stuff?"

"Sure! Dougle Darlin' is coming for dinner and I defrosted some pork chops. Why don't you eat with us and we can decide what to do tomorrow?"

"Perfect," I said, and smiled, relaxing a little for the first time.

All the way to the store, I talked to myself. *Okay, she has a website. Maybe she advertises for sex. Who knows? But it doesn't seem like it. It seems more like a lonely woman trying to amuse herself. Still. It is weird. Maybe not. What the hell do I know? I'm not exactly the man-expert of the western world, am I? What kind of champagne will I find on this island? But! She wants to celebrate! See? Lucy's an optimist and maybe I'm just a pessimist. Could be. But, damn, if Daddy knew she was doing something so downright scuzzy, what would he say? Should I tell him? Hell, no! Stay out of it, Anna!*

I headed right for the wine aisle and found some Napa Valley Chandon already chilled. Well, technically it wasn't champagne unless it was from France, but so what? It had bubbles. Besides, I didn't have the time, wallet or inclination to go on a search. I picked up a box of water crackers and a piece of hermetically sealed Gruyère whose freshness label said it would expire in 2006. Then I took a low-fat container of Boursin. One soft cheese and one hard. That would be Lucy's brain and my disposition, I thought. I paid for everything and left.

Driving home I found myself looking back over the years. I was back where I had started but way ahead of when I had left. I had a fabulous daughter, who was coming home in just a few days, my own new home, and every reason in the world to be excited about the prospects of my future. I had weathered more complicated situations than those before me. I would weather these too. I thought for a moment about

Arthur—the Cheese Whiz. I wondered if he was interested. I had thought I felt a twinge of electricity from him. I was sure of it. Well, leave that one to fate, I told myself.

Daddy's car was parked in Lucy's driveway, I noticed as I pulled into mine. I decided to throw on a dress, so I ran into my house to quickly change. It didn't seem right to go to dinner in shorts. Coming back out into my yard, I spotted Miss Angel from next door.

"Hey!" I called out. "How are you, Miss Angel?"

She turned, recognized me, and smiled, happy to see me.

"Hey, girl! What's all the news?" she said. "Miss Anna! You look so nice and fresh! You must have a new man in your life! I had a dream you were in love!" She sounded so young when she said that.

"Humph! Not me! You got a new man in yours?" I shot right back.

We burst out in good-natured laughter. It felt good to be familiar with someone whose sanity I knew was bankable.

"I don't need no man at my stage in this life, girl. No, ma'am. Just leave me be."

"Somebody told me today that what I was saving was perishable!"

"That's true and it's a sin to waste too, 'eah? Now tell me how your new little house is."

"Oh, Miss Angel, you wouldn't believe what's been going on."

I told her about the robbery and she just shook her head, saying, *What kinda fool thing going on in this world. Thank God you didn't get hurt.* When I told her about my new salon she looked at me with a certain surprise on her face. Her eyes were intensely focused on me as I went on about some of the details.

"You gone make out just fine," she said, as though she knew something I didn't. "If you decide you want to sell baskets, you let me know."

"Okay, I'll do that! Tell Miss Mavis I said hello."

"I will! You going over to Lucy's?"

"Yeah. She's helping me with the salon plans. She used to be married to a builder, you know."

Realizing that the Misses Angel and Mavis held their regard for

Lucy's intellect somewhere in the area of amoebas, it came as no surprise that she said, "That's nice, but look out, she's stupid."

"Nah, she ain't stupid, exactly. She's just, well . . ."

"Stupid!" She laughed again. "Just remember what I told you and think about baskets. They bring good luck and big money."

"Aren't big money and good luck the same thing?"

"I believe so!"

She smiled again and I waved as she disappeared in between the oleanders that separated our properties.

Baskets? Well, maybe I would sell her baskets. Why not? Angel had been making sweetgrass baskets all her life. Lots of Lowcountry women had basket stands along Highway 17. Weaving had continued since slavery, taught mother to daughter. They were made of long strands of sweetgrass from the marsh, coiled and sewn with strips of palmetto—magnificent! Some of the more complicated ones were in the museum collections and worth a small fortune. It wasn't a bad idea, really. If we were going to sell hair care merchandise, why not mix the display with Angel's baskets? If the tourists we hoped to attract actually materialized, surely they'd love one to take back to Ohio or New York.

Then again, maybe it would be nice if I had shelves to put the baskets on first.

Fourteen

The Palms Salon and Spa

O VER the following week, rummaging the ads in the *Moultrie News*, I discovered salon fixture heaven was to be found in Monck's Corner. Betty Hudson, who owned and operated Betty's Beauty Box in an extension on the side of her house, was retiring and anxious to convert the space to a playroom and bedrooms for her three grandchildren. She had some glass-and-chrome shelving that looked usable and four chairs from the seventies—retro cool. It didn't pay to move sinks, her dryers were too ancient, and just about everything else had seen better days. For an additional twenty-five dollars, her son-in-law threw them in the back of his pickup and brought them to the doorstep of the Palms.

"God! These are great!" Lucy said, referring to the chairs. "All you need to do is clean up them up a little and reupholster them. I know this gal at Lowcountry Interiors. They pick up and deliver too. Want me to call her?"

"Perfect," I said and checked that off my list. "Thanks."

Lucy and I, the ad hoc architect and decorator, had consulted with no one and decided how to best divide twelve hundred square feet. We allotted for a small reception area and boutique and space for the four chairs and two manicurists. That left us enough for a waxing room, two sinks, a coffee area, a small powder room, and a storage closet.

"You know," I said, showing Lucy my calculations on a legal pad, "we can probably save more money by washing our own towels than using a towel service."

"Why not?" she said. "There's enough room for a washer and dryer, isn't there?"

"Yeah, and Lucy, we still have to discuss this loan."

We decided to go to the Long Island Café for lunch and ordered salads topped with fresh fried shrimp.

"Lucy, here's the deal. I mean, you were *so* great, and I mean that, such a great friend to jump in and get moving and to do everything you have done. If, God forbid, you decide tomorrow that you hate my guts and never want to speak to me again, I'm still gonna love *you*. It's just that, I don't really want a partner, you know?"

"Hell, Anna, I don't want to be a partner! Is that what you thought? I just, I mean, I don't have a lot going on in my life right now and I guess I just wanted to do something to help, you know?"

"Yeah. Well, you sure did that."

She smiled and examined the shrimp on her fork, turning it, then popped it in her mouth. "Delicious," she said. "Absolutely delicious. You know, one time I went to a party in Philadelphia and all these people were eating these big old rubber shrimp that they thought were so good and they didn't taste like nothing 'cept cocktail sauce. Musta been frozen."

"Yankees don't get shrimp. You gotta eat 'em here. And what in the world were you doing in Philadelphia?"

"Chasing a man," she said and giggled. "Why else would you go there?"

"That's for sure," I said, agreeing as quietly as possible, hoping there weren't any tourists from Pennsylvania sitting next to us.

I mean, people from Philadelphia were perfectly nice; I had met lots of them over the years. But I couldn't imagine going there and if

I ever did, I sure wouldn't eat their seafood. Even they don't know how long it's been out of the water. See, what happens is that the fishermen catch the fish and ice them down. They could be out fishing for a few days before they return to port. Then the fish is graded by category and size, put on more ice, and shipped to a purveyor, who then eventually sells it to a restaurant. By the time it sees your plate, it's been dead too long to taste like anything worth the calories.

One of the many blessings of Lowcountry life was not only the availability of fresh seafood but the haunting sweetness of shrimp or fish caught that day. From childhood it was understood that what was in our waters was as good as it gets. And, it was.

"But, I meant it when I said I wanted to be the receptionist," she said, "and I'm not kidding either."

"You'd be great," I said.

What I was thinking was another matter. I only hoped we had enough clients call us to make having a receptionist necessary. I was wishing Carla would show up, offering her talent and experience to us, but she had not. She was so busy from morning to night that she probably never had a chance to think about leaving Harriet. I just hoped I could make Lucy see how important it was to book appointments correctly, because her job would be a little like being an air traffic controller. There was nothing worse than the wrath of an irate woman on a tight schedule made to wait because of a foul-up in booking at the front desk.

When the island drums carried the message that a new salon was on the horizon, disgruntled employees from other establishments and salesmen began to appear at our door. We hired Brigitte, a gal from Mount Pleasant who had a long list of clients she was positive would follow her, and Bettina, a high energy manicurist from Brooklyn who was married to a fellow in the Coast Guard stationed in Charleston. Bettina had a bag of skills—she could also wax anything, give pedicures, facials, and swore she did Reiki, reflexology massage, and aromatherapy.

"Lemme tell youse girls something, I can sell services like crazy," she said. "I tell 'em I used to work at Elizabeth Arden in New York and the next thing you know, their mustache is mine."

Lucy and I fell in love with her immediately and I said, "We believe you. Can you start when we open?"

My lawyer drew up a loan agreement for Lucy and me, and also the papers to incorporate the salon. That done, Lucy and I signed our agreement. Within days, the marble tile flooring went in, the Sheetrock was papered, the new sinks and reupholstered chairs installed, and finally, the mirrors and lighting went up. Lucy had called in every man she ever knew to help us and, sure enough, she delivered the legions of male muscle required to do the job in record time.

I was bringing in boxes and I could hear Lucy in the back area talking to the plumber, John. It seemed funny to me that the guy installing our toilet was named John, but then the whole world seemed to be spinning in a lighthearted orbit.

"John, darlin'," Lucy said, "you are so sweet to come and help us like this. I swear, you are. What can I ever do to repay you?"

"Don't worry," he said, "my wife does the billing. Just pay it."

Was it possible that there was a man impervious to her wiles? No.

"Lawsamercy, John! Of course we expected you to bill us! I just thought that maybe we could do y'all's hair on the house or something. Why don't I give you a gift certificate for your wife. What's her name now? Wasn't it Ruthie? Golly, I haven't seen y'all in so long, ever since Danny . . ."

I could hear her voice cracking, reliving the legend of how her husband, Danny, had unceremoniously thrown her out of his life like a beer can. It must have made John nervous.

"There, there," John said, "that would be awful nice and I'm sure she would be happy to give you some consideration on the bill, new business and all that."

Lucy's heels clicked along the new marble tile floor coming toward me. She stopped and whispered, "That should be good for at least ten percent."

"You're brutal," I said. "Throw in a pedicure."

That was how it went. Lucy flirted, cajoled, flattered, and squeezed every last one of her ex-husband's friends for a discount. It wasn't my style of doing business but I learned something. Every one of those gift certificates would bring a possible new client. The networking component of Lucy's campaign could prove to be very valuable.

"I put the salon on my website," she said later.

This was too much.

"You did *what?*" I thought I was going to have a heart attack.

"I mean, I linked it. Come on. I have a little bitty surprise for you."

She booted up her laptop at the front counter, went online, and in a few clicks we were at a website for The Palms Salon and Spa. I watched in amazement. The opening screen was a swirl of moss and blue-greens with our logo, which then faded out and back in with a list of our services and some head shots of models. That disappeared and the salon's address and phone number came up. All the while, the ocean and rustle of trees played in the background.

"Um, I know this was a crazy thing to do without asking you, but I was positive it would be a good idea so I just sorta did it. Anyway, I got reciprocal links from the Chamber of Commerce, Wild Dunes Resort, Caldwell Brokers, O'Shaunessy Rentals, Carroll Real Estate, and all the other real estate brokers on the island. I mean, it's just Power-Point. We can change anything you want."

"PowerPoint? Reciprocal links?"

Lucy was speaking Norwegian as far as I could tell. I could play solitaire and do a little Word, but that was just about the sum of my computer skills.

"Yeah, the software that made the slide show. It's not the most sophisticated thing in the world, but it's better than nothing. One night last week I was up all night worrying about how in the world we were going to let the world know the salon was opening."

"You're right. I mean, I haven't even called half my clients yet."

"And, plus, it's not like we have an advertising budget, right? But I owned the PowerPoint software so I started fooling around with it and did this. It's free and now we're linked all over the Lowcountry! I mean, I know it ain't great art, but hell, Anna Banana, you gotta start somewhere."

This woman was one unending stream of surprises. "Lucy? If you were a man, I'd kiss your face! What else can we do with your computer?"

"Email the world! I must have two hundred people on my buddy lists!"

"Go for it, sister. I wonder if we could get the summer rental brokers to include a discount coupon with their welcome package."

"I'll find out! What do you think? Twenty percent?"

"How about ten percent on products and fifteen on services?" Lucy would give away the ranch if I didn't keep an eye on her.

"We could get The Pig to stuff flyers in grocery bags . . ."

"The Piggly Wiggly grocery store? Isn't that a bit, I don't know, gauche?"

"Right! Too gauche! Harris Teeter?"

"I have to think about that. When Emily gets home Saturday, she can help."

"Oh, Emily! Yes! Oh! I forgot to tell you! My nephew is going to be spending the summer with me! David, my sister's boy from Greenville. He's adorable! Just twenty, and going to be a junior at Carolina in the fall."

"That's great." Very nice, I thought; she had a nephew to corrupt. "And Lucy?"

"Yeah?"

"You call me Anna Banana one more time, I'll give you a black eye."

"Got it, boss!"

That was how we made the telephones ring. And ring they did, right off the hook. Lucy made postcards on her computer announcing the new opening and sent them out to all my clients. Nearly everyone I spoke to seemed delighted to know I was going to be available for them.

Opening day was the following Monday. This was a calculated decision as most salons were closed on Mondays to give their employees two days' rest. We decided for the summer that we would be open every day except Sunday. After all, we had to maximize the tourist business.

By Friday afternoon, I was exhilarated. I made one last trip to Abide-A-While, the same nursery I had been using since Jim and I were married. Emily was arriving the next day at noon and I planned to pick her up at the airport and bring her home. I was thinking about everything and wound up buying five flats of pink and white geraniums and two flats of variegated hosta, thinking they would add something comforting to the look of our front yard. They weren't my first choice of planting materials, but they were the healthiest specimens available. At the last moment, I grabbed two pink mandevillas and two star jasmine vines. Anna the Tightwad had left the building.

Naturally, I had overlooked the fact that the beds on either side of our front door hadn't been worked in decades. From the first spade of dirt I knew I had to go back to Mount Pleasant to buy topsoil, vermiculite, manure, and mulch. On my *third* trip to Mount Pleasant, I bought drip hoses, a regular hose, and, in a moment of abandon, a new outdoor, double faucet with a pelican on top of it. On any other day I would probably have been feeling harassed by my short memory and the long list of chores ahead of me, but on that afternoon the world was my own perfect oyster.

I decided five or six inches was deep enough to dig and sift. After all, I didn't want the dastardly Atlantic Ocean flooding my yard and murdering my new beds with salt. My yard looked like a hurricane had hit it with all the equipment I had spread around. The small shed in the backyard had an old wheelbarrow, a shovel, a rake, and some spare screens. I took one screen and the other tools, threw them in the wheelbarrow, and rolled them around to the front of the house. I laid the flats in the shade, pulled out a big garbage can for all the weeds and trimmings I would produce, put on old clothes, and got to work.

Every shovel of dirt was thrown on the screen laid over the wheelbarrow to sift out rocks, old roots, and debris. I could hear my phone ringing and ringing inside the house but I just let voice mail pick it up, thinking that I would return the calls later. It was probably someone trying to sell me something. After all, it was suppertime for most people and that was when the invasion of telemarketers usually began.

"Leave a number and I'll call you back when *you're* eating!" I said this out loud to no one and continued to dig and sift.

Stage two was to dump the trash in a bag and use the same wheelbarrow to mix the old dirt with some good stuff to enrich it and then pile it all back in the beds. Next, I laid the drip hoses down the center and connected them to the faucet by way of a short hose tucked behind the foundation shrubs around the side of the house.

Inside my house, the telephone was still ringing so many times that I could imagine it flying off the wall and bouncing across the floor. I looked up and could see Lucy on her porch, so I knew it wasn't her calling me. I was covered in mud at this point and had no intention of tracking it all over my house, making something else for me to clean.

Ring! Ring!

"For the love of God! Give me peace!"

I was still talking out loud, probably not the most mentally healthy activity. I didn't care. I was almost done and amazed again at the amount of effort that went into accomplishing a task as small as this one was. I laid each of the plants in a small hole, staggering pink with white, pouring water in first, and gently covering them up. Then I put in the hostas on the edges, spacing them six inches apart. When the last one was planted, I spread the mulch over everything and then turned on the water.

"Now, when Emily gets here, be sure to tell her welcome home, okay? She's been gone too long, don't you think?"

"Who on God's green earth are you talking to?"

I looked up to see Lucy standing there with two goblets and a bottle of white wine under her arm.

"I *happen* to be talking to my new damn flowers. Got a problem with that?"

Then we burst out laughing.

"Honey, you need a glass of wine! You should see yourself!"

I stood up and brushed myself off a little, removing my gloves and taking a glass from her. My arms and legs were streaked with dirt. We raised a small toast to ourselves.

"Thanks," I said, "the sun's well over the yardarm!"

"Okay, you sly dog, who's Jim?"

"Jim?"

"Your daddy's been calling you and so has this guy, Jim. Jim is looking for you, girl! Apparently, he's in town and on his way over here to see you!"

"Holy shit! I gotta change!" I pushed the glass back to her and ran inside my house, slamming the door behind me. "If you'll put all this junk in the shed, I'll be your slave!"

"Anna? Who is *Jim?*"

I ran back outside, saw she hadn't moved an inch, and grabbed the glass back. "My ex-husband! You'll love him to death!" I took a gulp, slammed the door behind me, and headed for the shower.

Jim's rented convertible, a white Chrysler Sebring, pulled into my yard before I had a chance to finish dressing or to calm myself. All I could think was, *Oh, my God, how long has it been?* My hair was still wet, my face scrubbed to a clean shine, and, fast and furious, I threw on the only clean clothes I could manage to rustle up—black ankle-length pants and a black cotton V-neck sweater. I was sliding into my red open-toed mules when Jim walked right in the door. Jim with his short, gelled hair, sunglasses spinning in his right hand, perfect biceps, baggy khakis, woven leather tasseled loafers. No socks. His navy blazer hung from his index finger over the back of his shoulder.

"Anybody home?"

"You bad, bad boy! I can't believe you're here! Let me just look at you!"

We hugged and laughed and hugged again.

"God! You smell good enough to eat!" he said and delivered a gooey lick to the side of my neck. "But, about that hair . . . girlie!"

It was undeniable that the old familiar and very definite chemistry between us was still there.

192 DOROTHEA BENTON FRANK

"Take a bite, big mouth," I said, laughing. "I dare you!"

"Anna, Anna," he said, shaking his head and wagging his finger at me, "you know I gave up girls for Lent."

There had never been sufficient coal in his furnace to ignite the fire. Nonetheless, I loved Jim and he loved me. Always had, always would. Man, was he adorable, or what?

But when he didn't bite, or even nibble, I said, feigning a theatrical pout, "I'm crushed, what can I say? Come on! Let me show you my new house!"

"Great! Got any beer?" he said, looking around at the living room. "Got a guest room?"

"You're in it! Stand in front of the couch and visualize it with sheets and a blanket!"

"I thought this place looked small; but small is *good*. Small *works!*"

I said, "Listen, this palace is on the Isle of Palms, remember? Everything here costs twice what it's worth. *Besides, I just opened my own business!*"

"Yes! That's right! Ow! Ow! I can't *believe* it! You finally did it! Old Harriet must be *scratching* her mad place!"

"Scratching like a *dawg* fulla ticks!"

He threw his arms around me again and we spun around and around the room.

Woo-hoo! She's got a house on the island!

Woo-hoo! And her own salon!

She's rich! he said.

She's broke! I said.

He's dizzy!

So is she! Let me go!

I landed on the side chair and Jim collapsed on the sofa, after nearly toppling the coffee table and a fake (but very nice quality) palm tree. We were out of breath, laughing. He was the same old Jim. Thank God for small favors.

"Beer," he said in a mutter.

"You know what? I'm thinking . . ."

"You're always thinking, Anna doll."

"Yeah, but why is it people always ask me for beer and not wine or a cocktail?"

"Wet hair and no makeup?"

My wheels started turning like an express freight train headed from Topeka bound straight to Santa Fe. I could all but smell the smoke. No more Got-a-Beer-Anna. She had to die.

"Jim?"

"Yeah, baby?"

"You taking me out for dinner?"

Over the next hour and after the two-minute tour, I told him about Daddy and Lucy, the salon, and my terrifying debt. He was horrified when we rehashed the robbery. When I got to the part about getting fired, his blood pressure went up.

"You know what? Harriet must truly be insane! That's a lawsuit!"

"Oh, forget Harriet! Who cares now? It just made me crazy that she fired me, that's all."

"I'll thrash the woman if you want me to."

"God, I love you!"

He stood in the bathroom doorway while I blew out my hair and made up my face. We talked about Trixie—*She drives me crazy*—*She drives me crazy too*—*She doesn't know I'm here*—*She ain't gonna hear it from me!*—*Yeah, but I gotta tell her*—*Call her tomorrow.* I brought him up to date on Emily and her life. He offered to pick her up from the airport the next day, wanting to surprise her.

"She'll faint," I said.

"I can't wait to see her," he said. "Can you believe I haven't seen her in two years?"

"She's not a little girl anymore. Scary. But she's good, you know? No drugs or any of that weird shit they do in California . . ." I caught his eye from my bathroom mirror, turned off the dryer, and started laughing again.

"Hey! Watch it now!" he said and gave me a slap on the backside. "You're talking about the land of my people, you know."

"Oh, right! Gosh! Sorry! City of Saints, indeed. Help me pick out something to wear."

I went in my bedroom and opened the closet.

"I live in the aura of Saint Francisco, like you don't know that. Who are we hunting down? You ain't catching nothing but a sailor in that outfit, that's for sure!"

"The Cheese Whiz. His name is Arthur. Quit rolling your eyes. I'll explain in the car."

Fifteen

Really Cheesy

⁓

MAYBE it was that I was on the other side of thirty-five, but the hostess at High Cotton that night didn't appear to be old enough to work in a place that served alcohol. To her credit, she spun around on her ice-pick heels, led us to a great table by the windows, and seated us with the subtle flourish of a trained professional. I took a deep breath and scanned the room for Arthur. No sign.

Jim looked flawless. In his thirties, he had become a striking man with a movie star kind of élan. He told me I looked pretty divine too, for a girl, that is. He had dug all through my closet and come up with a black blazer, short black skirt and a lecture.

"What the hell has happened to you? You used to have this, like, whole costume department from MGM in your closet! This stuff looks like an undertaker's leftovers from a ragpicker's fire sale! Dreadful!"

I narrowed my eyebrows and thought about the truth of what he said. "Yeah, well, I haven't shopped in a while, I guess."

"Apparently." He shook his head. "Anna, Anna. I can see I have work to do on you, dearie. Next week, we shop."

"Next week, I'm opening my salon."

"Right. I'll shop. You work and I'll shop."

"We'll see," I said and thought to myself that a ragpicker's fire sale would be all my emaciated wallet could bear.

But my simple black skirt and single-breasted blazer saved the night. I usually wore it with a tank top but Jim said no.

"Use your pretty head, honey. This Arthur fellow is *standing* by his odiferous cart of decomposing dairy. You're *sitting* at the table, legs crossed, one extended for his viewing pleasure. If you lean ever so slightly, in a certain way, you *could* create a stir in the old codger's jewels. With a little luck."

"He's not old but your point's well taken." I reminded myself to cream the daylights out of my legs.

The fact was that I couldn't remember whether or not Arthur actually had said that this was where he worked but I did recall that he had made some reference to High Cotton. I told myself that even if this was the wrong restaurant, at least Jim and I could have a great meal. There were so many things to talk about and ever since Arthur had mentioned the place I had wanted to have dinner there. Just to see what it was like, you know? And I could immediately see why people lined up to get in—the restaurant was gorgeous, spacious, elegant, and, if what was on the plates of our neighbors was an indication of what our dinner would be, it was a safe guess that the food was fabulous.

Despite the fact that I had yet to lay an eye on Arthur, I sat to the side a little so that my crossed leg was discreetly positioned against the white tablecloth. The one advantage of being born with a body like an asparagus was that I had reasonably decent, long legs. I was getting crow's feet and I wasn't too happy about the recently arrived creases on either side of my mouth, but I still had a few guns in my arsenal.

Our captain arrived, all starch and protocol, handed Jim the twenty-two-pound leather bound wine list, and said, "May I offer you a cocktail before dinner?"

"Yes! Why not? I'll have a Gibson," Jim said. "How about you, Anna?"

Okay, I'm not a cocktail person. I start to giggle thinking of cocktails with naughty names—Fuzzy Navel, Sex on the Beach, Screw Driver—realizing I had to say something, anything, except to ask for a beer. The captain was waiting with limited patience and Jim's face was curious, wondering what was so funny to me.

"A Martini," I said, just like I had them all the time, looking at Jim evenly.

"Why not have a Cosmopolitan?" Jim said.

"A Cosmopolitan," I said, like a good parrot, wondering what a Cosmopolitan was.

"Very good," the captain said, nodding his approval, and walked away, clearly thinking we were a couple of jerks.

We opened the menus and scanned them. Sure enough, there was a cheese course among the desserts. Maybe this was the right place after all. If not, I was wasting enough nervous energy to light a small city.

"Did you even *hear* what I said?" Jim said.

"Oh, God, I'm sorry, Jim. My mind was wandering. Tell me again."

"If you're not going to pay attention to me, I'm going to make you pay half of the bill!"

I closed my menu and smiled across the table. "Oh, please don't be an old woman with me, just repeat it, for heaven's sake."

"I said, Gary left me."

Gary and Jim had been living together since Jim and I broke up.

"Good Lord! Why in the *world*? When were you going to tell me?"

"He's sick."

"Oh, God. Jim. I'm so, so sorry." I knew what that meant, at least I *assumed* it meant Gary was HIV positive. If Gary had it, there was every possibility that Jim did too. Before I could think another horrible thought, Jim spoke again.

"I'm not sick. I had blood work done and I'm fine. But, I can't *stand"*—his eyes filled up with tears and his bottom lip quivered—"the *thought* of . . ."

I reached across the table and grabbed his hand, squeezing it.

The captain reappeared, sighed deeply in ennui at the sight of our joined hands, and placed our drinks in front of us. Jim stood.

"Excuse me," he said, leaving the table to go to the men's room and compose himself.

Poor Jim! Poor Gary! He hadn't said much but what was there to say? His tears said it all. Over the years, just like the rest of the world, we had lost too many friends, men and women, all of whom contracted AIDS in different ways. In fact, I had arrived at the age where I had lost friends from all kinds of diseases. Breast cancer. Colon cancer. Early heart attacks. I knew that an insurance company's actuarial table would show that the odds were that x amount of people died in their twenties and more in their thirties and so forth. It didn't matter what statistics said, I had a terrible time getting my brain wrapped around the fact that young adults were dying left and right. And worse, who would raise their children and live their dreams? Never mind car accidents or suicides. Car accidents were arbitrary and suicides were another subject entirely. Anyway, true to form, I never went to the funerals but I always sent flowers and a card. Would I let Jim go to this funeral without me at his side? Would I always be a coward about seeing dead bodies? Probably.

I sat there staring at my glass, thinking that if I had my life to start over there was no doubt that my career would've been in medical research. How much longer would it be before we could stop these horrible diseases? The newspapers continued to report huge advances, but all around people still died way too young.

I wondered if Gary was taking the "cocktail," that now infamous jeroboam of chemicals designed to sustain the lives of HIV patients. But the way Jim had revealed the news implied he was too far along. God, I was filled with such sadness, not only for Jim and for Gary but for all of us. I just hated death. I hated it.

I needed to cheer myself before I slid into a maudlin pit, knowing I had to give Jim the compassion he deserved. I took a sip of the pale cranberry-colored drink that I decided was wrongly named a Cosmopolitan. It was delicious, but it should've been named something like Pink Quicksilver because it was going to slip down my throat with alarming speed. Jim had been right to think I would like this and that's how Jim had always been—the kind of man who thought about what you might like and then saw to it that you got it. I took a few more sips, thinking it didn't appear to have any alcohol in it.

I couldn't stop thinking about Gary. I wasn't overly fond of him, because he was the one who I blamed for jet propelling my life back to Daddy's house, but I most surely did not want to know the man was going to die a terrible death. It wasn't right.

Anyhow, I knew that if it hadn't been Jim and Gary it would have been Jim and someone else. Sometime after Jim and I broke up I had admitted that during the time we were together, my feelings for Jim had gone beyond friendship. I'd guess my heart began to change around the time Emily was born and we were playing house. Like pieces of a complicated jigsaw puzzle coming together over that first year, I fell deeply in love with Jim. I couldn't help it. We lived together in such an easy and natural way, sharing everything except a bed. It may have been a celibate marriage but it was not a loveless one.

It wasn't hard to make Jim happy. I kept things quiet so he could study, kept the house as neat as a pin, and I never nagged. The nagging part was something I had learned from my mother, who was the quintessential whiner, only to be outdone by Old Violet. Our domestic routine became more broken in and comfortable, much like a pair of shoes you never wanted to give up. On several different occasions after mucho beeros, I made attempts to show my affection and he gently declined all advances, peeling my arms from around his neck and directing me to my bed, tucking me in. When that happened, the next morning I would feel completely terrible inside. I knew he loved me. He knew I loved him. We were married. Why not give it a chance? No one would have blamed me for trying.

It just wasn't in the cards. Between his declining comfort level with my romantic overtures and my mushrooming frustration, he eventually zigzagged his way to Gary. After a while, all I had to do was light a scented candle and he would announce that he was going out for the evening. Those increasing late nights proved that the original terms of our agreement were how things were and always would be. Something in me defied his sexual orientation. The same kernel of stubborn will bamboozled me into believing that Jim might come around someday. But Jim had never deceived me; I had deceived myself.

"Would Madam care for another?"

The captain's eyebrows were somewhere in between the ceiling and the moon.

"Yes, Madam would, thank you." I wanted to say, Bug off, bubba. Madam is having some dark thoughts here and this is no time to piss her off. Who was this idiot?

By the time Jim returned I had drained the first glass, the captain had brought me a fresh drink, and I was well on the way to finishing it too. They were so good and my morbid veil was lifting, giving way to mild inebriation. I was calm.

"Okay, we have to talk about this," I said when Jim sat down.

"There isn't much to say." He took two sips of his Gibson and fished out the onions. "Thank God for vodka."

"Amen. At least I think it's got vodka in it. This is my second one of these babies. We had better eat something or else you're going to have to carry me out of here over your shoulder." I remembered that I hadn't eaten a single thing since breakfast. I broke my roll and ate a small piece. "So, talk to me. Did he move out or did you?"

"He did. I still have the apartment on Union Street. He's moved back to Ohio to be with his mother and his family. Funny thing is, I thought I was his family. Actually, not funny. I mean, we lived together for all our adult lives."

"Look, Jim, I'm no doctor or shrink but I think that when some-body is afraid and terribly ill, they want to be with their parents, if they're still around. And, not that it matters, but how did he get sick in the first place?"

"In the usual way. We had been fighting and sort of sulking around for a long time. Years, in fact. We probably should've gone our separate ways but for a million reasons, we just continued to live together as friends. But he was sort of shopping the market, you know? Anyway, he must have picked up someone and been careless. It's unbelievable to me that this could even happen to Gary. But you know how he is. The bars were his thing, not mine. For once in my life my laziness paid off."

"You mean, you weren't into going out anymore."

"Lord, Anna, the bars are stuffed with fierce young talent and tired old queens. What's more pathetic than an old queen cruising young boys with fake IDs who are looking for free drinks and a sugar daddy?"

"You're not even forty."

"I know that, but in my mind nearly forty-year-old men are supposed to be settled down or something. Hell, I've been in my own business for twelve years! And Gary's been in my life for so long, I wouldn't even know where to begin anyway."

This meant that Jim was coming back to me the same way Gary had gone to Indiana. He was here to fortify himself and my mission was to be his good friend. He would have to go back to San Francisco at some point to see about work. Jim, as you would imagine, had a very cool job. Maximizing his business degree and his love of all good things, Jim had become an expert on wine and ran a consulting business, buying domestic wine and importing wine for restaurants and hotel chains all over the country.

"Well, for the moment you don't have to do anything except relax and bask in Emily's youth, starting tomorrow. Have you called Gary?"

"Yeah, I called him. His mother thinks I'm evil incarnate and tries to monitor our phone calls."

"Like that will change anything."

The captain was returning to record and pass judgment on our culinary choices.

"Exactly. We'd better order."

I decided on the salmon carpaccio with a citron wasabi drizzle to begin. Jim ordered She Crab soup, a Lowcountry specialty and a second appetizer of quail stuffed with foie gras.

"Hungry?" I said.

"Famished," he said.

I didn't have a freaking clue what carpaccio was or in what direction wasabi drizzled. To me, wasabi sounded like a performance of African folk dance. Remember, I was the girl who preferred her food fried, served in a basket. Not the one who regularly ordered food speaking in tongues.

Jim couldn't decide between rack of lamb and the Chateaubriand so the captain stepped in.

"The seafood stew is very nice," he said.

"Let's have it, Anna, what do you say?"

I nodded my head and closed the menu, handing it to the captain. "Another executive decision made," I said. I picked up my glass and finished off my drink.

Jim was reading the wine list with the glacier speed of someone savoring a good book.

"May I suggest a Cakebread Sauvignon Blanc? The 1999 is very popular and reasonably priced," said the captain, with a repeat performance of high arch eyebrows, convinced that Jim didn't know anything about wine.

He didn't know Jim.

"No, I think not," Jim said, scanning the list with a little frown. "Oh! I can't believe you have this! Or do you?"

"Which one is that?"

"The '97 Clos St-Théobold."

"Would you kindly point out your selection?"

Warning! Eyebrows losing altitude and gaining speed. I suppressed major grinning by chewing my bottom lip. This was karma in action.

"It's right here. The Domaine Schoffit, '97, Rangen de Thann Vineyard, Grande Cru, Lot Number Ten. It has this residual sugar that's perfect for the heat of wasabi or for foie gras. Perfect. Anna, you're going to adore this wine."

"I adore *you!*" Jim had taken the prissy waiter's limbs apart by just being himself.

"I'll be right back with your wine, sir."

"Great! Bring a glass for yourself too!" he said and turned to me, flushed in excitement. "God, I was in Alsace last summer and found the Rangen de Thann Vineyard. It's this speck of a town in Colmat-haut Rhin—oh, fine! Here I go rambling on! Sorry, Anna."

"Please! I love it! I mean, it's so great that you can work in something you enjoy and make money doing it! I can't decide if I love you more for you or for squashing his grapes but good."

"Doesn't matter, as long as you love me."

And there it was—the admission from the guy who could give but not take, that he needed me. No problem, I thought.

The attitude of our captain had been replaced by a sudden solici-tousness. He uncorked the bottle with a sure hand and poured out a measure for Jim to taste, doing everything but presenting the cork on bended knee.

Jim drank, nodded his head, and said to him, "Pour yourself a glass. I think you'll find this to be slightly better than the Cakebread."

"I'm sure," he said and smiled, revealing a mouthful of birdlike teeth.

The wine was delicious. I assumed it would be sickeningly sweet when Jim said it had a sugar residual but it wasn't. We ate our first courses, neatly finished the bottle with the help of old Maurice the captain, who, practically salivating, had sidled up to Jim for another sample. Jim, generous soul, wound up pouring him two glasses and ordering another bottle for our entrées. This time it was another but very different Riesling, Domaine Trimbach, '83, a Clos St. Hune. Yeah, boy, it wasn't long before I was wondering how my fork was going to find my mouth. Must have been the Cosmos.

Jim talked nonstop and I listened, eating and trying to remain sober enough to give comments and consolation worthy of his troubles. When it seemed that Jim had talked himself out about Gary, I thought I could use a bit of fresh air. I was getting very sleepy. Must have been the Cosmos *and* the wine combined. I was doing heavy listening, most of the drinking, and not much talking. In my mind, I seemed fine, but I knew it would probably be a good idea to go to the ladies' room and pinch my cheeks to wake up.

"Jim? I'll be *rat* back. *Don'ge'up.*"

Jim stood anyway, the consummate southern gentleman, and as I stood I realized I was unfortunately as drunk as a coot.

"Are you all right?"

"Fine," I said and pointed my finger toward him for assurance.

By the grace of heaven, I wobbled to the powder room and sat on the toilet, intending to use it. The last thing I remember thinking was that a short power nap of five minutes would clear my head.

"Miss Abbot? Miss Abbot? Are you in there?"

I woke up midsnore and nearly fell on the floor. I could even hear the noise from myself and was mortified that I was snoring like a three-hundred-pound hog.

It was the officious but concerned voice of the hostess who had been sent by Jim to rescue me. Apparently, I had indulged in a forty-five-minute session with the netherworld and Jim had been a little worried.

"Okay! Yeah, I'm good!" I called out to her. "I'm fine!" I added. "Fine!"

I could see her spike heels under the stall door. She wasn't moving.

"Are you sure? Do you need anything?"

I sat up straight and pinched my face to get the blood moving to my cheeks. I needed an excuse quick.

"Um . . . you wouldn't, um, havatampon, wouldja?" Good one!

"Sure. You poor thing! I get horrible cramps too! I know just how you feel." I heard her rustling around, opening and closing a cabinet or something.

Her hand appeared under the door and I took it from her. "Thanks," I said, "I'll be *rat* out. Wouldja please tell ma husband I'm 'live?"

"Sure! Take your time," she said. "Glad you're okay."

I heard the door open and close. She was gone. I left the stall and looked at my face in the mirror over the sink. Cosmetic salvage was desperately needed. I brushed my hair, wiped the mascara from under my eyes, reapplied lipstick, then stared myself down in the mirror to measure my sobriety and knew I was in big trouble. I washed my hands, cursed myself to hell and back for being so stupid, and began my return through the bar and back to the table. I thought I felt much better. Stupid, but better.

From ten feet away, I saw Arthur. He and Jim were chatting away like old friends.

Try to be alluring. Walk carefully. Try to slink a little. Think cat. Big cat. Think stealth. Throw back shoulders. Appear casually interested. Don't trip over anything. For the love of God, don't drink anything else. Okay. Here we are. Go for it.

"Don' Ah know ya fra, fra somewhere'?" That was a pretty funny opener, I hoped. I thought I had got that out of my mouth without slurring too much. Very good so far. I took my seat and the now charming and attentive Maurice snapped my refolded napkin, handing it to me to drape over my lap, pushing in my chair a little. I smiled serenely and tossed my hair. Why did I do that? I hate hair tossers!

"Thought we lost you there, Anna. You okay?" Jim said.

"Hello, Anna. Your *husband* and I were discussing our favorites in the world of blue cheeses."

"Na ma husband. See?" I sort of turned my arm in midair to show him my ring finger and my body followed. I was heading for the carpet when the strong arm of Arthur scooped me up and plunked me back in my chair.

Arthur was smirking from ear to ear, as was Jim, and they both looked at each other, shaking their heads. Jim shot me a stern *Get a hold of yourself* grimace.

"Thanks," I said, "sorry." I struggled to regain some grace. I wasn't doing as well as I had hoped.

"Anna?" Jim said in a voice that betrayed both his trepidation and his determination to carry on. "I said that I thought we might enjoy a piece of the Chiabro D'Henry. It's a Sardinian sort of fruity cheese and maybe a slice of the French Fourme D'Ambert."

"And *I* said," Arthur said, "that I thought the Canadian Chaput Brique with the Rougerus from France were smoother and silkier."

I stuck my leg out from under the tablecloth and Arthur had little choice but to give my flailing limb a hard stare. Jim, watching me dig my hole deeper, could do nothing but look to the heavens for guidance.

"Namarried," I said, with what I was sure was the irresistible smile of a temptress.

Jim jumped out of his chair and grabbed Arthur by the arm. "We'll be right back, Anna. You just sit here like a good girl."

They hurried away and I couldn't have cared less why they did or where they were going. Arthur liked my leg. I was sure of it.

Maurice had cleared away the dishes and the space in front of me was empty. It seemed to me there was no reason why I shouldn't just rest my poor heavy head on the table for a minute or two. Hell, my hair was clean. Surely no one would mind.

Sixteen

Hair of the Dog

HEARD something piercing and offensive. Was there a hatchet in my forehead? *Ring! Ring!* A telephone. Instinct kicked in. Kill the intruder. I was buried deep in sleep, and still I reached out from the tangle of sheets and grabbed the receiver.

"Sleep well?" said the male voice with a hint of humor.

"Who is this calling at this ungodly hour?" The hatchet had moved. It was in the back of my head.

"It's Arthur, your wake-up service. You asked me to call you this morning and make sure you got out of bed early because you have things to do. Remember?"

Okay. I had no memory of that. In fact, the last thing I did remember was coming back from the bathroom at the restaurant. After that—black hole. Jim must have brought me home. I had been severely over served. I wondered how many apologies I needed to make.

"Oh, God, I am so sorry. You must think I'm a total drunk." Now was that the way to win a guy's heart or what? Give him something to tell his momma about the nice girl he just met. Remind him about your alcohol blood levels.

"No. I think you're single. Am I right?"

"Oh, God!" I buried my head under the covers and bit the back of my hand, remembering what a jerk I had been. It was hot under the covers.

"And, I think you're not accustomed to drinking wine."

"I'm not."

He had a great phone voice. It was breathy. Musky.

"And, I think you have great legs."

"Thanks, but that's small compensation for my shame and humiliation. Just tell me, did I have to be carried out on a stretcher?"

"Oh, Anna. No! You left willingly and in a very buoyant state. I mean, you were sleepy and waving around a little, but overall your performance of 'New York, New York' was relatively on key. The patrons loved it!"

"Tell me you're lying . . ."

" 'These little town blues . . . ' " He was singing.

"Shoot me, okay? Just shoot me and put me out of my misery."

"I thought you were pretty wonderful. And this Jim fellow is a decent guy. I mean, he told me how he had basically given you a brain dump of some major bad news and all. That's enough to make *me* drink. You were *married* to him?"

I knew he was asking the obvious. "It's a long story. Jim's great."

"Yeah, he seems like it. Okay, so I've done my job. You're up, I take it?"

"Yeah, I'm up. Thanks. Really."

"Okay. Say listen, if you ever want to go to, I don't know, an AA meeting or a movie or something . . ."

"Very funny. AA indeed. A movie? Maybe."

"Sunday?"

"Well, my daughter's coming home from school and I haven't seen her in six months, but . . ."

"Oh, okay, no problem."

He was going to hang up. He thought I wasn't interested.

"No! I was going to say, why don't you come over on Sunday afternoon around five and we can barbecue something or cook some shrimp."

"Great! Sounds good!"

"Great! Do you need my address?"

"Hardly. May I just say how fetching you look in your Carolina T-shirt?"

I looked down and sure enough the rag was bunched up on my body. "I want to die."

"I'm just teasing you—Jim was the one who helped you undress. *I* had the good manners to leave and go back to work."

"Arthur?"

"Yeah?"

"Thanks. I'll see you Sunday."

I hung up, crawled out of bed, and staggered to the shower, checking my living room. No sign of Jim but the couch was a wreck. He must've gone out to get a newspaper.

While the water ran hot, I took three aspirins and drank two glasses of water. I looked in the mirror over the sink and stuck out my tongue, which I was positive had been replaced by a sweat sock. I brushed my teeth to a fare-thee-well, said a good Act of Contrition to assuage my guilt, and got in the shower, letting the water run over my head. What an idiot I was! Never in my life had I done anything so asinine! Never again!

Obviously, he had seen me in some stage of undress. I cringed, fully aware that my abs (and most definitely when inert) weren't exactly off the cover of *Shape* magazine. I could only imagine that he had seen me in the least flattering of all poses—caked spit and lipstick lodged in the corners of my mouth, mascara and dried-up crud around my eyes, breath that could make a bulldog break his chain—God in heaven! Who knew? Had he seen my cellulite? Did I really sing? Shit! I couldn't carry a tune in a bucket!

I began to giggle. Well, I told myself, if he called you this morning and wanted to see you again, maybe it's not a total loss. At least I knew he had seen me at my absolute worst. I was musing about Lucy's face and how her mouth would hang open like a trapdoor when I told her this story. Perhaps it was better left untold.

Emily! What time was it? I wrapped a towel around myself and checked my alarm clock. Eight-fifteen. Okay. Her plane arrived when? Noon. I called Jim on his cell.

"Don't stress! I'll pick her up and bring her straight to the house! Do you want a decaf cappuccino? I'm stopping by Starbucks."

"Caffeine, please, yes, and a plain glazed Krispy Kreme doughnut."

"How's the head?"

"Fine," I lied. "I took a shower."

"Okay. See you in a few minutes."

I hung up, threw on some clothes, and looked around the house. Well, it was small and it wasn't over decorated, to be sure, but it was mine. Ours. Emily and me. My sweet baby girl, the same one who let the f-word slip on the phone with me, but the straight up the middle South Carolina girl whom everyone adored was finally coming home and her momma couldn't wait to throw her arms around her!

I decided to put flowers in her room and took my shears from the kitchen drawer. There was some honeysuckle by the shed and I could cut a small branch of pine, I thought as I looked around the yard for something worthy of a welcome. Snipping a bit of this and that, I heard a trunk slam shut and looked up to see Miss Angel. She was going somewhere. She had to be seventy-five years old but you could never have known that by the way she moved.

"Good morning!" I called out and started walking in her direction. "Isn't it a glorious day?"

"Well, good morning yourself, Miss Anna! And yes, ma'am! It sure is beautiful! How's everything? You cutting flowers?"

"Well, sort of. I haven't grown much to cut yet! But listen! My daughter's coming home today from Washington and I am so excited for her to see our new house!"

"I imagine so! Well, that's fine! Now, you come on tell Angel. Who's the man who slept over last night?"

"Oh, no biggie. Just my ex-husband."

"Your ex-*who*? You done lost your mind?"

I couldn't tell how she meant that, so I said, "Oh, no! It's not like that! He's gay." I didn't want her to think I had some guy in the sack all night.

She set her jaw so that her face showed neither shock nor humor and looked at me dead serious. It was clear she didn't know what to say. Time stopped. Then, rather abruptly, she said, "Come 'eah, see my baskets."

Well, okay, I had given her more detail than she had asked for, but for some peculiar reason Angel was the kind of person I thought required the blunt truth if you were going to be friends. I had never made it a habit to discuss anyone's sexuality, especially mine and surely not Jim's. On the other hand I didn't want her to think I just sort of slept around, either, because I didn't.

I followed her to her car and she reopened the trunk.

"I'm thinking about getting me a minivan," she said. "Holds more. Besides, this old thing is so low to the ground, I can't see nothing coming. All them killer folks in them big SUVs, gone too fast, talking on they cell phones . . . 'Eah, look at this."

She pulled out a stack of rectangular baskets—one that looked like a desk tray to hold printer paper or catalogs. The next size was for magazines and the largest one could hold newspapers. Then she pulled out a box of baskets, all of them the size of a small box of tissues.

"Miss Angel! These are so smart! I mean, you can really use them! They're wonderful!"

I had said the wrong thing again.

"What you mean, 'really use them'? Of course you can use them!" She shook her head and continued. "See them little squares? You put a four-inch potted plant in each one and line them up on your windowsill! I got them in all sizes to fit any kind of plant!"

"They could hold brushes too," I said. "And combs. And the big trays could sit on glass shelves and hold bottles of shampoo or conditioner, lined up like little soldiers."

Our minds were finally clicking along on the same wavelength.

"Where you got your salon at?"

"Across from the Red and White, next to the deli. Lucy's probably already there. Last-minute details, you know. We open Monday."

"It's gonna do just fine," she said. "Last night I dreamed about you and you had your arms full of collard greens. Greens mean money and you gone hab plenty, 'eah? I'll stop by and see what I got you can use."

We shook hands and the deal was cut. Miss Angel smiled at me and said, "All grown up with a daughter and a business! Do Lawd! Does my heart good!"

"Thanks, Miss Angel; I mean it."

I left her there and went back to my house, standing outside my back door for a minute, just staring at it. My chest rose with a sort of pride I had never known.

I put the greens and flowers in a little vase and placed them on the white wicker chest of drawers, stepping back again. Everything was ready, well, pretty much. Soon our house would be full of life and we would begin to write a new chapter for our family's history. We would refer to time as "before the house" and "after we moved." There would be Emily's homecoming today, then our first barbecue, birthdays, our first Thanksgiving and Christmas.

I heard another car door slam. Jim must be back, I thought. The front door opened and closed.

I took the cup from him and said, "Thanks! Jim, I am so excited about Emily coming home and everything, I can't begin to tell you. You know, I was thinking about Christmas and all these things that will happen here . . ."

"You know what, Anna?" Jim said, interrupting me. "You're right! This is so such a seriously momentous occasion. Think! What if I'd missed this? Ow! Here's your doughnut."

"Thanks. If you'd missed this it would only be half as good, that's what!" I ate it in two bites, scooped up his blanket and sheets from the couch and began folding them. "Hey! Do you have a camera? I never get pictures of anything and I want to see the look on her face, you know?"

"Done! I'll get a disposable on the way to the airport."

"Y'all up?" Lucy was squinting through the screen door. "I brought you a coffee cake. You know, I thought Emily might like it? When's your daddy coming over?"

"Oh, shoot! I forgot to call him! Lunch? Should I invite him for lunch?"

They looked at me and burst out laughing.

"You must be Jim," Lucy said, with a twinkle in her appraising eyes. "I'm Lucy. I live next door."

"I am Jim and it's nice to meet you," Jim said and shook her hand, then stood back and gave her a reciprocal once over. "My, my! The girl next door!"

"I'm sorry, I should have introduced . . ."

"God, girlie! Are you a mess or what? You call Doc and I'll pick up lunch on the way back," Jim said.

"Thanks."

"My plan was to leave now, stop by Trixie's and surprise her, and then zoom to the airport and zoom back here. Need anything besides a camera?"

"Nope," I said and gave Jim a kiss on the cheek. "Thanks. Tell Trixie I said hi."

We watched him leave and Lucy said, "He's a hottie, honey. Why'd you let him get away?"

"I couldn't convert him."

"All the gorgeous ones are gay. Damn. What a waste."

"No kidding. Well, soon my entire clan will gather and be given the chance to remark on how wretched I look. I am, despite my refined background, hung over like a walrus."

"In that case, let's fix you up, honey. You do look like you had a tough night! Don't let your daughter see! Admit nothing!"

"Don't worry. I'll be the perfect mother even if I get the DTs."

"Good."

I put on some makeup and all the while Lucy and I talked about Emily, Daddy, and the salon.

"You know what?" I said.

She looked up at me from the sofa, where she sat flipping between the Style Channel and CNN. "Huh?"

"It's just that, well, I can't remember a day when I've had so many things to look forward to."

"Life is but a dream, honey chile, shoo bop, shoo bop!"

"Yeah, well, you're the one who put the shoo bop in the dream for me, Miss Lucy."

"*Your* dream, girl. I only shoo bop with people I like!"

I giggled. "I'm gonna check my little garden out front," I said.

"I'll call Dougle," she said.

"I already called him."

"I'll call him again! I gotta go home and freshen up."

"Okay! See you later!"

I smiled from the inside out. We were in such a happy frame of mind. I watched Lucy rush home. She wanted Daddy to feel our happiness too.

I wasn't dressed for yard work. I had on side zip beige pants and a red cotton sweater with red sandals, all of it from the Gap. Emily loved the Gap and Banana Republic and every time it became necessary to buy clothes, we would scour their sales racks. She was a great bargain hunter and the outfit I wore was one she had surprised me with for my birthday last year. I wondered if she would remember that.

The garden appeared to have already taken root. That was strange. I turned on the drip hoses to give the flowers a morning drink. It was already warm and it felt like the temperature that day might rise to ninety. I loved hot weather. Shoot, let's face it. At that moment, I loved everything.

"*Anna?*"

I turned to see Miss Mavis coming down her steps with something in her hands, wrapped in newspaper.

"Hey, Miss Mavis! What you got there?"

She walked carefully across the yard, her arms behind her sort of like a chicken, until she came to a halt in front of me.

"I've been watching you!" she said, holding her parcel.

"You have?" What in the world?

"Watching you plant your garden! Looks like you know what you're doing too. Do you?"

"Well, like most things, some attempts are better than others. But, yeah, I like to plant things and make them grow."

"Well, so do I. But indoors. Here, stick this in the ground over by your power meter. Darn things are as ugly as the day is long. Don't know why they have to put them out there in the middle of a house, but they do. Stupid."

I unwrapped the newspapers to see a clump of a green vine, the ends of which had already been rooted.

"Is this a vine? I've never seen this before."

"What? Oh, good Lord! It's nothing but old Cherokee rose. This fool woman at the senior center gave it to me the other day. Thinks she's a big shot with all her Latin names and all. *Rosa laevigata* or something like that. Lord! I thought what am *I* supposed to do with this? And then I saw you digging like you were heading to China. Say *thank you.*"

"Oh! I'm sorry! Thanks! Really!"

"Humph. Well, fine then. I've got to go feed my kitties, 'eah? See you later."

"Thank you, Miss Mavis," I said to her back.

I could see her shaking her head, walking away just as smartly as she could manage. No doubt she thought my manners were hopeless. I decided to put her vines in the ground right then. She was absolutely right about the power meter. I imagined that if I were to ingest a hit of something psychedelic, it would be relatively easy to convince myself that the meter was a moose head with antlers. Ugly as a mud fence.

I got my trowel and dug a little hole, snitching some topsoil from the front beds to enrich the sandy earth. The soil quality of my side yard was probably a geological match for the Sahara. I had a thing for shrubs and plants the same way some women had it for shoes. Landscaping was expensive and would have to be done with prudence and over time.

While I waited for Jim and Emily to arrive, I rechecked every corner of the house. It seemed like the whole place practically vibrated with excitement. I couldn't decide whether to be in the house when they arrived or whether I should be at the front door or maybe in the yard. I was waiting for Jim and Emily like I had waited for Daddy to come home from work when I was little.

The car pulled into the driveway and I ran to the screen door. I couldn't help it. I was dying to see my daughter. Jim got out of the car and then her door opened. She was dressed in black. Black leather pants, a long black coat, a tight torn T-shirt, and her beautiful blond hair was dyed as black as pitch. She had on enough makeup to pass for the drummer from Kiss. I stood frozen in horror. Was this what they called Goth? She came up to me and gave me a casual hug. She was pierced and tattooed. She walked by me and into the house. She called out from the living room, in a voice too unkind for my already compromised nervous system.

"Yo, Mom. So this is *it?* Man. What a *dump.*"

Seventeen

Who's That Girl?

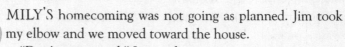

EMILY'S homecoming was not going as planned. Jim took my elbow and we moved toward the house.

"Don't say a word," Jim said.

"You mean, I should talk to her after I kill her?"

"It's a phase. That's all. She's having delayed rebellion. Our beautiful Emily is still in there."

I found her standing in her room, looking around. She was repulsed. I was reeling, trying to remember what the parenting books said about situations like this. I decided to remain calm and act as though she resembled a member of the Junior League.

"This is a *definite* problem," she said. "Like, there are so many kissy flowers on my sheets that I could die from an allergy attack, *okay?* I might get asthma!"

"Well, I suggest you get a summer job and use your money to buy what you want. I did my best."

"Yeah, if I was twelve, this would be fine. But this sucks, Mom, it really, *seriously* sucks."

She had been home less than five minutes and I was so mad I wanted to slap her face.

Jim brought in her four duffel bags and threw them on her bed.

"Home sweet home," he said and left. "Your mom went to a great deal of trouble here, Miss Emily. I suggest you show her a little appreciation."

"Why don't you just unpack and get settled, Emily? Oh, and don't come out of this room until you've transformed yourself into a civilized human being."

"Fine," she said. "Whatever."

She slammed her door. I can't have this, I thought. I hurried to the telephone to call Daddy and say that lunch would be delayed. He wasn't home. He was probably already on the way.

"Who're you calling?" Jim said, bringing in the groceries. "I got five pounds of shrimp from Simmons, coleslaw, red rice, and cornbread from the Pig. And three bottles of an amusing little Sauvignon Blanc, sure to raise your spirits. . . ." He was talking like everything was normal.

He looked at me and by the expression on my face he knew I was extremely angry.

"Okay," he said, "I'll go talk to her. There's more bad news. Trixie said she was stopping by to see Emily."

"I'm going to throw up," I said. "I'm going to kill that vampire in my daughter's room and then I'm going to throw up."

"Let me see what I can do first," he said. "Why don't you take a deep breath and set the table?"

I had just filled my stockpot with water and put it on the front burner. I tossed in half of a lemon, a tablespoon of dry mustard, and an Old Bay spice sack. It would take a while to reaching boiling, where I, on the other hand, had zoomed to boiling like a space shuttle. I heard Daddy's car door and then another. Within minutes, Daddy, Lucy, and Trixie were all in my living room.

"Anna? Where are you, honey?"

"What a precious *little* bungalow! It's *lak* an *itsy-bitsy* doll's house!"

"Don't you love her bookcases?"

Daddy stuck his head in the kitchen. "Where's Emily?"

I couldn't answer him at first. I just stood there, sweating.

"You okay?"

"Yeah, I'm okay. Emily's in her bedroom. She's talking to Jim. You'd better brace yourself."

"Oh?" He took a glass from the cabinet and poured himself a glass of tea. "Got a lemon?"

"Yeah," I said and handed him the lemon and a paring knife. "She's, um, she's changed." I left him there and went to greet Trixie and Lucy.

"Anna! Darlin'!" Trixie hugged me like she hadn't seen me in a thousand years. "Where's our girl? Ah can't wait . . ."

"Trixie? I think we are in for a long hot summer."

A lot of small talk went on, thirty minutes passed and still no Emily and Jim. Lucy helped me to set the table and I checked the water about fifty times. Lucy talked the ears off of everybody, kept Trixie's glass of wine filled until, finally, Jim came out of Emily's room.

"Mother," he said and kissed her cheek. "Dr. Lutz," he said and shook Daddy's hand.

"Well?" I said.

"Let's go ahead and eat. She's, uh, not hungry."

"Well! Ah would think she'd at *least* come out and say hello," Trixie said. Trixie, not known for her capacity to imbibe, was well renowned for her commentary. And the more she drank, the more she commentaried.

"She will, Mother," Jim said. "She's just finishing unpacking." Jim gave me a nod and I followed him to the kitchen.

"You know, Ah send her money *every* month! Not one month has passed without a generous check from me to her. Ah swanny, it seems *lak* all Ah do is give and give!"

"I know just how you feel," I heard Lucy say with a certain longing in her voice.

"Now, now, ladies, I am sure y'all are appreciated much more than you know."

Checking the pot, all I could think was that the last thing Daddy would want would be for Lucy to stop giving. The water was rolling so I put the shrimp in and removed it from the burner, covering it, letting them cook on retained heat.

I turned to Jim. "So?"

"She's a piece of work, Anna. I told her that I thought she was very rude and that she should apologize to you."

"And?"

"She said that she didn't need your shit, that she could've stayed in D.C. for the summer and lived with Frannie, who apparently is the one who helped her shop for her funereal wardrobe."

"Nice. Thanks, Frannie. And?"

"I told her if she wanted to look like that, it was her business, but that nobody in San Francisco had dressed like that in years. I said, 'So, look, honey, the whole goth thing is so *passé and finito.*' That pissed her off in paisley. She said, What did I know? I told her I knew plenty and if she wanted to spend the summer fighting with everyone, fine. But, I thought she was so capable of making a better effort than to barge in here and start finding fault with everything."

"So?"

"She'll be out in a few minutes. I told her to put on something lighter. Hell! It's hotter than two rats having sex in a wool sock! Rubber pants in June? Uck! What a sweaty misery!" Jim took a paper towel and wiped perspiration from his forehead. "This parenting thing is not exactly easy."

"It sure isn't. Thanks, Jim. Rats in a wool sock?"

"Yeah! Hey! Anytime! I'll pour everyone some more wine, okay?" He took a bottle and a corkscrew to the living room, where everyone was talking as though life was perfect and no monster was locked in the bedroom. "Decent wine makes high-voltage drama so much easier to bear."

"I imagine it does," I said.

"We need some music!" I heard Lucy say.

A minute or so later, I heard the *Sunday Brunch* CD I bought at

Williams-Sonoma on King Street. Was I old or what? I'd arrived at the point in my life where I bought my music at Williams-Sonoma. Worse, I liked it.

I drained the shrimp and arranged them on my largest platter with a bowl of cocktail sauce and lemon wedges.

"Let's eat," I said.

"What about Emily?" Daddy said.

"I'm coming!" she called from her room.

Honestly? The house was so small and the walls were so thin that you could probably hear someone change their mind.

We gathered around my table, which just seated a tight six.

"This looks absolutely da-vine!" Trixie said, adding, "Oh! Should Ah bring my glass?"

No, the waiter will.

"Please, yes," I said. "Y'all just sit anywhere."

Daddy took the head of the table near the back wall. Lucy sat on his left and Trixie on his right. Jim sat to my left and we saved the seat on my right for Emily. I was about to propose a toast when she appeared. Thank God, she had on long drawstring pants and a long-sleeve dark cotton shirt. Her tattoos weren't showing and her hair had been brushed up into a ponytail. It was still black, but at least it wasn't hanging in stringy hostility.

"Come sit, sweetheart," I said.

I wasn't optimistic about that meal at all.

"Hi, everybody," she said.

There was little to no enthusiasm in her voice.

"What on God's earth has happened to your *hair?*"

"It's a rinse, Granny. Don't stress yourself."

Trixie bristled and shot me a look of outrage.

Lucy introduced herself to Emily and Emily gave a slightly snide response: "Whoa!" It was more like she had said, *Oh, great. Mom's new friend is a stripper.*

"Emily? Please don't address Trixie as Granny and don't tell her how to handle her shock at your hair. It is black, after all."

"Fine. Sorry, Gram. I just get, like, really sick of people telling me what I'm supposed to look like. I mean, my hair is my business, isn't it?"

"Ah suppose," Trixie said. "But your blond hair was so attractive. Ask your mother. People spend good money to be blond."

"Thank God," I said. I was determined to get the show on the road and not spend the day speculating with Trixie on what had become of Emily's appearance and personality. "Anyway, I want to propose a little toast. I want to thank Daddy for all his help in helping me move. And Lucy for her generous help in my new business. . . ."

"Whut?" Trixie said.

"She's opening her own salon on Monday!" Lucy blurted. "Isn't that wonderful?"

"And I want to thank Jim for being just about the best friend in the entire world and doing more for me than I could even think of to ask for myself. . . ."

"Aw, shucks," Jim said.

"Your *own* salon?" Trixie said. "How on earth—Ah mean, where did you find . . . ?"

Lucy pulled a business card from her pocket and handed it to Trixie for inspection. "I made them on my laptop."

"Clever," Emily said in a flat voice and reached across the table for the basket of cornbread in front of Daddy.

It was unfortunate in the extreme that the shirtsleeve of her reaching arm receded enough to reveal an intricate design on her wrist that resembled some of the more complicated wrought-iron gates in the historic parts of Charleston. Daddy gasped, Trixie screamed, and I jumped up from the table.

"All right," I said, completely unsure of what I would say next until I looked at Emily's face.

Emily was smirking. If there was one thing I despised it was to see my only daughter smirk. Don't smirk at me, the mirror, or another person. No smirking allowed. Did she think she had won some contest to horrify her family?

"Emily! Come with me!"

"Whaaat?" she said. She didn't budge. She made that noise that sounds like *twick* and rolled her eyes.

Everyone stopped eating and all eyes were on Emily as they waited for her to get up out of her chair. Finally, she put down her napkin, left the table, and followed me to the backyard. I stopped by the shed and turned to face her. She stopped, crossed her arms, and tilted her head to one side.

"What's the matter with you?"

"Nothing!"

"Emily. Let me tell you something. I am prepared to be reasonable. You are not reasonable. I understand you're coming from dormitory life, where you have a lot of freedom. Our home is not a dormitory. I know our house is little and I can see now why you don't like your sheets. You have changed."

All the while I spoke to her she looked out past Miss Mavis's house toward the beach, realizing how close it was. She couldn't help but soften a little. "Yes, I have. I'm practically an adult. I've been living on my own now for a year and I do what I want."

"Oh? Are you paying all your bills?"

Her head spun around like a demon from a movie about possession. "*Noooo!* You *know* I'm not!"

"Lower your voice!" I lowered my voice as well. I had a fleeting vision of the Snoop Sisters and all my company with their ears plastered against the windows trying to listen. "If you're not paying your bills, you ain't on your own. That's just one small part of being an adult. The rest is basically how you conduct yourself."

"Can I go now?"

"No, you may not! You cannot go until you tell me what is the matter with you! Why are you so angry?"

"I'm *not* angry!"

"Okay. I'm going to attribute your pissy attitude to being tired from your trip. I'm tired too. I went out last night and probably partied too much." My head was pounding again.

"*You* went out? You *partied?*"

"Yeah," I said and noted the expression of disbelief on her face. "I went out and partied, well, had dinner actually, with Jim and saw this guy I had met before and I actually have a sort of date tomorrow."

"Holy shit! *That's* great! I just get home from school and you're not even gonna be here! Why did I even come home?"

"What?" What did she mean by that?

"I mean, I could've stayed in Washington. I could've, like, worked at the Gap. I could have lived with Frannie and had a very excellent summer. But, no! I start thinking about you and that you're probably lonely and that you probably totally need me. I get here, the house is crawling with all these people, you've got your plans. Know what? I should have kept mine!"

Suddenly I was struck by the fact that she thought I was all shriveled up like a crone and that I had no life. Was she saying that she was cutting me some slack by coming home *at all* for the summer? Well, we'll have none of this, I thought.

"Emily? From time to time you need to show up for inspection. You are not an adult yet. It is still my job to see that you haven't become a drug addict or an alcoholic and that your general health is good. And to discuss your course of study. What do I see? My beautiful daughter has gone to hell in a handbasket and looks like something from *Pit and the Pendulum*. You've got godawful dyed-black hair, and don't forget I am qualified to judge this."

"I like it."

"I don't! You've got four holes in each ear, one in your eyebrow, and God knows how many in other places. I don't much like that *at all*, but I do care about these tattoos. They creep me out, like you're fond to say. And what are you going to do about them when you're fifty? Don't you think tattooed women at fifty are pretty disgusting?"

"Henna."

"What?"

"They're henna paintings. They wear off in a couple of weeks. Everyone does it."

"Everyone at Gram's yacht club does *not* have henna tattoos; I can just about guarantee it."

"Yeah, well, they're all near death anyway. *Boor-ing!*"

I agreed with her about that but wasn't about to admit it. The yacht club was famous for its old codgers and its unwritten rule book. The members had so many rules about who could join and what to wear and who could eat in what dining room on what days—shoot, even if I had Donald Trump and Bill Gates's money combined, and I owned a huge boat, I wouldn't want to be bothered with all that nonsense. I had always believed that usually people formed private clubs to keep others out. Sometimes, that wasn't true. At that moment, I didn't really care about the yacht club. I was thinking about her dissatisfaction in a general way.

"Do you *really* hate the house?"

"It's dinky, Mom, but I guess it's okay. It's just that my room looks like it's for some little twit. I mean, look, I'm sorry, okay? I was just so pent up about coming back to a place I'd never seen and it was supposed to all of a sudden be home and I just didn't know. I just didn't know."

"If it would be?"

"Yeah."

"We can repaint your room."

"Okay."

"I mean, one of the reasons I bought this house was so that we could paint a room purple if we wanted to."

"A small feature."

"Puce. Paint your room puce for all I care."

"Really?"

"Yeah, puce and purple. Have a ball. And do you know that now we can walk around in our underwear? Think about it. Do you know I've never done that? I've been fully dressed for over thirty years!"

"Thirty-seven and counting. We run around half naked in the dorm all the time!"

I could smell peace sneaking up behind us. We stood there in the warm afternoon air, the stingy breeze, and wound up talking and temporarily putting our anger aside. At least we had a starting place.

"Look, Emily, I did my best. And, we gotta live together. Just be nice, okay?"

"Yeah, I know."

"Someday, when my ship rolls in, I'm gonna add on to the house. Another bedroom and a big bathroom and a study upstairs with porches all around, upstairs and downstairs too. Maybe a deck. I don't know. I'm dreaming, I guess."

Emily stared at the house, looking long and hard, trying to see the possibilities that I saw. She sort of smiled and turned to me. "It could work."

"Let's go back inside and make nice, okay?"

"Okay, I guess. Jeez, Mom, Gram is a such a phony, isn't she?"

"Honey, she's a nice lady, really. I mean, she's a little stiff, but she means well."

"I'll never be like her."

"Me either," I said and looped my arm around Emily's shoulder. We walked back inside together.

It was pretty obvious by their all-at-once chatter that they had been talking about Emily and how I would handle her smart-ass mouth. I gave them nothing, which was probably a disappointment to them. I just sat down and so did Emily and we started peeling shrimp.

"You girls okay now?" Daddy said.

"Yeah, we're fine," I said. "What did we miss?"

What we had missed was Trixie's sermon.

"Well! For one thing, Ah cannot believe that you weren't out here to greet us! So rude! And, the way you look, Emily! It's . . . it's horrible! You simply must do something! You cannot parade yourself around Charleston like this! And those tattoos . . . forgive me for saying so, dear, are without *any* taste or class!"

Emily lost it. She slammed her fist on the table and looked at

Trixie and said, "*Why can't you just keep your opinions to yourself? Why is that such a problem for you?*"

Needless to say, everyone became silent.

"I'm sorry, Gram, but it's true," Emily said in a strangely quiet voice.

More silence. Jim didn't tell Emily to apologize. Neither did Daddy or I. Lucy was still processing what had happened. Trixie, flushed and angry, blustered and then gained control of herself. She quietly put her napkin on the table and rose.

"Thank you for lunch, Anna. It was nice to see you again. Douglas? Lucy? Nice to see y'all too."

No one moved. Jim left the table to see his mother to her car. Emily sank into her chair. Daddy, Lucy, and I picked at a few more shrimp in an uncomfortable silence.

Jim and Trixie were outside for a few minutes longer than I thought Jim should have to suffer alone. I went outside to join them.

"She's a daggum witch," Lucy said, whispering. "Go save Jim."

"Good luck," Daddy said.

Trixie had finally shown her obnoxious self as I knew her to be, and everyone else agreed with that. Trixie was in the driver's seat of her new convertible Jaguar. She was crying and Jim was standing back with his arms folded, shaking his head and talking to her.

"Mother? You just don't come into Anna's house and call her daughter low rent! Why is that so hard for you to see? Emily is merely doing this to make some statement about her independence."

"Henna," I said to them.

What? What?

"The tattoos are henna paint and they wear off in a couple of weeks."

"But her hair?" Trixie said. "And the way she spoke to me? In all mah life . . ."

"Trixie? You blasted her hard and then expected her not to defend herself. That's really not fair, you know."

Trixie started her engine and looked at me.

"You have gone too far, Anna."

"Whatever you say, Trixie." I said in the most unemotional voice I could find.

"And don't expect mah support of your salon either!"

"I don't expect anything, Trixie. See you later."

I turned around and went back toward my house. Surprisingly, I felt pretty good about what had happened and knew it was proof of why I was right to buy my own damn house. Distance.

Eighteen

Rare and Well Done

~~~~~~

"SO am I grounded for the rest of my life? Because if I am, it's not fair!"

Jim and I looked at each other. I thought she would have been packing to run away from home but she was in the midst of helping Daddy and Lucy clear the table. Actually, she was holding a stack of dirty plates and standing by the door waiting for us to come back inside. And, given the moment, she was properly terrified. Daddy and Lucy were in the kitchen. If I knew anything about my father it was that he was already up to his elbows in suds and listening to every word.

"Not at all," Jim said, "that is, if I still have any influence around here. Mother can be intolerable and it is understandable for you to be upset by what she said."

"On the other hand, I can see it's past time for you to have a brush up in Grace and Poise. Let's start with Rule One in dealing with our elders."

"Come on, Mom. Is this serious?"

"Yes."

"Mom!"

"Listen to your mother," Jim said.

"Rule One: When older women have already proven themselves to be wicked old biddies, we do not attack them. It is unnecessary, as no one with half a brain listens to them anyway."

"Look, I know that's true, all right? But it's such bull!" She took a deep breath. "Okay. I know you're totally and completely correct, but I get *so* mad!"

"Verbally attacking old biddies is pretty rude," Jim said. "Your mom's right."

"I just don't understand how you can sit there and let her say whatever she wants and you just *take* it. This whole world is just taking whatever is flung at it!"

"You'll understand when you're an adult," I said. "Knowing which battles to fight is part of maturity."

"No! Okay! Maybe this is from living in D.C. on red alert! I know that, but at that moment, I just lost it!"

"Yeah, we all lose it, but you know you're going to have to apologize, Emily. You just can't treat Trixie like that. She's been pretty good to you all your life. Right?"

"Okay. Fine. Shit. Fine."

"Now."

"Can't I do it tomorrow? I'm pretty beat and I don't feel like going through it again."

"Call my mother now, Emily, before she gets home and leave a message on her machine." Jim smiled at Emily and me. "God, am I smart or what?"

"A certifiable genius, baby boy. Come on, let's get that kitchen."

"I'll be right there," Emily said. "God, I *hate* doing this!"

And that's what we did. Emily made the phone call and we stuffed our five fannies in my phone booth kitchen and put Trixie where she belonged—out of our minds.

To give you a recap—Lucy never said a word about any of it. All Daddy said was, "I understand it was difficult to hold your tongue, but I'm sure you and your momma will work that out. She had to learn the hard way too." Spare enough.

Everyone said the shrimp was delicious, how good it was to be together, and we all shook our heads over Trixie's behavior.

Later that evening, we were all supposed to go to Lucy's for another glorious sunset light show, courtesy of Lowcountry's Mother Nature. Emily and I were still talking about Trixie and so they went on ahead without us.

"Don't wait too long! You'll miss everything!" Lucy said.

"I'm going with Lucy," Jim said, and left.

The telephone rang. It was Satan's wife.

"Ah'd like to speak to Emily," she said.

I handed the telephone to her and we grimaced, knowing from the tone of her voice that a possible Armageddon was on the way.

"Hello, Gram?" Silence. "Yes." Silence. "I said I was sorry, didn't I?" Silence.

I couldn't stand it. I wanted to grab the receiver from her and tell Trixie to lay off. But I walked away, not wanting to hang over Emily. I wanted to see how Emily would handle her. I went in the bathroom and stayed for a few minutes and then came out when I heard Emily crying. She had gone into her room.

"What happened?"

Emily was spread out over her bed, sobbing. She didn't answer me so I sat down next to her and asked her again.

"Come on, baby, tell Momma." I leaned over and scratched her back. "What did she say?"

"Oh, Momma! She is the *meanest,* most hateful bitch in the entire world!"

"I don't know about that. I have a list of my own, you know."

"Oh, God! You're gonna kill me."

"I would do no such thing. I might wash that black shit out of your hair and I might scrub your henna decorations with a Brillo pad, but kill you? Never."

"She said I had seen the last nickel from her. Momma? I know, I know . . . I know we don't have a lot of money. . . ."

"She actually *said* that?"

"Yeah."

Trixie had no right to lay that kind of mental punishment on Emily. She should have told me and let me work it out. But, no, she had wanted to make Emily worry and suffer and she had succeeded. Temporarily.

"Well, screw her."

Here's where we revisited my theory about taking money from anybody. It always came back to bite you in the butt.

"You mean it?"

"Well, yeah. I mean, look Emily, when somebody gives you something like that, it's supposed to be a gift. People shouldn't give gifts with strings."

"And, in English that would mean . . ."

"It means that something else is attached to the gift—usually an expectation of some kind."

"Oh, and Gram expected me to grow up to be a debutante?"

"Ah reckon! If you really want to make her crazy, you should write her a real sweet thank-you note and tell her how much you appreciate all she's done for you."

"Yeah! *'Dear Gram, up yours!'*"

"Well, that ain't bad, but I was thinking of something a little sneakier and more underhanded. You know, say something like, *'If you don't want to help me or if you can't, I understand and really want to thank you for all you've done for me.'* That would kill her worse than anything."

Finally, Emily sat up and took the tissue I had for her. She blew her nose.

"Kill her with kindness, huh?"

"Exactly! Someday when we're both old ladies, I'll tell you some stories that will make your hair stand on end."

"Tell me now!"

"Hell no! You're still too volatile! You might use it against me in court or something!"

We smiled at each other and then hugged each other. If I closed my eyes, I could see her as a little girl, hanging on to me and hugging me so hard I had sometimes thought that she would never let go. Maybe that was why she had done all this to herself—she was trying to let go. I wondered why young people didn't just go their own way and why, instead, they had to push everyone away. I didn't care if her hair was purple or if her tattoos were real, she was still my daughter and I loved her with a kind of ferociousness I couldn't live without.

"You know what, sweetheart?"

"What?"

"Let's try to make this summer wonderful, you know? I mean, we're going to have to figure out what to do about Trixie's allowance. I guess I'll have to cut a few more heads and you'll have to get a job."

"I can do that. I don't know *what* I can do, though."

"We'll scrutinize the want ads tomorrow. Let's go watch the sunset and help Jim chaperone Doc and Lucy."

I stood and Emily rolled over and followed me to the living room. I started turning on a few lights so we wouldn't come home to a dark house. Old habit—make the robbers think you're home. Like we had so much worth stealing anyway.

"Um, Mom? I'm, like, really glad you brought that up. What in the world? Is he, I mean, are they, you know, dating?"

"It's hard to say. I think so. Lock the kitchen door, okay?"

"Okay."

"But so far, he hasn't taken her out anywhere that I know of. I think Daddy's too shy or something."

"Or maybe he doesn't want to be seen in public with a middle-aged Britney Spears."

"Whoever she is."

"God, Mom! Don't you watch television?"

"Yeah, all day every day."

"Well, you can say whatever you want, it just grosses me out to think of my grandfather with a girlfriend to begin with, much less one that looks like her."

"Go easy, honey. Old Lucy is really as good as gold. You'll see. Just give her a while."

We spent the next few hours at Lucy's, laughing, drinking frozen drinks, and it didn't take long for Emily to shine to Lucy. After the sun slipped away, we climbed down from her deck and then gathered in her kitchen to make a bowl of pasta for supper. I was chopping onions while the garlic sizzled in Lucy's frying pan. Jim opened three big cans of tomatoes and, using an odd little tool that looked like an arc-shaped blade, he hacked away at them in a bowl.

"Hey, Lucy?" Jim said. "What do you call this thing?"

"A tomato chopper," she said.

"Why did I bother to ask?" Jim laughed to himself and I just shook my head.

I slid the onions from the cutting board into the pan and in minutes the whole room smelled wonderful. Lucy was at the counter with her laptop.

"Come here, honey, lemme show you what I found on the web."

"What?" said Emily.

"This is the debate team from the University of South Carolina."

"Whoa! Not bad."

"Right?" Lucy said, and giggled.

I came around to see for myself. There was a full screen of great-looking young men and women, all of them very serious. Lucy pointed to a particularly adorable young man who looked like an Abercrombie & Fitch model. He had thick blond hair and penetrating eyes. I don't know if anybody besides Lucy still said *hunk*, but he was one.

"See that cute fellow? That's my nephew, David. He's coming to spend the summer with me. Tomorrow sometime. He's driving down from Columbia with all his stuff."

"Ohmagod."

"My sister lives in Greenville. I don't think David knows too many people his age around here. Maybe you could help me entertain him?"

"Ohmagod."

That was all Emily said about David and for the rest of the evening she was very quiet. We had our dinner and helped Lucy clean up. At what seemed to be the right moment, Jim, Emily, and I walked back to our house, leaving Daddy and Lucy alone.

"So, Anna, do you think they, you know, get it on?"

"Jim!"

Emily burst out laughing and I began chasing Jim around the yard, pretending that I was going to beat him up.

"Disgusting! That's what you are!"

"Em! Help your old man here!"

"You're on your own!"

We finally gave up and, out of breath, we went inside. Jim stood looking at the couch. He recognized it as his destiny for the night. Emily was standing next to him.

"Okay," she said, "sleep in my room. I'll sleep with Mom."

Jim hugged her wildly. "Thank you, child! Thank you! My back has been saved!"

"What do you mean? We paid two hundred dollars for that couch fifteen years ago! Don't you remember?"

"I rest my case," Jim said. "Yeah, and it belonged to the Marquis de Sade."

"There ain't a bargain in the world that ain't got my momma's fingerprints on it."

We said good night and when I finally turned out the light next to my bed, it was Emily and I, in the dark.

"Tonight was fun," she said.

"Yeah, it was."

"So what do you think about that kid David?"

"He looks pretty conservative, but he's very good looking. What did you think?"

"He's probably an asshole. I mean, debate team? Please!"

"Must you say *asshole?*"

"Yes."

So say it. At least she was talking to me about what was on her mind. I decided to tell her what was bothering me.

"Arthur is coming over tomorrow. What am I gonna wear?" It wasn't what I was going to wear that had me going, it was that he was coming over in the first place.

"Get some sleep, Mom. You don't want to look like a beat-up old bag."

"Oh, thanks a lot."

We were quiet for a few minutes or longer. I had so many things on my mind, but I was so sleepy I could barely keep my eyes open. Just when I was drifting off, Emily spoke again.

"Mom?"

"Hmmm?" I was sinking into my mattress and didn't want to wake up.

"Is Jim my real father? I mean, he's, like, this definitely totally gay guy. Was he always? I mean, did you, you know . . ."

My eyes shot open in the dark. In the first moment, I didn't know whether or not to pretend to be asleep. I decided to dodge.

"What kind of a crazy question is that? Jim is more than your father. And he's more than my ex-husband. Now, let's be quiet and we'll talk tomorrow."

Great. Just great.

After that, I knew I wasn't falling asleep in a hurry. Never lie. It's wrong. I waited until her breathing was even, rising and falling at predictable intervals. There was nothing so sweet in all the world than to have my girl next to me. My heart felt such relief that she was just . . . there.

I had never wanted to hurt Emily by not telling her the truth. I never wanted to hurt anyone. I wasn't a malicious person. There had just never been the right moment to tell her or a reason to tell her. I should have figured that the day would come when she would ask. I don't know why I thought we would get away forever with having the world accept that we were a regulation divorced couple. It was how I thought of us. But there was a difference. Jim had always been pretty open about his life.

I would discuss it with Jim in the morning. At some moment, and with certain delicacy, Jim and I would probably wind up telling her. I thought about adoptive parents for a while. My generation usually told their children they were adopted and at some stage the children were allowed and sometimes even encouraged to find their birth parents. But where was the textbook for this case?

I decided to say my prayers. Prayer always put my mind at ease. Maybe I didn't go to church every Sunday, but a night never passed that I didn't pray sincerely. I decided to ask the Blessed Mother what she would do if she had to tell her only child that her birth was the result of a rape. Wasn't Emily's life at a pretty precarious stage? She had come home so angry, ready to fight with anyone over anything. She had taken on her grandmother in a humiliating argument and lost not only her composure but her financial aid. I could tell by her remarks about Lucy's nephew how insecure she was about the opposite sex.

What really mattered was that I had my girl home, curled up next to me sleeping without a care in the world. She knew she was safe. I knew then what I would do. Sometimes the facts were too devastating. I would protect her from the dangers of truth for as long as I could.

Nineteen

Miss Mavis and Miss Angel Confer

I HAD been watching that house all day and there was enough funny business next door to alert the authorities. I was sure of it. All day long, cars coming and going and doors slamming and people yelling and carrying on.

"Oh!" I said and closed the curtains. "She almost saw me! That was too close for me! Angel? Are you there?"

Anna was going with that child of hers over to you-know-who's house again.

"No, Mavis, I was juss fixin' to go to Charleston and find us some men."

"What? I didn't make out what you said. Come out here!" She was always hollering at me like I don't know what, knowing perfectly well how impolite it was to yell from behind a closed door.

And, there she came, like the Queen, strutting across my floor.

"I'm righ' chea, Mavis. What's got your motor going now?"

"My motor's not going anyplace! You look down there and tell me what you see."

She stood to the right side of the curtains and slowly, slowly pulled
them back a little, staring at me the whole time like we were in a contest to see who would blink their eyes first. Then she moved across the
curtains and peered down and then across Anna's to that little hussy's
house. She was trying my patience, I can tell you.

"I don't see nothing, Mavis. Nothing 'cept a bunch of folks up in
that crow's nest of Lucy's."

"It's a widow's walk and you know it."

"I reckon they likes to watch the sun go down for the day. Something wrong with that?"

Well, there wasn't anything wrong with watching the blooming
sun set and I knew that.

"For heaven's sake, Angel, you're probably right. After all, Lucy's
been hanging off the side of that porch ever since that no-good bubba
she married took off. Just mooning and mooning! But you're right, I
am too judgmental and maybe a little nosy. Even Mary Magdalene
needed friends, didn't she?"

"Ooh! You bad, Mavis!"

Suddenly, I was wishing I could go up there too. But I was too delicate to climb all those steps and I knew it. After a certain age, there
are a few pleasures you have to forego for the sake of your own personal safety. That annoyed me too.

"Well! My mother always said, tell me who your company is and
I'll tell you who you are. I just don't like to think about Anna ruining
her reputation by going around with that, that . . ."

"Oh, go on, Mavis. Ain't nobody looking at who she going with
'cept us! And, she's all grown! Come on now! What's the matter?"

"Oh, Angel! I don't know. You remember last Sunday and how we
talked to her about her mother?"

"I do. I remember the look on her face too. She didn't want to hear
that her momma might be a good woman. Not no how! Makes a body
wonder what kinda nonsense they been feeding that child all she life,
'eah?"

"That's *exactly* what I mean! The dead can't defend themselves and just because her mother was caught with the wrong rooster doesn't mean she was *all* bad."

"You're right, Mavis! You are entirely right!"

"Don't point your finger at me, Angel. It's not nice to point."

"Humph. I—"

She opened her mouth to speak but I cut her off, as it was my prerogative to speak when it suited me. It was my house and Angel was my employee. I sat in my recliner and motioned to her to sit on the sofa, which she did.

"I remember! Yes, I do! I remember Mary Beth and how she was. She was a sweet girl married to an old man. Percy and I tried to befriend her, didn't we?"

"Yes, Mavis, y'all sure did do that. And I can tell you something I ain't never told no one."

"What?"

She sucked her teeth and said, "*I said that I can*—"

"I heard you fine, Angel! I wasn't asking you to repeat yourself! I was asking you what you knew!"

"Oh, sorry. Lawsamercy! One time my nephew was hanging around here wanting money from me. Had the car park in the yard, waiting. He couldn't make his car payment. And I was busy telling her about it and I clean forgot he was in the backyard. She left and when I finally got outside with my pocketbook, he say to me that he don't need a hundred dollar. Miss Mary Beth done give him fifty, so I only needs to loan him fifty."

"He borrowed money from my neighbor! The nerve! But, Mary Beth didn't have fifty dollars to give him! Where did she get it?"

"Shows what *you* know! She tell me later that she been cleaning out Doc's pockets and between the sofa cushions for years—and snitching from his wallet a little bit 'eah and there—and she had over three hundred dollars all saved up. I say she ain't supposed to give my nephew money 'cause none of us got it to give and she say to me that she ain't got no nephews and he just got married and she feel for him."

"My goodness! Yes, sir! That's how she was, alright. She wanted to go to school, you know, and Doc wouldn't hear of it."

"Yeah, 'cause he be afraid he gone lose her too, 'eah? She might find a young man and leave him!"

"Oh, Angel! I don't think so, but maybe! Maybe so. Who knows how men think? You know what she wanted to do? She wanted to be a practical nurse and take care of old people in the nursing homes. That doesn't sound like a cat on the prowl to me. Anyway, she was volunteering over at the rest home in Charleston, reading newspapers to old poops like us, and that's how she met that pharmacist in the first place."

"He was bad too, 'eah?"

"Oh, Angel. Can't you see how it could have happened? He was young like her and he probably made her feel alive and beautiful. I know what she did was wrong and, to tell you the truth, if she hadn't died, I don't see how she could have stayed married to *Dr. Douglas Lutz* forever anyway. It's just like that movie *Breakfast at Tiffany's*, except that Audrey Hepburn never got in the bed with a pharmacist and did drugs, of course. Anyway, it was a tragic loss of a beautiful young woman, and that poor Anna. I could just cry for her."

"Humph. Save your tears, Mavis. I think Miss Anna's gonna be just fine. People gots to work out their lives they own selves! She's got she girl home now and all kinda company coming and going. We might not be too fond of Lucy but Anna's old enough to pick her own friends."

"I know. I know."

"And if she wants to know about she momma? She gone ask. I say we be better off just being good neighbors and keeping our own business."

Angel was right. She started plumping all my little pillows and rearranging them on my sofa. They all had clever sayings on them that made me laugh. The good Lord knows, my life was pretty boring if I had to resort to pillows to amuse myself. One read I NEVER REPEAT GOSSIP, SO LISTEN VERY CAREFULLY. Another read IF YOU WANT THE BEST SEAT IN THE HOUSE, YOU'LL HAVE TO MOVE THE CAT. I just loved them all.

Twenty

Skewered

~~~

*Y*OU'RE going to think this is a bunch of bull, but it isn't. When I went outside in the morning to turn on my drip hoses, almost overnight my flowers had gone from tiny sprigs to lush and overflowing beds. I nearly fainted. For a minute I thought it was a joke, that someone had sneaked into my yard in the middle of the night and replanted everything. I even checked the dirt and the mulch. It had not been disturbed.

I walked around the side of the house to look at the climbing rose that Miss Mavis had given me. While it wasn't covering the side of the house, it had grown to a full bushy vine and was crawling up the water meter pipes. What in the world? In the backyard, the honeysuckle had taken off overnight as well. Everything I had planted was growing like weeds! I started to laugh. I didn't have a clue how or why this had happened. It was another one of those mysterious gifts from the Lowcountry's Great Beyond. I wondered if anyone else would notice. Maybe they had grown more than I thought and I was imagining things. Possible. I turned on the faucet and decided to go out and get the Sunday paper and some bacon and eggs. I would shop for dinner later.

It was only seven-thirty and Emily and Jim were still sleeping. I backed my car out of the driveway as quietly as I could and headed toward the Red & White. I was thinking about how nice it was to be together and about my salon.

The plan for that day was to have breakfast and check the salon again. With gargantuan effort, everything in the salon had been made ready. I planned to show it to Emily after breakfast. We would all— including Lucy—put the finishing touches on it and then cook something on the grill around five when Arthur arrived. It was hard to believe that we had done so much in such a short time. But that was the power of determination and a little luck thrown in. We had a pretty full schedule for Monday. I called Bettina and Brigitte and they would come in early to call customers when they weren't busy with the bookings they already had. True to their word, they had many appointments already on the books. So did I.

Before pulling into the parking lot of the Red & White, I swung into our parking lot to look through the windows. I'd admit that I held my breath getting out of my car and locked it for no reason. The parking lot was completely empty. I looked around at who our neighbors were and liked the way their offices and stores looked—neat as a pin. Our sign had been hung yesterday: THE PALMS SALON AND SPA. I looked through the windows and thought, *It looks beautiful.* The chairs were all lined up and waiting. Everything looked fresh and new. All the products were neatly arranged on the shelves. Miss Angel had given us some baskets on consignment and she and Lucy had hung them on the empty walls. They looked so rich and important. The reception area's nightlight made the entrance seem warm and inviting. Maybe it was corny, but I was so filled up with emotion when I stood and looked at it. I said the name out loud.

"The Palms Salon and Spa!" I was so proud!

To be honest, we were using the term *spa* loosely here. The only services we had resembling spa treatments were warm wax treatments for hands and feet, and standard waxing for legs, bikini line, and lips. But I had plans. If that little card shop next door ever moved, I would hire a team of aestheticians and rid the world of bad skin! Okay, maybe not the world, but the folks who vacationed here fried themselves on a regular basis. There were wonderful things you could do for sunburn—like aloe wraps. Not to mention massages, body wraps—but first things first. It was time for breakfast.

THE smell of bacon frying brought Jim and Emily to the kitchen.

"Hey, Momma. Whatcha cooking?" She put her arms around the back of my shoulders and gave me a squeeze. "Got any coffee?"

"Pot's over there," I said. "Pour some for your daddy too."

Suddenly last night's closing conversation about the nature of her birth came back to me. Thankfully, she didn't bring it up right then. Like most of us, she needed a cup of coffee before trauma, just to clear the cobwebs. Maybe she would forget. I doubted it.

"You get the paper?" Jim strolled into my kitchen in his boxer shorts and T-shirt. He snatched a piece of bacon from the paper towel and I slapped his hand.

"Bad dog," I said. "The newspaper's on the table."

"Ssgood!"

I loved breakfast—and I don't mean that I liked any old kind of healthy fiber and fresh fruit or freaking smoothies. That ain't breakfast. That's a medicinal therapy for personal plumbing. I mean we're talking bacon (not low sodium), sausage, grits, eggs scrambled in butter, biscuits dripping with butter (okay, I used the White Lily premix packages; so what?), and and a lot of rich coffee. We all know I didn't cook in the mornings, because why cook when you're alone? Too depressing. But a house full of life needed a full breakfast and that was what I served.

"Come on, y'all! Grits are getting cold!"

We gathered at the table and after the first bites, the conversation began in full force.

"So, what's the plan for today?" Jim said. "Pass the jam, please."

I pushed the jar of strawberry preserves in his direction and the biscuit basket too. He reached in for another one and hollered like he got stuck with a needle.

"Ow! What the hell is that?"

Jim had grabbed my sand dollar. I had this sand dollar that looked like a coaster. You put it in the oven with the biscuits and then placed it in the basket to keep them warm. At four hundred and fifty degrees, it could be mighty risky to grab it with bare hands. Usually, I put it under the napkin, but I'd been in a hurry and just stuck it in toward the bottom.

"You okay?" I asked and jumped up to get him some ice.

"Yeah, I'm fine. Don't get up!"

I was already up and in the kitchen, digging in my icemaker for some cubes to drop in a Ziploc.

"What is that thing? Some kind of weapon?"

"A biscuit warmer. I gotta renew my license for it."

"Mom's a riot, isn't she?"

"Watch it, kiddo." I handed the bag to Jim. "Hold this on the hot spot for a few minutes."

"I swear to God! I'm fine! Really!"

"Eat! Today is a busy day!"

"So what's up, Mom? Do we have any OJ?"

"Sorry, honey, I forgot juice. It's too healthy anyway. Right after breakfast, I am taking both of you to the *Palms!*"

"All *right!*" Emily said.

"We are going to do final inspection and then this afternoon, we are all having a barbecue in the backyard. Arthur's coming."

"Should I hide myself under the bed?"

"Very funny. No, I think he's probably cool with everything."

"I'll just be around, you know, alone and pouty, making sure you don't do anything risqué."

"I appreciate that."

Breakfast was over in one-tenth the time it took to prepare it. That was what annoyed me about cooking. First, you went to the store, then you hauled everything home, put it all away, took it out again, cooked it, and then everyone ate it in two seconds. Then, you got to clear the table, wash the dishes, scrub the pots, and take out the garbage. You could get exhausted just thinking about it. However, my little gripe session aside, it had been wonderful to look around the table at Jim and Emily enjoying something I had prepared. For a moment I felt like one of those fifties moms on *Father Knows Best*, except that on second look my daughter looked like a backup singer for Marilyn Manson and my ex-husband could do a wicked lip-sync to Barbra Streisand anything.

After the dishes were all done, the bedrooms cleaned up, and we were all dressed, I wanted to get everyone organized to go to the salon for last-minute anything. I called Lucy to see if she wanted to come along.

"Oh, honey! Can I meet y'all down there? I'm trying to find sheets and towels for David. He called me and should be here any minute."

"No problem. Can I get you anything?"

I was walking toward Emily's room with the cordless phone to pull up Jim's bed. Emily was in the closet, rummaging for something to wear.

"No, I bought enough groceries and beer for a football team! You know how boys eat! But thanks."

"Okay, see you later."

I clicked off and looked out the window at the red Saab pulling up in Lucy's driveway.

"Emily!" I said in a whisper. "Come here!"

Emily had put on ancient jeans and a tight black T-shirt from a Grateful Dead concert tour. She looked like Miss Defiant, USA.

"Wha . . . ?"

Holding back the curtain like spies, we watched the young man we assumed to be David unfold himself from the front seat of his adorable car. He stood up and stretched.

"Oh, shit. He's totally ripped."

"Yeah," I said, "he's worth a shot."

Emily cut her eyes at me and we giggled.

"You're a perv, Mom," she said.

"I most certainly am not! Well, maybe a little." I wiggled my eye-brows at her. "Come on. We've got tons to do."

"I'm just gonna quickly change, okay? Just gimme a few."

"No problem."

Apparently she decided her ensemble wasn't the most alluring combination to be caught wearing around a prospective date who, from across the yard and through our walls, was emitting the vibration of a screaming jungle animal. I had the distinct impression that I was about to witness my daughter in a way I'd never seen her. If it had been anybody else's teenager, it might have been amusing. We were still at the starting line, and I was not amused.

"Ask Daddy if we can take his convertible."

"Sure."

"I mean, I just think it would be more fun, you know?"

"Yeah, definitely."

"I'll drive," she said.

All at once I realized I was just as uncomfortable about my daughter and her sexuality as my father had always been about mine. Well! That wasn't very modern thinking, was it? I decided I wouldn't be an old poop, that I would take the wait-and-see approach. It seemed very sensible at the moment.

I didn't know if Lucy's nephew was watching as we got into Jim's car and pulled away, but Emily did enough posturing around the outside of the car to warrant it. Somewhere in her belongings she had come up with faded jeans (tight), a white T-shirt (tight), and it appeared that all body piercing ornamentation had been temporar-ily removed. Her hair was tucked up in a baseball hat and she had on sunglasses. Right out of the blue, I began to worry that he *wouldn't* find her attractive. How stupid! How pathetically typical. But if he didn't fall immediately in love with Emily I would be furi-ous with David, Lucy, and all their ancestors back to the potato famine.

We drove along the short distance never going over twenty-five miles an hour. Traffic was terrible, but that was no surprise. The day was fabulously beautiful and it seemed that everyone was coming to the beach for the day. I loved this time of year. This was when women were full of hope for a new love and realized it was time to do their roots. Maybe highlights? Be a little more blond? Cut their hair like Glenn Close or Gwyneth Paltrow or whoever was on the cover of any supermarket magazine? We can *do* it! I couldn't wait to open the doors.

"Whatcha thinking about?" Jim said.

"Just thinking that I am a happy woman, I guess."

"Watch out, Mom. Optimism kills."

I didn't know what she meant by that—probably some college slang meaning that the universe would slam you if you got cocky—so I said, "Thanks. I'll dispense my optimism in small doses."

It must have been the right response because she said, "Good idea."

We parked in front of the salon and they stood looking at the shop while I fumbled around for the keys. I opened the door, turned off the alarm, and pushed up the lights.

"It's beautiful," Jim said.

"Très cool, Mom," Emily said. She immediately plunked herself into one of the leopard print chairs and began to spin herself around. "I like it."

Jim walked from back to front, looked through the products and the accessories, and took a deep breath before he spoke. I could tell he wanted to put in his two cents.

"Spit it out," I said.

"Okay," he said, "here's the opinion of one businessman. This place is fab, absolutely fab! *BUT!* It looks too conservative, too clean, too new. It doesn't scream out, *Come in this place and change your bloody life!* In fact, to be perfectly blunt, it doesn't scream anything."

"What does it need?"

You have to understand that if anybody else had said this I would've given them a left hook to the right jaw, but Jim was a visionary and I knew I should listen to anything he had to say.

"Let me surprise you, okay? You stay here and fuss around. Emily and I are going shopping."

"Have at it, bubba! I have tons to do, but you gotta take me home to get my own car."

"Deal. Let's go."

We drove home and I was so excited by what Jim had planned, even though I didn't know what it was that he *had* planned. It was fine. Whatever. Part of me hated having the responsibility for everything anyway. I had always depended on Jim and loved the fact that I could relax and not worry for a while. I would wash my hair and do my makeup and finish grocery shopping for Arthur's dinner of seduction, I mean, for the perfectly innocent evening I had planned to make up for that unfortunate incident at High Cotton.

"Just gimme two hours!"

"Take three! Thanks! Love y'all!"

It was just noon. I called Lucy to tell her that we weren't going to the salon yet. "The salon is being held hostage by Emily and Jim until further notice. I think he wants to fluff it—you know, add this and move that to give it the exact look that Jim thinks it needs?"

"That's fine! I'm still feeding the boy! *Six* sandwiches!"

"God knows what Jim's up to! Anyway, I'm getting dinner together for Arthur. I went to the New York Butcher yesterday and bought out the place."

"The New York Butcher? This must be *serious*, girl!"

"It is. I'm insane over Bill, the guy who owns it. I said to him, 'Listen, I think Mr. Right is coming to dinner tomorrow. What do you have wonderful that I can put on the grill and make him fall in love with me?' So he says, '*Whatever you do, don't overcook the meat.*' I said, '*yeah*'—I started imitating a Yankee accent without even thinking about it. Somehow when he opens his mouth he sounds like, I don't know, something between Al Pacino and Tom Brokaw. I always think I'm talking to a movie star when I'm around him for some stupid reason. What's the matter with me?"

"Good grief, Anna! Tom Brokaw? Take an antihistamine! Maybe it's pollen?"

Sometimes, Lucy said the dumbest things.

"Probably. Anyway, I'm running out to The Pig in a few minutes to get salad and sour cream and a few other things. When I get back we'll go over to the salon, okay?"

"Fine, gimme a shout. So what *are* you making for dinner?"

"Um, let's see. I got three pounds of different sausages—Bill makes them—standard sweet Italian and some others with garlic and pesto and then chicken sausages with apples and onions. They're insanely excellent. Then I got some tiny New Zealand lamb chops and some pork chops stuffed with rosemary, mozzarella and garlic. I figured I'd grill all that and serve it with stuffed potatoes and a big salad. If that doesn't bring this boy to his knees, I don't know what will."

"And what are we wearing to drive him wild?"

"Who the hell knows? Whatever I can find that's clean. Maybe I'll buy a new T-shirt at the Piggly Wiggly in honor of all the pork that went down the tubes for our dinner. Wha'd'ya think?"

"You're a regular Pamela Anderson, honey. Why don't you stop by Banana Republic and get a V-neck something and a short skirt?"

"If I have time. Maybe."

And some thong underwear and a Miracle Bra . . . you know? I felt like saying, *Do you think it would be obvious to serve dinner with an air mattress strapped to my back?* I mean, I knew everybody in the world (except me) was obsessed with sex appeal and all that and yes, I was in the beauty business. But, I was in the beauty business from a *service* point of view. People needed their hair cut, I cut it. They wanted color, I colored. Trim? I trimmed. I didn't believe in promoting personal insecurity. I prided myself on conservative advice and promoted healthy skin and hair. Boy, was I boring or what?

I thought about my boring persona up and down the aisles of the Piggly Wiggly, blaming overexposure to my father as the culprit. He was the most conservative man on the earth. I confess I had always thought it was the best way to be. Nice and safe. But did he seek out conservative mainstream women? No, he didn't, did he? They came to him, arms wrapped up in hope and chicken parmesan, thinking they were simpatico, that they could fill each other's voids. No committed relationship had ever materialized from any of them. No, when Daddy was following his natural instincts, his hunt was quite different. He liked beauty queens like Momma and tarty babes like Lucy.

By the time I got around to the bread aisle I realized Daddy had a glaring weakness for commercial beauty. Maybe most men did. Maybe I was another divorced idiot who had always praised substance over style and finery over fashion. The burning questions were, Could my self-respect (*insecurity*) keep me warm at night? Would my principles (*gross fear of rejection*) give me comfort? I had to face it. I was going to be single for the rest of my life or I was going to have to loosen up. I paid for the groceries and went straight to Belk's.

Now, Belk's wasn't the sexiest store in the world, but it had very nice merchandise for the sensible woman. It took me two seconds in the Ralph Lauren department to realize I needed something besides black pants and another black top. To hell with sensible for once. I walked out and went to Banana Republic and decided to buy something young and fun. It seemed that every article of clothing was the same price. Inside of half an hour I had tried on and bought an aqua tank top with spaghetti straps and a thin short cardigan that matched; a beige stretch cotton short straight skirt with a little slit; and low platform aqua slides. I felt like a whore but the salesgirl assured me that her mother had the same outfit. This did very little to lift more than my left eyebrow. (Note, if I ever go into the retail clothing business—Cut off tongues of all sales job applicants under twenty-two. And it might not be a bad idea to slap them silly once a day.)

I went home to organize my kitchen and grill. I laid the clothes on my bed and looked at them. How could this little bit of fabric and leather cost over two hundred dollars? Was I crazy? I *never* spent money like this!

That's why you're single.

Oh, fine. What would Jim say? Emily? They would say nothing because if they did I wouldn't feed them. It was three-thirty. I called Jim's cell.

"Hey! How goes the war?"

I could hear hammers in the background. What in the world was he *doing?*

"Everything's good! Hey! I had an idea. . . ."

"What else is new?"

"Let's have cocktails here. What do you say? I actually picked up some champagne and pâté at the wine store in Towne Centre. . . ."

Bang! Bang! Bang! Hammer! Buzzzzzz!

"Jim? Do I hear a chain saw?"

"Um, yeah. A little one. So, come over around five? Five-thirty?"

Despite the fact that Jim muffled the phone, I heard a man in the shop say, *"Mr. Abbot, where do you want us to run the plumbing conduit for the cappuccino machine?"* My heart started pounding. Then another voice said, *"Do you have a minute to look at the magazine racks?"*

It was too late to panic. I took a deep breath and said, "I'll see you around five-thirty."

I called Lucy again and told her to relax, that we would go over together when Arthur arrived.

"Fine with me," she said. "David's still eating."

While I was dressing I thanked God I had a daughter and not a Hoover like David. I spent some time in thought about Arthur, deciding he was a better diversion than obsessing about the salon and Jim's formidable theatrics. Whatever Jim had done, I would rave about it, say he was wonderful, and change it later if I didn't like it.

The doorbell rang and my face and neck got hot. I checked my lips in the mirror, gave my neck a squirt of Chanel No. 5, and went to the door. Arthur was standing there with a bunch of grocery store flowers and a package wrapped in white paper. Even through the screen door, he smelled delicious.

"Hi," I said, "come on in."

"Hey," he said. "God! You look great! Really great."

"I do?" *I didn't look like an ass? This was good. Okay. Breathe.*

"Yeah, here—these are for you and I brought us some cheese."

"Thanks! That was so sweet of you!" Suddenly I didn't know what to do with him. Should I tell him to sit on the couch? Show him the house? What—two bedrooms and the spot where he stood?

Tell him to come with you and open the wine.

Right. Thanks.

"Come with me and help me open the wine."

For God's sake, Anna, don't show him the bedrooms.

He followed me to the kitchen. I opened the refrigerator and leaned down to get the wine from the bottom shelf; realizing my behind was probably showing, I quickly tugged at my skirt. I felt his hand on my wrist.

"Don't worry," he said, "I'm not looking at your beige-lace-covered perfect, um, pardon the word, ass. I'm a gentleman, remember?"

I stood up slowly with the wine in my right hand and turned to look at him. I could feel a tingle in every part of my body. I was all at once mortified and excited. This Arthur person was quite possibly the most powerful male energy I had tripped across in years. And, he had taken a shower for me and put on some deadly cologne. Yeah, boy, hot night ahead. All it takes is a shower? Take it easy, I told myself.

I was standing right next to him and could feel the heat of his body.

"This kitchen's pretty small," I said, "and I'm not used to skirts. The corkscrew's in the drawer there." I pointed right behind him and bit my lip, thinking I might die any second.

"Did you say *screw?*" He started laughing and then I did too.

"You know what? You already think I'm a drunk. Could you please not think I'm a slut too? Jeesch! Men!"

"Good save, Anna," he said, rifling the drawer until he came up with the corkscrew, "but let's face the facts. You and I both know there's some wild energy here and neither one of us is going to be able to concentrate until we find out what it is."

"Okay, Casanova, look," I said, feeling witty for having called him Casanova, which should give you a clear picture of what a dope I am, "there's heat for sure, but don't you prefer the fantasy? I mean, isn't it more fun to wonder for a while what I taste like?" Good one, Anna.

"I did that last night," he said and popped the cork. "Where's your daughter and Jim?"

"They're at the salon," I said and gulped, "why?"

He poured some wine into two goblets I had placed in front of him. What a stupid question. *Why? Why? Was I serious?*

"Because I didn't want to have them walk in the room while, um, if, I mean . . ."

Well, I told myself, at least he had the good grace to flounder around and not just say something stupid like *I didn't want them to come in and find my hand under your sweater.*

"If what?" I said.

"I just wanted to be alone with you for a few minutes. I mean, I know this sounds like something out of a Bogart and Bacall movie, but all last night I couldn't sleep. I kept thinking I wanted to sort of, I don't know, stand around you and just feel what that was like. I just, I mean, there's this feeling you give off or something. I don't think I've ever known anyone like you."

My eyebrows arched at that part. *Never known anyone like me?* He almost had me going until that dumb statement.

"Except for Sheila. Now there was a *woman!* And except for Andrea! Andrea was . . ." His eyes drifted off through the window.

"You're a jerk, you know that?" I started to giggle. He had dimples.

"And the romance is off to a great start!"

"Maybe," I said. "Cheers." I loved dimples.

We clinked our glasses and looked at each other over the tops of them. We were going to have a blast together. (Blast furnace.)

I put my glass down on the counter and said, "Soooo, we're supposed to call Lucy, my neighbor, and tell her when we're ready to go down to the salon to see it. Emily and Jim are serving cocktails there at five-thirty. They've been decorating all afternoon."

He slid his arm around my waist and pulled me to him. God, he felt good! I could tell he was smelling my hair. I felt him kiss the top of my head. Just a light kiss. So sweet.

"Then, we can't keep everyone waiting." He pushed me back and looked in my face. "Can we?"

"Five minutes one way or the other won't kill them."

"Let's take the cheese down there!"

"Fine. The cheese. Right."

To hell with the cheese. Jim had cheese. No, Jim had pâté. Oh, who cared? I wanted to hang in Arthur's arms and let him hold me up. I wanted to sink to the floor and have him follow me. I told myself this all-consuming feeling was merely wanton lust. And then I told myself that lust was a worthy and wonderful thing, a chemical fact that had preserved the species and who was I to deny it? It was proof of God and the devil, heaven and hell.

"We'd better get out of here," I said, "you're dangerous."

"You sure?"

Fate reached out and delivered Lucy and David to my front door, banging and yoo-hooing.

"Come on! Let's go!" Lucy said.

I could tell she had come in the door and was headed for the kitchen where we stood, just as though a heat-detecting chip was imbedded in her forearm. We dropped our arms and stepped away from each other, clearing our throats and assuming the polite smiles necessary for the sake of social grace.

"We're in here," I called out, "come on back and have a sip of wine with us!"

"Do we have time? Is the bottle open? Y'all, this is David! My nephew!"

I took one look at David and said, "Don't come anywhere near my daughter. I'm not kidding."

"Anna!" Lucy said. "You don't mean that!"

"Of course I don't! Just kidding, David. Nice to meet you. This is Arthur."

I meant it. I didn't want this David anywhere near Emily. He was too good-looking for all of us. Nothing but trouble.

Twenty-one

A Little Help from My Friends

LUCY, Arthur, David the Young and Dangerous, and I jammed ourselves into Arthur's car and arrived at the salon in what seemed like a flash. It wasn't that Arthur drove too fast; it was one of those mysterious encounters with time speeding ahead because you were so caught up in conversation. We were all excited for different reasons.

Lucy wanted David to meet Emily and she was dying to see what Jim had done. David wanted to see what Emily looked like and he could have cared less about the salon. Arthur was politely curious to see the salon, but only because it was mine. I already knew that Jim had performed some magic and I was more than a little on edge with anticipation to know how the evening would progress with Arthur. The guy was frigging *hot*—what can I say? Something in me knew that this was going to be a decisive day—one I wouldn't forget.

I wasn't really paying attention to the salon front as we pulled into our parking space. We were all chatting away like a bunch of birds on a wire. I grabbed my purse and was talking to Lucy about dinner when I noticed the look of surprise on her face. I turned toward my salon and nearly fainted from shock. I hardly recognized it and I'm not exaggerating.

The clean front now sported two oversized clay planters. The bases of them were encircled with three-inch bamboo poles held together with intricately tied hemp and twine. They held two of the most glorious deep green, luscious dwarf palms I had ever seen. They must have cost a fortune. Men were coming and going from the entrance with tools, cables, and garbage headed for their trucks. And our awning, which had been a basic aluminum overhang to provide shelter from rain, was now covered in a thick layering of breezy palm fronds.

That wasn't all. Oh, no. You might recall that the salon had clear glass windows, floor to ceiling. You could look through to the receptionist desk, a tiny waiting area, and the display of merchandise. Not anymore. The windows were now covered in two five-foot bamboo walls and I could only imagine what was behind them. I took a deep breath. Then, another.

"Keep breathing," Lucy said, and patted me on the arm. "Let's go in."

If Lucy had some reservations, can you imagine where that left me? All Arthur said was, "Cool."

We stepped inside between the gorgeously toned men in tight T-shirts, with excellent haircuts, who were coming and going, obviously finishing up. They were too fabulous looking to be anything but friends of Jim.

"Excuse me, ma'am."

"Pardon me, ma'am, I just have to get this through the door."

All I could do was look at them and sigh.

There must have been fifteen people bustling around and no sign of Jim. Emily rushed over, gushing, and her face was flushed with enthusiasm.

"Isn't it awesome, Mom? Come see!"

"Oh, my God!" Lucy said. "It's fabulous!"

But my feet were rooted to the entrance area. It *was* stunning. No, it was mind-bending! Our bare-bones décor had been morphed into something from a fantasy. I was in a high-tech jungle. The bamboo wall to the left of the front door held pale green thick glass shelving, with bull-nosed edges, suspended from the ceiling by brushed steel cables. Every other shelf held one of Angel's baskets, filled with the merchandise we had bought. Displayed this way, you wanted to pick up each item and take them all home.

It was the lighting! I looked up to see tiny lamps descending from the ceiling on bendable cables so that you could adjust the spots in any direction. The bulbs were an amber color, which explained the warmth they spread over the tortoise-patterned bamboo. The left wall now held a stainless steel cabinet that could have been from a professional kitchen. On the bottom were two doors I imagined were for supplies and on the top was an elaborate cappuccino machine—the kind you see in restaurants—with copper tubing and glass canisters, shining and beckoning. On the left and right were smaller glass shelves that held slim black mugs and chrome accessories—a sugar bowl, another bowl filled with sugar substitutes, and a cylindrical container with tiny spoons. I pulled open the bottom doors and saw that one side held a small refrigerator and the other was for supplies and waste.

To the right, opposite the wall of products and against a low wall of the same bamboo, was a low-back, black leather bench with chrome legs where three people could wait in relative comfort. Across the top of the bamboo wall were bushy ferns in sweetgrass baskets. He had sacrificed my waiting space by a hair, but in all truth, whether or not we would have people waiting still remained to be seen.

I turned to the reception desk, which was the same, but resituated on an angle. A matching bench sat against the outside bamboo wall and floor-to-ceiling cables, installed like a ladder, held every latest magazine, for clients to read.

Jim appeared from the back room and gave me a huge hug and shook hands with David, whose eyes were riveted on Emily, who was oblivious to him.

"Hey! Don't you love it? I said, Jim, son, this place needs some excitement. It's small, you know? So I was thinking, *African Queen*—right? I mean, some combination of tropical and mysterious but slick, hip. Right? So what do you think?" He was talking a million miles an hour.

I was stupefied. It was incredible. It was unbelievable. It was a classic Jim maneuver.

"I adore you! That's what I think! To the extent that it's possible to think at all . . ."

"There's more! Come see!"

"Jim! You're a regular Houdini!" Lucy said. "I swear you are! Isn't he a Houdini, y'all?"

We followed him and listened while he described each detail.

"Okay, the cappuccino machine is leased. It's free, actually. You just have to buy coffee from them, which comes in these little pods for forty-five cents each. It makes divine coffee, by the cup, in thirty seconds. Or you could make cappuccino if you feel like frothing milk, but puh-leez! Who has the patience?"

"Not me," I said. I shook my head.

"Me either! I got the glass and cable from a guy I used to know who does display for Dillard's and he and his team put them up for us for nothing because I sent him on a wine tour all through Burgundy and Épernay three years ago. I couldn't go—had the flu. Remember when I was so sick? Anyway, he owed me, massively. He did the lighting too—left over from a store renovation. Those were all his guys you saw when you came in. I bought the bulbs at Lowe's—I was thinking rose, because rose lighting could flatter the worst bulldog, but they didn't have rose and actually, I think amber is better, what do you think? It's warmer."

He was babbling like the proverbial brook.

"Jim!"

"What? Something wrong? Oh, God! She hates it!"

I started laughing and so did he. "It's beautiful!"

"Are you Emily?" I heard David say to her.

I turned around, realizing I had forgotten to introduce them. Emily narrowed her eyes at him with suspicion all over her like gnats at dusk.

"Yeah, I'm Emily. You're David, right?"

"Yeah."

"Cool."

"Yeah. Cool."

I looked at Lucy and Jim and then at Arthur and we all shrugged our shoulders, sort of guffawing like old farts do when they realize they're old farts and there's another generation ramping up to take our place. *What do they know? They're so young! What harm could there be? Ah! Youth! Wasted on the young!* We shared simultaneous thoughts. I probably would have given it higher focus at another place in time, but at the moment I was so busy looking at the changes to the salon, that I let their attraction slide, telling myself that Emily would have no more than a passing interest in him anyway. He wasn't her type. He was too normal looking.

"Does this ship have a galley?" Arthur said. "I brought some hors d'oeuvres."

"Oh! Did you bring wine? I could use a glass of something, I think," Lucy said.

"I've got champagne! Veuve Clicquot, of course—the chateau's run by a woman, you know. Thought it was appropriate!" Jim said. "Come on, Arthur, I'll show you the catering facility."

I knew Jim was kidding but followed them through the salon to the back, thinking, *who knew?* The four stations were relatively unchanged except for the same bendable lights that surrounded the mirrors like Medusas and each station had an elliptical clear glass vase of lucky bamboo. It was just what they needed.

The ceiling of the shampoo area had posters of tropical destinations, affixed by decoupage. I guess he thought people should have something to look at while they had their hair washed. Why not? At the back, where I had the small washer and dryer, Jim had put up overhead racking, which now sported at least sixty inexpensive wineglasses and a small refrigerator in the closet. We opened the cheese on the washer and put it together on a cutting board Jim had obviously bought, along with cocktail napkins. Arthur handed me the box of water crackers, which I opened.

"Amazing!" I said. "You're too marvelous for words, Jim!"

Jim popped the cork, singing the old Cole Porter tune, throwing in an occasional *It's so true!*

"My God! Emily! I forgot to buy a stereo!"

We cracked up again. He filled glasses while Arthur offered everyone crackers with two different and delicious cheeses. We sipped before toasting; we toasted a thousand times and sipped some more, refilling glasses all around. It was a very exciting moment, and another sign of Jim's generosity and affection for us.

"Congratulations, Anna!" Jim said.

"Thanks! But, please! It wouldn't be this without *you*, you know. I guess I'll have to be an organ donor for you, huh? Thanks to you this place looks as exciting as I feel! And thanks to you too, Emily! I'm sure Daddy worked your butt off!"

"You wouldn't believe!" she said and rolled her eyes for David's benefit. "He had me running and making a thousand phone calls! I called towel people . . ."

"I ordered two hundred black terry cloth turbans with embroidered gold metallic palm trees," Jim said, "my treat! They'll be dee-vine!"

"Good Lord!" I said. "Thanks! You're too much!"

"And the smocks!" Jim said. "Emily, tell her about the smocks!"

"Oh, Momma! They're so outrageous! They have pockets! Leopard print, with the new logo up here, and the best is—"

"New logo?"

I looked at Jim, who quickly uncrossed his arms, covered his face, and peeked through his fingers.

"Well, this was Emily's idea, Anna. It seemed to us that with all this glorious new theater here that you needed a more exciting name for your business, you know?"

"Such as . . . ?" I said.

"Anna's Cabana? The sign's coming tomorrow—fuchsia neon! Big rush job! My treat too! I know, I know, that means you have to change your business cards."

"Already done," Emily said, "be here Wednesday. And your invoices and letterhead. I'll order checks tomorrow. Bank's closed. Sunday and all, right?"

"My treat too!" Jim said.

"Great God Almighty!" I started giggling and couldn't stop.

Arthur gave Jim a playful punch on his arm.

"You are something else! I gotta hand it to you!"

"This is a helluva lot cheaper than alimony, believe me!"

Arthur silently mouthed his surprise to me. *No alimony?*

I shook my head and shrugged my shoulders, indicating that it was fine with me.

There was a commotion at the front and a man's voice called out for attention. He had a huge box on a hand truck and he looked harried.

"Where do you want the smoothie machine?"

Smoothie machine? "Hang it from the ceiling! Jim? Have you gone insane?"

"It only does one flavor and it's supposed to fit right next to the cappuccino machine. I measured twice! So now you can offer a daily smoothie for your clients in the morning and vino in the afternoon! *N'est-ce pas?*"

"I love smoothies!" Lucy said. "They're so good for you too!"

Jim and Emily went to help the delivery man with Lucy and David on their heels. I looked at Arthur and he looked at me.

"*N'est-ce pas,*" I said, "ever since he started going to France years ago he's been *n'est-ce pas*-ing the world ever since. Is he wild or what?"

"I got some *n'est-ce pas* for you, little girl."

Arthur's eyes were dancing, his dimples were showing again, and I thought he was the most adorable man in the world.

"Oooh! Am I supposed to be afraid?"

It was easy to be a big old flirt with people all around. Five minutes later I would wish I had said something slightly more conservative. But, hell no. Not with Arthur. Couldn't say something coy like, *Oh, hush, you bad boy!* Then, I wondered how in the world we would find five minutes to be alone anyway when it seemed the evening had enough people in it to cast *The Ten Commandments*. And, naturally, Daddy would be there, adding one more pair of eyes. Safe. I was safe. And, it crossed my mind that I had better keep an eye on Emily and the young Mr. Hot Lips.

We soon peeled ourselves from the salon and within the hour actually moved dinner from the grill to the table. There was so much going on, not only in my head but with all you have to do to feed seven people. How had Jim done it? Did I remember to buy half-and-half? I couldn't recall anyone who had ever thrilled any person I had ever known the way Jim had just knocked me off my feet. I never could have imagined what he had done and maybe that was one reason why we had always been so close. He was a daredevil with vision.

When Daddy arrived, Lucy drove him back to the salon to see it. He came back home whistling through his teeth. He sat down in my living room and Lucy sat on the arm of his chair, handing him a Beck's. Just so you know, she had wrapped the bottle in a paper napkin. Her second career seemed to be Spoiling Daddy.

"So? What do you think?" I said, standing there with a platter of grilled meat.

"'Anna's Cabana'? That's one helluva sideshow you got there, honey. You won't get many men in there, though. Too weird."

"Glad you like it, Daddy. Let the men keep going to Causey's! They're too cheap to pay for our talent anyway! We're gonna eat in about two minutes, okay?"

Causey's Barber Shop was one of the great institutions of Mount Pleasant and had been around since the Flood. No straight man I knew would spend forty dollars for me to cut their hair if they could get it done for twelve dollars at Causey's. It made perfect economic sense. But that was how Daddy was. Slightly negative, too critical, and always looking for the holes in your plan. He couldn't help it. To be honest, if my salon wasn't for clients like Daddy that was probably, no, *definitely* a good thing.

I put the platter of meat on the table next to the salad bowl and the bread basket. I just had to evacuate the potatoes from the oven and my first official dinner party would be in progress.

Emily was in the kitchen with David. My good child was putting sour cream in a bowl for the table. I had to put out butter, salt and pepper, and chives and remember to eavesdrop.

"So, how's Carolina?" she said to him.

"It's all right, I guess. How's Georgetown?"

"Hard as hell but completely excellent," she said, slightly smug that admission to her school was more difficult to gain. "I thought summer would never get here."

"Yeah, me too. What are you gonna major in?"

"Dunno," she said. "Mom? You want me to mince the chives?"

"That would be great, honey," I said.

Safe. Benign. So far. I took the potatoes to the table thinking that Emily, who never lifted a finger unless I threatened to cut one off, was mincing chives. Man, I thought, are pheromones powerful or what? Giving the table a last check, I decided that everything looked fine.

"Okay, y'all! Let's have dinner."

Jim was the first to step·up and fix himself a plate. I leaned over to whisper in his ear.

"I really love you, you know," I said.

"As well you should!" he said and kissed my cheek. "This looks delicious and I deserve to be fed!"

"Anytime, old boy, the door's always open. Just sit anywhere."

Lucy was right behind him. "Can I sit in your daddy's lap?" She giggled and batted her eyelashes.

Old Lucy had been spending secret time with Mr. M, as in Martini.

"If you want, be my guest!"

Jim shuddered and walked away.

"I was thinking I might wear a coconut bra and a print sarong to work. What do you think, Anna?"

"I think *NO!*" I said, without a second thought.

Arthur appeared with two opened bottles of red wine and said, "I think YES!"

"Gee whiz, Anna, it was just a joke," Lucy said with a pout.

I gave her a little knock in the arm. "I knew that."

Emily put the sour cream and chives on the table and David, a dead ringer for a vulture surveying his next roadside picnic, loomed over the sausages and chops. Sniffing. Sniffing and rubbing his washboard stomach in small circular movements.

"Man! I'm starving," he said. "This looks really, really excellent!"

"Dig in!" I said, when what I should have said was *Hang on, cupcake, let the old people live. Your Aunt Lucy warned me about you.*

Somebody must've taught the boy some manners because he said, "Nah. Y'all serve everybody else first."

I must've looked askance because he added, "Seriously!"

Well! What a nice kid!

A short while later, I looked around my living room to check the temperature. Arthur was talking to Emily and David. Lucy was entertaining Daddy and Jim. I took the last lone lamb chop, half a potato, and a spoon of salad and sat on the floor next to my coffee table, passing the bread basket around.

"A toast!" I said. "Not to get too mushy or anything . . ."

"Ah, come on, Mom! Spare us!"

"Emily? Darlin'?" Lucy said. "Let your momma say wha'ever she wants! Okay?"

I reminded myself to make coffee. Regular. Negotiating the yard could be dangerous.

"Um, I just want to say thanks!" I looked from face to face. "I mean it! I love y'all and thanks!"

"Here, here!" Emily said and raised her Diet Coke.

"You're welcome." Jim said and blew me an air kiss.

"We love you too!" Daddy said.

"Gee! Do you love me too?" Arthur said.

Everyone stopped and looked at me.

"Jerk. Just eat, okay?" I said.

"Ah, God! Now I'm gonna cry," he said.

The women snickered and the men shook their heads. Arthur, despite his dopey sense of humor, was trying to be a part of things. And I, who had been without a man since before Lucy's last (or maybe first) surgical procedure, loved it.

Dinner was, thank the Lord, delicious. You know how baked potatoes can be crispy-skinned and all but collapsed inside? That's how they were. Personally, I think it depends on the potato and the humidity or something like that. And the meat was a perfect medium rare and juicy. The salad was crispy—it's critical to pick the correct bag—and the bread was fresh and tasty. A good first dinner. The wine had made us all comfortable enough with each other for stories to flow. I had heard it said many times that a great party is dependent on the guests and I could see then that it was true. My small gang ran the gamut. The mix was perfect.

Lucy and Daddy left first. Lucy made some statement about having to change the website right away but we all knew better. David and Emily went off to Wal-Mart to buy a mini stereo for the salon, saying they'd be back in an hour. Jim insisted on doing the dishes and told Arthur and me to go for a walk on the beach. As much as I wanted to do just that, I knew Jim was exhausted and we wound up cleaning the kitchen together. Once the dishwasher was humming, Jim excused himself, leaving Arthur and me alone in the kitchen.

"So? Wanna go for a walk?"

"The beach is where I saw you for the first time," I said. "But, do you think we should wait for Emily and David to get back?"

"Nah, screw 'em. They're fine."

"Right. To hell with 'em. I'll get my cardigan."

Arthur improved my mood. Where I worried about everything, he seemed not to worry about anything.

We walked across the dunes and were struck by the enormity of the night, the dazzling dark sky, and the song of the ocean. The moon was full and prominent, throwing a faint light all over the beach, the kind of light I saw in my dreams—not day but not night either. We walked near the edge of the water, our shoes left behind at the path. Our hair was blowing like crazy, our faces were damp with spray, and I thought this must have been the most romantic moment I had experienced in my entire life. It wasn't long until he stopped and pulled me toward him by my waist. His pant legs were almost in the surf and the tide was coming in.

"Okay, Anna Lutz Abbot, I'm going to kiss you now."

"Fair warning," I said, for no reason at all, sounding like a celibate nerd at an auction house.

When his lips touched mine I thought, *Okay, just throw me down right here. I don't care.* I might never get tired of Arthur's lips, I said to myself. He smelled right, he tasted right and he felt right. God in heaven, I thought as my heartbeat increased, I'm in trouble now.

We stood in the water's edge, kissing, stopping to look at each other now and then and then kissing some more. We moved away from the water so we wouldn't get soaked and continued kissing like teenagers.

"Arthur?"

"Hmmm?"

"I haven't felt like this in forever," I said, letting my feelings hang out there to be abused.

"I want to make love to you, Anna."

Oh, God! Now what, big shot? Now what are you gonna tell him?

My voice squeaked. "I can't," I said.

"Why not," he said, "you got a headache?"

"Worse," I said, "I got a teenager."

"Right, we had better get back? You want to go?"

"Not yet," I said.

Neither one of us moved. I put my hands on his face and traced his jawline with my fingers. I swore to myself that he had the ideal jaw and the perfect chin. He grabbed my wrist and kissed every fingertip and then the center of my palm. The tide washed over our feet and we stepped away again. This time I leaned into his chest with my arms around his waist and he held me close. I could have stood there for a very long time, maybe until sunrise. I felt like I was falling over the edge of the world.

Later, as I tossed myself around the bed, trying not to rouse Emily from her sleep, I told myself the feelings I had for Arthur were just physical. On the other hand, I really liked him. He was adorable, attentive, smart, solvent, had a dumb but lively sense of humor . . . I had a whole list going in my head when suddenly another country was heard from.

"Did you kiss him?"

"Yeah," I said, "big time."

"That's good, Mom. Now, let's get some sleep, okay?"

Twenty-two

Show Time!

◦━━◦

*D*O I need to tell anyone here that I was in the salon at seven-thirty, dressed to kill—okay, maybe to maim— makeup on, drinking my third cup of coffee, and I had already read my horoscope and Liz Smith? Bettina and Brigitte were coming in at eight-thirty, followed by Lucy, Jim, and Emily at nine. I checked the book. Brigitte had appointments all morning, Bettina had appointments all day, and I had a few, scattered over the morning and the afternoon. *Anna's Cabana* (heaven help me with that idiotic name) was almost open for business.

I looked up when I heard Bettina's ancient Chevrolet come moaning and chugging into the parking lot, looking for a place to die. It lurched forward, and with each lurch a considerable amount of dark fumes billowed from underneath it. When she threw it into park, it appeared to give out its last gasp. Fanning away the clouds of stench, Bettina was dwarfed by the sheer size of her car. She opened the enormous trunk and pulled out a heavy box. I called out to her as she crossed the empty parking spaces, her back arched from the weight, taking quick steps on her platform sandals.

"Hey! That's some *vee-hickle* you got there, sugar! You want me to call Father Michaels to give it the Last Rites?"

"Yeah, right? I told Tony, I said, 'Look, if I get a ticket for causing a health hazard from The Yacht, you can pay it! Not me!'" Then she saw the salon entrance. "Holy whopping shit! What the hell happened?"

"My ex-husband got in a mood. Come on in and see. Here, let me help you with that." The Yacht, indeed. More like the Kon-Tiki.

She went back to get another box. Bettina from Brooklyn had arrived and she was moving in. The one I carried must've had a thousand bottles of nail polish in it. I dropped it on the bench by the door. She was right behind me with another box.

"I ordered polish. I guess I forgot to tell you."

"I owned it so I brought it. What the *hell* . . . ? This place looks like something outta Vegas!"

This made me nervous, to say the least. I was insecure enough as it was. "Do you think it's too much?"

"Whaddya nuts? It totally rocks! I love it!" She stood there, little skinny chicken that she was, in her black stretch capri pants and black halter, clacking away on her gum. She looked all around and was grinning from ear to ear, commenting on everything. "Would you look at this coffeemaker? All we had at my last salon was a Bunn machine! And this bamboo? Jeez! I'm in the rain forest here! All these ferns? Gorgeous! It's the hills of Costa Rica!"

"Really?"

"I swear to God, Anna. This is gonna be all over town by tonight! We might make CNN with this joint! *People* magazine! Who knows?" She stood with her hands on her hips, shaking her head. "So. Where do I put my table? I gotta do tips on Mrs. Milligan at nine-thirty. Wait till everyone sees this! Hot shit."

"Put it in between the chairs on the left, I think." Her small manicuring table could roll anywhere. "Actually, put it wherever you like the light."

"There ain't much light in the rain forest, right? Well, I'll pull a couple of those bottom hoses around to light my table. The good thing about this table is that I can bring it to the client, you know? You don't *have* to tell me *why* your *ex-husband* did this. I mean, it's none of *my* business. I always mind my own business. Learned that lesson in New York, if you know what I mean."

"My ex-husband is as gay as a goose and he loves to create . . . I don't know, scenery?"

"He's *what?*"

"Listen, Bettina, here's what I'm thinking. This salon has gotta have the seal of confession between us girls. We're gonna be living together, right? We're all gonna be telling each other everything sooner or later. So, yeah, my ex-husband is gay, but there's a story that goes with it. . . ."

"I'll *bet* there is!"

"And, I'll tell you all about him and me. Eventually. In fact, he's coming in this morning. You'll *adore* him. Everyone does."

"Jeez, my Bobby thinks decorating is the same thing as making a pyramid outta his empty beer cans! Right? Ain't it the truth?"

Bettina began to laugh and sort of snort like crazy and her whole little body shook when she did. It was the kind of contagious laughter that I had been starving for, but I sure hated to think about her cussing in front of clients. I never did that and I hoped she wouldn't. I made us two cups of coffee and handed one to her. We clinked the rims and toasted.

"Welcome to Anna's Cabana," I said. "My husband and daughter changed the name."

"You're shitting me, right?"

"I never shit anybody, Bettina, and never say 'shit' in front of the clients or you gotta put a dollar in the cussing box."

"No problem. You ain't gonna get my money."

"Good! Mine either!" Well, I thought, I hope that takes care of that! "Yeah, so they changed the name and ordered a new sign. Sign's supposed to be coming this morning. Then we'll have two. This one's neon, no less. We're gonna have a little confusion over that, but I figured what the heck. They were so excited and full of beans over it and I don't care too much."

"I woulda done the same thing. After all, they built you a movie set and everything."

"Exactly!"

"Shit! I got it! Here's what we gotta do! We gotta make T-shirts! We can sell 'em! On the front they can read ANNA'S CABANA and on the back we can put FORMERLY KNOWN AS THE PALMS SALON AND SPA FOR ABOUT FIVE MINUTES!"

"Definitely!" *Definitely not!*

Well, I thought, shoot. I'm holding a one-way ticket to Tacky Town and the train's leaving the station. Too late to get a refund. Maybe everything would all work out fine. I sure hoped so because I had everything I owned—and *didn't own*—riding on it. I showed her how to use the coffeemaker and then we began arranging our work areas. It was about eight-fifteen when Brigitte arrived.

Brigitte was the total opposite of Bettina and that was probably a good thing. Too many nut bags in my tiny *cabana* would drive me out of my mind. She swung in the door and stood there looking around in astonishment, which I completely expected.

"Okay. Help me here. Am I in the right place?"

"It's a long story, but yeah, you're in the right place. Pretty crazy, huh?"

Brigitte was quiet for a few minutes while she thought about her response—a quality I would no doubt come to value, given the velocity of Bettina's mouth.

"Yeah, but you know what? Every single salon in Charleston looks the same—boor-ing! This place has personality!" She took the cup of coffee I handed her and gave a low whistle at the bamboo walls and waiting area. "I like it; I really do. In fact, I like it a whole lot! It reminds me of a boutique from the seventies or something, but, like, these lights and everything are from *The Jetsons*. You know what I mean? The *real* question is when did you do all of this?"

"My ex-husband is a Whirling Dervish. He got a bunch of friends of his together and they went insane."

"Tell 'em the next time they get bored they can take it out on my house! Man!"

"You can tell him yourself; he'll be here shortly."

Brigitte was a total professional. You could tell by the way she dressed. She wore black linen trousers and black leather slides with a starched white linen shirt. Somehow, she wasn't wrinkled, a miraculous feature given the humidity. Her collar was open and her sleeves were rolled up. Her makeup was natural looking, and her brown bob was shining and moving. This was a woman of some no-nonsense style who could handle anybody—meaning an irate client—with a cool head. I hoped.

At eight-thirty, in rolled the rest of the troops—Emily, Jim, and Lucy.

"Hey! I brought Krispy Kreme doughnuts! Y'all come have one!" Lucy said.

Everybody said hello, everybody had a doughnut, and, inside of thirty minutes, we had our first client in Brigitte's chair and another at Bettina's table. Jim, who had clearly established himself as everyone's darling, hooked up the stereo. Pretty soon Frank Sinatra songs filled the air with nostalgia and romance.

I was combing out Mary Meehan's freshly washed hair when the door opened wide and who stood in the entry but Miss Mavis.

"I've come to make an appointment with Anna for a wash and set," she said to Lucy. "Does she do pin curls?"

You could tell by the way she held herself she didn't much like having to deal with Lucy.

"Well, hey, Miss Mavis!" Lucy said. "If you want to maybe read the paper for a few minutes, I'll bet she could squeeze you in right away."

"Not today?" Miss Mavis said, and leaned in to hear what Lucy had said repeated.

"I said, *Yes! She can take you in a few minutes! Why don't you have a seat and I'll get you a cup of coffee?*"

Unfortunately, Lucy's reply was a little too loud for Miss Mavis.

"You don't have to shout, young lady, I'm not *deaf*, you know."

Miss Mavis drew herself up in a huff and turned away, taking a seat on the far side of the reception area.

I took a deep breath and rested my hands on the back of the chair for a moment. I had known my client, Mary Meehan, forever.

She giggled a little and said, "Who in the *world* is that woman?"

"She's my next-door neighbor." I just shook my head. "I'll be right back, okay?"

I went up front as fast as I could. Miss Mavis was sitting in a knot, as far away from Lucy as possible. If body language could be used as a weapon, Lucy would have been missing a limb. I sat down beside her. I knew now that when I talked to her I had to be sure she was watching my mouth as I spoke. I took her hands into mine and I said to her what I thought she needed to hear from someone who cared about her sensitivity.

"I'm so glad you're here, Miss Mavis! What a wonderful surprise! I just need ten minutes, okay?"

"That's fine," she said, "and I think I *would* be glad to have that cup of coffee now. Just black."

Lucy, whose face was tomato red, jumped up to get it. Miss Mavis shot her another blow dart.

"You just stay right there, Lucy. Anna will get it for me, won't you, dear?"

I already had the pod in the machine and the coffee was beginning to drip. I winked at Lucy, which made her feel somewhat better, and smiled at Miss Mavis.

"How about a doughnut?" I said to her.

"Oh, I couldn't!" she said, waiting for the slightest encouragement.

"Come *on*," I said. "They're still warm."

"Well, all right. One can't hurt much. Gotta keep my figure, you know."

I handed her the coffee and a doughnut on a napkin and went back to Mary, who was deeply engrossed in a cell phone call with her husband.

"Just put Sophie in the house," she said.

Sophie was her dog, not her daughter.

"*Sorry!*" I whispered to her.

"*That's okay.*"

I started to blow out her hair and noticed in the reflection of the mirror that Emily was standing around doing nothing. When I was through with Mary, Emily and I were due for a chat. It made me crazy when she did this. *Idle hands are the devil's workshop,* as Sister Guilt used to say. If there was one thing I truly detested, it was sullen teenagers standing around collecting attitude like metallic filings. She needed to find something to do or else she was going to drive me crazy.

"Emily? Honey? Go get Daddy, okay?"

Jim was in the back unpacking another box of something he had bought to enhance the *Cabana.* He came over with four bottles of hair product.

"This stuff is guaranteed to keep your hair straight like the runway girls," he said.

"Yeah, sure!" Mary said. "In this weather?"

"Well, we've got that spray, you know," I said, not really paying attention. "Is that shampoo?"

"Heads up, just for a minute. That's salon talk, you know." Jim gave one of his irresistible grins that made Mary swoon a little. "First, you wash with this." He held out the open bottle for me to smell.

"Fruit cocktail!" I said. "God! You could drink it!"

"Lemme smell!" Mary said. "Wow! I love that!"

"Then, you apply this serum and this conditioner that you rinse after five minutes," he said. "Last, you spray one shot of this stuff on the roots and comb it through. They swear it gives you flat straight hair that shines like glass."

"Where'd you get this stuff?" I said.

"Why should I tell you?" he said with a wink. "Actually, if Mary will be the guinea pig, and *if* this stuff works, I was thinking you might want this to be your salon private label shampoo and treatment line. They do it for curls too!"

"Straighten me out," Mary said. "I'm game."

And so Mary got straight hair and Miss Mavis got pin curls and then I asked Jim to show Emily how to use a broom, which she began to use.

"You want spending money for the summer, don't you?" I said.

"Yes," she said, shocked that someone of her intelligence had to push a broom to pay for her henna tattoos and eyebrow studs. "I guess so."

"Well, it's the best I can offer you. You can take lunch orders for clients, straighten out perm rods, Windex the glass shelves, keep the magazines straight."

"Anything else?"

"If I think of it, I'll let you know."

She didn't really mind being in the salon. She was more or less pretending to be put upon. In addition, considering her loss of funding from Trixie, she wasn't about to argue. Lastly there was Lucy, the direct link to David and therefore a social life. David had a job at Barnes & Noble in Towne Centre for the summer. I imagined they would wind up seeing each other after work. My secret was that I hoped David being around would cause her to change her hair color back to blond. It wasn't that I had anything against her experimenting with hair color. How could I? It was that she looked more like me when her hair was its natural color and I wanted that association to be more obvious.

The phone rang all day and at about three o'clock, a delivery man from Abide-A-While showed up with a palm tree with a stuffed toy monkey hanging from one of its limbs.

The card read:

> *Let's monkey around!*
> *Congratulations and good luck!*
> Love, Arthur

Well! I said to myself, this is a good omen. A promising one. I called him to thank him.

"You didn't have to do that, but I loved it. Thanks."

"Well, I just thought you needed to know what was on my mind."

It had been so long since I'd been pursued by an eligible man, that I couldn't find words to respond. I could feel myself blushing.

Finally I said, "Yeah. So? Um, well?" There I was, the adult with the cool head, reduced to a pigtailed schoolgirl with Band-Aids on her skinned knees, stuttering.

"Well put. So how's your first day going?"

I knew he was snickering at me, which only made me feel all the more lamebrained.

"Really good. Yeah, really good. Lucy brought in doughnuts."

What a stupid thing to say! Tell him how much you loved the walk on the beach last night. Tell him how you thought about him when you were trying to sleep. Hellfire, girl! Doughnuts?

"Krispy Kreme."

"Well, that's pretty special."

Dead silence.

"You there?" I said.

"Anna?"

"Yeah?"

"I can't get you out of my mind."

"Shit. Me either."

Bettina perked up from her table. "That's one dollar," she said. I could see her shoulders shake with laughter.

"I want to see you later, okay?"

"Okay," I said, "me too. Around nine?"

"Sure. I'll pick you up."

I hung up the phone and looked around. Bettina, her client, Lucy, Brigitte, Jim, and Emily were all staring at me.

"Holy hell," Emily said, "Mom's in love."

"One dollar!" Bettina said.

"Don't be ridiculous," I said. "I have a date. Period."

"Sit," Brigitte said. "I'll blow out your hair."

"I'll do you a manicure," Bettina said.

"Anna," Jim said, "I'll be back in an hour."

"Where are you going?" I said. *Was he jealous?*

"Berlin's, honey," he said, "*you* need a *dress!*"

Before I could stop him, he was out the door. He wasn't jealous. He was a generous saint.

"I wish I had an ex-husband like him," Brigitte said.

"Don't we all?" Bettina said.

I had two more clients that afternoon, and three walk-ins showed up from the real estate office in our shopping center. Bettina left at five and Brigitte was all done at six.

"Not bad for a first day," Brigitte said as she straightened up her station. "I'm too tired to eat and that usually means I worked! Anna. I think this is going to be a very busy place!"

"Thanks. I kept having nightmares that I opened for business and nobody came—you know, like that lonely Maytag repair guy?"

"Hardly. I think we had better find two more stylists and quick! When June rolls around and all the touristas show up, this place is gonna be a crazy house."

"I hope you're right! Tourists! Ugh!"

"The girls from the real estate office threatened to tell all their renters about us."

"Well, we gotta take the good with the bad, I guess. See you tomorrow."

Overall it *had* been a promising day. I began the business of closing details—wiping out the sinks, wiping down the counters. Emily was helping me.

"Daddy never came back," she said.

"Call his cell," I said. "Tell him if he doesn't get here, I'll just meet him at home."

"Okay," she said and went up front to call.

Lucy came toward the back sinks where I was trying not to chip my French manicure that I adored.

"Here's your appointment list for tomorrow," she said. "I gave this one an extra half hour because she wants a perm or highlights or something that sounded like it needed more time."

"Good plan," I said, "thanks." Then I looked at the list. My day started at eight and I was booked solid until seven. "You trying to kill me?"

"No, just protecting my investment!" she said. "Don't y'all think it's time for cocktails? Oh, Emily? David called and he wants to know if you want to go to the movies tonight. I told him yes, you would. Is that okay with you?"

Now all eyes turned to Emily, whose face was stricken with panic.

"Sure," she said, "why not?" She went to the powder room, closed the door, turned on the fan, and screamed.

"AAAAUUUUUWWWWW! I hate grown-ups!"

Lucy and I burst out laughing. The door opened and she came out.

"I'm fine now," she said with a decided smirk of delight over her date with David.

"Good," I said, "let's get out of here. We've got hearts to break."

Twenty-three

Long Walk off a Short Pier

J IM showed up at the house around seven, loaded with
enough shopping bags to kill a camel. I was just getting
ready to serve another gourmet dinner ("gourmet" meant to
be humorous) of this crazy pasta that Emily loved when she was a little girl. First, you fry four pieces of bacon until it's really crispy and
then drain it. In some of the same grease—not too much or your heart
will explode—you cook a chopped onion and dissolve a chicken cube.
Then, you throw in a can of tomatoes and crumble the bacon back in
it. Cook and drain the pasta, throw it in the sauce, stir around some
Parmesan cheese, and, baby child, it's Yum Yum Time.

Add frozen garlic bread, salad in a bag, and I'm feeling like the
fastest cook in the East, or something. Oh, yes, I was swimming in the
excellence of the day. New business, possibly a new boyfriend, and
here was Jim to change my image with something wonderful to wear.

"Okay, girls! Gather 'round! Gather 'round! Daddy's home with
lots of goodies for his women!" He threw the bags on the floor and
himself on the couch. "I'm dead. All my bones ache! My feet are
arthritic! I'm an *old, old* man. Wow!"

He played dead, bringing on a fit of giggles from Emily. Moody as she could be, Jim knew the exact location of her funny bone.

I poured him a glass of wine and brought it to him. "Here, precious!"

"Did you buy me something too?" Emily said.

"You know I did!"

Emily pulled off his shoes and rubbed his foot and I took his other foot and tickled the sole.

"Stop! That drives me nuts!" He laughed and tried to twist away from us. "Why do you vixens torture me like this?"

"Oh? You're ticklish?" I said. "I'm sorry, honey! I didn't know that!" Then I rubbed his foot. "You hungry?"

"I could eat a horse," he said and sat up. "Actually, I ate horse once. It was quite good. It's a delicacy in some places, you know."

Emily looked at him hard, searching for the liar within. Realizing he was speaking the truth she said, "Euuu. Euuu. Euuu. Gross."

"For this I spend a fortune in tuition? *Euuu?* Let's eat."

"Eat first, review the booty later?" Jim said.

"Yeah, it's getting cold."

We served our plates in the kitchen and remarked on what a good thing it was that we were all on the skinny side.

"If you ever expand this house, Mom, the kitchen is so definitely on the top of the list."

"Gotta cut two thousand heads first!" I said, and went to the table with my plate and the salad bowl. "Somebody get the bread from the oven, okay?"

At the table, everyone ate and I thought again about how happy I was. Looking around, just seeing them was so very nice. Man. Some days were poetry.

"Today was fun, wasn't it, Mom? God, this is so good."

"Today was wonderful," I said, and paused for a moment. "I just don't want this dinner to go by without me telling both of you how much I love you." I don't know what got into me, but I burst out into tears. "I'm sorry," I said, "it's just that I'm so *happy!*"

Emily got up to get a tissue for me and Jim said, "Women."

Emily handed me the tissue, I blew my nose like a thunderous storm, and we all laughed. Emily rubbed my back around and around, exactly like I used to rub hers and I wanted to cry again.

"What a day," I said.

I looked up from the dinner table and saw David the Young Turk standing at the door. He was obviously confused by my tears as I was sure he had heard me boohoo and blow my nose.

"Come on in," I said, still sniffling. "Did you have supper?"

"Hey! Is this an okay time?" Then he said, "Um, I didn't exactly eat. Aunt Lucy was getting dressed for a date and I sort of . . . gee, that smells good."

"I'll fix you a plate," Emily said, "come sit down."

"Uh, thanks."

I assumed Lucy had a date with Daddy but something inside also told me she had a date with somebody else. Before I had the chance to think about it too much, the awesome clothes, shoes, and accessories were displayed, an outfit was chosen for me for that night, Emily was out the door on David's arm, the dishes were done, Jim was in bed snoring like a wild animal, and Arthur was at the door. If nothing else, I smelled good. Jim had sprayed me from head to toe in Chanel's Allure. Well, chemical allure was better than none at all.

"Hey," I said, "glad you're here! What a crazy day."

But he didn't come in the door. He just stood there on the other side of the screen and looked at me like something in shrink-wrap in the butcher's display at the Piggly Wiggly. At least that was what I hoped his look meant.

"You look beautiful," he said.

How could he say that? I thought I looked like a hooker in the tight dress Jim and Emily insisted made me look fierce. But when I looked back at him, I forgot my insecurity and saw someone I wanted more than I had wanted anyone in a long time. Maybe ever. It was appalling to be so undone. Time was suspended in anticipation, while Perrier bubbles raced through my veins.

"Thanks," I said, opening the door for him, "you smell like something, um, something really wonderful."

"You're not very slick at this dating opening line thing, are you? Come here."

"Uh, I guess I'm a little out of practice."

There in my doorway, in my new house, on the day of opening my new business, my new boyfriend kissed me with his perfect lips. I tried to remember the last person I had kissed whose lips matched mine so perfectly and I couldn't recall a soul. I decided to capitalize on this opportunity and let him kiss me all he wanted. You'll be glad to know I moved him inside the door to the living room. I wasn't just gonna hang my sex life out the door for all the world to pass comment. I do have some sense of propriety, you know.

I pushed him down on the couch and my new navy cotton and spandex dress that fit like a sock began to hike itself up my legs. What was the difference? He was leaning back into the cushions and pulling me over to crawl on him. He couldn't see my behind anyway. He was busy feeling whatever he could feel and so was I. It was getting very warm. We were kissing like, God knows, a couple of nymphos desperately in need of some moderation therapy and one of my new red sling-backs went flying across the room, landing with a thud. I didn't even look up. Then the other shoe took flight. His shirttail came out and I wondered for a split second if we would even make it to the bedroom. There was a lot of heavy breathing, one long look of consensus, and the kissing started again, this time in a way that was slightly less anima and more evenly paced. But, oh God, I was heading to hell on the super slide of sin and loving the ride. We were not going to make it off that couch until I said so. His hand was square on my backside and my hand was working its way from his belt buckle to his zipper. To hell with shy, I thought. I heard someone scream.

"*Oh! My! God! I'm gonna puke my guts out! Jesus, Mom! Get a room!*"

Emily and David had returned home. I sat up in shock, not looking their way, and tried to recover my hairdo and composure. My body temperature was about three thousand degrees. Arthur struggled to sit, dumping me on the other cushion. I pulled my dress down the best I could.

"Um, I'll just wait outside," David said as he turned and left, snickering.

Emily's bedroom door opened and closed. *"Disgusting!"* she said in a most guttural voice. Then the bathroom door slammed. A minute passed. Then it opened and slammed again. Then my bedroom door slammed. *"Ahhhh!"* she screamed. Then it opened. Then it slammed. Then she rushed past us, slamming the door.

Arthur and I looked at each other. We heard David's car pull away. It was almost dead silent except that the sound of Jim's snore penetrated the walls and the mood. How he had slept through all this carrying-on was a mystery.

"Your girl sure knows how to bust up a party," Arthur said.

"I could die," I said. "That's never happened before. I mean, if I had caught her in the same position, she'd be grounded for about a hundred years."

"Then let's not get caught," he said. "Come on. We're going to my house."

"What about dinner? I already ate, actually." Was that the dumbest thing I could say or what? Boy, when my passion cooled, it sank like a stone to the freaking South Pole. "I mean, are we going to be late? Should we call somebody? I mean, not that I *want* to call anybody . . ."

He was standing in front of me with his arms crossed, shaking his head, dimples showing and eyes twinkling.

"You know what? You're making me insecure over here. I already ate, too. Why don't you just get your purse and let's get out of here."

Well, then I felt like an ass. A complete, world-class ass.

We drove to his house, or rather his friend's house. It was another old island home, much like the one where I grew up, except that it was on the Intracoastal Waterway and the front of it faced the water. I could hear the dogs barking wildly from inside the house.

The house was elevated from the ground and the screened porch was casually strewn with old painted rockers of varying sizes on either side. The overhead light was corroded from the salt air and the door could have used a coat of paint. I wasn't being critical. In fact, the imperfections were comforting. I followed him through the door into the kitchen on the left. Nikki and his other setter were jumping all over us, begging for a scratch or a cookie or to be let out. I was never sure about what dogs wanted. I had enough trouble with people.

"Come on, girl, get down. Come on, Ringo, cut it out! Glass of wine?" He stuck his head in the refrigerator. "Beer? *Cos-mo-pol-i-tan?*"

"Very funny. God! Will I ever live that down? A glass of wine would be perfect. Ringo? The dog's name is Ringo?"

"Yeah. My friend is a huge Beatles fan. So am I."

"Me too."

He smiled at me, probably because it was reassuring to know we had something in common besides this raging desire to rip off our clothes.

"I was thinking we could sit on the front porch and watch the lights and maybe take a walk on the dock if the bugs aren't too bad."

I exhaled and said, "I'd love that. There's a nice breeze."

I was relieved that he wasn't going to try and pick up where we had left off on my couch. Emily and David's return had my nerves all jangled and, frankly, it had given me a chance to think about rushing to the mattress mambo. Yes, I wanted to sleep with him but the old-fashioned Lowcountry girl in me told me to hold out. I knew the world jumped into bed the first chance they got, but I didn't want to do that. I liked him too much.

I watched his hands as he uncorked the bottle. They were large and beautiful, manly hands. Naturally, I wondered about the implication of hand size and his—well, you know what I mean. I had read about that in *Cosmopolitan* magazine but I sure didn't have much field research to back up their claim. I told myself that I should be ashamed and then I giggled, not ashamed one bit.

"What's funny?" he said and handed me a goblet.

"Everything," I said. "I was just thinking about what Emily must have said to David when they left." This was a complete lie, but not a bad recovery. "Can you imagine?"

"It's your job to give your kids something to get over, isn't it? Cheers."

"Man. I'll bet she's still stressing about it!"

"Well, I'm sure we were a pretty scandalous sight to her. Come on."

I followed him down the center hall of the house and he paused to turn on a few lights. It was a pretty nice house, but clearly a man's place. I stepped in the living room behind him. The sectional couch was black leather, and from its sheer bulk, I guessed that it probably had a pullout bed. There was a large-screen TV for ball games and the two recliners were positioned to watch Clemson attempt to kick Alabama's butt. The coffee table was empty and there wasn't a framed photograph of a human being to be seen—only wildlife and landscapes—or a live plant in sight. The dining room on the other side had a dark Victorian table and was covered in mail. The chairs around it looked like no one had used them in years. I didn't see any bedrooms and assumed they were upstairs but I wasn't asking for a tour. I was back on my good behavior. Temporarily.

"Ah! The porch! I'll bet you I've spent more late nights on this porch since I've been here than anywhere else."

For the record, the porch was wide and long, furnished with oversized chairs on one end and a hammock on the other. It was the best feature of the house and no doubt the reason his friend had bought it in the first place. I stood looking at the twinkling lights across the water and the small boats that shifted in their own wakes. What a night for dreaming, I thought.

"This is really beautiful," I said.

"Come sit down," he said. "You know what I've been thinking?"

"Well, there's just no telling."

"I'm thinking that although this is the third or fourth time I've seen you, I don't know anything about you except that you used to be married to Jim, you have a daughter who's a knockout if she'd get that shit out of her hair, that you can't drink vodka worth a damn, and that you own a new house and a new business. Who are you, Anna?"

"What do you mean, who am I?"

"Just what I said. I want to know what you think about, what your childhood was like, how many guys you've slept with . . ."

"*What?*"

"I'm just kidding about the other guys part. Come on. Sit next to me and tell me all about yourself. What's your passion?"

Passion?

"Like I'd tell you anyway?" Another clever retort designed to dodge the question.

I caught my breath and took a seat next to him. Now, I'm a chatty gal, but all at once I was at a loss for words. I was fixated on his question and wondering when the last time was that someone had asked me about myself. Maybe it was because of the kind of business I was in but I was *completely* used to listening to others talk about themselves. I was the one who took care of other people's problems, dispensing advice with every twist of a round brush.

And passion? Did I have any beyond a physical one? Now that my geographical passion for island and my desire for autonomy had been met, what was next? What else, if anything, did I crave?

It wasn't that I thought no one cared about what went on in the deep recesses of my head—certainly Daddy, Jim, Frannie, and even Crazy Lucy would have gladly listened to almost anything. This was different. Arthur's question presented a chance to try on my new persona, that independent-woman cloak I started wearing when I signed my mortgage and lease.

"Cat got your tongue?"

The breeze was blowing all over the porch and the air smelled sweet. I was trying to find the way to tell him what I wanted him to think about me. I decided I would just dive in and let my thoughts of the moment rip. It was easier to tell the truth in the dark, whatever that truth had become on that night.

"No, it's just that it's been a long time since anyone asked. A lot has changed. I mean, I just threw my life into forward after spending most of it in reverse, or neutral."

"You have an automatic transmission in that tight little dress somewhere?"

"Yeah, and you're a comedian."

"Come on. Tell Uncle Arthur about Anna's secrets. I won't tell a soul!"

"Okay, here's a secret about me. I love porches at night and I have to be on this island to be happy. I don't know what it is about the Isle of Palms."

"Does that mean you don't want to live with me in Nepal?"

"Is that north of Columbia?"

"Yeah, way north."

"Then, I can't go. I'd die." I smiled thinking about running away with him.

"Damn. I really love Nepal too—yak cheese and all that. So, is it this island? Or do you think it could be the Atlantic Ocean that has this mysterious pull on you?"

"No, it's this island. Definitely." This swung me back to childhood and I had a memory of something amusing. At the same time, I was trying to decide whether he wanted the real goods or he wanted to be entertained. I opted for entertainment. "Okay. You're gonna think this is stupid."

"I'll be the judge of what's stupid around here."

"Okay. When I was little, really little, I used to think I wanted to be a pirate when I grew up. To be more specific, I wanted to be the one who found Blackbeard's trunks of gold that are supposed to be buried on this island."

"You're kidding, right? Blackbeard?"

"Yeah, Blackbeard. You know, some people think this is just a little sandbar but it isn't. The Isle of Palms has great historical value."

"Yeah, right."

"I swear, it does!"

"Look, I'll give you Sullivan's Island and Charleston. I mean, even a Yankee foreigner like me knows they dug up the *Hunley* here. I thought all the pirates were in Barbados or someplace like that."

"Well, they were there too, but Blackbeard's ships actually worked as Charleston's first navy, guarding the port, with a lot of pillage and plunder thrown in."

"I never heard that one. So, what would you have done if you had found a trunk of gold?"

"Tough question. I think I would have just been rich. You know? A great bicycle, better toys . . . that sort of thing. My brain was young at the time. I mean, I wouldn't have called a broker to discuss setting up a portfolio."

"Right." He sighed and stood up. "Don't you know, little girl, that money is the root of all evil?" He refilled my glass.

"Money can make people wicked, that's for sure. Thanks. The way I figure it, *enough* has always been about twice as much as I had at any given point in my life."

"Me too."

Then there was silence and I sensed he was disappointed that I hadn't given him something more. And maybe, just maybe, it would be nice if I got interested in what he wanted to tell me. People often asked questions they wanted you to ask them, didn't they?

"So, what are you doing in Charleston? Where are you from, anyway?"

To my surprise, he positioned a large footstool with a big cushion under my legs and I stretched out, kicking off my shoes for the second time that night. If I had realized we'd be porch sitting instead of going out to the city, I would have worn shorts. But if I'd worn shorts, the dress I was wearing could never have delivered its deadly effect. There was something much sexier about bare legs hanging out of a tight dress than khaki shorts.

"Well, I was born in Connecticut and then I went to school in

New York when my parents got divorced. They got divorced when I was a kid."

I was right. He wanted me to know him. "Any brothers? Sisters?"

"Nope. Just me."

"Another only child. Me too."

"Anyway, I got a degree in business from NYU and then I got interested in the food business when I was managing a restaurant with a friend and then the next thing you know, I was up to my neck in cheese. Cheese is a trend thing, you know."

"Seems like everything has its little moment in the sun, I guess. Like quiche and all that? Jim would probably agree."

"Exactly, I mean, ask him about the Chardonnay fever versus Sauvignon Blanc grapes recently. And, Merlots versus Cabernet. Same thing."

"So, have you ever been married?"

He heaved a deep sigh and confessed the bare minimum. "God, yes, I was married. I'd never do that again."

Me either, I thought. "Children?"

"One son. He lives with his mother on the Upper West Side. I have a studio in the Village on East Tenth Street. I've always liked downtown Manhattan better."

I said, "Umm. I've never been to New York, but I think I'd like downtown better too. I mean, you always hear it's more charming and less chaotic."

"Yeah, but it's never as quiet and peaceful as this. You might be right about this island. Come on. Let's go look at the night."

"Okay," I said, and watched Arthur reach for the bottle. "How old is your boy?"

"He'll be eighteen this fall. You want to have another splash?"

"Sure," I said, standing to leave with him, "why not. So, what's he like?"

"He's better than me."

"I doubt that. What's his name?"

"Charlie. He wants to be a child psychologist, of all things. But he's probably trying to sort out all the emotional crap he endured while his mother and I were trying to ruin his childhood. He has a huge heart."

"I doubt that you ruined his childhood. I mean, if he knows you both love him, that's a lot."

Then I saw Arthur's eyes and, even in the dark, they told me he had failed to give his son that most basic requirement of all parents—confirmation that he loved him. I wondered why.

"Come on," he said, "the moon's rising."

There was the opening creak and a closing clack that came with a screen door on any old island porch I had ever known. All doors of this type would swell with rain and shrink with cold. They never hung quite right or worked completely to keep out bothersome mosquitoes. But they were a sound I identified with something soothing. Someone was coming or someone was going. You wouldn't hear the person walk across the damp grass of their yard but you would hear the creak and the clack of their screen door. It was a safe sound.

We walked down the wooden steps and at the bottom he took my hand.

"Watch where you walk," he said, "the ground's uneven."

I was definitely wearing the wrong shoes. It wasn't long before I stumbled and he steadied me. So for the third time that night, I took them off and hooked the heel straps over my finger.

"You do realize that at this rate, you'll never wear out those shoes?"

"Very funny, bubba. I don't know where I thought we were going."

"Well, maybe we'll go to the Boathouse for a nightcap later."

"We'll see," I said. "It's already pretty late."

We walked down the slope of the yard, me moving like an old woman navigating cobblestones. Reaching the end of the floating dock, we sat on the edge, swinging our legs over the water. The tide was coming in.

"Where's the boat?" I said.

"What boat?"

"Arthur, even a Yankee boy like you must know that there's no point in having a dock if you don't have a boat."

"I don't know. Mike doesn't have one. Maybe I should rent one. Take us sailing under the Carolina moon. Actually, my neighbor uses this dock sometimes. Maybe we can borrow it."

"Ask. Let's do that. I'd love it. I'll pack us a picnic or something."

Something was wrong. Arthur had become distant, as though his thoughts were far away from here. I guessed he was thinking about his ex-wife and I wished I hadn't asked him about her or about his son.

"Tell me what you're thinking," my inner masochist blurted.

"That I wish . . . I don't know," he said and pulled me to him, "that I wish I knew how to *really* love. There's something wrong with me. Anna?"

"Hmm?" I was so lost in the breeze, his arm around my shoulder, the moon, the sparkle of the salty water, that he could have been saying *I'm sorry; it was blown off in the war.* And I would've heard that we were perfect, anything else but what he had really said. To me he had said he wanted to love. Not that he couldn't love.

He kissed me again as all the surroundings insisted that he should. I mean, you got a girl on the edge of a dock in the moonlight and what else are you supposed to do? You kiss her again and again and your heart speaks to her and she hears you cry for her to heal you.

"Don't get involved with me, Anna," he said, "I can't deal with it."

"You must be kidding," I said, lying through my teeth, "I never get involved."

If it was the last thing I ever did, I'd make Arthur love me. He needed me. I was sure of it.

Twenty-four

The Hole in the Bottom of the Sea

❧

I HAD become Madame Ovary. During the rest of the week, Arthur was taking over my brain. He was my first thought in the morning, my last thought at night, and the rest of the time, I fantasized about him. It was those darn lips of his and those dimples. Not to mention the way his arms felt, the way he smelled, his eyes, the way his eyebrows grew, the spray of freckles across his nose, his height, weight, complexion, and did I mention how it felt to be kissed by him? Other than these minor but frequently distracting thoughts, I was in full control.

We hadn't seen each other since Sunday night—between his work schedule and mine, life was a cyclone. More importantly, we had not slept together. Somehow, when I realized how late it was, I had said something stupid about the time. We were still on the end of the dock, fooling around.

"Oh, my Lord! It's eleven-thirty!" I said.

"Is it? Come on, I'll take you home."

Take me home? What was I supposed to say then? *Oh, my mistake! It's too early?* Right.

The man had my mind in a French twist. Get it? French twist? Okay, that was stupid. But look, I couldn't decide whether he was really serious about not getting involved. Weren't we already almost there? We had talked briefly on Thursday—I called him, actually, because I got antsy (read: *possessed*) that he hadn't called me. It was all right to call him, I told myself, because this wasn't like the fifties or something. I was a liberated woman. Anyway, I got my satisfaction because we made plans for Sunday again. I was also nervous because even though he wanted to see me that weekend, he sounded less enthusiastic than he had when we were together on Sunday. Well, when the next Sunday rolled around, I would be at my best and he would see what he was treating so casually was seriously worth having. And, I would talk about it with Jim. And Frannie. Not Emily, who had been hanging around with David every single night after work. Why was it so easy for her? Shoot. Young people.

It was Friday and the salon had been extremely busy all week. The neon men had shown up and installed the new sign, the stationery had arrived, Lucy had changed the website, and the phone rang all day long. *Anna's Cabana* was a wild thing, honey.

Shock of all shocks, Lucy had flowers on her desk from whom, Daddy? I had never known Daddy to send anyone flowers, but Jim and I decided they'd probably had some kind of a tiff and he had sent them to make up. I imagined it was over the past weekend, but we didn't ask. I figured Lucy would tell me if she wanted me to know. She did.

I was in between clients. Jim and I were discussing his return to San Francisco while eating tuna salad sandwiches standing over the washing machine, which was another demonstration of the unglamorous reality of salon life. Lucy came back to download, thinking we were curious to know where her flowers had come from. We had assumed correctly.

"I don't want you to think I'm dragging you into this, Anna," she said, "but I got mad with your daddy."

"He probably deserved it," I said, not missing a beat.

Jim arched his eyebrows. "What did he do, the onerous cad?"

"Well, it's just that I like to go out and he doesn't. He just wants to play house, *if you know what-I-mean.*"

"Please! *TMI!*" Jim said, throwing his arms in the air. *Too Much Information.*

I shuddered as the briefest of all thoughts of Daddy in the rack with Lucy tore a hole through my brain.

"Well! It's the *truth!* I just gave him a piece of my mind. I said, Dougle, darlin'? I don't mind making dinner and all that but, shoot, I like to go to restaurants too!"

"Sounds fair enough to me," I said, and tried to not look her in the face.

"He said that he couldn't imagine anyplace better than my house and that I shouldn't tell him how to spend his money. Is that the rudest thing you've ever heard of? So, I went out to dinner Saturday night with somebody else."

We tsked and shook our heads.

"Sounds like him," I said. "It's not the absolute *worst* thing I ever heard. But it ain't great."

"Classic Dougle," Jim said. "He's tighter than a gnat's ass."

"Who'd you go out with?"

"A very nice man I met in a chat room," she said. "He took me to Cypress and paid for it too!"

A chat room. One of these days she was gonna get herself in trouble. She trotted away, vindicated by our support and twenty-five dollars' worth of hideous pink carnations. I have always hated carnations—they reminded me of FTD and sick people who get flowers from people who left it up to someone else to understand their obligations and impotent emotions. I could barely even acknowledge Daddy as sexual and, believe me, impotent was nothing I cared to consider. Carnations said it all. Gee, God.

Yeah, Jim was bailing out on me, returning to San Francisco, and I just hated it.

"Have you told Trixie when you're leaving?" I said.

"Yup. The Queen Mother is still chewing her cuticles over Emily," he said. "How much of a bind will her rescinding of dinero cause? I mean, I can help, you know."

"Precious, you have already done too, too much! Besides, she's earning some money. I say we let her sweat it for a while. There's a good lesson in that."

"God, you're tough. When did you become so tough?"

"Okay, I'm gonna let you in on a secret. Mothers know that demonic possession of their teenage daughters arrives on the coattails of the first pimple. So, I guess I started toughening up when Emily was about twelve."

"Hmm, I seem to recall her phoning me around then, crying because you had slapped her just because she called you an asshole? Does that seem right?"

"Yep. That's when the party began. God. I think you could raise ten boys for the energy it takes to raise one girl."

I know it seems strange that Jim didn't pay regular child support and normal that he didn't pay alimony. How could I have ever asked him to do that? It wouldn't have been fair. Anyway, it had always worked out all right. When I had needed anything all I had to do was peep and a wire transfer was there. Jim was the only father Emily had ever known and even though she had voiced her suspicion about that, we were still all letting it ride.

I took a huge bite of my sandwich and washed it down with gulps of sweet tea. Jim and I were eating like it was a contest. I had an appointment in ten minutes and he wanted to do some errands in the city. Every time I reached for a potato chip he slapped my hand.

"Don't eat those! Cellulite! Here! Do you want my pickle?"

"I used to until I met Arthur," I said, knowing I should wash my own mouth out with soap.

"GIRL! You are so terrible! So what's up with Monsieur Camembert? Anything to report? I thought by now you'd have him sniffing around twenty-four/seven."

"I wish. This guy is one curious specimen."

"Curious specimen? How curious is he?"

"Okay. We go for a walk on the beach after dinner last Sunday night, right?"

"Right, I remember."

"And, he's all romance and kissing me and smelling my neck and everything."

"So far, this doesn't sound like a problem."

"And then he sends me this tree with the monkey . . ."

"Adorable . . ."

"And, you dress me up and we go out again. This time to his house, after Emily earns ten years on a couch. . . ."

"She told me. Honest to God, Anna! Aren't you a little old for that?"

"Oh, shut up and pay attention, you old priss!"

"Well!"

"Just listen, 'cause I gotta go do Mrs. Stith's highlights. So we're on his dock, drinking some wine, and he's putting the major make on me. I'm loving it and I can tell he is, too. Then, all of a sudden he tells me not to get involved with him. Like, what the hell does that mean?"

"Age-old man-ploy to get woman to fall like a redwood. Pure and simple. Women always want what they think they can't have."

"Jesus." And, I thought, if he thought I wasn't going to be infatuated with him, he'd want me more? How utterly stupid! "Jim? Lemme ask you this. Why can't two consenting adults just enjoy falling in love or lust or whatever it is? How long do people play games with each other?"

"Forever. Your whole problem is that your expectations of relationships are too high. Men are in love with themselves and their Johnsons. Period, end of story. They fall in love when it's too late to back out or if they can't get in your shorts. And, unless you spend the rest of your life stroking their ego, they're gonna fall out of love. Them's the facts, sweetie."

"Man. That's pretty cold, isn't it?"

"Anna? Your appointment's here." Lucy's voice sang through the little intercom from Radio Shack.

"Life's rough, Anna, you know that. Look at me and Gary. Look at you and me."

"Yeah, but we love each other, don't we?"

"That's different. We've known each other all our lives and we have a child. Starting a new history with a new partner at our age is optimistic, at best. You're hot for the guy, right?"

"Smoldering."

"Then, just go screw your head off with him and forget about it. Have fun, you know?"

I walked away thoroughly discouraged. Was that really how it was?

I did Mrs. Stith's highlights and Mrs. Clarkin's perm and cut four more heads that afternoon. All the while I was trying to figure out if I knew anyone who had married and stayed in love for decades. I thought about Daddy and Momma. Daddy had loved Momma with a great passion. Everyone knew that. But, why? I *knew* why! The ugly truth was that he loved her because of how she made *him feel,* not because of who *she was.* Was that the nature of a man's love for a woman? Not what you bring to the table, but how you make him *feel?*

I was drinking a cup of coffee when my last client of the day arrived. Caroline Wimbley Levine.

Miss Tall Pines never made an appointment without using all three names. Stuck up, rich, and a bit of a pain in the behind, she had been a client for about a year. I was surprised that she was willing to drive to the Isle of Palms just for me since she lived near Jacksonboro on her momma's plantation. Well, actually, it was hers now, ever since her momma died. God, I had loved her momma, Miss Lavinia. What a sweetheart she was! Caroline couldn't shine her shoes, at least not in my opinion. But, money was money and I could perform miracles on her stringy hair because it was just like mine. She was in my chair, combed out by Emily and waiting.

"Hey, Miss Caroline," I said, pleasantly, "thanks for coming all the way over here." I pressed the pump with my foot and raised her chair.

"Anna! This place is unbelievable! I love it! I absolutely love it! Was that your *daughter*? She's brilliant!"

Maybe she wasn't such a bitch after all.

"Yeah, that's my Emily. She goes to Georgetown. Home for the summer."

"Oh! I didn't know they had a college in Georgetown, South Carolina."

"No. She goes to Georgetown University in D.C. Gonna be a sophomore."

"You're kidding. How in the world did she get in *there?*"

Okay, she was still a bitch.

"Her great-great-grandfather's uncle was John Carroll, who founded it." That was a complete lie and I didn't even flinch. "Plus, she made pretty good grades and got a sixteen hundred on her SATs." While you're lying, why not go whole hog? "Yeah, we're real proud of her. She's a whip." Stuff that up your pedigree!

"I guess you *are* proud of her!" Her blue eyes were Frisbees. "I would be, too. You know my son has a pack of learning disabilities."

Okay, not a bitch.

"No, I'm sorry. I didn't know that."

"Oh! He's very smart and all that, but he's always had a problem with writing. Verbally? He's amazing. A vocabulary like I don't know what. But your daughter goes to Georgetown. That's really fabulous. What a kid!"

I smiled at her in the mirror, thinking this conversation with her was proof of why it was better to listen than to talk, and said, "Yeah. Want a smoothie? Cup of cappuccino?"

"Cappuccino would be great! Gosh!"

"Thanks," I said and walked over to the coffee machine. Bettina was standing there, hovering below boiling, having heard her and ready to kill.

"Just who the hell is *that?*"

"She's a good client," I said, "stay cool." I put the pod in the coffee machine and foamed the milk, waiting for the coffee to drip.

"Lemme give her a *Brazilian* bikini wax, Anna. *That'll* fix her."

"Simmer down, Brooklyn." I gave her a light punch on her little arm. "Why don't you offer her a manicure? You busy?"

"I'm on it."

Before I could return to Caroline with the coffee, Bettina was standing there.

"You know what, sweetheart? You oughta let me do your nails for ya."

"Well, all right, why not?" Caroline said. "I haven't had a manicure in weeks!"

"Here we are," I said, handing her the mug. "Now, what are we doing today?"

"I need an updo, I think. I have a wedding tomorrow morning and it's outdoors. In this humidity, I need my hair practically nailed in place. I have these little waves here and here." She pointed to her forehead.

"Or, I could rebond your hair. I mean, it takes a while, but you'll have stick straight hair for six months."

Her eyes went from normal back to Frisbees again. "You mean for six months, I don't have to use a straightening iron?"

"Yep. Guaranteed. It's no bargain, but it's foolproof. And, you'll be here until about nine tonight."

"How much would it cost? Shoot! Who cares? Go ahead! Lemme just call my boyfriend."

She pulled a shiny cell phone from her bright red Louis Vuitton bag and hit speed-dial for the Man.

I went to mix the conditioner and solutions I needed, thinking about her wallet. *How much could it be? How's four hundred dollars—one hundred extra for keeping me here until nine o'clock.*

She was still talking to him with her free hand when I returned.

Bettina had moved in on her and was filing away at the same speed she chewed her gum. I would have to talk to her about that gum.

"Jack says hello," Caroline said, smiling up at me.

Jack says hello. I don't know Jack and you don't know Jack either! "That's so sweet! Tell him I said hey and to come on in here and let me make him look like Tom Cruise," I said, thinking that one day I would accidentally get a mind reader in my chair and then the jig would be up.

"He *already* looks like Tom Cruise!" she said, in that girly gush voice that men loved. "Well, maybe Tom Cruise's older brother."

"Yeah?" Bettina said, piping up, "then tell him to *definitely* come on in here! I'll give him a massage on the house!"

She started that snort laugh of hers and we couldn't hold back the giggles. I was getting punch-drunk tired. The problem was that our giggles—mine and Caroline's—had an empty sound, like we were all starved for something to laugh about, and maybe we were. Maybe there was something I had in common with Caroline Wimbley Levine—some kind of starvation.

I saturated her hair with heavy conditioners and put her under the dryer for thirty minutes. That was to protect and prepare her hair for the process. I handed her the latest issues of *Skirt*, *W*, and *Town & Country*. She was oblivious to what we said under the hum of the hood.

It was just after six o'clock and most of the staff were ready to leave for the day. Brigitte was the first to say good night.

"How early can I get in here tomorrow?" she said.

"When's your first appointment?" I said.

"Wedding party. They'd like to start at seven. Bride, six brides-maids, mother of the bride. Ugh. I hate wedding parties."

"Want a hand?"

"Would you? Oh, God! Thanks, Anna. I owe you one."

"No sweat. See you at seven! Bring doughnuts!"

"They need manicures, don't they?"

"You bet!" I said.

"No problem!" she said and out the door she went.

I watched Brigitte leave, thinking to myself that she had worked constantly all week, one client after another, and that she was quietly bringing in tons of new business. On the aggravation meter, wedding parties only ranked slightly higher than prom girls. The stress of a bride and her mother were bad enough; add one pregnant bridesmaid, one cranky sister-in-law-to-be, and at least one other newly married-someone-cuter-and-with-more-promise-than-the-bride's-intended to the lineup. It was enough nervous anxiety for a stylist to keep Zoloft in the drawer. It also meant that by ten in the morning we would all be fried for the rest of the day, but with a substantially fatter wallet. You'd have to be an idiot to turn away a wedding party, from a business point of view, and anyway, there was something really nice about being a part of someone's wedding day.

Lucy did the bank deposit for the next day and turned to Emily.

"Y'all going out again tonight?"

"Yeah. We were gonna go eat Mexican food and then see a movie. You wanna come with us? David wants to see *Star Wars*."

Lucy and I eyed each other. She was flattered. I knew better. For Emily to invite Lucy on her date carried meaning. Either Emily was trying to score points with Lucy for a reason beyond fathom or she didn't like David anymore. She was crazy about David and didn't care what Lucy thought. Everyone knew that. Or, and this one had the highest probability, it was that they intended to sneak off someplace after the movie but invited Lucy so Aunt Lucy and I would think, *Aren't they great kids*, when they sneaked in the house at one in the morning.

"Emily, I want you in the house by eleven tonight. I'm gonna need you in the morning bright-eyed and bushy-tailed."

"*Damn it!*" she said.

Did I know this kid or what? "David will understand. You have a job, right? We have a wedding party at seven. Put a buck in the box."

"*Damn it!*" Emily repeated as she stomped to the back to get her purse. "Well, there goes the movie. That's just *great*."

"Two bucks!" I said.

"What does all that mean?" Lucy said, in a whisper to me.

"It means you don't have to sit through *Star Wars*," I said back, under my breath.

"Well, thank God. Em, honey, thanks for the invitation, but I think tonight I'm just gonna put my feet up. You and David go on and have a good time, okay? Come on, I'll give you a lift home."

I was checking Caroline's timer when I heard the door open.

"*Well, hel-looo!*" said Lucy.

I looked up to see a very handsome man, late forties, with a bad haircut, looking all befuddled.

"Jack!" Caroline said from under the dryer. She lifted her hood and stood up to greet him. "Y'all! This is Jack!"

Bettina and I said hello to him. I caught Jack's eye and something mildly electric passed between us.

Hustle your client's boyfriend, Anna. That's classy.

I averted my eyes immediately, hoping he would let it go.

"What kinda salon is this? Who owns this place? Tarzan?" He started laughing, thinking he was hilarious.

"Nope, it's mine. You can call me Sheena. Can we get you something to drink?" I said. "Coffee?"

"Uh, no, thanks," he said and turned to Caroline. "What are you doing? Spending the night? I thought we were going out for dinner."

When the irate *other* shows up and begins to bark, the smart stylist steps away and makes herself busy doing anything so she won't appear to be eavesdropping, even though she never misses a single solitary word.

"Oh, honey, I'm sorry," Caroline said, "it's just that I had a chance to straighten my hair and Anna had time, so I said okay. Why don't we go out for dinner tomorrow night?"

"Tomorrow night I'm on call," Jack said.

Hmm. Doctor. Not bad, I thought, and then quickly dismissed the thought of being Mrs. Doctor Jack. Besides, HMOs have ruined the lifestyle. It didn't take much to push old Arthur aside. *Still . . .*

"Well, can we go late?"

"What time will you be done?"

She was standing on her tiptoes, which was entirely unnecessary, and kissing his cheek when I came back around the corner.

"She'll be out of here by nine-thirty," I said. "God, I'm sorry to have ruined your plans. I didn't know." Now, first of all, I meant what I said. I don't know why I felt obligated to apologize to them, except that I didn't want this Jack to think ill of me. "Unless you want to do this another time."

"Oh, that's okay, Anna. We go out to dinner all the time; don't we, sweetheart?"

"Yeah, we do," Jack said. "It's true."

"Jack? If you'd like, I have a nice bottle of wine in the back and some cheese in the refrigerator. Bettina? Why don't you show him where it's at and let's make this whole process as painless as possible?"

Jack brightened a little so Bettina said, "Come with me, doll."

Jack shrugged his shoulders and said, "Why not? I could use a glass of wine." For a second we all seemed to be watching Bettina wiggle as she walked and grinned as Jack followed her.

"She's a little number," Caroline said, "is she married?"

"I wouldn't worry about Bettina trying to snag Jack in the back room. She's as safe as they come and *very* married."

"Okay. If you say so."

It occurred to me that if she was so worried about Jack why was she willing to throw away dinner with him?

I rinsed her hair, put her in my chair, combed her out, and blew it dry.

"Alright. Before we start this, I have to give you follow-up instructions. No ponytails, bobby pins or clips, or shampoo for forty-eight hours, okay? You can't even put your hair behind your ears. Do we agree?" I stood there stirring the chemical soup in my mixing bowl like one of Macbeth's witches.

"Okay. But why?"

"You'll make marks in your hair with rubber bands and a shampoo

will neutralize the whole deal, just like you're not supposed to shampoo after a perm."

"I'll tell you, this is some world we live in, isn't it? My momma used
to always say, Pride knoweth no pain."

"Your momma was right about pride and everything else too. I
loved her to pieces."

"I miss her so bad I could die."

"Well, if you die, at least you'll have great hair in the box," I said,
and began to section her hair.

I applied the straightener section by section, waited ten minutes,
and towel-dried her hair until it was bone dry. Then I ran the flatten-
ing iron across each section with the neutralizer to seal it, taking an
occasional sip of wine while everyone chatted away. I couldn't
remember if this was the exact order of steps I was supposed to use,
but it seemed okay since her hair wasn't falling out on the floor. That
was a relief. Bit by bit, Caroline's hair began to shine like it was waxed
and we all marveled at it.

"Amazing," Bettina said. "Can you do mine too?"

"Yeah, but not tonight," I said, "next week."

Bettina had already talked Jack into a shampoo and a neck and
shoulder massage on the house.

"Go tell everybody you know that Bettina gives the best massage
you ever had," she said, throwing all her weight into Jack's muscles.
"Man! You're tight! Lotta stress?"

"Yeah, I guess. That feels so good!"

"Well, I guess I'll have to learn how to do that too!" Caroline said.

I was trimming her now stick-straight hair into some layers to give
it movement. If Jack had been mine, I would've known every muscle
group he had by name. Some women had all the luck.

Her hair looked wonderful and even she agreed.

"Gosh, Anna! It's a miracle!"

"Yes," I said, "it's rather stunning! I'm glad you like it."

"You look gorgeous, Caroline. Let's pay the bill and let these ladies
have what's left of their evening."

Bettina cleaned up and was turning out the lights. I handed Caroline a bill for four hundred and twenty dollars. It was nearly ten o'clock and I was dead on my feet. She handed me her American Express card and when the machine accepted it and expelled the receipt for her to sign, she added a fat tip.

Bettina came up beside me and handed me my purse. She turned on the night-lights and turned off the coffeemaker. I just stood there watching him open the door of her car and making sure she was safely inside. I was jealous of her and ashamed of myself for it.

"That guy is adorable," I said.

"That's how life is with rich women," Bettina said.

"How's that?"

"They never suffer for anything, you know?"

"Her son is learning disabled."

"And she's really nice too?"

"She's a doll."

"Damn it!"

"Come on, Brooklyn, let's call it a day. And tomorrow you owe the box a buck."

All the way home, I wondered about happiness. What would it take to make me happy besides all the blessings I already had? What passion was I still hiding in my heart, not addressing? I knew the answer. A good, solid, long-term partner. And, what did I have? Arthur. Arthur, the Cheese Whiz, who didn't want to get involved.

Twenty-five

Hello and Good-bye

SATURDAY, the salon was crazy. We took care of the wedding party and one client after another without a break. Over the groans of Emily, the aerobic workout of Bettina's gum, phones ringing nonstop, blow dryers blasting, cell phones playing everything from "Claire de Lune" to "The Mexican Hat Dance"— these were the sounds of a viable, healthy business with great promise and if I hadn't been so exhausted, I would have celebrated.

I remember at one point, Lucy stuffed a bit of a bagel with tuna salad in my mouth. At another point, someone delivered a plant— probably a gift from Daddy to wish us well, or from Bettina's husband or an admirer of Brigitte. I could not have cared less who sent the thing. My legs were throbbing. By the time I got home that night, I was too tired to eat. It was seven-thirty and all I could think about was the bed. It wasn't even dark and I was under the covers. I had to depend on Emily to be responsible and Jim to entertain himself. They never woke me up but I remember at some point I heard them talking.

"She's worn out," Emily said, "let's let her sleep."

"Maybe I should get her some vitamins," Jim said.

It was the morning sun that finally roused me from dreams so deep that when I woke, I didn't know where I was. Emily was sleeping next to me and the house was quiet. I slipped out of bed and washed my face, deciding to walk on the beach, something I had not done all week.

It wasn't quite six o'clock, but the birds' morning music and fevered conversation were in full swing. The air was thick and damp, almost wet. I crossed the dunes and looked over the scene before me. As always, it took my breath away with its sheer power. The tide was almost high and the ocean roared its way to the high watermarks of seaweed mounds and knocked aside the odd piece of driftwood without a care.

High tide on the Isle of Palms was so overwhelming that it could make you feel like something was coming to get you, pull you away and devour you. It seemed more appropriate to sit and watch than to try and walk the sinking sand of the water's edge. I would only get drenched, so I walked a short way and settled down on a palmetto log.

Well, I told myself, *I think my business is gonna be okay. We sure have enough clients and no one's complaining about the pricing. That's a huge load off my mind.*

I was seeing Arthur late that afternoon. Arthur. *Don't get involved.* And then I remembered Caroline and her boyfriend, Jack. Here was this gorgeous man and woman. How did he treat her? He made sure she got in her car safely and told her how beautiful she was and gave me the eyeball at the same time.

I kicked off my flip-flops and dug my feet into the sand. It was what we did in the Lowcountry when we found ourselves alone on the beach. We would sit, stare at the water, kick off our shoes, and dig our feet into the sand to stay cool. With the ocean rolling all around me, I could look at life from different angles.

The sky gradually gave up its blanket of deep gray to pale blue with golden edges of light, erasing the last traces of night. And over the next half hour or so, the sky would become brilliant blue again. The water changed from deep steel to sparkling navy as the morning sun climbed into position and another day began. On the turn of a tide, a new era had begun for me as well.

It looked as though I might be successful enough to remain independent. What I lacked was a love. Loving Emily was wonderful and all-consuming. The love I felt for Jim was special. But, Arthur had put his finger on it. What was my passion? I thought about this for a while and decided the real question should have been, *Where* or *Who* was my passion?

I was deeply troubled when I looked back at all the years gone. So many years had passed without an affair, or a *passion*. Suddenly, I was hungry for it. I wanted to make Arthur look at me the way Jack looked at Caroline. Jack burned for her in the way I wanted someone to burn for me. Maybe it *was* about making men feel like they were king, like Jim had said. Well, I would try it on Arthur and see how we fared.

By the time I walked home, Emily was up and in the kitchen making toast.

"Hey! Morning!" she said and gave me a peck on the cheek. "Where'd you go?"

"I went to the beach to watch the sun come up. It was beautiful," I said and poured myself a cup of coffee. "Not much beach at high tide, though. Pretty wild looking. Jim sleeping?"

"Sawing logs. Man, can he snore or what?"

"Pretty impressive. Want some eggs or something?"

"Nah. Thanks. Mom?"

"Hmm?" I was peering into my refrigerator like the secret of life was on the second shelf.

"I gotta do something about my hair. I can't stand it anymore."

"David? Prefers blonds? Big surprise."

She went from zero to one hundred in two seconds. "*Mom!* How can you *say* that?"

It's too early, I thought, but here we go anyway. I hated hostility before breakfast.

"Sorry. Just a knee-jerk reaction."

"If you think I would change my hair for some *stupid* boy, you just don't know me at all, *do you?* I mean, how could you possibly *think* that? *Uhhhhhhhhhh!*"

"Lower your voice, Emily. Your daddy's sleeping."

"And that's *another* thing. Don't you think it's a little bit *weird* for you to be dating some guy while Dad's here? Are you trying to make him feel like complete *shit*, or what?"

"Watch your language, young lady. Your father and I have been divorced for a million years and he actually *wants* me to find somebody. I have never had a better friend in my life than Jim and what goes on between us is nobody's business but ours." Now I don't know why I threw that last comment into the mix—I guess I just didn't feel like her jumping to the next topic, which, in the back of my mind, I knew would've been the nature of her birth.

"I have the most *screwed up* life of anybody I know. Did you *ever* think about *that?*"

"Emily? Do you think we could discuss your screwed-up life a little later? I just got up and haven't even finished my first cup of coffee."

"Fine. When you're mentally ready to be *a mother*, email me. I'm going for a walk."

"Don't slam the door."

SLAM!

"Whoever sold women on the idea of motherhood was one sadistic bastard," I said to the empty kitchen.

I peeked out the back door and watched her cross the yard in the direction of Lucy's. *Good*, I thought, *take your anger to somebody else's house for a while. You wear me out.*

By the time I had made the bed and had a shower, Jim was up, whistling in the kitchen. I smelled bacon and thought to myself that a perfect world would be one where you could eat all the bacon you wanted and not raise your cholesterol.

"Morning! Whatcha cooking?"

"Omelet? Cheese and onions with bacon?"

"When you go back to San Francisco, I'm wearing black for a month."

He smiled and turned a small perfect omelet onto a plate, handing it to me. "Go sit, I'll be there in a minute."

"You'll get no argument from me. When did you learn to cook like this?"

"Ah! There are many things about me that you don't know. That's why I'm an international man of mystery."

"Ah! The real Austin Powers at last!"

I put my plate on the table and went to the kitchen to pour us some orange juice. The omelet was golden and fluffy. I decided to use cloth napkins. In my world, cloth napkins designated the event as extraordinary. I even threw bread in the toaster and ran outside to cut a few blooms and put them in a bud vase for the center of the table, along with jam, sliced butter pats on a little plate, and cream and sugar in my best containers. By the time Jim joined me, it wasn't just breakfast we were having, but a Sunday morning event. At least it was to me.

In between bites, we began talking about his plans for leaving.

"I thought I'd see if I could get a flight Thursday. I've got a bunch of stuff to do for Hyatt and I probably have a foot of mail."

"And, you thought you might stop off in Ohio to see Gary. Am I right?"

"Yeah, you're right. You know, Anna, I just can't let him sit in his parents' house and rot away while his parents tell him he's going to hell when the day comes."

"If they won't let you in the door, call me."

"They think he made a 'sinful lifestyle choice' and that this is his *fault*. It's his fault, all right, but being careless isn't the same thing as committing a sin that would damn you to hell for all eternity. I just don't believe that. Tell me this. Who on this earth would *choose* to be gay? When is the world going to realize that some people just are?"

"I don't know, Jim. I don't. I mean, there are all these fundamentalists who say that with massive therapy it can be overcome. But look, I love *you* and I don't *care* what people do in the dark. Shoot. You've been a wonderful friend to me all my life and a great parent for Emily. I have nothing but love for you. You know that."

"Yeah, well, I say true Christians don't judge, that's what."

"You're preaching to the choir here, bubba."

"Yeah, I know."

"While we're on the subject, Emily asked me the other day just how she was brought into the world."

Jim spit his coffee all over his fresh lavender Ralph Lauren golf shirt. *"What?"*

"To be specific, she wanted to know if she was conceived by you and me in the regulation manner."

"Holy shit! *What did you tell her?"*

"If I recall correctly, her exact words were something like, *'Is Jim really my father? Did y'all—you know?'* I said, *'Lemme tell you something. Jim is more than a father, now go to sleep.'* It was one of those late-night chats. She hasn't said anything else, but, sooner or later, she's gonna."

"Then what?"

"Then, I think we noodle and figure out something. I mean, I don't want to lie to her. She's entitled to the truth, but honestly Jim, she's so hot and cold lately that I'm *afraid* to tell her. She won't understand."

"*Who* won't understand *what?* Morning, y'all!"

It was Lucy. She had walked right through my back door without knocking. I hated when someone did that and knew I'd have to say something. This wasn't the right moment to do that.

"Hey! Get yourself a cup of coffee and join us," I said. "We were just discussing Emily and her temper."

"She gets that from your daddy, I can tell you that much. Do you know that now he's mad at me *again?"* she said from the kitchen.

I pushed my plate back and put my forehead down on the table. "I can't take it," I whispered to Jim.

"There now," he said and patted my head.

Lucy came in and sat down. "Yeah, he's as hot as a goat's fanny in a pepper patch."

Jim burst out laughing. "Goat's fanny? What did you do to the poor man?"

"His nurse found my web page on AOL. She showed it to him. I said, 'Look here, Dougle, when you cough up a rock for this finger, then and only then do I quit dating!' He thinks he *owns* me!"

"That's Daddy!" I said.

"Men assume ownership of women like dogs do of chairs. If they get settled in it, it's theirs."

"Y'all making Bloodys?" Lucy said. "It *is* Sunday morning, isn't it?"

"Girl? I slept for twelve hours last night and one vodka would put me back in the bed for another twelve. But if you want one, be my guest. Everything's in the kitchen."

"Don't mind if I do," she said, "otherwise how will I ever get my nerve up to ask you about how Emily *did* make it into the world. She's over there with David, watching *Star Trek*. They're not coming over here for at least an hour. We can talk."

Jim and I stopped breathing, staring at her in disbelief. *Was she giving me* permission *to tell her what hardly anyone on the earth knew?*

"I'm sorry, y'all, I heard everything." She stood there in front of us in her bulging turquoise halter and white pants that were like second skin. "Believe me, I won't tell a soul."

I didn't believe that for a minute.

"Why don't I make a batch of Bloodys for everyone?" Jim said.

"Good idea," I said. "Okay, Lucy. Sit."

Over the next half an hour, Jim and I told Lucy the story of Everett Fairchild, Emily, and us. Even Lucy was shocked and then she wept.

"First of all, can I just tell y'all how much I respect y'all for loving that girl and keeping her. I never told you this either, Anna, but when I was a little girl, just twelve, my daddy and momma ran off and left me and my little sister—David's momma—in a cold trailer with no money and no food. We were living in the country outside of Greenville and lemme tell you, it was the scariest thing that has ever happened to me. We wound up living in foster care until we finally got my daddy's momma to come get us. I think it's why . . . I think that's why . . ." She started to sob. "Oh, shit, y'all, I'm sorry. Why I never had any kids of my own. I was too scared. How could somebody like me take care of a child? I never saw my own momma and daddy again.

They might be dead for all I know. That's one reason I learned how to use the Internet, you know? So's I could try and find 'em."

"Jesus. There are too many stories like yours, Lucy," I said and blew my own nose. The woman never ceased to just clobber my opinion of her. "And too many unhappy children in the world. I mean, even though Jim and I were never, well, you know . . ."

"Shit," Lucy said. "Who cares about that?"

"Well, Anna drove me bullshit trying to get in my bloomers, if you must know."

"Must you tell every person in the universe about that?" I said.

"I don't blame her," Lucy said.

It was a droplet of comic relief. We all smiled.

"Another Bloody?" Jim asked.

"Sure," Lucy said, "what the hell."

"Not for me, thanks. I have a hot date this afternoon, you know."

"Anna," Lucy said, when Jim went to the kitchen, "I swear on my life I won't tell anyone."

"Please. We haven't told Emily and it would be devastating to hear something like that from anyone other than us."

"Well, since you brought it up," Lucy said, "why haven't you ever told her?"

"I just couldn't find the right time or the right words. But I will."

Later, Emily and David came waltzing through the house as though nothing had happened earlier that morning. Actually, that was okay with me if Emily wanted to forget about her tantrum earlier in the morning. Teenagers had flash flood tempers. We both knew that and sometimes it was just better to let the little geysers evaporate.

"We're going to the beach," she said, "be home by five."

"Wear sunscreen!"

"Miss Anna?" David said. "I don't want you to worry about Emily when she's with me. Really."

"I always worry," I said.

"I know, all moms do, but seriously. I wouldn't let anything ever happen to her. I'm a careful driver and a strong swimmer. We don't go in the ocean if there's a strong undertow and I won't let her go over her waist."

"Really? Okay. I'll worry a little less."

He grinned at me and I grinned at him and I thought, Wow, what a nice young man.

They left and Jim and Lucy both said the same thing.

"Okay, he can marry her," Jim said.

"Isn't he something?"

"Yeah. He really is."

Jim went to see a friend of his West of the Ashley and I decided to work in the yard for a while. The yard had continued growing like nothing I had ever seen. Must have been the Miracle-Gro. I was digging up hostas to separate when I felt someone looking at me. Just on some general principle, I decided not to look up. It was probably Miss Mavis. It was.

"Go to church today?"

"No, ma'am. I didn't."

"Didn't think so."

I heard her rustle through the bushes, going back to her house. I wasn't very nice to her, not that she was nice to me. But old ladies like her didn't think they were required to be that nice. They just said whatever popped into their minds. It was sort of an amazing phenomenon that old people believed in as a privilege of certain years.

I heard the rustle again.

"Had dinner?"

This time I stopped and stood up to face her. "No, ma'am. I didn't."

"Well?"

"Well, I appreciate the invitation but I'm kind of a wreck here, all covered in dirt."

"Your yard looks nice. Go wash your hands and come on over. Five minutes. All right?"

What could I say? "Thanks, Miss Mavis. I'll be right there."

Twenty-six

Miss Mavis Says, Cluck, Cluck

I WAS reclining in my pink chair, reading about all the latest weddings in the *Post & Courier*. Heavenly days, some of the brides were so fat and some of the dresses were so tacky, it made me wonder where their mothers were. It truly did. And, their hair! Mercy!

Speaking of hair, I thought that child Anna would eat us out of house and home. I know her life is none of my business, but there's something funny going on in that house. Funny business, that's what. That girl is carrying too much on her shoulders. Entirely too much. As a good Christian woman, I had an obligation to help her. But I didn't know where to start, besides a good meal once in a while and some advice. Well, I could discuss it with Angel.

"Angel? Angel?"

No answer.

"Answer me!"

"I heard you, Mavis, what now?"

"What?"

Angel stood right in front of me with her hands on her hips, looking at me like she was going to spit. I hated her when she did that.

"I said, I hear you the *first* time. I was just drying my hands. Lawd, I wish you'd get yourself a hearing aid."

"I don't need a hearing aid, thank you."

"Humph."

"No comment from the peanut gallery, if you please. Sit down for a minute. I have something to discuss with you."

"You want a glass of tea?"

"No, thank you. If I drink too much tea, I have to run to the little girls' room and I'm plenty comfortable right now."

"You want a cookie?"

"No! Can't you just stop for a minute and sit? Good grief!"

Finally, she put her bony bahunkus down on the hassock opposite me, and folded her hands in her lap.

"All right, Mavis. Tell me what's on your mind now."

"Anna. We've got to do something."

"What are you talking about?"

"That child has too much on her plate. Did you see the way she ate? Good Lord! And, she's so skinny! And why is her ex-husband staying in her house? What are they doing? And Lord in heaven with all His angels and saints, what did he do to her salon? It looks like a bordello! And her daughter?"

Well, don't you know that she started laughing so hard I could all but see her tonsils and a gold crown that she had on a back molar. Not a pretty sight, let me tell you.

"Come on, Angel. Quit laughing like a fool and talk to me!"

"Oh! Lawd! Mavis?" She paused to catch her breath. "Don't you remember what it was like? Now, you ain't never had no business to run like hers, but you sure had a pain-in-the-butt husband and your two chillrun sure 'nough did give you a run for your money! Did you already forget what it was like to be busy all the time?"

"Well, she worries me. Turn down the air conditioner, will you? I'm having a hot flash."

The next thing I heard her say under her breath was, *"You ain't had no hot flash in thirty years, old woman!"*

"I heard that!"

"Well, you ain't."

"Fine. Just turn it down. Thank you." I fiddled with my afghan until she sat down again. "Now, you tell me this. What kind of example is it for her ex-husband to be sleeping there? What could her child think? Isn't it immoral?"

Suddenly, Angel looked at me like I was an incompetent old ninny. It was the expression I hated the most.

"Mavis? I'm gone tell you what and I mean for you to listen to me. I'm your oldest friend, right?"

"I suppose."

"Do you know how to spell trouble?"

I just looked at her.

"B-u-s-y-b-o-d-y! That's what this is. You're all the time looking for something where there ain't nothing and, as the Lawd is my witness, you ought to know by now that sticking your nose in other people's business ain't gone do nothing but bring trouble to your door. Yes, ma'am. Just tell Trouble to come right on in and sit chea on your sofa."

"You listen to me, Miss Know-It-All. Last night when I got up to powder my nose, it must've been two-thirty. I heard a rustle outside and looked out the window and what do you think I saw with my own eyes?"

"There ain't no telling."

"I saw her daughter, that Emily—who she thinks is such a saint—walk out the back door and go off with that boy who's staying at Lucy's. They were off and over the sand dunes in the blink of an eye!"

Angel's eyes grew wide. "You *lie*. Please tell me you *lie!*"

"I do not and you know it."

Angel let loose a long whistle. Personally, I have always thought that to whistle was very unladylike.

"Her momma gone cut her behind iffin she find out. Oh! Do Lawd!" Angel raised her arms up over her head and brought them down, slapping her thighs. (Another gesture I have never used.) "You ain't gone tell her, are you?"

"I don't know yet, but I do know that sleeping with a man you've divorced can't be a good example for a young girl with overactive hormones."

"She ain't sleeping with that little skinny thing."

"And just how do you know that?"

"'Cause she tell me she self. He's gay. Yes, sir. He's one of them gay men."

"My stars! Do you mean to say that he is a homosexual?"

"Yes, indeed. That's right."

Angel and I stared at each other, each of us in our own state of shock, I can promise you. Finally, I decided that Angel understood the need for action.

"Well, now I know why she divorced him," I said.

"Amen."

"That poor child! That poor child! There's Anna working herself to a pulp, while her daughter is running around doing what she shouldn't be doing with that Lucy's houseguest, and her ex-husband can't even do anything for her nerves, if you know what I mean."

"Yes, ma'am, I do. I do indeed."

"No wonder she's so skinny." I stopped to take a tissue from my pocket and blow my nose. "Angel? I have an idea."

"What's that?"

"We're gonna have Father Michaels pay her a visit."

"Do Jesus! Help us and save us! Miss Mavis gone stir the pot now!"

"Well, help me up," I said, and Angel pulled me up out of my chair. "You don't have to yank my arm off, you know. Good gracious! I've got to get busy."

"And just what are you fixin' to do now?"

"Call the rectory?"

I looked at her and her face just dared me to do it. Meddling. That's what I was about to do. "Oh, dear, Angel. I can't send the priest to her house! What can we do?"

"I say we just watch and wait. Next time you see that girl running the road with that boy, you tell me and I'll take care of it, 'eah?"

Twenty-seven

Rock the Boat, Baby

I ATE so much dinner I thought I wouldn't be able to zip my pants. Gosh! Could Angel fry chicken or what? So good! I put away all the garden tools when I got home, thinking all the while that tonight was probably the night old Arthur was gonna go for my knickers. Was I going to put up a fight? No, I was not. There was a line of protest in the game of love. He says nothing but starts undoing your blouse or something and you say, *Oh! I don't know if we should be doing this* . . . and then, as he knows you're not seriously objecting, the fun begins.

What would I wear? Something difficult? A hook-and-eye challenge? Did I have decent underwear? Probably not. That nagging little voice in my head—the one that needed a muzzle—reminded me that Arthur had made this whole stink about getting involved. Fine. We would see what we would see.

After rummaging my drawers and deciding I didn't have any lingerie I'd even wear to my own car wreck, I got in my car and raced over the connector bridge to the Towne Centre. In a hair of the time it took me to find a parking spot, I was already on my way back to the

322 Doroth

house with two bras and two pairs of panties all wrapped in pink tissue from the store that had no secrets. Both of them could cause cardiac arrhythmia, I decided, pleased to death.

I took a shower, shaved every square inch that needed it, and when I got out, I inspected my armpits in the mirror to make sure I hadn't missed anything. Then I creamed myself with After Tan. Now that may not seem too glamorous, but it didn't attract bugs. On my island, it was all about bugs. I was in a towel, hair still dripping, wiping the steam off the bathroom mirror, when the phone rang, almost scaring me out of my skin. I was busy in another world, envisioning myself with Arthur.

"Hello?"

"Wow! Your voice is pretty husky there, ma'am. Did I interrupt something?"

It was him. I cleared my throat. "Nope." I giggled. "I just got out of the shower."

"Oh. Good! Showers are good!"

God. He was as much of a dork as I was. "Yeah, well, I was working in the yard."

"Ah! So. Um, what time are we getting together tonight?"

"What time is it now?"

"Six."

How about 6:01? "What are we doing?" A *leading question* . . .

"I dunno. I was thinking dinner, a good wine, some moonlight, and then we'd see. How about I pick you up around seven-thirty? We can watch the sunset."

"Sounds great," I said. "Dress code?"

"Something comfortable—I'm making dinner for us."

"Fabulous!" I said, and we hung up.

I was at war with my closet when Emily came in. She was covered in sand and I could smell beer. Needless to say, she was sunburned.

"Good Lord, Emily! What happened to you?"

"Volleyball in front of the One-Eyed Parrot, lots of laughs, and too much sun. Uhh. I need to lie down. David wants to go to some party tonight, but I'm too tired."

"Get a shower, take two aspirin, and lie down for a while." Somehow aspirin could ward off the nausea and headache that came with overexposure to the sun. Not to mention beer.

"Yeah. I'll do that right now. You going out?"

"Just over to Arthur's—he's making dinner for us."

"Have fun. I'm dead. Where's Dad?"

"I think he's out with some friends—he'll be in at some point."

"Okay." The bathroom door closed and I heard her start the shower.

I pulled out a pair of black silk tapered pants that looked pretty good despite their age and tried them on with a slinky horizontal black and beige pin-striped, double V-neck pullover with three-quarter sleeves. It was one of those knitted tops that felt good to touch—the first and most essential consideration. But it looked innocent and at the same time, could slip from one shoulder to reveal the lacy strap of an—at best—marginally concealed weapon. Ooh. I was so bad. I blew my hair out straight, applied very natural looking makeup, except for my eyes. I knew we'd be back out on that dock again and unless I did something a little dramatic with my eye makeup, he wouldn't be able to see me hypnotizing him. *You're feeling very relaxed. Your guard is down. You want to fall in love with me. You want to lionize me. . . .* I decided then that the courtship, or the pursuit, or whatever they called it these days, would be as much fun as the capture. I hadn't felt so ripe for a hunt in, well, forever. This time I wore flat sandals.

It was seven-fifteen. Emily was already snoozing. David had called and she told him to call her back at nine and if she was alive, maybe they'd go out for ice cream or something. That sounded reasonable and I had tucked her in, closing the blinds. I heard Arthur's car and went to the door to meet him so we wouldn't wake Emily up.

"Hey!" I whispered, "Emily's sleeping—too much sun."

"Hey, yourself. Let's go."

He looked me up and down and seemed a little self-conscious and nervous. This was a good sign. We drove to his house, making small talk, him looking over at me and when I'd catch his eye, he'd look away.

"I set up dinner on the dock," he said.

How romantic! "Sounds like fun," I said.

We walked through the house to the porch and I could see that he had gone to considerable trouble to set a stage. There was a small metal round table at the end of the dock and two chairs. On it was a silver ice bucket with a bottle of something. A little hibachi, resting on the dock's edge, was sending out smoke signals from its smoldering coals, next to a cooler that I guessed held dinner, protecting the food from bugs and us from salmonella. There was nothing like the smell of lighter fluid to remind me of a more nostalgic time, when everyone used briquettes and didn't worry about cancer every two minutes. Beside the ice bucket was a small cutting board covered with a clean dish towel over some snacks.

And, there was a boat at the dock.

"This is one very groovy picnic," I said.

"Yeah," he said, while he poured two glasses of wine, handing me one.

"Thanks. Whose boat?"

"Oh, the neighbor's boy I told you about."

It was a pretty decent boat—brand-new fiberglass with a fore and aft deck and what appeared to be an area below to sleep. There was a serious fishing chair on the back.

"Look at the sky," he said and looped his arm around my waist.

The western sky held radiating streams of light, coming from the sun through the clouds. Streaks of indigo and gold were spread across the sky where, by the second, the blistering sun was slipping away. The summer sun didn't disappear into the horizon, but in the lower half of the sky, there seemed to be a fiery line that would open in every shade of heat. The white sun was surrounded by huge stains of red and deep fuchsia—like some great artist had brushed the sky with a paint of opaque jewels. The hotter the day, the more extravagant the sunset.

I stood there with Arthur and stared, the same way I had when I'd climbed to Lucy's lookout so many nights, filled with awe to take it all in.

"Fabulous," I said. "You know, it makes you wonder."

"Wonder what?" he said.

"About everything."

"Are we about to get heavy?"

"No. It's too early for philosophy. Besides, you promised to feed me and I am ravenous."

"I like my women hungry."

"Then you should adore me," I said, without thinking.

"That's exactly what I worry about," he said.

I ignored that and said, "I could eat like a man. And, of course you should adore me," I said, "I'm the perfect woman." That was pretty outrageous to say so I punched him lightly in the side to show him he needed to lighten up.

He smiled and so did I.

"You are?"

"Yes! I am!"

"I can't wait to hear what qualifies you as perfect."

"Well, you have to consider the market of what's available. First, I'm old enough that you don't have to put me through college."

"Which implies . . ."

"That too many men your age are chasing skirts young enough to be their dependants."

"Oh, dear! Can that be true? Butta-bing."

"Butta-boom. You know it's true. They don't know your music and they heard about your childhood from their parents. Okay?"

"Ouch!"

"So much for dating girls instead of women. Secondly, I don't want anything from you."

"You don't?"

He pulled me to his chest, held my arms behind my back, and licked my neck, giving me goose bumps and weak knees.

"Well, besides the obvious."

We exchanged knowing smirks and then he let me go.

"I'm gonna cook our veal chops before it gets too dark. Medium?"

"Whatever you think," I said. "See? That's another thing. I'm agreeable. Most women are always giving orders and nagging. Not me."

"Well, if there's one thing I truly hate, it's somebody getting in my face and telling me what's wrong with me. That's the fastest way to get rid of me."

"Me too. Growing up I had nuns for teachers and a grandmother who didn't like one single thing about me. Mainly because I look like my mother, who she hated."

"Ah! Here's comes the flaw! Emotional baggage!"

"Negative! I keep my baggage to myself, thanks. I'm old enough that I'm over it."

"Really? Nothing bothers you about your past?"

(For the rest of this date, the role of the Seductress will be played by the Liar.)

"Nope."

"Wow."

"And, I don't want to get involved either. I mean, I'd like to have a guy friend, maybe with privileges."

"Privileges?"

"You know. . . ."

Even in the fading light, I could see him smiling, thinking he had just struck pay dirt.

"Well, that seems completely reasonable. After all, we're two adults, right?"

"Exactly."

I took the plastic container of salad from the cooler and mixed it with the dressing, refilled our wineglasses, and watched him cook as the day disappeared. Over dinner, which was so good I couldn't believe it, we talked about him. If there was one thing I had learned, it was that men liked to talk about themselves.

"Really? You came to Charleston for the summer because it's boring in New York? That's a new one."

"Well," he said, "the regular restaurantgoers leave for the Hamptons on Thursday or Friday so the city is left to the tourists. And August is almost completely dead. Anyway, I always wanted to see what Charleston was like and it was a good time to do it."

"So what do you think?"

"I think Charleston is the best-kept secret in America. I mean, everybody's heard of it but they don't know how cool it really is. If I didn't have my son in New York, I might stay forever. Who knows? And, the people are nice."

"Yes, we are."

Dinner was finished and I stood up to take his plate, thinking I would just put everything in the cooler and help him carry it back up to the house. I thought we'd probably do the dishes and then sit on the porch. Maybe I could get him in the hammock with me. He had other plans. When I reached for his plate he put his hand around my wrist.

"Not so fast," he said, "it's too nice out here." He pulled me to his lap and I put my plate back on the table.

"What did you have in mind?"

"You."

Well, that was it. We picked up right where we had left off the last Sunday. Next thing I know, he throws a beach towel on the dock and we're lying on it. Thank God it had become dark. Next thing I know after that, we're both naked and about to get it on, right there on the damn dock for all the world to see. I couldn't continue. It was too bohemian.

"Arthur!"

"What?"

"We can't do this on the dock!"

"Why not?"

When I didn't answer, he got up and pulled me to my feet.

"Get on board."

It was the perfect solution. Without a word and without a stitch of clothes, we climbed on the boat. Sure enough, there was a small cabin below with a couch that converted to a bed. We pulled the back cushions away and *resumed*. For the next two hours, there was a whole lot of moaning and gymnastics and you name it.

"Arthur!"

"Anna."

Not a lot of chitchat. But he said my name and I loved hearing it the way he said it. It sounded like he was saying, *Finally. At last.* It was enough. I didn't need a running commentary. You know the old *actions speak louder than words*? Arthur was amazing. The fact that we were in such a tight space and the boat rocked with the incoming tide only added to the wildest—well, let's just say it was amazing and be done with the details. Except for this—at one point, my heart was beating so hard, I thought I might die. And, if there had been an Olympic medal for endurance, Arthur would've taken the gold.

Alright, that was more than I intended to say.

We were lulled by the water's movement. The cabin smelled like us and I loved the smell. He looked so innocent! Who knew? Occasionally, I would hear the sounds of gulls and then the water lapping against the hull finally put me into the deepest sleep. It had to have been after two in the morning.

I was dreaming one minute and the next minute I heard something like a horn. Arthur got up.

"You folks alright?"

Shit! Shit! Shit!

I peeked out the tiny window. There was a Coast Guard boat with two men right next to us and it appeared that we had floated down from our dock on the Isle of Palms to the Ben Sawyer Bridge on Sullivan's Island. It was morning. I was naked. Arthur was naked. The sun was up. We were in the worst sort of compromised position. There wasn't a beach towel or a T-shirt anywhere to cover ourselves. Were we going to be arrested? I panicked and covered myself with a cushion, hoping they wouldn't come on our boat. No such luck.

"Want to put on some pants, sir?"

The voice came from just a few feet away. He was *on* our boat.

"It seems I left them at our dock and it appears that we floated quite a ways and, um . . . my wife's in there, sir, and she's, um, in the same situation. Wedding anniversary."

Wife? Wedding anniversary? PLEASE DON'T LOOK IN HERE!

"I see," said the official who could and probably would ruin my at life any second. "Can you start the boat?"

"Um, it actually belongs to my neighbor. I don't know the first thing about boats."

I wanted to die. There were no curtains. Nothing. A seat cushion. Now I find out that I am with the King of the Screws and he can't start a freaking boat. Great. I was already visualizing our pictures in the paper with some sensational headline. LOVE BOAT COUPLE FOUND NAKED AND ARRESTED.

"Lower the engine and turn the key!" I shouted. "Anybody got a T-shirt or something?"

"Harry! Gimme my windbreaker," I heard the man say and then saw a windbreaker fly through the opening, landing not far from my foot. "Well, if this ain't the goddamndest thaing I seen in a long time. Why don't I follow you folks home and let's just verify a few facts."

I stuck my leg out and pulled the jacket toward me with my toes. We were going to be arrested for stealing a boat, public nudity, and who knew what else? I contemplated suicide. I put on the windbreaker and at that same second, I spotted a yellow box of garbage bags, the big black kind. I pulled the windbreaker around myself and grabbed one. I tore a hole in the top for my head and two more in the sides for my arms. Stepping aside from the opening, I took off the windbreaker and put the bag on over my head. Nice dress. Jim should see me now, I thought. I fixed another bag for Arthur and handed it out through the opening.

"Pull this over your head, nature boy."

"Thanks."

I caught the eye of the Coast Guard officer and saw that he was snickering. Well, if he thought this was funny, maybe we wouldn't get in trouble. I decided to play along, thinking that if we entertained them, things would go easier when we got back to the dock. I went on deck in all my black plastic splendor. My hair was all in knots and I could feel my lips were swollen. I must have been some sight.

"Can you start this boat, ma'am?"

"Of course I can! I'm *from* here, unlike my Yankee husband!" I turned the key and lowered the engine into the water, then revved it up. "Pull in the bumpers, okay, honey? And the rope?"

I watched Arthur pull the white bumpers and the soggy rope over the side and into the boat.

"Honey? When we get home, I'm gonna kill you. You know that, don't you?"

"I'm sorry, baby," Arthur said, "I should've checked the knots."

"Well, darling, this sure was the most unforgettable anniversary we ever had."

"How many years you two been married?"

"Ten," I said, at the same time Arthur said, "Twelve."

"What's your name, Officer?" I said, pretending there was nothing out of the ordinary going on.

"Oh, I'm sorry, ma'am. I'm Chief Bill Benton. Happy anniversary."

"Thanks, Chief Benton. Nothing but bliss for all these years."

As the boat sped up the Intracoastal Waterway, all I could do was hope to God I could remember where the dock was. Arthur stood next to me and elbowed me when it was time to slow down and make the turn. Chief Benton helped me dock the boat. When he saw our clothes and the table and all our things on the dock, he smiled and shook his head. We climbed out and shook hands with him.

"The boat belongs to the son of our neighbor over there," Arthur said and pointed to the house. "What time is it?"

"Five-thirty. I don't want to wake them up. Boat looks okay. You know, I shoulda done this with my Patsy thirty years ago. She woulda loved it."

"Well, it seemed like a good idea at the time," Arthur said.

"Maybe it's not too late!" I said, pretending to be his new friend.

The chief winked at me and said, "No harm done, I suppose. You folks stay happy, okay?" He flagged his partner to approach the dock and in a minute he was pulling away, laughing at us.

Arthur turned to me and we just started laughing, laughing so hard that tears ran down our faces. I was pulling my underwear on under the bag like a contortionist. Then, I had one leg in my pants and then the other. Finally, I put on my top and ran my hands through my hair.

"I wish I'd had a camera," I said. "Oh, my God! You shoulda seen your face!"

"And yours! When you came out in that bag, I lost it!"

"I thought I looked pretty darn good! Some anniversary!"

"Want a divorce?" he asked.

"Are you crazy? I want to know what we're gonna do for an encore!"

I went home and sneaked inside. Emily and Jim were sleeping and I thanked heaven for that small favor. I took a shower and since it was too early to get up, I decided to lie down on the couch with a quilt. All I could think about was Arthur and what had gone on between us. Coast Guard rescue aside, I knew I would never get him out of my system. I had fallen in love and in lust and I don't even know in what order. Not get involved? Yeah, good luck.

Twenty-eight
Incredible Odds

I DRAGGED myself into the salon by nine, grateful that no one knew what had happened last night. But on a curious note, I wanted to tell somebody about my "cruise" because without question, it was the funniest thing that had ever happened to me. It was even more insane than a Lucy story, and those were my benchmarks for the outrageous. Nonetheless, I said nothing, thinking maybe I would tell Jim and Frannie. It was too fabulous to file away and repress.

"Here's your schedule for today," Lucy said, handing me the list. "You look worn out, girl. What'd you do last night?"

"Hot date with the Cheese Whiz."

"Isn't it always about men?"

"Seems like it." The mystery plant was on the floor next to Lucy's desk. I had all but forgotten about it. "Who sent this thing?"

"Dunno," she said, "no card."

"Where'd it come from?"

"Belva's."

"If you have a minute, why don't you call Belva's and see who it was."

Somehow I got through the day without giving myself away and, of course, promptly forgot about the origin of the plant. Besides, Mr. Don't Want to Get Involved called around three.

"Wassup, Ms. Abbot? You busy?"

"Not at the moment. What's on your mind?"

"I was just thinking about you. You know, last night and everything."

"I'm never getting on another boat for the rest of my life."

I could hear him laugh a little and instantly I began to relive the other, more intense episode that made me sleep like the dead in the first place. I couldn't decide whether I had better never see him again or put him on a leash. Who was I kidding? I wanted him all to myself.

"Did you hear what I said?"

"I'm sorry, Arthur, I was just thinking about last night and this place is a little noisy. What did you say?"

"I said, I don't have to work Thursday night. Do you want to go do something?"

"Sure," I said, and then remembered that Jim was leaving Thursday. "Wanna cook or go out? Movies?"

"I was thinking about this restaurant I found downtown. It's pretty charming."

"Sounds like a plan," I said.

"And, Anna?"

"Yeah?"

"I enjoyed last night, I mean what happened between us. I enjoyed it very much."

"Me too."

We hung up and I was so pissed off I thought I would spit fire. He *enjoyed it?* What was I? Dessert? He couldn't say something like, *Wasn't it incredible?* No. This unromantic dumb-ass was thanking me like I had given him a piece of pie instead of my body and soul for hours on end *and* I'd wound up dressed in a garbage bag, humiliated beyond description.

He *enjoyed* it.

Well, isn't that *special*. I had to assume that him calling me was slight headway. Actually, given his politics, a phone call from Arthur probably should have been considered hot pursuit/stalking. Was I taking a crumb he tossed my way and making something larger out of it?

Yes.

This whole dating thing made me truly insecure.

I turned my attention to planning something for Wednesday night to say bon voyage to Jim. I knew he needed some uplifting. It sounded like it was going to be all but impossible for Jim to have a civilized visit with Gary's family. I realized that my stupid, almost obsessive, musings over Arthur were pretty low on the scale of real issues like the one facing Jim and Gary. Once again, my relationship with Jim had helped me put things in perspective. I decided to go all out and have a big cookout in the backyard.

I called Frannie on the off chance that she might be free to come and surprise Jim. Besides, I was dying to see her myself. It had been far too long since we'd made the effort and Jim was a great excuse for anyone to go the extra mile.

"Hey! Frannie! It's me. You got a minute?"

"Girl! *Where* have you been? I've been missing you! You got your house and opened your business and I suck so bad, I didn't even send you a plant! How's it going?"

I brought her up to date, leaving out the story of Arthur and the boat. Then I told her about Gary and how upset Jim was, that he was going to try and see him.

"I think he needs us, Frannie."

"Whoa. No shit. And, I expect that Miss Trixie knows nothing."

"Probably not. I didn't ask him if he had told her or not. I should call her and ask her to dinner for Wednesday."

"Lemme get this straight. You're calling me on Monday to see if I can be there Wednesday?"

"Yeah. No can do, right?"

"Wait a minute. I have to be in Raleigh on Friday—tobacco business—don't ask. I could leave on Wednesday, fly to Charleston—can I spend the night at Chez Anna?"

"Of course!"

"Then I could fly out Thursday night. Let me see if there's a flight. I'll call you back."

In an hour, it was all done. Frannie was coming.

I called Daddy and invited him, after checking with Lucy to see what the temperature of their relationship was. They were back in love. Naturally, I invited Brigitte and Bettina and her husband and I assumed Emily and David would be there. I should have told Arthur, but he probably had to work. Everyone agreed to help and we kept it a secret to surprise Jim.

After work, Emily and I took a long look at the backyard. I didn't have a deck. I only had one tiny charcoal grill. I didn't even have a hammock. All that existed there was beach grass, a shed, and a ton of flowering bushes and plants. I looked at my checkbook and the story was pretty dismal. However, I did have a Visa card with a liberal limit that I almost never used. Once again, since leaving the watchful eye of Daddy, I was about to blow the bank.

"Emily? Let's go to Lowe's and just see what it would cost to make this yard look like something."

"Can we stop at Taco Bell?"

"You bet."

Six tacos and two Diet Pepsis later, while strolling the aisles of Lowe's, Emily and I calculated that we could get a table with an umbrella, six chairs, a medium-sized Fiesta gas grill, and a small Pawley's Island rope hammock on a frame for right under a thousand dollars. This "Sydney" collection of furniture wasn't out of *Lifestyles of the Rich and Famous*, but it would do the job.

"What the hell, Mom," Emily said, "go for it."

I did. For another forty dollars I bought enough citronella torches to make the backyard look like we were having a luau.

"I don't want to point this out, Mom, but you got six chairs and ten people."

"We'll use the chairs in the house."

"And, you gotta have food. What are you gonna cook?"

"Obviously, something from the grill! Don't wreck my good mood, missy. I'd hock my jewelry for Jim."

"Um, you don't have any jewelry."

"Well, if I did . . ."

"Whatever."

By Wednesday morning, I had a menu, courtesy of Bettina and Brigitte. I had seven pounds of baby back ribs marinating in Lucy's refrigerator for the grill. And I planned to serve steamed shrimp to pick on while the ribs cooked. Brigitte was bringing salad and a watermelon basket. Bettina was bringing meatballs. Lucy was bringing her blender.

And I had invited Trixie. It went like this.

"Trixie? Hi! It's Anna."

There was a sigh, punctuated with silence and another sigh. "Well, hello," she said, "how are you, dear?"

In Trixie's vocabulary, *dear* was a name reserved for those she held as slightly putrid. I thought, Oh, screw her, let me just invite her and be done with it.

"I'm fine, thanks, busy. You know."

"Ah'm sure you are. Bless your heart."

"Anyway, the reason I called is that you know Jim's leaving on Thursday . . ."

"No, Ah didn't know. Is he going back to California?"

"Uh, yes. So Emily and I thought it would be a good idea to do something like have a cookout for him Wednesday night and we were hoping you could join us."

"Ah'll have to let you know. Ah'm not sure of what's on my calendar and I'm just running out the door now. Call you later?"

Call me never for all I care. "Sure. That's fine."

Why was it that certain people in my life made me feel guilty over every single thing? Was it my fault that Jim hadn't told her he was leaving? No. After the way she had treated Emily I should have just reduced our relationship with her to greeting cards on required occasions. But, hell no. The good little Catholic girl in me was always willing to turn the other cheek. The Queen of Darkness in her was always willing to give that cheek another slap. I'd never accept that Trixie was just as committed to inflicting personal pain as I was to reconciliation. Intellectually, I wanted to be nice to Trixie for Jim's sake and I wanted her to have a place in Emily's life. And, years ago, she had tried awfully hard to help me, so I owed her something.

She called later to accept. She asked if she could bring anything. Now we would be eleven. Maybe she could bring a chair.

On Wednesday, I sent Jim off with a list of things to do. Most of them were just silly errands to keep him out of the house so he wouldn't know I had anything going on that night. Lowe's called at three to say they were ready to deliver the furniture so Lucy and Emily took off for home to make sure it was in the right place, level with the ground, and wiped down with Fantastik. By the time I got home, the table and chairs were immaculate, the umbrella was raised, the hammock was hung, and the citronella torches were in place. It looked like I was having a party except for one thing—no word from Frannie. She was supposed to have arrived by four. Maybe her flight had been delayed. I asked Emily to call the airlines and check.

"Air traffic controllers delayed the flight because of some storm system that they think *might* get in the way, Mom. Nothing she can do about that."

"Storm system, bull. It's eighty-five degrees and clear as a bell. Probably a security thing." We went outside and looked at the skies. Not a cloud in sight in any direction. "Well, let's hope she makes it tonight."

Lucy went home to shower and returned at six thirty with an aluminum folding table to use for a buffet, hauled by David, who had

taken a bath in some kind of loud cologne and couldn't take his eyes off Emily, who had stripped the color out of her hair that afternoon and begged Brigitte to apply a platinum blond toner, which she did and finally Emily looked like Emily. In fact, Emily looked like she'd never left the Lowcountry, thus beginning a pronounced change in Emily's appearance and attitude. Maybe the clothes she wore had been in her closet all the time, but she had on a baby pink T-shirt and white shorts, which were too short, but I said not one word about it. With all that swinging blond hair and those green eyes of hers, she looked her age and she looked pretty.

"You got a white sheet?" Lucy asked me.

"Toga party?" Emily said.

"No, Klan meeting," I said.

Emily got this look on her face.

"Oh, for pity's sake, Emily. She needs a sheet for a tablecloth! Go look in the linen closet!" Lucy and I exchanged looks of mock despair. *Adults are not allowed to make jokes that aren't one hundred percent politically correct. Adults are not allowed to have a sense of humor that is counterpoint to the teenager's. Adults should admit they're old and boring and just go someplace and be quiet, except when teenagers need money, car keys, or rescue from any number of things.*

"Kids," she said.

Bettina and Bobby arrived with a covered pot, so hot that Bobby carried it with pot holders, rushing ahead of Bettina, who was fishing something out of her trunk.

"Hi!" I said.

"You gotta be Anna," he said, "heard a lot about ya."

"I'm so glad to meet you, Bobby. We love Bettina to death!"

"Nice place," he said, nodding his head at my flower beds. "Where do you want me to put this?"

"Oh! Let me take it for you!"

"Nah. Too heavy," he said, "I'll just put it in the kitchen."

Manly. Very manly. Whew.

"Got my CDs and my boom box," Bettina said and whizzed past

me on her wooden platform mules. "I brought eighties dance club music from New York!"

Well, I thought, there goes the shag contest. Guess I'm gonna have to learn how to Hustle.

Next came Brigitte with a huge watermelon, carved to look like a basket with a handle, filled with strawberries, cantaloupe, and all kinds of chopped fruit.

"Holy cow! Did you make this?"

"This is what a sporadic sex life does to you. Your freaking Martha gene rears its highlighted head and you start carving rosettes out of radishes."

"I'm single and, lemme tell you, honey, I couldn't make one of those if life and limb depended on it. But I can garden."

"My point exactly," she said, standing there with the watermelon balanced on one hip. She looked hard at the explosion of flowers that were all but growing up the sides of my house and into the windows. She turned to me with an arched eyebrow and said, "This place looks like the freaking Charleston Botanical Gardens!"

"It's all about the dirt," I said.

"Sure."

"Let me help you," I said.

"Here," she said, "I'll go get the salad."

"Okay, we're out back." I went inside and out through the kitchen to the backyard.

I had a cooler in the backyard filled with beer and a few bottles of opened white wine. Emily was spreading a sheet over the table—pink and gray plaid, which actually looked pretty good next to the gray-and-white-striped seat cushions around my new table.

"Yeah, first I grabbed a contour sheet," she said, "figures. But you have to say this looks, like, completely perfect."

Lucy was unwrapping the plastic tumblers, plates, and paper napkins and, when Daddy arrived, the blender started to hum. The new grill, which we rolled over to the folding table, was fired up, and soon the ribs were spread across the grate filling the air with the scent of

Stubb's barbecue sauce and pork fat. There was nothing to compare
with the smell of melting brown sugar, mustard, and meat cooking.

Trixie strolled in with preruffled feathers and Daddy immediately
went to her side and was the consummate diplomat. Finally, she spoke
to Emily.

"There now! Don't you look nice?"

"Thanks, Gram," Emily said. "I decided blond hair was better for
the summer. I was gonna put some blue streaks in, but I didn't have
time."

"I heard that," I said to her, grabbing her arm as she tried to escape.
"Was that necessary?"

"Yes," she said, "good one, huh?"

"You're my girl and don't ever forget it," I said to her in a low
voice.

"Learned at the knee of the master!" she shot back and took off
in the direction of David, who Lucy had breaking up ice in the
cooler.

I turned back to see Trixie holding her bosom and Daddy shaking
his head.

Then I heard him say to Trixie, "You know, these young people
always want to get our goat, don't they?"

"Ah imagine so," she said, with her chin raised and her lips pursed
as tight as a cheap perm.

Daddy took her arm and led her to Lucy, who was mixing rum
drinks and fruit in her blender, which was attached to my kitchen by
the longest orange extension cord I had ever seen. *Just give her one of
your frozen bombs, Lucy. Set her mind right!*

Bettina had her music blasting from her boom box and was dancing with Bobby, who was a dead ringer for John Travolta in *Saturday
Night Fever*, the way he moved. Good Lord, I thought, this is not your
typical Lowcountry party. No one was wearing Weejuns or Pappagal-
los and there wasn't a stitch of Lilly Pulitzer in sight, except for Trixie,
who was fully swaddled in a watermelon print with a matching green
sweater set. I realized that times had changed. The rest of us looked

like we could have been from anywhere in the country. The Low-country had been invaded once again by Yankee apparel chain stores. We were in danger of losing our fashion identity. Then I giggled because I would rather have gone naked—*and I had done that, hadn't I*—than look like Trixie.

By the time Jim arrived, there was a party in full swing.

"Surprise!" everyone said.

"Have y'all gone completely mad? Where did all this furniture come from?"

"Where do you think?" I said, taking his arm and bringing him to the gathering little crowd that we were.

"Girl! You shop Lowe's like other girls shop Saks!"

"Ah was beginning to think you weren't coming," Trixie said.

"Hi, Mother!" He kissed her cheek. "You look like a picture of summer!"

Trixie smiled and twisted her pearls.

Jim was delighted. Everyone came up to Jim to wish him well on his trip, to tell him what a marvel he was, to say that they would miss him, and to ask when he was coming back. He spotted Emily with her new hair and smiled, obviously liking what he saw.

"You look beautiful, Emily," he said, then turned to David, who had his arm around her shoulder. "Watch yourself with your arm, young man. That's my only child in your possessive clutch. I can always come back here and—"

"Oh, Daddy," Emily said.

All she had to do was say *Daddy* and Jim dissolved into a sputtering mush ball.

"Well, there's a hand attached to it." He took her by both shoulders and said, "Oh, Emily, I'll miss you, sweetheart." He threw his arms around her and hugged her until I thought she would wind up with cracked ribs. "You know my cell number, right?"

"By heart," she said.

"Use it, okay? Call me if you need anything—especially if you're thinking of doing something *stupid*." He shot David a look that said it all.

"We're not doing anything stupid, sir," David said, blushing deep red.

Emily took David's hand, and they walked away.

I lifted the last of the ribs from the grill, put them on a platter, and placed them on the table, thinking it would be a thousand years before I ever got the grill clean.

"Smells good," said a familiar voice.

I looked around to see my oldest girlfriend.

"Frannie! You made it!"

"I wouldn't have missed the chance to see all this! Wow! You have a house and a yard and everything! Saints preserve us! How'd you do it without me?"

"I had Jim."

"Where is that old dog I dragged my behind all over hell's half acre to see?"

"He's here and he's gonna faint when he sees you! Oh! I'm so thrilled to see you, you just don't know. Where's the other half of you? How much weight have you lost?"

"A billion pounds! Stress, a new man, and Weight Watchers. But you are not half as thrilled as I am! I can't believe I'm here!"

I hugged her so hard I gave myself a chiropractic adjustment. "Is he single, I hope?"

"No, but getting separated. . . ."

I looked at her with disapproval and she gathered up one side of her mouth.

"Well, this one is actually *seriously* in the process. . . . You know, in Washington, they're all a bunch of liars. It's not so easy at our age. You just hope for the best and tell yourself it's their mortal sin and not yours, right?"

"I don't know, Frannie. Dating stinks. Let's get you a drink and go find Jim."

"Is that Frannie?" Daddy said, coming through the crowd with Lucy's arm intertwined around his. "Well! What a nice surprise!"

"Yes, sir, Dr. Lutz. Great to see you again!"

They shook hands and by the look on Frannie's face, it was clear she was amused by Daddy's proximity to Lucy. It didn't take long for Lucy to clarify.

"Hey, I'm Lucy, Frannie," she said, "I live next door and Dougle Darlin' is my sweetie-pie."

"Well! That's great! Really!" Frannie said and, turning to me, mouthed *Whoa!* "About that drink?"

Jim was at the cooler, pulling out a beer.

"Hey, ugly," she said, tapping his shoulder. "What's this I hear about you abandoning the East?"

"Oh, ho! Look who's *here!* And, who *you* calling ugly, ugly? Give me a meaningful hug!"

"Look at you with all this nasty gel in your hair! Go take a bath!"

"What? Look at all your hair! Ain't you never heard of a beauty parlor?"

"Bump you!"

"Yeah? Well, bump you!"

This continued as I knew it would until they decided to really talk to each other. They were teasing and laughing like they were ten years old again. Same old tune, new lyrics. I was so excited to have a night with them and suddenly wished everyone else would leave. However, I had to feed the crowd.

I needn't have worried about moving things along because as soon as they saw the platter of ribs, everyone fixed themselves a plate. Some people sat at the table and others stood by the buffet, laughing and talking. Trixie was thoroughly entertained by Daddy and Lucy, and of course, Jim spent some time with her. Soothing Trixie and her cat fits were requiring more effort than I thought she was worth. If Jim wanted to suck up to his mother, I understood because after all, she was his mother. But I, perched on my high moral ground, would have no part of it. Anyone who abused my child was dead in my heart.

And then I thought about Daddy. Soothing his cat fits would probably have looked like more effort than he was worth to Jim. Funny how we excused our own relatives everything and our in-laws had to twist any sort of forgiveness out of us like they were asking for a kidney. But maybe it was because they set the tone for vengeance the first moment they laid eyes on us and continued for years to be suspicious over whether we were good enough for their children? Ring a bell? Yeah, like freaking Big Ben.

I looked around to see where Emily was. David was in the hammock and she was pushing it. They were talking and laughing—probably about what a bunch of old geezers we were—but they seemed to be having a good time. He was a nice young man and I thought a pretty good influence.

Finally, around eleven, everyone went home until it was just Jim and Frannie in the kitchen, taking over the clean-up mission, and Lucy and I in the yard. Daddy had left first to follow Trixie over the Cooper River Bridge. She announced that she would feel safer driving by the drunken scum who convened nightly at the foot of the bridge on the Charleston side if she had a charming escort. Emily and David had disappeared. If I had to guess I would say that they had stolen a six-pack and had run to the beach as fast as they could. Just a guess, you understand. Brigitte, Bettina, and Bobby all left together, but not before they gave Jim a gift.

"Open it!" they said.

Bobby rolled his eyes and said, "I ain't had nothing to do with this. Nothing."

It was a T-shirt with our logo on the back and on the front, on the breast pocket, was printed in one-inch pink letters: BIG JIM, HEAD BANANA.

"Do you realize what this will do for my social life in San Francisco?" he said good-naturedly.

"Oh, ma Gaaad!" Bettina said. "I didn't think of that! I sware ta Gaaad, you guys!"

"You're just a scandal, Jim," Brigitte said. "Come on. We all gotta work tomorrow."

"Y'all, thanks for coming," I said to them out front by their cars, "I think this meant a lot to Jim."

We all stood there in the moonlight feeling pretty good about ourselves. More than that, we had established ourselves as our own little tribe. We belonged to each other and we belonged together. Even Lucy. Emily. Jim. *Anna's Cabana* had bonded some unlikely characters. If I had known that independence could cause this kind of adrenaline rush, I probably would've tried to strike out long ago.

An hour later, Lucy was still hanging around, drinking wine with us. I thought that maybe she didn't see that I wanted my old friends to myself and so at first, I was a little annoyed that she didn't leave when everyone else did. I helped myself to a beer from the refrigerator, my first of the night, and went out to the backyard where she was with Jim and Frannie. It was so nice to see them around my new table, relaxed and talking, but they seemed serious. Too serious.

"What's going on? Did somebody die or what?" I said.

"No," Frannie said, "but you might when you hear what Lucy just told us."

"What? Emily?"

"Emily's fine. Sit," Jim said, "I don't feel like picking you up off the ground."

I looked from face to face. The news was obviously horrible—too horrible for Jim or Frannie to tell me.

"What happened, Lucy?"

"Anna? You ain't gonna believe this."

"Okay, what?"

"On my life, Anna, I never meant to interfere in your business."

"Get to the point, okay?"

"Well, remember how I told you that I used the Internet to search for my parents?"

"You found them? Why that's wonder . . ."

"No, I didn't find my momma and daddy. I found Everett Fairchild."

"WHAT?"

"All I did was go to Google and type in his name. He's a Sea Pro dealer in Clearwater, Florida."

It *was* a good thing I was sitting down. I could barely breathe.

"Guess what else?" Lucy said.

"You're not gonna like this," Jim said.

"No kidding," Frannie said.

I waited.

"He's the regional sales manager and he's coming here in August for a sales meeting at Wild Dunes. It's all on his website."

"You *will* both be back in August?" I said to Frannie and Jim.

"Nah. Too hot here in August," Jim said.

"He's screwing with you, Anna. Of course we'll be back. But we need to talk this through and then we need a plan." She was the same Frannie—capable and in charge.

"Holy Mother. What were the odds on this?" I took a long drink of the beer. "I've got some serious thinking to do. Lucy, did you tell Daddy?"

"Hell no!" She rolled her eyes all over her head. "I've been sweating all night debating how to tell you this anyway! I wouldn't tell him!"

"Good. Please don't. For the moment, I think it's best if we just keep this to ourselves. This is my issue and I have to think it through. I knew this would happen one day."

"That's not all," Lucy said. "I found the card that came with the plant. It must've fallen out and slipped under my desk."

"Well?" I said, waiting for what couldn't be any more unnerving that what she had just told me.

"Well, it was weird to me. It was from some guy named Jack Taylor. It said, *'I loved meeting you, Sheena. Let's be friends. Jack Taylor.'* Who the hell is Jack Taylor?"

"He's the boyfriend of one of my clients. Good grief. What's that about?"

Twenty-nine

Plan for the Mother Lode

WHEN Lucy finally wandered back through the yard to call it a night, it was after eleven. Jim, Frannie, and I—the Unholy Triumvirate—were left at the outdoor table to assess the night, the bomb Lucy had dropped, and to generally try and make some sense of life. Jim poured himself a glass of Chablis, draining the bottle he had kept for himself on the side. Frannie pulled out a pack of Parliaments from the folds of her linen pants and lit one with a Bic lighter.

"She's a trip," Jim said, referring to Lucy. "Anybody want anything?"

We shook our heads. I was too stunned to even know if I could swallow another drop of anything.

"I'll say she's a trip," Frannie said, sending a little cloud into the night air. "On top of that, she's a regular private investigator."

Frannie's cigarette smelled wonderful, but I gave her a little hell anyway. "When are you gonna quit smoking?" I said. "That shit kills, you know."

"If you lived my life, you'd smoke too. I have my laptop inside," Frannie said, taking a deep drag of her cigarette. We watched her smoke spiral above us and then, like a tiny fog in a dream, it slowly rolled away on the breeze. "Wanna go see the dirtbag's website?"

"Definitely," Jim said, and stood, "let's go."

I shivered all over, from just the slightest thought of actually seeing the face of the man who in one evening had altered my future, Jim's future, and brought my only daughter into this world. Still, I followed them inside.

"I don't know," I said, the screen door closing behind me. "Maybe I don't want to know anything about him."

Everyone was quiet for a minute. This was déjà vu of my worst nightmare. I wasn't so sure I wanted to revisit the past. Not so sure at all.

I had always thought of Emily minus Everett. The only justice I had was that Everett had been denied acting as her father. He didn't even know Emily existed and had probably forgotten about me as well. He didn't know he had a gorgeous daughter with his spooky green eyes and his platinum hair. And, suppose we dug him up? What would that do to Jim? I'd been planning Emily's wedding since the day she was born and Jim was the only man I could envision walking Emily down the aisle. Everett would ruin the pictures, to say the least. What possible good could come from Everett Fairchild at this point in our lives?

What would it do to Emily? She had voiced some suspicion about Jim but she had no clue that her birth was the result of a rape. Resurrecting Everett would make the truth necessary.

"Well, you don't have to look," Jim said. "I will."

"You're afraid, aren't you?" Frannie said.

"Hell yes, I'm afraid. Wouldn't you be?"

"Yes. Yes, I would be afraid. But that wouldn't keep me from looking. I guess that's how I am."

"Yeah, balls, up there under that skirt somewhere. You've got 'em. I don't. Look, y'all," I said, "I wrote this criminal out of my life years ago, and with your help, I'd like to add. Why in the world would I want to know how well he was doing? Personally, I hope he's living in a hell of his own."

"Well, he might be," Jim said, "you never know."

"On the other hand," Frannie said, her jaw squared off like it used to when we were children and she was ready for battle, "*you* have the power to make his life a living hell."

"Now, *that's* worth looking into!" Jim wrung his hands and shifted his eyes around the room, impersonating the evil landlord.

"You're right." I took a deep breath. "I guess it's now or later, and later I'd be forced to go through this with Lucy. I guess this is the lesser of two evils."

"Oh, thanks a lot," Frannie said. Standing by my dining table, she plugged her laptop into my phone jack and booted it up. "Come on, thing! God, I hate waiting!"

"I'll go get the chairs," Jim said. "Laptops take forever."

I went with him to help. The night was cool and quiet. I could hear the tide rolling in and the air smelled like it always did—pine, jasmine, salt. How could the world be so normal when my insides were turning flips?

"I don't know about this, Jim," I said.

"When the future is uncertain, it's best to face it. Since when are you a coward?"

"Since always."

"Yeah, like Eleanor Roosevelt."

We each carried two chairs and struggled a little by the door, finally getting them inside.

"What if Emily walks in?" I said, getting more nervous by the second.

"I'll switch the screen to MSN or something. Come on. Don't hyperventilate. All we're gonna do is look at his site."

First, she typed in SEA PRO, the brand of boat he sold, and arrived at the official website for the company. Then she clicked on "Dealers," "Florida," and "Clearwater." There it was. Just like that.

There was Everett Fairchild, older but suntanned and smiling, wearing Ray-Bans and a knit shirt, standing by a row of boats on trailers. I would have known him anywhere. There was his phone number, address, directions to his dealership, testimonials from satisfied customers, and links to see all the models he carried. It had taken mere minutes to discover the whereabouts of the *worst* person ever foisted on me by fate. And he was going to be on the Isle of Palms the second week of August. What in the name of heaven was I going to do?

"Oh, my God," I said, "it's him." My voice had no emotion.

"He still looks like an asshole," Frannie said.

"I'll bet he still is one too," Jim said. "Come on, Anna, what do you think?"

"I think I have to go to bed," I said. "I feel sick."

"Me too," said Frannie, and she began closing screens. "Jim, you get the couch tonight. Sorry."

"Doesn't matter. I'm packed."

"Good night, y'all, love you!"

It wasn't thirty minutes before Emily tumbled into bed next to me, smelling like the contents of a brewery.

"You know what?" I whispered to her.

"What?" she said.

"When you take your momma's beer and you're underage, you're supposed to brush your teeth so she won't smell your raunchy breath."

"Saaa-wee, Mommy."

"Bad girl. Bad, bad girl." I'd lecture her tomorrow, I thought. "How's David?"

"Fabuloso. He is soooo amazing."

I imagined that meant all was well. "Good, honey. Let's get some sleep."

I thought it would be hours before sleep would come, that I was going to be tortured all night by thoughts of Everett Fairchild. I decided to say my prayers. I wasn't someone who drove the good Lord crazy with endless petitions; I really didn't. I saved my begging for rare and desperate occasions and this certainly qualified as one. Maybe if I asked for some guidance, it would come. Fortunately, guidance was the last thing I remembered thinking about and I rolled over to hit the snooze button on my alarm. It was morning. I had slept so hard it surprised me. Maybe God figured I needed beauty rest more than advice.

351

Breakfast was our last meal together for Frannie, Jim, and me. Emily was sleeping until the last possible minute she could. Teenagers could sleep like nothing I'd ever seen. Anyway, breakfast wasn't anything glamorous, just cereal and toast, but the coffee was as rich and strong as the conversation. And, I didn't feel as badly as I would have about them leaving because Jim and Frannie talked loud and long about their plans to come back in August.

"You know," Frannie said, "August is dead in my business. All the pols are in the Hamptons or on a boat somewhere, enjoying a weekend with major party donors, under the guise of campaign strategic planning."

"I hate politics and politicians," I said. "I don't know how you put up with all those powermongering egomaniacs. Jeesch. Too much bull for me."

"Easy. I get paid enough to overlook the fact that I'm like Ralph Kramden's buddy, working the sewers. It's a dirty job, but somebody's gotta do it. That is, somebody's *gonna* do it and get paid, so it may as well be me. It's a living, not a calling."

"Well, I can identify with that, except what the heck does that say about us? I enjoy making people look better. I really do. But it doesn't exactly feed my soul."

"I don't think very many people have the luxury of a career that pays the bills *and* feeds the soul," Frannie said. "Maybe artists, movie stars, Broadway stars, rock stars, journalists . . ."

Then Jim piped in, "People who cure terrible diseases, opera singers, museum curators, art dealers on Madison Avenue, international fashion photographers, great chefs, architects, some teachers—probably at the university level—anthropologists . . ."

"Everybody but us," I said.

"Basically," Frannie said.

Jim jumped in. "What about the great vintners of Europe, Napa, and Sonoma? Great wine feeds the soul, the senses *and* pays the bills, doesn't it? And what about decorators? Lots of them make fortunes and love what they do! And antique dealers?"

"Yeah," Frannie said, "it sucks to have to do something every day that doesn't really fire you up inside. I mean, I help these suits protect their agendas and get what they want. I justify it by thinking of myself as a missionary or a guide, you know? I lead the innocents through the fires of hell without them getting burned."

"You should've been a litigator, Frannie," Jim said, "you could argue anything and make the world believe it."

"Yeah, the world needs another lawyer."

"I don't know what I'd do if I could plan my life over," I said. "Maybe I'd be a landscape architect or something."

"I think I'd run away from the world. Maybe I'd have a resort on a remote island like Fiji or someplace like that," Frannie said. "Jim? You could run the restaurant and Anna could rearrange palm trees and flower beds until her last breath. Then we could push each other in rockers and read all the great books."

"Sounds awfully boring—truly dreadful," I said. "I'll stay here and run my little salon and make smoothies for all the tourists. Y'all send me a postcard."

"Not me, honey," Jim said. "I ain't going to the South Seas unless the IRS is after me."

"Well, for the moment," Frannie said, "I'd settle for just one long weekend of lying in the sun and reading one of the books I've bought but haven't had time to read. It would be so great to just hang out together and really get back in each other's lives. You know?"

"Definitely," Jim said. "I've got this awful feeling that by August I'm going to need some heavy doses of cheer."

"Y'all know what all this means, don't you?" I looked from Frannie's face to Jim's. "It means we need to take an oath that we'll see each other more often. We're practically family—at least we used to be."

"Anna's right, Jim. I mean, shoot! Look at us! We're not getting any younger. Life is traveling faster than light these days. Pretty soon those idiots at AARP are gonna start jamming my mailbox with coupons for, God knows—adult diapers! Ugh!"

"She's right. We're getting older by the second," Jim said. "Frannie ain't got no husband. In fact, none of us do, but at least you have Arthur. How's that going?"

"He's great, but he doesn't want to get involved, even though he's involved. And because I know you're dying to know, the boy is hot, okay? I'm seeing him tonight." I picked up my plate, taking it to the kitchen. "Y'all want another pot of coffee? I gotta get to work."

"No more coffee for me," Jim said. "I'm going to the beach. Okay?"

"Anna," Frannie said, "Jim and I thought we might spend the morning on the beach and I was hoping you or somebody in your salon could do something with my hair this afternoon before I have to fly out of here."

"No problem! I've been dying to get my hands on your head for about a million years, girl! Y'all go to the beach and I'll see you around three? You can't leave here without seeing the salon anyway!"

"Can I go to the beach too?" Emily said, coming out from the bedroom, yawning and struggling to open her eyes.

"Forget it," I said, "you're lucky I'm not tearing up your behind for last night."

"Mother Superior! You're a tough nut!" Jim said. "Let her come! I never get to see her! How about I bring her in at noon? I have to be at the airport by two." He looked at Emily. "What'd you do, you little wench?"

"Nothing," Emily said, face flushed.

"She and David ripped off a six-pack and she sneaked into bed, half trashed, after midnight," I said. "She smelled like a derelict."

"Emily!" Jim said. "I am *shocked!* If this young gentleman can't provide the contraband for your entertainment without reducing you to common thievery, I say, dump the lout! Like that!" He snapped his fingers in midair and flicked his wrist. "What's the drinking age around here anyway?"

"She ain't there," Frannie said, "but neither were we when we used to buy cases of beer with fake ID."

"Good point," I said. I didn't approve of underage drinking one bit, but the fact was that we had all done it. "Okay. You get yourself to the salon by noon, 'eah?"

"Okay," Emily said. "Whatever."

I loved when she said *whatever*. What did it mean? That she didn't care what I said when I knew she really did?

I sailed into the salon before nine-thirty. Bettina and Brigitte were gathered around Lucy. The hair on my neck stood up. I knew I had been betrayed. It was obvious she had told them about Everett and was squeezing every drop of sap from the story for them that she could. Murder crossed my mind. After swearing up and down she wouldn't say anything, she had told them. I couldn't believe it. It wasn't my imagination, because they all looked nervous and guilty.

"Morning, Anna," Brigitte said, walking away from them, reaching for a tissue to blow her nose. "Excuse me. Allergies. Thanks for last night. We had a great time, didn't we?"

"Oh! Yeah!" Bettina said. "I never saw Bobby eat so much! Those shrimps were fan-tas-tic!"

Lucy slithered toward the bathroom, like a snake from the bottom of the swamp.

"Morning, everyone," I said, and threw my purse in the cabinet next to my station without looking at them, closing the cubby door harder than I should have. "Lucy? Can I have a word with you?"

Silence.

"Sure! I just have to powder my nose, okay?"

They knew I was angry. I looked in the mirror and rubbed a trace of mascara from beneath my eyes. For a split second I imagined myself the founder of a nonsmearing mascara company for humid climates. I stood there and ran a comb through my hair, over and over.

"I'll be waiting," I said to her back. "Anybody got today's schedule?"

"No," Bettina said, at the same time Brigitte said, "It's right here," and handed it to me.

"Looks like we have another wild day ahead of us, right?"

The front door opened and the first two clients of the day walked in, saving Bettina and Brigitte from certain embarrassment. They made themselves busy with them and I waited at my station for Lucy, who had been in the bathroom long enough to change the wallpaper, her mind, and her story. Finally, I walked to the door and rapped on it lightly with my knuckles.

"Do I need to call the plumber?"

The door opened and she was in there sniveling into a tissue, chest heaving, silent sobs. Classic Lucy.

"Come on, Judas," I said, and took her out through the back door into the rear parking lot. "First of all, calm yourself down. We have a business to run."

"I'm sorry, Anna. . . ."

"Don't say one word or I don't know what I will do to you." I was so enraged I thought I might actually hit her. "Just listen, okay?" She seemed to understand that her life was hanging by a thread so I continued. "We're talking about trust, Lucy. Knowing about my life is not a license for you to wiggle your tongue for the ears of anyone who will listen. This is my child's life, my life, and our privacy. It was my deepest secret—mine, not yours—you've revealed and I can't imagine that I'll ever trust you again. I want you to go home and when I calm down, we'll talk some more."

"Am I . . . fired? Oh, God! I am so sorry! It just came out!"

"Right. It just popped into your brain and rolled off your tongue, just like a sliding board. No, you are not fired but I am so upset right now that I know I can't spend the day with you. So, go."

As she walked away from me, her shoulders were shaking so hard I knew that everyone in the salon must've thought somebody died. It would be impossible now to keep it from Emily. I was filled with dread and a heaviness in my chest that was so awful, I thought I might die on the spot, falling dead on the floor.

I watched her push the front door open and go toward her car. I wished that Jim wasn't leaving. Or Frannie. I needed to talk to them. I couldn't tell Daddy. He would just go to Lucy with it and the damn story would spread like kudzu. I had to put a lid on it right away.

For the next two hours, I answered the phones, took care of two walk-ins, and stayed busy. In between clients, Bettina and Brigitte avoided my eyes—knowing they were sharing space with a nuclear warhead with a short fuse. Neither one of them asked me where Lucy had gone. Eventually, I began to calm down and took them aside.

Brigitte's client was under the dryer and Bettina's was drying her nails, sipping a smoothie through a straw; both of them were unaware of my trauma. I took Brigitte and Bettina to the towel area in the back.

"Look. Emily is going to be here any minute. One word, one funny look from any of us and she's going to start asking questions I'm not ready to answer. I don't know what Lucy told y'all, but she shouldn't have said anything. It wasn't her place."

"I agree," Brigitte said, "and to tell you the truth, I didn't want to know anyway."

"Well," Bettina said, "I, for one, understan' Lucy, you know? She's a dumb-ass and can't help herself. The world is loaded with dumb broads. Don't be pissed at her, Anna. We probably woulda weaseled it out of ya eventually anyway. No way we wouldn't have heard it sooner or later. You woulda told us, right? Am I right, or what?" She looked from me to Brigitte, who shrugged her noncommittal shoulders.

"Probably," I said, "but in my time, not hers."

"If it's timing that's giving you agita, don't sweat it. By the end of the day you'll owe us two Oscars for Best Actress. Am I right, Brigitte?"

"She's right. Emily will notice nothing out of the ordinary."

"All right. Let's get back to work."

When Emily arrived, we put her on phone duty and I went outside with Jim, after he had said his good-byes to Bettina and Brigitte. The sun was raging overhead and I knew I couldn't stand the heat for long. I felt very emotional as we stood by his rental car. He got inside and turned on the air conditioner and got out again.

"Your nose is red," I said.

"Because I have aristocratic skin."

"Yeah, right."

"In five minutes it'll be ten below zero in there," he said, smiling at me. "That's one thing about Detroit—they understand air conditioners. German cars? Forget it."

"Oh, Jim, I wish you didn't have to go," I said. "The cat's out of the bag and I need you worse than ever."

"What cat?"

I told him and he said, "Oh! *That* cat! Well, listen, Anna. We've been saving each other's behinds since fifth grade or something like that and this is just another challenge in a long list of ones that have been met and dealt with."

"I know but, damn! Why did she do it?" I didn't really expect an answer to that, I just needed to figure out what to do so that Emily wouldn't find out until I wanted her to.

"Because Lucy is as thick as a post. Don't you worry. I'll think about it and call you tomorrow, okay? Tell Frannie. See what she thinks." He shook his head. "That Lucy is a nice gal, but, man! She's got all the judgment of a two year old playing with matches."

"Exactly. God, I'll miss you. Good luck in Ohio. I'll be thinking about you every second." I knew his anxiety over Gary must have been eating him alive.

"I'm kind of a philosophical guy, you know? I mean, I think things will work out because they always seem to. That goes for you too. Don't fret—it gives you wrinkles, and we don't want wrinkles."

I shook my head at him as he got in the car and put it in reverse, lowering the window for a final word.

"I love you, Anna. Count on it."

"I do. And I love you, Jim. Until we rot and after that too."

I kissed my fingertips and wiped them all over his face. He hollered and raced to raise the window on my hands. I shrieked and jumped back, laughing. We waved at each other as he pulled away and I thought, once again, that I had never known a better friend. I would count the days until his return.

The rest of the day flew by until Frannie arrived, greeting everyone like she'd known them all her life. She fit right in like the final piece of a jigsaw puzzle, making the place seem complete, with her wise-cracking humor matching Bettina's and her poise on par with Brigitte's. Frannie had plenty to say about the salon. After about fifteen minutes, a smoothie, and a cappuccino, she finally got in a robe and into my chair.

"So, I got out this magazine and started wondering if you could make me look like Julia Roberts and then I decided that it wasn't really my hair that kept me from looking like her. Right? Soooo! Then I started thinking about Elizabeth Taylor and how she used to look and all. *National Velvet?* And I figured that was hopeless too. Can we do a supermodel thing?"

"Sure, I'll just take a little off the sides," I said. "Want another cappuccino?"

"Why not?"

"I'll get it. My pleasure!" Bettina said. "And then I'm doing your nails! Maybe I'll airbrush Brad Pitt on your pinky!"

"God, don't you love her?" Frannie said.

"To death, but let's talk hair for a few minutes, okay?"

I removed the rubber band that held her enormous chignon in place. Her thick hair, shot with silver threads, tumbled past her shoulders in uneven lengths. She had the kind of hair a girl like me would kill for.

"Look at this! Jee-za-ree! When's the last time you had a haircut?"

"When Dubya's daddy was in the White House. What do you want for my life? I'm busy!"

"What do we have? An hour and a half?" My mind was racing. "Let's get going."

I put a single-process mahogany glaze on her hair, just enough to bring out the fire in her natural color. When I blew it dry, it was a full three inches longer. I loved the color too.

"Woman? You got too much hair! Jeez! You got hair for four women!"

"Then, cut it!"

"I'm painting your nails red," Bettina said. "With your kinda sass, you need red nails!"

I rewet Frannie's hair and started to cut, bringing it up to right above her shoulders and giving her some long layers in the front. When I blew it out it was swinging and glossy.

"Wow!" Frannie said. "I'm going on a manhunt! This is too good to waste!"

"You look gorgeous!" I said, watching Bettina roll her cart over to another client. "You get on that plane, make some man pay for the pleasure of your beauteous self, and call me when you get to your hotel. We gotta talk."

"Something happen?" Frannie whispered.

"Yeah."

"Lucy told the troops?" She whispered again.

"Yeah."

"Shit. I could smell it."

"Yeah."

"I'll call you as soon as I can."

"Good."

We hugged like best friends do and I watched Frannie leave.

I started to worry about Emily seeing David that night. I knew that if I went out with Arthur and she went over to Lucy's to watch TV, there was a huge window for trouble. It was an awful thing to have to worry about someone like Lucy betraying me again. And, it made me mad all over again.

I decided to call Daddy and see if I could talk him into taking Lucy out for the night or maybe he could just go over to her house for the evening. If he was around, she wouldn't dare take it on herself to start telling Emily anything. She would doll herself up and make Martinis and maybe, in all her drunken stupidity, she'd forget what she knew for the night. Nothing like wishful thinking.

I went out to the parking lot and called Daddy on my cell phone.

"Daddy? I'm in a pickle again. I need your help."

"What's up, sugar?"

"It's about Lucy and her tongue that's as long as I-95."

Daddy cleared his throat, and I realized I had either given Daddy lewd thoughts or he already knew. He already knew.

"She called me about an hour ago," he said. "That's the whole problem with women. They talk too much."

"Not all women, thank you," I said. "This one in particular thinks she's obliged to tell it all like the *National Enquirer*. I could kill her, I'm so mad."

"Well, I don't blame you for being angry and I'm not sure it means you have to tell Emily anything. At least, not yet."

"But soon," I said and choked up thinking about it, "soon I'm gonna have to pay the devil."

"Maybe not," he said. "I think we can figure out a way to present the truth and leave the devil out. Right now you're upset and can't think straight."

I hated it when he said things like that, implying female hysteria. "I'm thinking pretty straight and here's the immediate problem." I told him about Arthur and that I intended to keep the date I had with him, but I was concerned about what could happen that night.

"So, you want me to put some static on her line? I can do that. I'll call her back and see if she wants to go out to supper."

"Then all I have to worry about is Emily and David doing what they shouldn't with no adult present in the house."

"Good Lord, Anna," Daddy said, "listen to you! What are you worried about? Unprotected sex? How old is Emily? Do you really think she's so promiscuous that she'd hop in the bed the minute she could?"

"You know what, Daddy? She's old enough that she's going to do what she wants anyway. I just don't like the idea of providing the opportunity by leaving them alone in a house with beds. It seems like an invitation to go crazy."

Daddy roared with laughter and I realized that I sounded like my grandmother. Then I started to laugh too.

"I'm an idiot," I said. "Violet lives!"

"You . . . oh, God, that was funny . . . you never heard of the backseat of a car? Honey, if young people want to have sex, they find a way!"

"Just take Lucy out to dinner and then hang around for a while, okay?"

"Okay. Now quit worrying so. We will figure this all out, because at some point, you have to tell Emily the truth, you know. She's entitled to some version of the truth, Anna."

He was right. I had waited too many years because the truth was so entangled and ugly. I wanted to know that Emily was strong enough to take it like an adult. I had hoped she would be so happy with Jim and me as parents that she wouldn't want to know about anything else.

"Are you listening to me?"

"I'm sorry, Daddy. What did you say?"

"I said, I'll call you later, okay?"

"Thanks. Daddy? I love you, you know. A lot."

"You have to learn to forgive, Anna. People make mistakes. Lucy can't help it."

It was true. I wasn't very forgiving. But he wasn't exactly perfect about forgiveness either.

Later on that night, after a great dinner and a lot of wine, I was lying in bed with Arthur, enjoying the ol' afterglow. I told him what had happened with Lucy, which led to telling him about Everett. I thought he might have some advice for me. I waited for him to say something but he was strangely quiet.

"What are you thinking?" I said.

"I'm thinking that this is what I hate about relationships." He rolled over on his side, propped himself up on one elbow, and faced me. "You see what I mean?"

"No," I said, uncomfortable with what I knew I didn't want to hear from him that was coming as sure as morning. "Tell me."

"This is the *getting involved* shit that I don't want to deal with. Why can't two people just be together and enjoy each other? I mean, why does everyone feel like they can dump everything on each other just because they have a few nights together?"

I had made the large mistake of assuming Arthur wanted to know what was on my mind.

"Because, um, I don't know. I guess because sleeping together implies a certain kind of intimacy? You know? Share your body? Share your soul? Or don't they do that in New York?"

"Not like southern women do. Yankee women are more independent," he said with an undercurrent of minor disgust. "I mean, you're not as needy as *some* women I've met. And, you wouldn't want to hear about them any more than I want to know about this."

I got up and started dressing. As far as I was concerned, the party was over.

"Well, you can call me oversensitive, but I feel offended. And, you want to know what I think? I think some women are just willing to take less because less is better than nothing. I don't think it's got a damn thing to do with Yankee stoicism."

He watched me buttoning my shirt and said, "I never meant to offend you, Anna. I told you how I was, didn't I? I don't like getting involved."

"Then why are we sleeping together?"

"Because we want to. Because we are attracted to each other. Because we enjoy each other. Shouldn't that be enough?"

He got up and went to the bathroom. I didn't answer him. No, his reasons weren't enough for me. I knew that. This guy needed some remedial lessons in the art of romance. I looked around his room, anxious to leave, realizing I could either take Arthur the way he was or walk away before I got hurt. Before he'd started his "terms of engagement" lecture, I'd been sure I could make him fall in love with me. His repeated profession of his lack of interest in love had spurred me on. What was the matter with me? Was I so desperate for affection?

"Come on," he said, "I'll drive you home."

"Okay."

I was quiet in the car and when we pulled into my driveway, he said, "You know, Anna, it's not you. It's me. I had a marriage and I got killed. I don't ever want to be that vulnerable again. I'm sorry."

"Whatever," I said and got out. "Good night."

Whatever summed it up. It was Emily's term and it was perfect. I'd have to remember to tell her I had learned something from her. Arthur may have been the King of the Screws, but he'd seen my bloomers on his floor for the last time.

Thirty

Culture Gap

"HEY, Anna? Sister Francesca here. The confessional is open for business. I'm still in Raleigh, but all snuggy in my bed at the lovely Ramada Inn with two cans of Diet Coke and a whole pack of cigs."

"Hey, Frannie."

"I'm poised to hear the details of your personal life and give you my inestimable advice."

She had called as promised. It was Saturday night and I was home alone, showered, and ready to spend the night with an old movie and popcorn. I was polishing my kitchen counter (not because I was waiting for Arthur to call—yeah, right—but because it needed it—yeah, sure) and sipping a glass of wine from the stash that Jim had left for me. Arthur had not called—no surprise there. Emily was doing temp work at Barnes & Noble, helping David take inventory until midnight. Lucy had gone to Myrtle Beach after work to spend the night with God only knew who, which suited me fine as I was still furious with her.

"I don't know where to start," I said. "Should we begin with Lucy or Arthur?"

"Well, I never laid eyes on Arthur when I was there for my drive-through visit, so let's start with Lucy. I had a thought on the plane."

"Tell it," I said.

"She deserves to die."

"At first I thought so too, but then I decided that of all the things I'd be willing to sit behind bars for, murdering a pea-brain wasn't one of them. Then I thought about drugging her and secretly removing her tongue."

"Too disgusting," Frannie said.

"I could hire somebody."

"Possibility. Hang on, I have to get ice." I heard her rustle around and then pick up the phone again. "You know what? Hotel chains are this bizarre exercise in brand identification. I had this same exact room in Peoria last month, right down to the view of the parking lot. Spooky."

"I can't tell you the last time I stayed in a hotel," I said.

"That's another thing. You need to get away from Charleston once in a while. But back to Lucy. Here's the net net. When it was just a few people that knew about Everett, it wasn't a big deal. Now this genius has made it a topic for conversation. The chances of Emily now hearing about it from someone else have just quadrupled. And, of course, the larger question is what *are* you going to do about him coming to Wild Dunes?"

"To tell you the truth, I've been so upset and so busy that I haven't given it a thought."

"Well, Anna girl? Here's what I think. You can do two things. One, do nothing and leave it to chance. Your risk of bumping into him is small. Two, you can set the fucker up and blow his world to smithereens. I have a strong preference for the second choice, because look, you have to tell Emily the truth eventually, right?"

"What's telling Emily got to do with blowing up his life?"

"Because telling Emily the truth is gonna blow up *yours*—temporarily."

"I know. That's why I never told her."

"Anna, listen to me. Someday soon, Emily is going to want to have her own family. At the very least, she should know Everett's medical history. And if she finds out the truth there's no saying that he's going to try and barge his way into your life. I imagine he would be shocked as all hell for a while and then he'll crawl back under his rock. Look, it's always infuriated me that this guy did what he did and went on with his life like it was nothing. I mean, who in the hell does he think he is? He's a bad guy! Very bad!"

"Frannie, I got over being angry about it years ago and consoled myself with the idea that Everett couldn't touch us, couldn't talk to us, couldn't see Emily's dance recitals, her graduations, class plays, Christmases, and all those things. I've had Emily to myself all these years. If I let him know she's alive and she's his daughter, then I have to share."

"No, you don't. Emily's a grown woman over eighteen. *Emily* would have to decide if she wanted to get to know him. Not you. And there's always the possibility, however remote it might be, that he's got a long-term wife, other children—I mean, who knows? Maybe he's become a born-again Christian, which would be perfect, so he could start sweating eternity in hell right now."

"I don't know, Frannie." My stomach lurched and I thought I was going to be sick. "This makes me very nervous."

"Well, I say you need a plan. You know what I'd do? I'd enlist Bettina and Brigitte. Neither one of them is stupid and that Bettina is one slick gal—a little rough around the edges, but slick. They already know anyway."

"The problem would be keeping it from Emily."

"Well, I'm just telling you what I'd do. Now tell me about this Arthur person."

I told her about the last date with him and she made all the correct remarks.

Men are pigs! Tell him to buzz off! I'd let my fingers rot away before I picked up the phone to call him!

"Just how many lives does he think he can skewer, hiding behind the pain of his first marriage?" But then she asked the critical question. "How is he in the sack?"

"If I told you, you wouldn't believe it."

"Try me. I'm a woman about town, you know."

"Frannie, you know I never discuss this kind of thing. Nice girls don't talk about their lovers."

"Nice girls have nothing to discuss."

I giggled. She was right. "Okay, I'm gonna say this and then I want you to forget you heard it, okay?"

"Okay."

"Never before in my entire life have I even heard about anybody having this kind of sex. *Never.*"

"What exactly do you mean? Is he, you know, weird?"

"Oh, no! Hell, no! I mean, when it was over, I thought I was dead!"

"What?" Frannie started laughing. "What did he do? Hold you upside down in the air and bang your head against the mattress?"

"No! God, you are so stupid! He just, I mean, oh, hell! It's just that it went on *forever!* And it was *amazing!* I thought I was flying off into outer space or something! I'm not kidding! For the love of God, Frannie! I *perspired!*"

"You?" Frannie was howling, laughing so hard I could hear her nose getting stopped up. "You *perspired?*"

"*Yes!*"

"Don't you *usually?*" she said and snorted, laughing all over again.

"Usually *what?*"

"Perspire?"

"Hell, *no!*"

"Hold on, I gotta grab a tissue."

I could hear her in the background saying, *"Oh, dear Lord! I gotta take her to Club Med or something!"* She blew her nose, coughed, laughed, and blew her nose again.

"It's not *that* funny, Frannie. I'm trying to tell you something here and it's not easy when you keep laughing, you know."

"Come on. I'm sorry. Tell me."

"Look, I guess the question is this. Jim says that men only care about their money and their Johnson, and that they're in love with themselves. Is it wrong to have a relationship with a man only for sex and, just as important, can you do this and not get involved?"

"Men do it all the time."

"Really? I guess they do."

"Women have sex to get love and men have sex to feel good."

"Good Lord. Whatever happened to romance?"

"Anna? You want romance? That's what Jim is for. He lands in Charleston, redoes your salon, buys you a new wardrobe, tells you how fabulous you are, how fabulous Emily is, and how fabulous your house is. If that's not romantic, I don't know what is. I think it was Harry Truman who used to say that in Washington, if you want love, get a dog. And you always have me. I love ya—not like on the wild side, but like a sister. And as for this guy Arthur . . . ?"

"Yeah?"

"Next time, don't perspire. Sweat like a hog!"

"Okay."

"You never get it all with one man, honey. You don't get love, romance, great sex, *and* money."

"I know. All the gorgeous men are gay and all the nice ones are married."

"Yeah, and what's worse is that we're at that rotten age where the nice guys are still married to the bitches and are hanging in there waiting for the last child to go to college. In five years there should be a flood of available men, according to my statistics."

"Yeah, but those same guys in five years won't want women our age."

"Don't be morbid. I say let's concentrate on Everett Fairchild and take out your frustration on Arthur's sheets."

"Good plan. Hey, good luck at your meetings and thanks for coming down. Jim was thrilled."

"So was I. Did he call from Ohio?"

"No, but that's how Jim does. You know. He sorta disappears and reappears. He'll probably call me when he goes back to San Francisco."

"Right. God! It was so great to see you and Emily and your dad and all. Think he's getting it on with Lucy?"

"Everyone keeps asking me that. Parents don't have sex, don't you know that? They have little mounds like Barbie and Ken dolls."

We laughed and said good-bye, promising to plan the Fairchild Offensive together.

I said to Frannie that I agreed with her about just seeing Arthur for sex, but I didn't mean it for a minute. I wanted to see Arthur in the worst way and it killed me that he didn't call. I looked at the telephone, debating dialing his number. What would I say? *Oh, Arthur? When I got out of your car on Thursday night, remember I said, Whatever? I meant that whatever kind of shallow and demoralizing relationship you want to have is fine with me . . . ?* I was still embarrassed that I had told him everything and he hadn't cared. I couldn't believe that you could make love to somebody and then lie there next to them and not care about them.

I looked at the clock. It was eleven-fifteen. Arthur would be home from work any minute. The kitchen closed at eleven. Maybe my problem had been that I had expected too much from him too soon. I mean, if he didn't want to get involved, I could understand it. After all, he was only here for the summer. It made sense. If he actually lived here then it would be very different. Maybe I should pack a midnight picnic and be waiting on his steps when he came home. Yes. That would be nice. I'd take a bottle of wine over there with something to eat and show him that he was wrong, but very gently. There wasn't really any reason why I couldn't have a summer fling with him and then say good-bye, was there? I mean, hadn't I dated other men and they hadn't worked out when I thought they would? So why should I walk away just because he wasn't promising to love and honor me forever on our second or third date?

Poor Frannie was such a cynic. Her failed love affairs had made her calloused. I still believed that you could have love and romance along with a committed relationship. It just took time to build it. Although, looking around my life, there weren't many successful marriages in evidence. That didn't matter, really. My attraction to Arthur was so exciting that I was sure it was a good thing. All I had to do was think of him and my insides fluttered like a young girl. I was willing to take the risk of his rejection a second time. I would be careful. If I didn't ask for anything from him he wouldn't run away, would he? No, I knew he was attracted to me. Definitely.

I pulled on a pair of white Levi's and a navy golf shirt brushing my hair up into a stretch band. I scribbled a note for Emily that I'd be gone for a couple of hours and got in my car with a chilled bottle of wine and a bag of lime-flavored Doritos. The Doritos were the best I could do.

His car was in the yard. He must've left early, I thought. The dogs started barking when I got out and the porch light went on.

"Hey!" I said. "Want some company?"

"Sure," he said and smiled at me. "Come on in. I just got home."

He held the door open for me. I climbed the stairs and greeted him with a light kiss on his cheek. I was planning to walk by him and into the kitchen, but he put his hand on my left arm and held me there. Oh, yeah, here came his lips! Lord, this man could kiss.

"You know what, Mr. Big Cheese?"

"What Miss, um, Midnight Rider?"

"I love the way you kiss me." I held the bag of Doritos in the air. "Come! I've brought us a feast."

"I was just gonna make some eggs. Want eggs?"

"Nah, thanks. I brought some wine too. Jim bought me a case of something he thought I'd like. It's a New Zealand Sauvignon Blanc— Fairhall Downs—whatever that is. Got a corkscrew?"

"Did you say *screw*?"

"Very funny and no, precious, I didn't come over here on a late-night nooky hunt or something." I ripped open the bag and took a bite of a chip. "God, these are terrible. Don't eat them. I wanted to talk to you."

"I'm sorry to hear that," he said, pretending to be disappointed. He reached into the drawer. "Here. Hand me the bottle. Does this mean you don't want to sleep with me anymore?"

"Good grief! Is that all men think about?"

"Hell, no! We think about football, wrestling, money, power—do you really think we're all just a bunch of shallow bastards?"

"Yes, but that's okay because at least we women know what they're dealing with."

"Ooooh! Ouch! Let's go on the porch."

The air was thick with fog. We couldn't even see the dock.

"Is the boat out there?"

"You mean the Love Boat?"

"Good Lord." I sat in the same chair I had before and Arthur handed me my goblet. "That was the most unbelievable night of my life."

He took a chip from the bag and dropped the bag on the footstool. "It was pretty funny, the Coast Guard and all." I watched him pop the chip in his mouth. "You're right. These are disgusting."

We were quiet for a few minutes, enjoying the mysteries of the night, and then I broke the silence.

"So, I've been thinking, Arthur."

"Yeah? Whatcha thinking?"

"Well, I think we should be friends. I mean, I'm not saying we shouldn't sleep together, but I think the main thing should be that we become friends."

"Aren't we friends already?"

"Yeah, but I don't want us to not see each other because of this commitment thing. I mean, I get it. At first, I thought it was a little screwed up but then I began to understand. Anyway, what's the difference? You're just visiting here, you're going to be leaving in August, and you're right."

"Getting involved with someone a thousand miles away is stupid, not to mention damn inconvenient."

I felt my heart sink a little but plunged ahead. "Look, I figure if we just forget the whole *involved* thing, who knows? I mean, you might want to visit here again and need a couch. . . ."

"A couch? You'd make me sleep on the couch?"

"No, of course not, unless Emily was there. But I might want to go to

New York sometime. It would be nice to know I could just call you and see you without the burden of some disappointment hanging over us."

"I'm glad you're telling me this. I really am. It was how I hoped you'd feel after you had a chance to think about it; I mean, I felt pretty bad about what I said on Thursday. I know it seemed, I don't know, selfish or something."

Yes. Selfish would be the word, Mr. Me Generation.

"Not at all," I said. "Look, if you lived here things might be different. But you don't, so this is what we've got."

"What have we got?"

"We're friends."

"Right. Friends. Good."

Well, don't you know old Arthur gets up and pulls me to my feet and started moving on me. I'll tell you, I was snickering inside so hard I couldn't believe I didn't burst out laughing. Instead I let him kiss me all he wanted. Yes, I did. He had a handful of my left breast and I loved that too. But then I decided either I was going to jump in bed again or I was going to give him something to think about. So, in the tradition of the classic southern tease, I let his temperature rise to the appropriate level and stood back from him.

"Arthur? You are so hot you make me feel like all I want to do is crawl all over you, but I gotta go."

"GO?"

"Baby-boy, you are the sexiest man I have ever met in this world and absolutely hell to resist, but I have a teenage daughter who's probably drinking all the booze in my house and I gotta get up early tomorrow."

"Tomorrow's Sunday, sweetie."

"That's right. I have to be in church by nine-thirty. Night, daarlin'. Let's try to see each other this week, okay?"

"You working Monday? I need a haircut."

"Yes, you do!" *Right after I braid your short hairs.* "Come by! No problem!"

I don't know what *he* thought but all the way home *I* thought about him trying to sleep and I couldn't stop congratulating myself. The first battle had taken place and the hard-hearted Yankee had been bested by the belle. Shoot! He didn't know who he was messing with. There hasn't been a southern woman born worth her salt who couldn't bring a man around to her thinking by merely withholding her favors.

Thirty-one
Waxing Eloquent

ARTHUR, with renewed desire, became more attentive and I saw him twice that week, beginning with the Monday he came in for me to cut his hair. Bettina bubbled all over him, saying, *I'm from New York too, ya know*—every other sentence, not understanding that Arthur still considered himself to be from Connecticut and therefore slightly more important. Now, that almost went completely over my head because Arthur didn't realize that if you were from the Lowcountry, anyone north of Columbia was suspect. But he kept saying, *Actually, I'm from Connecticut*, and Bettina would say, *Yeah, well, same thing*, to which Arthur would reply, *Actually it's quite its own place*, until I finally realized that Connecticut wasn't the melting pot that Brooklyn was. I never thought about New York, Brooklyn, or Connecticut. Why would I? But Arthur wanted the rest of us to know that he was of another, more rarefied social stratum than Bettina. I thought it made him look stupid to think he had to point that out in the first place and I worried that he might insult Bettina. To her credit, Bettina was actually baiting him, trying to decide if he was worth my energy.

When he left she came over to me and said, "Connecticut. Big hairy deal."

"Well, I guess that about sums up how you feel about him."

"You got it."

Lucy and I patched things up because I knew we had to and she was grossly unhappy that she had caused me so much anxiety. Daddy was calling her less and less and I knew she thought that her betrayal had caused it. For my part, being mad with Lucy was a little like staying upset at your dog for peeing indoors when it was pouring rain outside. The dog couldn't help it and regretted it. What were you supposed to do? I told her I'd duct tape her jaw if I found it flapping around again. She took an oath.

"Cross my heart," she said, almost breathless. "I'd rather die."

"Okay. Don't make me hold you to it."

And Jim finally called about a week after he had left.

"Hey, you! I thought you'd never call! How was Ohio? Are you back in San Francisco?"

"Yeah, I'm home and it seems awfully empty. In a word, Ohio was horrible. Gary's parents are completely destroyed by the reality that they're going to live to bury their son. They were pretty nice to me— I imagine that Gary had told them that this illness was of his doing, not mine. When they saw that I really cared about him, they were more hospitable. But this is complicated by so many issues, you know?"

"Yeah. I can only imagine."

"I called Hospice for them."

"Is he that close?"

"You know what? I can't tell, but he seems to be at peace about his death and I just figured that, from what I've read, that's when things start shutting down. His parents aren't handling it well at all. His mother is crying all the time and his father barely speaks. Hospice does all sorts of counseling and I really called them for his parents. Plus, I think Gary would benefit from the comfort of professionals."

"Jim, I am so sorry about Gary."

"I know that. I mean, I know he caused you some misery years ago. . . ."

"That misery was my fault, not his."

Jim was quiet for a few minutes and I wondered what he was thinking. "You're good to say that, Anna, in many ways."

"I'm always here for you, Jim."

"I know that and it's helping me get through this. You know, I travel so much that my world has grown small and, outside of Gary, I have always been so grateful to have you and Emily and Frannie too. There's just nothing like shared history."

"You're right. We're another definition of family, I guess. Unlikely souls struggling together, separately."

"Yeah, well, I'll call you soon."

Time moved on through July, measured by the flood of tourists and the incessant heat. The Isle of Palms sun boiled, scorching everyone and everything. The late afternoons brought dark skies, sudden downpours, and then the light would reappear until the sun set around eight-thirty.

David and Emily had their share of flaring tempers and then reconciliation, but for whatever reason, they were well matched as friends and as young lovers too. I had come to a place where I let her almost come and go as she pleased. It was wrong and I knew it, but each time I would say, *You have to use your own judgment,* she seemed to grow up a little more. That was the goal—to have her grow up as much as possible before Everett Fairchild came to town. I still hadn't decided if I was going to do anything about it, when fate stepped in.

I hadn't seen or heard from Arthur in awhile and I thought, Oh, great, we're playing games again. It was the beginning of August, late one night, and I went over to his house. I knocked on the door and the dogs started barking. After a few minutes, a man in pajama bottoms and a T-shirt came to the door, scratching his head, obviously roused from his sleep.

"Can I help you?" he said, squinting to see if he knew me.

"Oh! I'm sorry! Is Arthur here?"

"No, he's gone back to New York. Is there something I can do?"

I stood there for what seemed an eternity, lost for words. Finally I said, "No, that's okay. I'm sorry I woke you." I started down the steps and he called out.

"If he calls do you want me to tell him anything?"

"Yeah, tell him Anna's not surprised."

Now, given my state of mind, I thought I was pretty cool about Arthur just pulling up stakes and heading north. The weasel. He hadn't even called. Well, maybe something had happened with his son and eventually he would turn up. Maybe not. I didn't care. It's a very telling thing about me—this art of quick recovery. But by the time you're in your thirties, having traveled a sidewalk pockmarked with personal disappointment, you learn that life goes on. I knew there was a lid for every pot. Unfortunately, every lid I had found was a little warped or maybe I wasn't the right pot. It didn't matter because he was gone and a prolonged examination of his exit was a waste of my time. After all, he was living up to his promise of not getting involved. Besides, in his defense, I didn't have enough information to make a judgment.

Without Arthur around to distract me—and this was after I had the good cry I will admit I had over being dumped—I began to focus my vengeance toward Everett Fairchild. The following week, Brigitte and I were working late, finishing with our clients around nine. Everyone else was gone and we were closing up the shop.

"Hey, you wanna grab a bite to eat?" I said.

"Why not?"

"I'm not starving, but I could go for something small. Wings?"

"Dunleavy's?"

"I'll follow you," I said.

With that, we got in our cars and followed each other to the tiny pub at the corner of Station Twenty-two and Middle Street on Sullivan's Island. Parking was a problem but we finally found spots and met up at the front door and eased our way through the crowd. We were greeted by Vicki, the waitress.

Now, you have to know her to fully appreciate the experience. Vicki, a vivacious buxom redhead with the map of Ireland all over her face, should have been working on the *Daily Show*. She was probably the funniest woman on the island and everyone loved her. And Dunleavy's could be crowded, with lots of people standing between the tables watching any of the four televisions suspended from the ceiling, while yellow Labs and small children wandered in between them. Sometimes there was music but there was always fun to be had and where there was fun, Vicki was in the middle, directing traffic and taking orders at the same time.

We found a small table and parked ourselves, knowing that when she showed up we'd have to shout our order to be heard.

"What'll it be, ladies?"

"I'll have a Harp and a dozen wings—medium hot," I said.

"I'll have the Peel 'n' Eat Shrimp and a glass of Chardonnay," Brigitte said.

She took notes and said, "See that guy over there?"

We followed her gesturing and noticed a precious fellow a few years younger than all of us.

"In the blue shirt?" I said.

"Yeah," she said, "if he's still here at eleven, I might—just maybe—give him the thrill of his life."

"So would I," Brigitte said, squinting in his direction. "He must be a tourist. Too starched."

"Who cares?" I said. "He's adorable."

"Get on line, girls," Vicki said. "I'll have your drinks out in a second."

How funny that there was a place in this most conservative society that women could talk about men like they had been talking about us for eons. We were kidding, of course. Not really.

Brigitte and I went through the wings, the shrimp, and a pile of Wet-Naps and finally the crowd thinned out so that we could talk and hear each other.

"So, Brigitte, I gotta ask you something."

"Shoot," she said.

"You know this whole deal about Everett Fairchild and him coming to the Isle of Palms in two weeks?"

"I'm glad you brought it up instead of me. What are you gonna do?"

"What do *you* think I should do?"

"Well, as I'm not obliged to produce a pot roast every night, I've had the time to ruminate."

"Ruminate. Good word."

"Thanks. My father was an English professor."

"Ah."

"Well, here's the problem. If you were a vicious person, this would be easy. You could deliver fifty pictures of Emily to his condo and attach a note that says, *Does this child look familiar? Call this number.* But you're not like that. And you don't know enough about his life and who he is, you know what I mean? I mean he could be a superb man, though I doubt it. Or he could have a fabulous wife, although I doubt that too. But if I were in your shoes, I couldn't live without knowing how he had turned out. I'd want to see the creep."

"You're right," I said, "I don't want to wreck anybody's life. I wouldn't get any pleasure out of that. But I would like to know what he's like now."

"So, if we went to the special events manager at Wild Dunes and offered them a full day of beauty for a raffle prize or drawing or something—haircut, color, manicure, pedicure—the works for the lucky wife or meaningful other, you could get a long look at his wife. Better yet, you could have her before-and-after pictures taken with Emily and send them home with her."

"Oh, my God," I said, and my heart started to race. "Well, one thing's for sure, if we got her in the salon, Bettina could get the goods on his marriage."

"No kidding," Brigitte said, "you'd know what he ate for breakfast by the time she was done with her."

"What if he doesn't have a wife?"

"What if he does?"

"What if she doesn't win?"

"Anna. Calm down. We *fix* the drawing."

"Right. I knew that. I just wanted to see what *you* were thinking."

"Sure."

Vicki came over for refills. "Y'all want another drink?"

"Yeah," I said, "I think I'd like a Cosmopolitan. Just one."

"They're *dangerous*," Brigitte said.

"*We're* dangerous," I said.

"Well? I got a man waiting for me, honey."

"I'll have one too," Brigitte said.

"That's the spirit," Vicki said, and walked away sticking her pencil behind her ear.

Brigitte was one smart cookie. Over our drinks—which I sipped *very slowly*—we planned the details of our scheme. The brilliance of the plan lay in its simplicity. It would give me that window of time that his wife was in our salon to decide whether or not I wanted to take the next step, which would be to let Everett know that Emily was on the planet. Maybe this was stupid, but I knew that I would arrive at that decision based on what kind of wife he had. If she was smart and nice, I mean really nice, I would probably be more inclined to let Everett's wife have the truth. A smart wife, a savvy wife, would understand and take it better than some gal who wasn't secure in herself and her marriage. Brigitte agreed with me on that point.

"You're right," she said. "If his wife isn't the right kind of woman, telling Everett about Emily would bring all kinds of trouble into Emily's life and there's no reason to make her unhappy. Life's complicated enough as it is."

"Boy, you can say that again," I said. "The last thing Emily needs is to have a woman pitching fits. She has a grandmother for that. Jim's mother loves to make Emily feel badly about herself."

"Great. I had an aunt like that." Brigitte rolled her eyes, remembering. "Okay, so, let's say the wife is a decent person, seems to be well balanced, and we like her. Then what? I mean, you can't just tell her, can you? How are we going to get the information from her to Everett?"

"Good question. Unfortunately, I think—and please tell me if you have a better idea—I think I'm going to have to pick up the phone and tell him. The only other way would be that she recognizes Everett's eyes in Emily's head, and I think that's asking a lot."

"Well, how do you feel about calling him?"

"What are you? My shrink? I'd be scared out of my mind! What did you expect?"

"I ain't your shrink, honey. I told you I've thought about this. A lot. And if I were you I'd be terrified too. But when I thought it through I came to another conclusion. He's the one who should be scared. Not you. You could prosecute, you know."

"What if he says he doesn't remember me?"

"There is such a thing as a paternity test. Simple enough to get a court to order one. Although if what you tell me about his eyes and Emily's is that obvious, all he's going to have to do is look at her."

"Well, if I decide I'm too chicken to call him, I could slip a bunch of pictures of Emily in his wife's goody bag, right?"

"I think you should do that anyway. Let her get home and ask him why she was given the pictures. She'd stew over that for a while and eventually confront him. Wouldn't you?"

"Hell, yes," I said, "I mean, she has to know he went to school here and it wouldn't be beyond any wife's imagination that her husband might have left a little bundle behind while sowing his youthful oats."

"And you know what else we could do?"

"We could give a free haircut and massage to a man. . . ."

"And that man would be Everett? But I'm not sure I have the nerve for that one."

"Me either. The vodka has spoken. We'd better go home before we decide it's a good idea to send him pizzas at three in the morning."

"That's actually not such a bad idea," Brigitte said, obviously done in by her cocktail.

"Time for the check."

I knew the plan would work. If I were to describe the state of my nervous system from that moment on until the day his wife walked in our salon I could only say that there wasn't any combination of medicine on the planet strong enough to give me emotional equilibrium.

Naturally, I had discussed it with Jim and Frannie. Jim was going back to Ohio and couldn't come to Charleston until the last minute. Gary was almost at the end and was asking for him, but still hanging on. But, as usual, despite the rest of his life, Jim had a great idea.

"Get a photograph taken of the whole staff and frame it. Make them group head shots—in color. Put that in her goody bag. It would seem more normal, you know? Write out a card that says something like, *So you won't forget your friends at Anna's Cabana.* Place Emily in the middle of the lineup and tell whoever takes the picture that you want them to really come in close on Emily's face."

"Brilliant. I'll get the girls in the deli to do it with Lucy's digital camera. You're right. I mean, we were just gonna drop in some pictures in an envelope."

"That's why you never do anything major without consulting me first to help fine-tune the play."

I called Frannie, who was filled with advice and her customary abundance of mirth and excitement over the adventure.

"Jaysus! Me granny is spinning in her grave! I need a smoke! Hang on!" I could hear her rumble around and then she picked up the phone again. "Okay. Give me the plan again."

I told her that Lucy had called Wild Dunes and spoken to the head of guest relations. She told them that we would like to be their premier salon for tourists. For the month of August, we would have a drawing and give away a free makeover, sun exposure treatments, and a manicure and pedicure—the works—to one of their guests once a week and ten percent off to all their other guests.

"They went nuts! They thought it was wonderful!"

"You and those gals are so funny," she said. "Okay, are you going to throw in lunch?"

"Good idea."

"What about a limo to pick them up? Champagne in the backseat and all?"

"Open container law in South Carolina."

"Then just give her a split with a note attached to it that indemnifies the salon against any problem if it's opened."

"Too complicated."

"Then give her a note that says, *Drink me!* Two glasses will loosen her tongue enough so that when she arrives, you can go to work. What questions are y'all gonna ask her?"

"Gee, God, I hadn't even thought about that. What do you think?"

"Well, for Pete's sake, the first thing you need to know is if they have children! I mean, don't you want to know if Emily has half brothers or sisters?"

"Come on, Frannie, I'm not a total idiot! Of course that's the most important thing!" I had never considered it. She was right. "But besides that, what should I ask her?"

"Well, as long as we're channeling the devil, why don't you get Bettina to somehow start a chat to find out what their sex life is like. And while Bettina is warming her up, check out her jewelry, shoes, handbag—see if she and old Everett have any dough to speak of."

"Heaven help me, Frannie, their sex life is the *last* thing I want to know about."

"No, it isn't; because if they're not happy then you might not want Emily to get entangled with them. I mean, Anna, this woman could be a total, screaming, nagging bitch. Or a lunatic. Or overpossessive of Everett. Or who knows? Maybe she's such a tightwad that she wouldn't let Everett give Emily ten cents for college."

"God, Frannie! The thought of money never even entered my mind!"

"Then, hang on, lassie, I'll call Rome on me other line and have you put on the short list for sainthood."

"You're so funny," I said and giggled.

"Look, here's the point. The more you can get her to talk, the more you can make a better guess on what kind of man he turned out to be. And whether or not you want Emily to find out about him now or later."

"What do you mean now or later?"

"Look, Anna. Let's say his wife is the salt of the earth and you love her to death. Okay, then you might want to take Emily aside with Jim and tell her that you have found her birth father and ask her what she wants to do about it."

"Well, that's about how I had figured it, which is why it's so important for Jim to come. If that happens, I don't think I should spring this on Emily without him."

"Absolutely. It wouldn't be fair. And if she's a bitch from hell, you don't have to tell Emily right away. Do you? Is she suspicious about anything?"

"She thinks I'm just nervous because we've been so busy, and upset because King Arthur went back to New York."

"He what?"

"Yeah. Skipped town and took Excalibur with him."

"Excalibur? Is that what he calls his . . ."

"No. It's what I called it."

"Excalibur? Whew! Really? Whoa!"

She was killing herself laughing and I was turning every shade of lipstick in my makeup bag, including the free samples.

"Don't bust a gut up there in Yankee territory, girl! Wait till you get here and I'll tell you all about him, if I have the courage. I'm going to hell, right?"

"Who gives a shit? Just pray he's there! Anna?"

"Yeah?"

"Excalibur?"

"Yes. Get over it, okay?"

The trap was ready. Now all we needed was a victim. We had our trial run on the first Saturday in August with a precious older lady from Birmingham. The concierge gathered the names of all the guests who had a Saturday night stay at Wild Dunes that week. All we had to do was stop by and pick them up. We took the names back to the salon, pulled a slip of paper from the fishbowl, and we had a winner. We then called the concierge back to arrange the appointment, giving him three different times. Wild Dunes was happy because they had a little bonus to offer their guests. We were pleased because Mrs. Dan Gaby of Birmingham bought three of Angel's baskets, for almost five hundred dollars, and a twenty-five-dollar bottle of aloe for her husband's sunburn. There were benefits to this that I hadn't even calculated. Besides, I knew she would come back to our salon if she came to the Isle of Palms again. It was always interesting to meet new clients—especially if they liked to talk. Women don't go to the beauty parlor expecting to keep their business to themselves.

"Dan liked to burn himself half to death out there, deep-sea fishing with all those silly men," she said.

"Did he catch anything?" I said, while I was painting color on her roots. She was easily on the other side of seventy-five.

She started to chuckle. "Catch anything? Well, nothing much besides sun poisoning and a hangover. He's up to the condo right now, lying on the couch watching the Golf Channel. Is that the most boring thing in the world? The Golf Channel? Why, I'd rather clean closets than waste my time watching golf on the television."

"Sometimes I think fishing is just an excuse to drink beer," I said. "And, I wouldn't watch golf on television or in person. Puts me to sleep!"

"Me too!"

She was pleased as punch with her hair and her purchases and we were one week away from facing Mrs. Everett Fairchild.

Thirty-two

La Bomb-ba

~~~~~

IT was early Saturday morning, the second week of August, and I couldn't shake my dreams out of my head. I was a teenager, riding in a pale yellow convertible with some friends, heading from Breach Inlet toward Fort Moultrie on Sullivan's Island. My mother was in the back of a van in front of me. She was wearing a lavender dress and jacket and she waved at me, smiling. I was aware that she was dead and I kept saying in the dream, *There's my mother! See her? She looks so great!*

Most dreams I had seemed to be a clearinghouse for whatever was on my mind during the day. Even though I had been born in the Low-country and had grown up in the Gullah culture, combined with my peculiar brand of Catholicism—which was highly driven by saints and novenas—I wasn't completely convinced that all dreams of my mother were spiritual visitations. I only hoped they were. I may have had a garden growing out of control, but my imagination was in check. Still, I'd had enough of these dreams to know something was about to happen and if it was indeed her, that she wanted me to know that she was around, pulling for me.

Well, yes, something was about to happen because this was the day that Everett Fairchild's wife was coming into the salon.

Frannie had canceled her return emotional support trip because of business but Jim would hopefully arrive that night. Among the many things on my list, adding to the very worst case of nervous anxiety I'd ever had, was the most harrowing of all burning questions.

How does one get their act together emotionally to meet the wife of one's rapist?

I hadn't given my own state of mind much consideration because, compared to the possible ramifications of the day before me, it seemed like I had accepted the plan as it came together. But I hadn't. When I woke up and realized everything was on schedule, I was terrified.

I wanted this woman to take me seriously. Who wouldn't? I kept thinking that, if and when she found out that her husband had fathered Emily, she wouldn't believe it was a rape; she would say it wasn't his child; and finally she would say that if her husband left some little nothing hairdresser with a baby, so what? That I was nothing but a redneck hairdresser and people like me did white trash things like this all the time.

I mean, I would have felt better about myself if I were a world-famous neurologist and she was coming to me because of migraine headaches, you know what I mean? I thought that I had made peace with myself about being a hairdresser instead of a doctor or a lawyer, and I had. I was wildly proud of myself. Until that morning arrived, that is, and then I was wildly insecure. Well, at least I owned my own business and that was a substantial something to console me.

Was there anything in my closet that would send the message I wanted her to receive? Exasperated with my own self-consciousness, I finally settled on a midcalf white linen tank dress with a lavender linen overshirt. I put on every piece of faux turquoise jewelry I owned, which wasn't much, and white sandals with a low platform. How odd that I had chosen white. I looked pristine and innocent. It was another reminder that before I had been targeted as the aircraft carrier of Joanne Fairchild's husband's stinging crash landing, I had been innocent if not pristine.

For all the thought I had given to how and what I should do to fix my life, I had never figured Everett Fairchild into the equation. I wasn't convinced in the least that seeing his wife would bring me closer to a decision on whether it was right or wrong to circle his planet. The whole thing made me a complete wreck.

That day I would have to begin the process of deciding if his marriage looked hospitable enough to allow my daughter to enter their lives. How could I even concentrate if my hands wouldn't stop shaking? I wished that Jim was going to be there.

The group picture had been taken and framed. Emily was right in the middle, her father's green eyes plainly visible. We put it in a gift bag with some shampoo, conditioner, and a T-shirt, of which we now owned many dozens. I decided then and there that if I didn't like Joanne I would just remove the picture from her bag before I gave it to her. Easy enough. Our small cast was ready. Everyone, that is, except Emily.

It was only eight-thirty in the morning and already over ninety degrees, as it had been all week. Emily didn't want to come to work. She slipped into moodiness, as she was unaware there was a landmark occasion hovering to which she should rise. She and David had argued over something—probably sex or power, which at their age were frequently the same thing.

"He's a total jerk," she said.

"Men mature later than women," I said, "you know that."

"Except Lucy," she said, "he's just like her. I'm not working today. I've had it."

Who knew what that meant except that she didn't feel like dealing with Lucy? I didn't want to know what had happened—and I imagine she didn't want Lucy asking her what had happened either. Tough noogies, O young, petulant one.

"Honey? It's Saturday! It's our busiest day! I need you!"

"Then tell Lucy to stay out of my face, okay?"

"Okay."

I understood. I really did. Unfortunately, this was not the day to abandon ship.

I wobbled into the salon and everyone was already there, playing opossum. The most difficult part had been not telling Emily and I hoped we would be busy enough that she would slide through the day. Lucy, Bettina, and Brigitte were cool and greeted Emily and me as though it was another normal unspectacular day.

But we knew better. Joanne Fairchild would be there in twenty minutes. She was bringing a friend who had booked a long appointment while their husbands were playing in a golf tournament.

The front door opened and in they came, stepping up to Lucy's desk to announce themselves. One was stunning, right out of a magazine, and the other one was, well, bless her heart, dowdy. She wasn't overweight, just frumpy, the kind of woman who never got a second look or even a serious first glance. I assumed correctly that the one who suffered from the overzealous personal stylist and trainer was Joanne. And, because Lucy took her over and introduced her to Brigitte.

I gave Joanne the eye. She wore cobalt tissue linen drawstring pants and her black knit halter top left a great part of her rock hard midriff exposed. Her arms were toned from the rigors of weight training, her wrists a chorus of thick gold bangles. Her four-carat diamond stood out like a midnight beacon against her deep tan, flashing little rainbows against the walls every time she moved. She had almost jet black hair pulled back in a clamp and I imagined she had dark, heavily mascaraed eyes hiding behind her large Chanel sunglasses. She was the complete antithesis of me. She was dark, flashy, and she reeked money. And she was self-absorbed. Fault Number One: egocentric.

Yes, Brigitte was handling Joanne. Before everyone starts saying, *Why? This was the opportunity of your lifetime*, may I just say that this was going to be nothing like a high school catfight in the girls' bathroom. It was choreographed to be dead serious and innocuous at the same time. Way before this day actually dawned, I knew that when

Joanne Fairchild arrived, Brigitte would have the most composure of any of us. Besides, Brigitte was no nitwit and I trusted her to ask the right questions. I would be four feet away the entire time and listening, ears twitching. It was the most I could bear. I think it was the most any woman in my position should have been expected to bear.

Lucy brought the other woman to me and introduced her as Marsha, before they were swept off to change into salon robes. Brigitte was shampooing Joanne and I put Marsha in my chair. Bettina was warming the wax and making the treatment room ready, her heels ticktacking back and forth across the floor. Lucy offered them drinks and magazines.

As soon as Marsha sat down I could sense that she seemed uneasy. Her appointment was obviously more important to her than it was to me. How could she have known that I only wanted to fall in a hole, pass out cold, and have them tell me what had happened later? Anything. But, hell, no. My middle name should have been Be the Pro and Face the Music.

"I think, I mean, I've been thinking that maybe I'd like red hair. What do you think?"

Oh, God, not today! Why did I always get the desperate-to-be-saved on days I could barely think?

"Well, let's see what you have here," I said and pulled the rubber band from her ponytail.

Her shoulder-length hair tumbled and settled around her shoulders like wisps of goose down from a pillow fight. Women thought they knew what they wanted but it was my experience that I could serve them better if I knew what they hoped would come of a few hours in my chair. Sometimes a client would badger you into some wild new look that would be great on a rock star but looked like holy hell on their triple chins, broken veins, and trifocals. And, I mean that in the best way. I'm not in the business of being cruel. I'm in the business of serving up someone's most flattering appearance.

Whenever I gave in to duplicating the hairstyle of a magazine picture of some glam gal a client had carried folded in her wallet for months, she almost always regretted it. Sometimes they sat right in my chair and cried. I was in no state of mind to have that happen.

"Well, we can do red. I mean, honey, I've got a war chest of colors that would scare Rembrandt. I can make it any color you want." I looked at her face in the mirror as I stood behind her and thought about it for a minute. She had obviously colored it a lot—at home— because it was straw and didn't have much elastic to it, except at the roots. What she really needed was a good cut. And to lose the blue metallic eye shadow.

"Marsha? If what you want is a new look, I think it's more about the cut and the condition of your hair than the color. But, I'd go blond. Blonds are hot this year. I can give it some highlights and glaze it to give it body and to make it shine and I can cut away all the dead stuff."

"Well, as long as I leave here looking like I've been here, I guess that would be okay."

"Does that mean cut it and condition it?"

"I guess. Look. Here's the thing." She lowered her voice and said quietly, "My husband works for Joanne's husband. I'm always hearing about *Joanne this* and *Joanne that* from him. It would be nice if my husband would look at me the way he looks at her. You know what I mean?"

I thought, Whooo baby, it didn't take long to start getting the skinny on Joanne Fairchild. Fault Number Two: Joanne flirted inappropriately with the help.

"Done," I said, "Blond it is. I can show you some makeup tricks too, if you're interested."

"I'm interested in anything but let's not announce what we're doing, okay?"

"You can count on that, Marsha. This chair is sacred like the confessional at the Vatican. I'll be right back."

I went to the back to mix some color and some bleach, thinking about the scores of women I had known over the years. They spent

more money in one week on groceries and more time on volun-
teerism in a month than they spent on themselves in a year. They
forgot that men don't care how many committees they chaired or
whether or not the chicken soup was made from homemade stock.
Men liked their women to be good looking and stylish. Women forgot
that they didn't have to sacrifice themselves on the road to quality
homemaking.

I knew what I would do to resurrect her face. I was going to give
her a single process and then some highlights. Bettina caught my eye
and followed me.

"So, what do you think the first thing is *she* says when Brigitte
starts washing her hair?" Bettina said, practically hissing and spitting.
When Bettina was annoyed, it showed like the lights on the tree at
Rockefeller Center.

"I give up," I said, whispering, stirring color around in a plastic bowl.

"She says of all the women in the group they're traveling with,
wasn't it funny she won? She said she needed to win the Day of
Beauty *less* than any of them. Augh! Is she stuck on herself or what?"

"Be nice. Bait her. Don't challenge her."

"I know, I know," Bettina said, "but you know me. First impressions
and all. I'd like to slap her! I *hate* women like her!"

I put the bowl on the counter and faced her, whispering. "Me too,
but don't judge her, Bettina. That's death. We need to get her to talk,
remember? Concentrate on how you're gonna find out about her sex
life."

"Right." Bettina's eyes glistened at the prospect of her assignment.
"It will all come out in the waxing room." She inhaled, raising herself
up to her full height, and walked away as though nothing had passed
between us. *Go wax the hell out of her,* I thought, *and while you're at it,
cut her cuticles up to her knuckles.*

Fault Number Three: *massively* egocentric. I returned to Marsha,
who was deeply engrossed in conversation with Lucy.

"I just said to Marsha, Anna, that she needs to jazz up her

wardrobe with some color. Marsha, honey, you're too pretty for beige! You remember that Color Me Beautiful thing? Well, if you had on a hot pink knit shirt . . ."

"What's Color Me Beautiful?" Marsha said.

"Don't worry about it," I said to Marsha. "Lucy? Her whole appearance is about to morph so don't waste your breath! Come back after I color her hair, okay?"

"Oh! Silly me! Who knows? You might come in as a Winter and turn yourself into a Spring!"

"What's she talking about?"

"Ancient history," I said, smiling at her in the mirror. "Okay. Are you ready to change your life?"

"Without a doubt," she said.

Standing behind her to her right, I continued to stir the color like it would eventually become mayonnaise. I was trying to think of the most exciting thing I could do to her head without her having a nervous breakdown. She needed her hair cut off at the roots, it was so fried. But she had good cheekbones and a nice jaw. With some makeup, we could bring out her eyes. I was itching to get started.

"All right," I said, the professional in me kicking in at last, "tell me about your lifestyle. Are you in the sun a lot?"

"Are you kidding? We live in Florida! I play golf, tennis, and the rest of the time, I'm on a boat. We're in the boat business, you know."

"Right. So you need a low-maintenance style."

"Yeah, I don't have a lot of time to fix hair that's gonna blow all over the place anyway."

I began to section her hair and paint her roots with a medium blond color. I knew it looked brown to her, but she didn't say a word. Her eyes went from the mirror and back to her magazine with a genuine smile for me, every time she looked up. I liked this woman and wanted to make her look beautiful.

"So, what are we doing today?" Brigitte said to Joanne.

"Just a blowout," she said. "I don't need a makeover."

Everyone who heard her hated her guts.

Neither one of us would have admitted it, but Marsha and I were listening to Joanne Fairchild's chatter with Bettina and Brigitte. Bettina sat by her side, doing her fingernails.

"That's a gorgeous stone," Bettina said, remarking on Joanne's paperweight, while she removed her old polish. "Your husband must be a pretty fabulous guy, huh?"

"Yeah, sure," Joanne said, "he's all right. I'm terrible. I mean, after fifteen years, I'd probably get sick of Brad Pitt."

"Not if he gave me rocks like that, hon!" Bettina said and I shot her a look. She recovered by saying, "But I know what you mean. My husband, Bobby? He ships out for months at a time, so we don't get tired of each other. But if he was around all the time, he'd make me crazy. I'm *sure* of that!"

"That's why I'm single," Brigitte said, coming to the credibility rescue. "I never have dated anyone who didn't eventually bore me to tears. Who needs it? I have my nice house, my nice car, and nobody tells me what to do. Life's good."

"Well, my husband can't tell me what to do. Rhett, that's my husband's name—short for Everett—"

"Jeez! Rhett Butler! I *knew* he was alive!" Bettina laughed and snorted, making everyone giggle just at the noise she made, if not the joke.

"Oh, no! Puh-leese! Everett Fairchild is no Rhett Butler! Are you kidding? When Mr. Fairchild is selling a boat he is the most utterly charming man you can imagine, but that's because his livelihood is involved. But when he comes home? Boor-ing! He's too tired to do anything except eat dinner and fall into bed. Anyway, the house is my business, not his. I do what I want."

I'll bet you do, I thought, and looked at Marsha in the mirror, who raised her eyebrows and twisted her lips to one side in agreement.

"Well, that's how it should be," Bettina said, adding, "another French?"

Joanne said, "French is fine."

"So, where do ya'll live?" Brigitte said. "Got kids?"

"No, no children, but that's okay. We live right outside of Clearwater."

"Kids are a pain in the behind," Brigitte said. "But, I love kids, don't get me wrong—I have a ton of nieces and nephews and they're fabulous. But they go home at night, you know?"

"Yes. I'll tell you something else," Joanne said, "we have a lot of friends who don't have children and they are quite happy, thank you. I mean, you have kids and you have to give up your whole life!"

San Andreas Fault. Doesn't like kids? That did it.

"Well, I'd like to have six," Bettina said. I sent her a death ray and she caught it, coming back to her senses. "But I can understand why someone like you wouldn't want to be tied down, because you're right. Kids are nothing but a noose!"

"Exactly! I mean, I'm on the go all the time and I like my life like it is."

"Me too," Brigitte said, smiling. "So what do you do for fun?"

"Oh, the usual stuff. I like to shop and have lunch with my friends, but I play tennis for our club and that's a pretty big deal. I belong to a book club and an investment club and I volunteer for different things around town. This year I'm chairing the fund-raiser for our library. It's going to be fabulous. Pat and Sandra Conroy are coming."

"No kidding," Brigitte said, honestly impressed.

My timer went off and I combed the color in Marsha's hair out to the ends.

"Five more minutes," I said.

"No problem," Marsha said. "I'm taking this quiz in *Cosmo* on how you can tell if your lover is cheating on you."

"Come on," I said, "wait till he sees you tonight! He's gonna drool!"

"Good!"

Brigitte was finished with Joanne's perfect hair, spun her chair around, and handed her the mirror to check the back.

"Fine," Joanne said, without a trace of gratitude. "Thanks."

Bettina and Brigitte held their breath for a moment, sort of not believing the tone of Joanne's voice. She had delivered that *fine* and *thanks* as though she was picking up a burger at a drive-thru. Fault? She was an ingrate.

"Okaaay!" Bettina said. "Let's wax next."

"I'll follow you," Joanne said, "maybe someone could ask that lazy kid over there to get me a Coke from next door?"

"Sure," Bettina said.

My face was burning. That *lazy* kid? That *kid* was her stepdaughter and that *kid* was my family. I said nothing. Fault? Ungracious and thought herself to be the queen, that's what.

"Come on," I said to Marsha, "let's get you rinsed."

I put her in a seat by the sink and motioned for Emily.

"Whatcha need, Mom?" she said. "I'm helping Lucy address postcards for the mailing."

I reached in my pocket and handed her a dollar. "Run next door, baby, and bring me a Coca-Cola in the can, okay?"

"Sure," she said and left.

Marsha had a funny look on her face. "Is that your daughter?"

"Yes, that's Emily. She's home for the summer from school."

"Oh."

I realized that she had seen Emily's eyes and, knowing Everett as she did, she was startled but didn't ask any more questions. I wondered what she thought but I wasn't about to ask her. All I could think was, *Oh, no, what if she blows this before we can play our cards?* My heart began to beat a little faster and I could feel the back of my neck break out in beads of perspiration.

In a few minutes, I had Marsha back in her chair and Emily had returned with the Coke.

"Whaddya want me to do with this?"

"Put it over ice in a glass and take it to the lady in the waxing room. Knock first, okay? Thanks, honey."

" 'Kay."

Marsha now had a look of complete disbelief in her eyes, as though she'd seen a ghost.

I just ignored it and said, "Okay, now we're gonna highlight your hair and cut the dickens out of it." I should've been a poker player.

Marsha wound up with a precious, short, layered haircut that took ten years from her face. I made the back sort of flipped and gave her long thin straight bangs.

"God! I love it!" Marsha said. "How can I thank you?"

"Tell your friends," I said. "You really do look wonderful. Now let's do some makeup."

Joanne Fairchild hadn't noticed a thing at all about Emily's eyes and apparently Marsha had decided to keep it to herself. By the time they left, both of them buying one of Angel's baskets and tons of skin care and hair products, I was completely wrung out and could've slept for a month. Joanne tipped no one.

Final Fault? Tightwad.

Marsha, on the other hand, tipped until she ran out of cash, even giving Emily five dollars.

"What's this for?" Emily asked.

"Because you're a great girl," she said and smiled at her.

When they went out the door, we all heaved sighs of relief. Three people came in without appointments. The phone rang. It was David for Emily. She took the portable phone to the back of the salon. The rest of us whooped and slapped each other on the back, relieved that our charade was ended. The clients were waiting, looking at us like we were crazy. Brigitte was right. I knew we needed another stylist as soon as possible. Maybe two.

Emily returned, all smiles. David had apologized for whatever infraction had been committed and wanted to catch an early movie.

"Can I go?"

"Sure. Get home at a decent hour."

"You're the best, Mom. Thanks."

We closed at six and hung around for half an hour, cleaning up and getting set up for Monday.

"So what'd y'all think?" Lucy said. "I didn't like that Joanne much."

"She's never touching Emily," I said, "not in a million years."

"I hated her guts," Bettina said. "Know what she said in the waxing room?"

"Tell it," Brigitte said.

"So she says to me, 'You ever have an affair?' I said, 'What do you mean an affair? You mean, since I married Bobby?' She says, 'Yeah.' I says to her, 'Whaddya crazy? You don't know Bobby! He'd break every bone in my body!' Then she laughs, this weaselly little sneaky laugh, like, heh, heh, heh, and I say to myself, *Oh, brother!* Then I say, 'What? What's funny? Did *you* ever have an affair?' And you know what she says?"

"What?" Brigitte, Lucy, and I said all at once.

"She said, 'Who, me? Why, I'd never do a thing like that.' All innocent and everything. So right there I decide that she's a lying piece of adulterous shit. If you ask me, I think she's sleeping with that nice lady Marsha's husband because she all but said so."

"Who cares," Brigitte said. "I didn't like her way before you waxed her."

"She's got pubes like an animal," Bettina said. "Disgusting! Right outta the zoo. I waxed her but good! Then I plucked the strays with the tweezers. That always gets them."

"Good!" Brigitte said.

"Bettina! Good Lord! Well, I don't like her either," I said, thinking I would go to bed as soon as I got home. "She's horrible."

"Worst of all, no tips! What kinda woman takes a manicure, pedicure, bikini wax, and a blowout on the house without tipping the help? She's tighter than a bee's butt, honey," Lucy said, "and y'all know me. I hate cheap."

I started turning out the lights and then I completely freaked out.

"Oh, no!" I almost screamed it.

"What?" Brigitte said.

"She's got the picture of Emily! Shit! If Everett sees it, then what?

I have to deal with her? Emily gets tangled up with her? I don't want that woman to ever get near Emily!"

"It can't happen!" Brigitte said.

"You don't know my luck!" I said.

"Anna? Quit worrying! She probably already threw it in the garbage," Lucy said.

"Yeah," Bettina said, "she probably kept the frame and dumped the picture."

"God. I hope you're right," I said.

What had I done?

When I got home there was a message from Jim on my voice mail. He couldn't come. Gary's parents had called and said Gary was asking for him. He said he'd call me as soon as he could.

Thirty-three

Love's Labor Found

~~~

USINESS was fabulous but August was a bummer. It was hotter than it had ever been in the history of mankind. Even the weatherman on television had joked that the only thing that separated Charleston from the fires of hell was a screen door. Think about *that* for a while. We're talking scorching, blistering, oppressive heat with humidity that made even my hair look like Don King's. There was a thunderstorm every afternoon and then the mosquitoes would rise from their fortresses and swarm the islands. You'll never hear that from the Department of Tourism, but you can take it from me. If you ever decide to vacation here, leave all perfume at home. And that SSS stuff from Avon? Ha! Lowcountry bugs guzzle that stuff like bubbas at a kegger.

So, on yet another hot-off-the-charts, manless night, I was stretched out on my old sofa, shoes off, watching *Saturday Night Live* reruns. Steve Martin and Dan Aykroyd were doing the Wild and the Crazy Guys skit and there I was all alone, laughing my guts out, thinking I'd love to cut their hair. Emily was out with David, but I expected her soon. The phone rang. It was Jim and his voice was cracking, heavy with emotion.

"Gary's gone."

My heart sank. I couldn't stand it that Jim was so sad and even though we knew Gary was going to die, it was somehow still surprising that he had.

"Oh, Jim. I'm so sorry."

"Yeah. Me too."

We talked for a long time about everything—his parents, how they were handling it and how it had been at the end. Gary was angry about dying and didn't want to let go. Jim had held his hand, telling him over and over that it was all right, that he would help his parents with his estate or anything that needed to be done. He had fought for his last breath and the trauma of being a witness to his friend's death had a profound effect on Jim.

"It was the most awful thing I've ever seen," Jim said.

"Not everyone has a peaceful death. I am so sorry, Jim."

"Yeah, well, poor bastard. His body just stopped and you know what? No matter how strong his will was, and it was *strong*, there was nothing to stop the inevitable. He was nothing but skin and bones, Anna. It just broke my heart to see him like that. He was a good guy, you know? Nobody deserves to die like that. I just feel so bad."

"Shit. I wish I could do something, Jim."

"Oh, hell, what can anyone do? But thanks. I feel better just talking to you."

We talked for a few more minutes and then I said, "So do you want the dirt on Joanne Fairchild or what?"

"God, yes! I was just going to ask you about that. What happened?"

We wound up giving only a few minutes to the subject of Joanne Fairchild. A rehash of her visit was unimportant in light of Gary's death. Besides, there wasn't much more than fizzle to be said.

"Oh, God, Jim," I said, "you know how we all plot and scheme? We think we're so smart and we're gonna fix everything with the truth? In this case, the truth is that his wife is a self-centered, materialistic snob. You and I wouldn't want her in Emily's life for love or money. And, she's probably running around on him anyway. At least, there was some allusion to her extramarital sporting events."

"Great, that's just great," Jim said. "Well, we tried. But, you know what? It doesn't change the unfortunate fact that, as long as you know who Emily's birth father is, she has some right to know as well. Even if his wife is a cheap and tacky bitch. Don't you think?"

"Yeah. I mean, I guess I'm trying to figure out the details of how we should tell her. And when. But, thank God, Emily's not asking, so what's the rush?"

"I don't know. God, I'm not looking forward to the next few days."

"When's the funeral?"

"Tuesday."

"Do you want me to come?"

For me to offer to attend a funeral was a first, but I would've done anything for Jim.

"No. I'm okay."

"Do you want to come here afterwards for a few days? To sort of decompress?"

"Nah, thanks. I gotta go back to work, which I am completely not in the mood to do. Why don't we call Frannie and see if she wants to come Labor Day? I have to be in Burgundy on September fifth for a tasting, so I'm flying over on the third."

"Come here first!"

"Yeah, that's what I was thinking. I could fly to Charleston first. Probably should see Trixie too. She hasn't been feeling so great."

"Oh? What's the matter with her?"

"Who knows? Probably done in by the heat. Or lonely. She's always complaining about something. That woman is a bona fide conundrum. With all she's got, you'd think she'd find a reason to celebrate something every five minutes. But not her. I don't think she's got a note of music in her soul. Anyway, I could stay for a couple days and then head to France from there."

I assumed that Trixie didn't know about Gary yet and that when she found out, she would find it beneath her interest. I told Jim he could come when he wanted and stay as long as he liked. I'd be his brick.

When he asked about Arthur, I told him he'd escaped without a good-bye and he said, "Honey, there are a million Arthurs out there. When I get to town, we'll go trolling together."

"You know what? You are some kinda guy, Jim Abbot. Even in your lowest moments, you find a way to make me feel better. I still can't believe I haven't even heard a word from Arthur, though. Isn't that a little screwed up?"

This unleashed some shadowy thoughts in Jim's mind.

"Are *you* screwed up? No. Is it screwed up that he didn't *call?* Yes. Let me tell you something about men who can't commit to relationships. They *don't* call. They live their whole lives looking for excuses on why they can't have a relationship with anyone. You're too tall, you're too short, too fat, too thin, too ugly, too pretty, too smart, too stupid, too rich, too poor, too *something!* The only thing they value is themselves. They are emotionally bankrupt pretenders."

"You go, honey!" When Jim got on a tear it was like mashing the pedal to the floor in a Ferrari.

"It's the truth."

"I know. I just miss him, you know?"

"You really liked him, didn't you?"

"I guess. Yeah, I guess I did. The bastard."

"That's my girl."

"Jim, what's the matter with people?" Another invitation for a lecture but I knew it was good to just let him talk. Anyway, filling my night talking to Jim was good for me too.

"I don't know. I think that people just don't understand, Anna. And they don't have strong values. They don't understand what's worth it and what isn't. And, they put themselves first." He stopped for a second and sighed. "I'll tell you what. I'm gonna miss Gary every day for the rest of my life and for the rest of my life I'll be damn glad I was here with him in the end. There just aren't that many people in your life who ever really love you. You know?"

"That's for sure," I said, and thought about how much I loved Jim. And Daddy. And Emily. And Frannie. "I can count 'em on one hand, just like they say."

"It's true. They know you inside and out including all your evil ways and they still love you. That's what you gotta hang on to. The rest of these players are just not worth our sweat."

I knew he was right, but I still wished Arthur would call and give me some reasonable explanation for dropping off the map. Like that he was shopping for a diamond for me and he got kidnapped, conked on the head, and was in the hospital with amnesia.

I spent my Sundays going to Mass and gardening—which involved cutting flowers from my wild and woolly garden to fill every container I owned. My garden had reached warp-speed progress. I would take flowers to the salon, to Lucy, and to the Snoop Sisters next door and they grew back almost overnight.

On that Sunday, after talking to Jim, I had dinner with Miss Mavis and Miss Angel, which I heartily enjoyed. Later, I was in the yard again working. Emily and David were at the beach. When I gardened I was my most serene self, thinking through my life and seeing it for what it really was. Mentally, I was still savoring the warm apple pie Miss Angel had served for dessert.

Our dinner conversation had centered around the island in the old days, when there had been a Ferris wheel, a merry-go-round, cotton candy, and Jones bingo. I laughed listening to Miss Mavis talk about the dried lima beans people used to mark their numbers on their bingo cards and the teddy bears, radios, and horrible Nubian lamps you could take home, if you won the "cover all." When she was barely married to my father, my mother had gone with her several times and she said they'd had a grand time. On one occasion, Momma had won a Scotch plaid metal ice chest.

"She was so excited, you'd have thought she'd won the Irish Sweepstakes! I can still remember her eyes sparkling when she chose that prize. The man who called out the numbers was named Gabe, which is an unheard-of name in these parts. He was Italian, I think. *B-12! Under the O-64!* He had the most masculine voice! Don't you know that Yankee winked at your mother and she liked to have died? Oh! We laughed so!"

I remembered that cooler being on our back porch, slightly rusted on the hinges of the handle. I used to sit on it when it was full of ice because it was cool.

Miss Mavis talked about the trolley that brought her parents from Charleston, all through Sullivan's Island to the Isle of Palms, and how they fell in love with the place.

"I wasn't even born but I heard the stories so many times, I remember them like I was there. My momma and daddy would go to the foot of Cumberland Street to catch the *Sappho*—that was the name of the ferryboat they took. The ride across the harbor was so beautiful, the wind blowing Momma's hair and Daddy hanging on to his hat. Momma had a hamper filled with sandwiches and their clothes for the beach. They'd dock in Mount Pleasant and take the trolley up Railroad Avenue on Sullivan's Island—that's Jasper Avenue or Boulevard now—and then over to this island. The Fourth of July was so beautiful with all the fireworks. They were so wonderful, Momma said. And they'd always have some special entertainment, like men jumping out of airplanes in parachutes—one year some fool stunt pilot got himself killed. Oh, yes, I remember hearing about that. Terrible!

"There was a long boardwalk where she'd walk with Daddy under the stars. The big bands would play and Momma and Daddy would dance in the pavilion until it was time to catch the last trolley car home. They always took the very last trolley."

Her parents had loved the island so much, they had built one of the first summer cottages there. It had no heat or plumbing but it did have electricity. I was such a sissy, I couldn't imagine agreeing to that kind of inconvenience and calling it fun. But those were the stories of the past, and how wonderful that women like Miss Mavis's mother had valued the great beauty of the island over something like running water.

The richest conversation and the best advice came from the oldest people you knew. I wondered why we seemed to let their wealth of knowledge and experience go by the boards. But we had become a country of youth goals. Women of sixty were supposed to look thirty while they worried about women who were actually thirty snatching their husbands of sixty-five. Go figure.

As far as I could tell, the Isle of Palms hadn't completely sold out to the outside world of consumer noise. People still dropped in on their elder neighbors, not out of a sense of duty, but for the genuine pleasure of their company. It was what I loved best, I suppose, that no one was really alone on the island. Life made room for everyone.

Daddy and Lucy were all patched up again and they seemed to be getting serious. And even though Lucy was heavily invested in the media bull of Botox, nip and tuck, liposuction to reduce, saline to enhance, Love@AOL, Barbie clothes, excess alcohol, and the sporadic use of psychotropics to alter her state of mind (whew!), I couldn't really blame her. My daddy was drawn to outer beauty and considered any other good that came with the package to be a bonus. If Lucy was going to be attractive to a man, it would only be an older man and she would have to do everything in her power to be the young girl of his dreams. No matter how big a man's paunch, how thin his hair, most men wanted their women to be as good looking and youthful as possible. If some women committed the sin of valuing themselves through men, some men found their immortal virility through a woman's looks.

As much as I didn't like those realities, I understood them. Nobody—except the hopelessly depressed—really wanted to die. All these seemingly neurotic and shallow acts were really about survival. Maybe there was an element of survival tactics in what I gave to the women who were my clients. Certainly, I had even helped Marsha from Clearwater feel better about herself.

While I weeded the front flower beds, I was chewing on that thought and wondering if Joanne Fairchild had thrown out our photograph. I was also thinking that maybe a walkway with mondo grass borders would be nice—give the front of the house some warmth. I looked up to see Emily returning from the beach with David.

David was rushing across the steaming asphalt, barefooted, carrying two beach chairs and a small cooler. Emily, who had had the brains to put on her sandals, had a beach bag on one shoulder and sandy beach towels over her other arm. She followed him, laughing at his antics. They were beautiful and happy, without a care in the world. And even though Emily insisted they were nothing more than friends, I knew my daughter. She was in love.

"I'm gonna rinse off under Lucy's shower, okay?"

"Hey, Miss Abbot," David said, "the beach is fabulous! You should go for a swim!"

Lucy had smartly installed outdoor showers for all sand rats returning from the beach. I should do the same, I thought, then I wouldn't think twice about my daughter being in a shower with a boy, even though they had on their bathing suits. But I also knew that Emily wouldn't be so stupid as to do anything sexy twenty feet from my nose. Would she?

"Yeah, good idea! Get the sand off and then come right home. You're as red as a beet!"

"Okay! I'll be home in ten minutes!"

One of the many things I liked about Emily's relationship with David was that they dealt with each other as equals. He was a year older and she was a little bit more accomplished. He had his own car, she knew the lay of the land. They were nearly the same height, both lanky but toned, and they looked like they fit together. He teased her, she teased him, and, as far as I knew, they split expenses. They were both film hounds and had seen every movie that had come out during the summer. They both loved books and had finished their summer reading already. They liked crossword puzzles and bought the *New York Times* from Barnes & Noble on Sunday, spending the late afternoons lazing around in hammocks, trying to remember a four-letter word for a three-toed sloth. If they *weren't* in love, they should've been. They had been off and running since the moment they laid eyes on each other and she'd dropped her "angry woman" act and gone back to looking like and being herself.

What a summer it had been. I stood up from the ground and arched my back, looking at the sun. Maybe I would take a swim and then shower up. I wondered what Lucy was doing about supper. When I went into the house to change into my swimsuit, I called her.

"Hey! Wanna go for a swim?"

"Sure! This weather is so sticky! Gimme five minutes!"

True to her word, in minutes, Lucy was at the door. She had on a red bandeau bikini with a man's red Hawaiian print open shirt. She wore an enormous straw hat and oversized red sunglasses. Needless to say, her sandals were red too. She was ready for the French Riviera.

She held the shirt open and said, "Hey! Look at me! I'm censored in red!"

"Lucy? I swear! You must be the most exciting thing to ever hit this beach since the Seewee squaws!" There I was in a black tank suit, flip-flops from the Gap, a baseball hat, and Ray-Bans. At the last minute, I had grabbed a cotton T-shirt in case my skin started to burn.

"Who? Thanks!"

"When the English landed up around Awendaw, the Seewee squaws ran out to meet them. They were wearing skirts made out of Spanish moss and check this out—they were topless."

"You swear?"

"Yep. Cross my fingers, hope to die! Let's go."

I took two beach chairs from the shed and we walked the short distance, crossed the dunes, and looked for a place to settle. The tide was coming in and the beach was shallow. We decided to park ourselves in the soft sand, facing west toward Sullivan's Island. The sky behind us was growing dark, a sure sign that within the hour we'd have a thunder boomer to cool off the night. Over Sullivan's Island, the sky was as clear and beautiful as it had been all day. Lucy and I chatted, reminiscing over what the summer had brought.

"I'll tell you what," she said, "if somebody had told me a year ago that within a few months I'd have a real job and a real man, I woulda said they were crazy as hell, 'eah?"

"And, I'll tell you what, if somebody had told me a year ago that I'd have my own house and my own business, I would have said they were crazy as hell too!"

"And, I'd be in love with my boss's daddy?"

"And that my daughter would be head over heels over your nephew?"

"And that I was the one who would locate Everett Fairchild?"

That stopped me for a second.

"What's the matter?" she said.

"I don't know. I guess it's that his wife was such a turnoff and I had hoped she'd be different than she was. Just disappointed, I guess."

"Well, you know what, Anna? I've been thinking about this. Look. We set her up for the kill. She didn't know she was being interviewed, did she? Maybe if she'd known what she was walking into, she would've shown us her best side instead of her worst."

I looked at Lucy and realized that once again, Lucy had sliced it just about as thin as you could. We, or I anyway, hadn't wanted Joanne to be a good woman. We had all but tricked her into sarcasm and cynicism. Maybe under all her hoopla there was a decent person. I hadn't played fairly. I had hated her before I ever saw her.

"Damn it, Lucy. You're right. You kill me when you say these things. Why didn't I think of that?"

"I don't know, but she really might be a big old bitch just like we thought, you know. Let's not forget that she *was* pretty horrible. No tips?"

"That's true also."

I felt a little better. Her second comment had left me in a place where I could excuse myself for plotting against Joanne, and justify the judgments I had made against her. My capacity to rationalize my worst behavior was not something I was proud of. But there it was. Just like the rest of humanity, I had my warts too.

We were quiet for a few minutes and then, out of nowhere in particular, I said, "I went to Mass this morning. Nine-thirty. The choir was amazing."

"You did? I used to go to church when I was real little. I loved to sing. Haven't been to church in years."

"You know what's really crazy, Lucy?" I said that and then thought to myself that asking Lucy a question about craziness carried with it possibilities of a new understanding of the team.

"What?"

"Well, maybe crazy isn't the right word. But have you ever noticed that you live your life by hurdles? I mean, I used to say that as soon as I got my own house, my life would begin. As soon as I got my own business, I'd be my own woman. As soon as I did this or that, then I could do the next thing on my list. Why I haven't gone to church all these years is a mystery to me. I mean, I was sitting in the back pew this morning and thinking about how lucky I am and saying thanks to God for a million things. It made me feel so good. Just to be there. I don't know, I felt connected, you know?"

"I haven't been to church in years. But I do know what you mean. When I come out here or when I watch the sun go down at the end of the day, I think about my life. I do. I think I'm pretty lucky, you know, everything considered."

"Yeah, me too."

We were quiet again for a few minutes, watching the little sandpipers run around the water's edge and then scramble away from the easy flowing waves as they washed the shore. They were so busy and so determined to get their supper.

"Anna?"

"Hmmm?"

"Let's have us a Labor Day party. Jim and Frannie are coming, right?"

"Yep. They are."

"Well, remember the cookout we had for Jim? Let's do it again. He's been through hell. You've had a rough summer too, with all the stress of that Joanne and just everything—moving, opening a business . . . what do you say? Emily's going to be leaving for school and I could invite my sister down from Greenville. When does Emily go back?"

"Her classes don't start until September ninth. She's leaving on the freaking third, unless somebody blows something up."

"Good Lord, Anna! Don't even think that!"

"Right. Sends bad vibes to the universe."

"Exactly! Listen, it'll be great. Hell, I'd even invite the old biddies next door! We're closed Labor Day anyway, aren't we?"

"Yeah, but Lucy? Here's the problem."

"What?"

"If you do the cooking, we'll all wind up dead in the morgue."

We started laughing.

"Oh, Lord! Isn't that the truth? Do you remember when I first met y'all? And I brought over that awful casserole? It had been in my freezer for two years! I can't cook worth a S-H-I-T! But I'll make you a deal."

"What?"

"You cook and I'll buy the food. We'll tell everyone to bring an appetizer or a dessert, like we did for Jim's party. We'll put Dougle in charge of the grill, set up a self-serve bar, and do everything buffet. What do you say?"

"I don't want to listen to Bettina's disco music, okay?"

"Then let's call it a Lowcountry barbecue! All beach music! Come on! What do you think? I'll even make invitations on the computer! Hey!" She sat up in her beach chair and looked at me.

"What?"

"Did you ever call that Jack Taylor guy to thank him for that ugly plant?"

"Hell, no! He's probably married to Caroline by now!"

"Well, then, let's invite them and find out. In fact, it would be great to invite a few clients. Why not?"

"Fine. You make the list and call them. Hey! Jim could teach Bettina to shag! Oh! I can see it now! My house or yours?"

"Both! I have a bigger kitchen. And the deck. But we can share the yard, right? We can watch the sunset together. I just bought another digital camera. I'll take pictures of everyone. You could invite Harriet!"

"Have you lost your mind?"

"Just a thought."

"Right. Okay. Let's do it. But no Harriet. We need to do something to mark the end of this summer with a party. You're right. It's a good idea."

"If you entertain clients and employees, you can deduct it!"

She was right. Good old Lucy.

Sunday morning, September first, Jim was snoring on the sofa, Frannie was snoring in Emily's room, and Emily was snoring in my bed. I couldn't sleep with all the honking going on so I got up at six. Luggage was everywhere. Glasses, bags of potato chips, and Burger King wrappers were all over the table from our late-night powwow. Frannie and I had listened to Jim talk himself into a stupor over Gary's death, sympathizing and consoling at first and then, as the night wore on, we became deeply philosophical, deciding there were no accidents and that we were all in each other's lives for a reason. At one in the morning, I had been convinced of destiny. At six in the morning, I was convinced we had all had too much wine.

The day had just broken, light slipping through my windows in angular shapes, soft at first, becoming stronger and brighter with each passing minute. I decided to get the paper and take it down to the beach with a container of coffee. I tiptoed around the mess, got the coffee going, dressed, poured myself a mug, and sneaked out my back door, so that I wouldn't wake Jim. He looked more haggard than I'd ever seen him and I wanted him to rest. I picked up the *Post & Courier* from my front yard, and then decided to leave it by the door.

I looked at my flowers and shrubs. Jim had called it Turbo Eden. It was true. I now had bougainvillea and jasmine growing up the sides of the house with so many deep pink blooms, it was almost like they had something to prove. I thought about Miss August, the lady who owned the carriage house Jim and I had rented when Emily was born.

She had been dead for years and I thought it was probably her hand from heaven that was the cosmic cause of the insane growth of my entire yard. I could almost hear the lilt of her laugh and it seemed as though she was there, right beside me.

This Lowcountry connection with the other side was thriving, healthy, and not really a topic for deep discussion with tourists. Tourists may have thought we were a little crazy to begin with but let me tell you something, they bought those volumes of Lowcountry ghost stories like they were contraband from some secret society of Saint Germain! When clients from Indiana or some such place would ask me about the Gray Man at Pawley's Island, or the Summerville lights, my matter-of-fact response made them think I was holding back Lowcountry secrets. When you lived here you just took these things for granted.

In the early hours of morning, I thought about all kinds of things. First and always, there was the splendor of the empty beach. It didn't matter how often I went over the dunes, it had never been the same twice. I thought about Miss August again and wondered if she could see me. Remembering her was so pleasant, I made a note to do it every day. What a happy woman she had been. Then, I thought of my mother and the dream I'd had. I missed her and I wasn't even sure why. Maybe it was because she'd left me with so little of her, except for the way I looked. But maybe that wasn't true at all. Was I like my father or my grandmother? No, I wasn't. Didn't she love to garden? And hadn't my mother been ambitious? I mean, even though she rode a tiara out of her hometown to marry Daddy, what life would she have had otherwise?

Marrying my daddy was a rather brave thing to do when I looked at it that way. She was only a kid, really, a kid Emily's age, who considered her options and took a chance. And I had done the exact same thing.

I stood there sipping my hot coffee with the ocean flooding my feet and decided, okay, Momma had made a mistake. She was full of life and, as Miss Mavis had said, when she found herself stuck on this end of the island and pregnant, it probably all but blew her mind. If a game of bingo and winning a cooler had brought her a big thrill, how dull was her life? Pretty dull.

I looked down toward Sullivan's Island and there wasn't another living soul to be seen. I remembered seeing Arthur that first morning and told myself to get over him for once and for all. If he really fit the profile Jim described, he'd never come back to me. Speaking of men, Lucy had really invited Jack Taylor and Caroline Levine to our barbecue. They had said they'd be there, but I doubted it. Surely, with their money, they had better things to do than hang around with a bunch of hairdressers and their families. I wondered, though, if Susan Hayes would bring Simon—I'd never met him but, boy, did I know a lot about him! The things she had told me in the chair! Amazing.

I walked along the shore, the beach to myself, and thought myself to be a very fortunate woman. I had a terrific daughter who delighted me at every turn, wonderful friends who sustained me, great neighbors who welcomed my company, a loving father who had finally come around, and I had the Isle of Palms. What else could a woman need?

Thirty-four

Chicken Dance

A S it turned out, there was something else *this* woman needed. A caterer. When I went over the guest list with Lucy Sunday afternoon, it seemed we had seventy-five people coming. How was I supposed to take care of a crowd like that? I had planned on cooking but forget it! Seventy-five people? Had she gone crazy? Jim and Frannie stood with me in the living room, listening to Lucy explain.

"Well, you know how it is, don't you? You invite somebody and they say, Oh, but my brother is visiting with his wife and kids and you say, Oh, what the heck! Bring them too! Right?"

"Seventy-five people?" Frannie said, "Are you *sure* that's it?"

Lucy clenched her teeth and squinted her eyes. "Better make it eighty, just to be sure," Lucy said.

"I'm going to Lowe's," Jim said. "Frannie? Come with?"

"Sure. I'll get my bag."

"Good Lord!" I said, "What are we gonna do?"

"You and Lucy go get the food, paper products, and the drinks and Frannie and I will handle the rest. Let old Jim worry about this."

"I adore you," I said and blew them a kiss.

I called Brigitte immediately. "Kill three watermelons," I said, "we got a cast of thousands coming tomorrow."

"Glad to have something to chop," she said, "cures anxiety. Hey! Do you need a folding table? I have one."

"Yes, yes, yes. Do you have any folding chairs?"

"No, but I can borrow a dozen from the library. Want me to call Bettina?"

"God, yes! Can you ask her to get a sheet cake from Sam's?"

"Consider it done. In fact, I'll tell her to get brownies and a slug of chicken wings for an hors d'oeuvre. And a ton of chips and salsa."

"Just get me the receipts."

"Okay."

"Brigitte? Thanks. I mean it."

"Hey, you give my life purpose. I was gonna spend the evening sorting through old *National Geographics*, looking for pictures of nude male tribal dancers."

"Wow. That's seriously pathetic."

"Yes, it is. Especially considering that I just went through a catalog gawking at all the male models in their tight underwear. I'll call you later."

"You need a man, honey."

"Gee. Think so? Ever since I told Evan to hit the road, there's been a drought."

Brigitte had revealed herself to be the undisputed wit of our gang. I hung up the phone and turned to Lucy. She was biting her lip from nerves.

"Lucy? Don't worry about the party. We'll be fine. Get out your little black book. If we don't find Brigitte a willing victim by tomorrow night, her panties might have a self-combustion issue."

"What does that mean?"

"A *man*, Lucy. Find Brigitte a *man*."

"Oh! Sure! Okay. I have some guys I can call, but shouldn't we go to the grocery store first? The Pig has a sale on soft drinks but Harris Teeter has a special on paper products."

"Right! Fine. Get in the car! Where's Emily?"

"Next door, watching a DVD with David. They're sitting there like zombies, staring at the tube."

"Do me a favor. Tell them to start cleaning up the yard. It needs to get raked and the table and chairs need a good cleaning."

"Okay—I'll be right back. If you have a second, can you take this over to Miss Angel?"

"Sure. What is it?"

"Twelve hundred dollars from basket sales. I figured she might like to get paid."

"Wow! I thought they were selling, but twelve hundred dollars?"

"They ain't cheap and, honey?—we ain't got a blade of sweetgrass left in that shop."

"Wow," I said again.

Lucy trotted off to her house and I made a list of what we would need. We needed a lot. I stuck the list in my purse and hurried over next door. I tried Miss Angel's door downstairs first. After a few minutes, she opened it.

"You ain't one of them Jehovah's Witnesses, are you?"

"No, I'm the bearer of good news," I said, handing her the envelope. "Guess we need some more baskets."

She lifted her reading glasses up to her nose and opened it to count it. "Come on in," she said, "my pit bull's at the groomer."

"You don't have a pit bull," I said.

"And you ain't got no sense of humor, 'eah?" she said. "You want a glass of tea?"

"No, thanks, I gotta hustle my buns to Mount Pleasant to grocery shop. We have about seventy-five people coming tomorrow."

"You want me to keep Mavis at home?"

"Heavens! No!"

"All right then. I'll bring two pound cakes. I had a dream you were going to a funeral."

"No!"

"What's the matter with you? Girl? Don't you know that means out with the old and in with the new? Shuh! How long you been living 'round 'eah?"

"All my life!" I threw my arms around her and hugged her tight. "You're wonderful! Thanks, Miss Angel! Everybody will faint when they taste your cake!"

"You're right," she said, "I expect they will do that. Better invite a doctor, 'eah?"

"We did. Three in fact. That I know of anyway. I'll see you later."

Two hours later Lucy and I had barbecue, baked beans, coleslaw, and biscuits ordered to be delivered in serving containers with warming candles from Mr. B's, the best barbecue place on this earth. Our trunk was filled with paper plates and napkins, plastic cups and flatware, cases of soda, beer, and wine, and enough bug spray to wipe out every bug in the Amazon. I was getting excited. It dawned on me that besides Jim's, I hadn't been to or given a full-scale party in years. I couldn't wait.

By one the next afternoon, my backyard was in celebration mode. Daddy was outside hanging the twenty-five strings of lights Jim had bought at Pottery Barn. There were ten lights to a string and each one was covered in a miniature Japanese paper lantern.

"You need a deck," Daddy said. "A deck would be perfect out here because the ground is so uneven. If you're gonna have these cookouts all the time, you need a deck. We could build in the grill with a little refrigerator and sink. You could have nice counters and outdoor storage. Then you could put benches and planters along the other sides and people would have a place to sit."

"You're right," I said and gave him a kiss on the cheek, thinking there was a deck in my future. "If you want to build me a deck for my thirtieth birthday, I wouldn't object."

"You were thirty a long time ago."

"And, what did you give me?"

"I don't remember."

"That's the point." I giggled and he laughed with me.

"You've got the devil in you, Anna. Maybe we'll go to Home Depot or Lowe's next week and have a look around."

"I'd love that, Daddy, I really would."

"You could have a hot tub too, you know."

"Get Lucy a hot tub. What would I do with it? Sit in there by myself and read *Salon* magazine?"

"Lucy? Actually, that's not a bad idea!"

I groaned at the thought of Daddy and Lucy in a hot tub together and then thought, well, why the heck shouldn't they do whatever they want?

But at that moment, there was no hot tub and no deck. Jim and Frannie were arranging the tables. David was bringing heavy clay pots of flowers from all around our house and Lucy's to help decorate the back stoop and the tables. That kid was a doll, always pitching in. Emily was spraying the bushes with bug killer to hold the mosquitoes and no-see-ums at bay.

"I'm getting eaten alive!" she complained.

"Keep spraying!" I said.

I heard a truck out front and went to see who it was.

It wasn't the delivery van from Mister B's Barbecue. It was another van. On the side it read TAYLOR SLACK'S BEACH MUSIC UNLIMITED. A good-looking young man got out to greet me.

"Are you Mrs. Abbot?"

"Is my husband responsible for this?" I couldn't stop shaking my head.

"I believe so, ma'am. Is he here?"

"Come on around to the backyard, Taylor," Jim said and looked at me with his best bad-boy face. "Well? Are we having a party or aren't we?"

"You're incredible," I said.

"I came early to put down the dance floor, sir. Is there someone who could give me a hand with the risers?"

"No problem, son, just come with me."

Dance floor?

The next truck to arrive was from Margaret Egan's Nursery. I went outside with Jim on my heels.

"I've got forty red and yellow hibiscus bushes and twenty palms. Where do you want them?"

"What?" I was shocked.

"Don't worry," Jim said, "they're rented. Where are your Christmas lights?"

"I don't have any," I said. "But Lucy might."

By five o'clock, I had showered and changed into the lethal dress I wore the night Arthur and I sailed the River of Sin.

"Damn, sister, you look fierce!" Jim said.

"Thank you!" I said and did a little spin. "Don't you want to feel the goods, big boy?"

"At moments like this? Yeah."

"Come on!"

"Ahem!" Jim said, clearing his throat, "but rather than mangle a perfectly good platonic relationship, whadaya say we check out the party scene?"

"Right!" I said and gave him a *Charlie's Angels* handgun shot, blowing off the tip of my smoking finger. "Let's go!"

As always, Jim had worked his magic. My yard looked so amazing with all the twinkling hibiscus bushes and palms I thought we were ready for a wedding. The dance floor was only twelve inches off the ground, but the risers were adjustable, so even though my yard was uneven, the dance floor was level. And, it had steps to get to it so people didn't kill themselves getting on it. Young precious Taylor, who Emily had half an eye on, put skirting around the sides with a staple gun and Jim placed the lit plants along the sides, creating walls. Citronella tiki torches were everywhere, lit and doing their job.

"Doesn't it look incredible?" Lucy said. "I gotta go change in a minute, but what do you think?"

"Jaysus! She's been bossing me around like Sister Torture teaching me times tables!" Frannie said, on her way to the house. "I'm needing a shower!"

"I thought she was Greek," Lucy said.

"Her mother was Irish," Jim said.

"Ah," Lucy said. "Come on and let's check this all out, then I gotta go do my face and all."

The deejay had his own generator, which was a good thing. I had visions of losing power and all these people bumping into each other in the dark, getting black eyes and going to the emergency room. But this guy was prepared for everything. He had boxes of maracas, leis, straw hats, crazy sunglasses, and glow-in-the-dark necklaces. Jim was so crazy and fun—he'd probably start a limbo contest. I would not encourage them.

Mr. B's had delivered and the food was all in place. The beer was iced down in a giant garbage can and the soft drinks were in another. Everything was ready.

Just then, Brigitte appeared with a carved watermelon basket in her arms.

"It's déjà vu all over again," she said to Lucy and me.

"I've got six men coming to meet you," Lucy said.

"Well, that's a start," Brigitte said, completely deadpan. "Here, take this. I've got two more of these babies in the car."

Bettina was pulling up with Bobby when we got back to Brigitte's car.

"I'm so excited!" Bettina said, slamming the door of the Yacht as Bobby winced. She had on white capris with a pale blue chambray shirt over a white halter and she looked radiant. That girl was as cute as a bug. "I got a bucket of salsa! Only five ninety-nine! Such a deal! And I got six bags of Doritos, ten dozen brownies, and a sheet cake with an American flag on it—think that's enough? Wait till you see the cake! It's gorgeous!"

"This party is all she's talked about all week," Bobby said. He gave me a kiss on the cheek. "Same drill? Food out back?"

"Yeah," I said, "thanks."

People arrived, the music started, and our guests wandered back and forth from Lucy's widow's walk as the sun went down. Our party took on a life of its own. Lucy's blenders whirred while she stood back and shimmied. Yes, Lucy was wearing one of her fringed "outfits." Daddy watched her in fixated fascination.

Miss Angel and Miss Mavis slipped through the oleanders with platters of sliced pound cake. I went to greet them.

"Oh! Miss Angel! This looks so delicious! Thank you so much! And Miss Mavis! You look so pretty!"

"Hush, girl, take this platter and find me a place to sit. At my age I could drop dead any minute."

"She hasn't been to a party in years," Miss Angel said.

"What did she say?" Miss Mavis said.

"I said that the dress you're wearing is my favorite too!" Miss Angel said.

"Oh! Well, thank you, Angel."

I took the platters from them, Emily took them from me, and I sat the two women at the table with the umbrella.

"Can I get y'all something to eat or drink?"

"Don't fuss over us, Anna, go be with your young friends. We'll be fine and *I'll* take care of Mavis," Miss Angel said. "Hey! I like this music!"

"Under the Boardwalk" was playing.

"What's that?" Miss Mavis screamed.

Miss Angel shot me a look of loving exasperation and turned back to Miss Mavis. *"I said, This music makes me feel like dancing!"*

"Well, you go on and dance then. I can't! Can't afford to break a hip, you know."

I left them to their squabbling and looked around. The yard was filling with people I hadn't seen in ages and people I hadn't ever seen. Probably Lucy's friends, I thought. Everyone seemed to be having a wonderful time and I was thrilled.

I spotted Carla Egbert, the receptionist from Harriet's House of Horrors, and worked my way over to talk to her.

"Carla!"

"Hey! God! What a night for a party! Anna! I love your house! Thanks so much for inviting me!"

"I'm so glad to see you!" I was. "So, how's it going? Old Harriet still mad at me?"

"Anna, I caaan't staand her another minute! Gimme a job!"

The very words I had waited to hear.

"When can you start?"

"Are you serious?"

"You bet! Wanna run the place?"

"I'll do *anything!*"

"That's the whole point, Carla, you *can* do anything! Tell Harriet to kiss my big fat pink fluffy behind and come in tomorrow!"

"You mean it?"

Was she kidding?

"Uh, yes. I mean it. I open at nine."

"Deal!"

We hugged and I thought, Okay, this is going to be a truly wonderful night.

Everyone was dancing and the blistering heat of the day became one of those famous Lowcountry balmy nights. You could smell salt and even over the music—which was pretty loud—you could hear the ocean's roar. True to his word, Jim was teaching Bettina to shag and Frannie was teaching Bobby. They were all wearing sombreros and laughing, having fun.

David was running around with Lucy's digital camera, with Emily by his side. I have to say this again. This David was an excellent influence. His plan was to fill the memory stick, download it, erase it, and continue taking pictures. All the prints would be in the salon next week for everyone to claim. What a great idea! I looked up a few minutes later and saw Daddy doing a slow fox-trot with Miss Mavis. Miss Mavis was in heaven.

"Get a picture of *them!*" I said to David and he went off and snapped a dozen, knowing it was important to document it.

Trixie had arrived, wearing a pale yellow linen sleeveless dress. She worked her way around the crowd, arriving at where I was standing after some time.

"Hello, Anna," she said, offering me her cheek.

I gave the old goat a little peck and said, "Oh, Trixie, I'm so glad you could come."

"Ah understand my son had a little setback," she said as though Jim had clipped a bothersome hangnail.

I could smell gin. I wasn't serving gin. And, I wasn't sure if she meant Gary's death or not. "Do you mean Gary?"

"Of course Ah mean *Gary*," she said with noticeable discomfort.

She was snockered. "Well, yes. Gary was a great friend to Jim for many years. I'm just glad Jim was with Gary and his family at the end. I think it made it easier for all of them."

Trixie looked at me like she had no earthly idea what I was talking about and I worried for a moment that I had given her some information that Jim didn't want her to have.

"Ah see," she said, "Ah'm sure it did. My son is a very compassionate man."

"Your son hung the moon, Trixie, and he's spent the better part of his years teaching our daughter and me how to arrange the stars."

"*Our* daughter? Come now, Anna. When are you going to let go of that little fantasy?"

I stared at her. "Give me your car keys."

She opened her purse and handed them to me. "Why? Am Ah blocking somebody?"

"Yeah, the rescue team from Betty Ford. Don't even think about driving, okay?"

"How dare you! Why! Of all the *crust!*"

"Emily is our daughter and you don't know shit, Trixie. Put that in your pipe and smoke it."

I walked away before I hit her. She wasn't going to ruin this fabulous night. She could take her anger to a counseling center and stew in it for all I cared. I managed to get about ten feet away from her when I bumped right into Jack Taylor.

"Well, hi!" he said, "this is some great party!"

"Hi!" I said, trying to recover my good humor. "Hey, I never got a chance to thank you for the plant, but it was awfully nice of you. Not necessary, but very nice. Where's Caroline?"

"She's around. You want to dance?"

"Why not?" I said. I tossed the car keys to Jim and said, "Hang on to these!"

The deejay was playing "Carolina Girls" but we'd danced for about two seconds when he switched to the Righteous Brothers' "You've Lost That Loving Feeling" and the next thing I knew, Jack Taylor had his arm all the way around my waist and I could smell his aftershave. I liked it and I liked the way he held me too. *Oh-oh. No, no, Anna. Don't go there!* I straightened up a little and he looked at me.

"What's wrong?"

"Oh, nothing! Just that I don't feel like having Caroline whupping my ass at my own party, that's all." *Well,* I thought, that *was a very ladylike thing to say, Anna, good job.*

He burst out laughing and said, "What? You must be kidding! Look over there!"

Sure enough, when I looked around, Caroline was engaged in some serious flirtation with one of Lucy's castoffs. She apparently was trying to read the embossing of his cowboy belt through the hips of her silk dress. You know, like Braille? Whew! Still, it didn't seem right to snag her date.

"We're really just friends," he said. "I mean, we used to be more, but we decided friendships lasted longer. And what about you? Isn't that your husband over there?"

"We're divorced," I said, "and he's gay."

"Ah!" he said and his eyes danced, "that explains a lot."

I didn't know what that meant but it didn't matter.

When the music stopped he said, "Thanks. Can I get you something to drink?"

"Sure. I'll come with you."

We stepped down from the dance floor and moved toward the bar. He took a bottle of wine from the cooler and poured some into small plastic cups for us. He was wearing a white shirt with rolled cuffs and navy trousers and somehow had managed to remain wrinkle free. That was proof that he was a little prissy. Although when Brigitte showed up unwrinkled it seemed fine. And, how did he know I didn't want a beer? Was it because he thought women should drink wine? I got annoyed and in the same breath, I got annoyed with myself for getting annoyed with him in the first place.

"Here we are," he said, handing me the cup, "cheers!"

"Cheers!" I said and clinked his cup.

What was the matter with me? Here was a perfectly nice, attractive, single man, a doctor no less, interested in me and I had only the most minimal attraction to him. I liked the way he smelled, the way he danced, and the way he looked, but he didn't have that electricity thing that Arthur had. He was as dull as a bucket of green paint. *All* doctors were boring, I thought. Daddy included. At least it seemed that Jack was dull. Why was I rushing to this opinion about him? I'd had two whole minutes of conversation with him and already decided he wasn't for me.

"Beautiful night," he said.

"Yeah, it was hotter than the roof of hell today. We got lucky that it cooled off." I couldn't sound like a lady if my life depended on it.

"I'd like to have dinner with you sometime, I mean, take you out to dinner, if you'd like to, that is, if you want to. That didn't come out right."

He just sort of blurted it out and then stumbled all over himself. It was the first right thing he had done in my eyes. *Okay*, I thought, *give him a shot.*

"Sure, that would be great. In fact, this week's good. My daughter's going back to college in the morning and I'll need some cheering up."

"You have a daughter? Where?"

I pointed to her and saw him do a double take. "Her name's Emily. She's goes to Georgetown." Then, in the true courteous fashion that all overprotective mothers possess, I decided I needed more information about him. Maybe he was a pedophile for all I knew. "What kind of a doctor are you?"

"Why? Are you ill? Should I check your pulse?"

"No! I was just wondering, that's all."

"Dermatologist. Graduated from the Medical University of South Carolina. And I'm a Citadel grad. I'll have to show you all my plaques sometime." He was smiling.

"It's very important to know about potential serial killers before you have dinner with them, don't you think?" I said.

"Most definitely! But I assure you, my serial killer days are over. Right now I'm focused on taking two points off my handicap. Do you play golf?"

"Golf? Honey? I'd rather take a needle in my eye! No, I don't play golf."

"All righty then. I won't be taking you out on the links! We'll just start with dinner."

Out on the links? How old was he? A thousand?

I spotted Marilyn and Billy Davey walking over to us. I was hoping she would come.

"Here comes my real estate broker! Hey!"

"Anna? This is my husband, Billy."

"Hey, nice to meet you. I'm not her husband. I don't know why she tells everyone that."

"Shut up, Billy! I don't know why he says these things! We've been married for almost thirty years!"

"Nope!" Billy said and shook hands with Jack. "You married to Anna?"

"Not yet," he said. "Think I should ask her?"

"Hell, no," Billy said, "getting married is the quickest way to wind up with an old woman."

"Billy Davey! You embarrass me!" Marilyn turned on her heels and started walking away.

"Marilyn? Come on back, darlin'! I was just kidding! Come on . . ."

Jack and I started laughing.

"What a perfect match! He's a mess, 'eah?"

"You sounded just like Susan Hayes when you said that. Where are they?" He looked at his watch and then around the crowd. "There they are!" He waved them over.

Susan and Simon came through the crowd, Simon pulling Susan along by the hand. They were both tanned and smiling.

"Hey!" Susan said. "You are so nice to have us! What a night! Did y'all eat? I'm starving!"

"She's always starving!" Simon said and introduced himself. "You must be Anna. I'm Simon. Thanks for inviting us."

"How did you know who I was?"

"Because my lecherous friend Dr. Taylor said that I would find him with the prettiest girl at the party. That's how."

"You boys are some smooth talkers," I said. "You fill a girl's head!"

"How about filling my stomach before I faint?" Susan said. "Come on, Anna. You're too skinny. Let's feed you."

Susan and I walked away from the men arm in arm.

"Marry him tomorrow," I said, "he's adorable."

"Nah! Then I have to start picking up his clothes off the floor. God, this barbecue smells like heaven! Did you make it?" She heaped a spoon of it on her plate.

"Yeah, right! Mr. B's on Coleman Boulevard. I cook, but not for this many people. You want a roll for that?"

"Me either. No roll. Carbs. I'm doing Atkins." She picked up a piece of meat and popped it in her mouth. "Whoo! Hot!" She took a long drink of her wine. "Damn, honey, this is good! So what's the occasion for the party?"

"End of summer? You know? Just wanted to thank everyone for all they did to help me start up my salon and all."

"What a great idea! So are you loving being on the Isle of Palms or what?"

"You wouldn't believe how great it is."

"The city's so hot you could die for a breath of air! Actually,

Simon and I have been talking about moving over here, that is, when we take the plunge."

"Come on with me, I'll introduce you to my broker, Marilyn Davey. She's a sweetheart."

"Marilyn Davey? Hell, honey, I've known Marilyn Davey since the sandbox! Went to Bishop England with her and Stella Maris! She's the best! And that husband of hers is crazy as a bedbug, 'eah? He's fun!"

"You know it. Did you know I went to Stella Maris and Bishop England too?"

"No way!"

"Small world, huh?"

I took Susan to Marilyn and they started an animated conversation that would probably lead to a house sale.

"Just make sure you invite me to the wedding," I said before I left them. "I gotta go check on Daddy."

"Let's get together, okay?" Susan said. "We can double-date!"

"Great!" I said and thought to myself, Well, if I did go out with Jack tomorrow night, being with Susan and Simon would be the optimum situation.

I met up with Brigitte at the bar.

"Lucy find you anything interesting?"

"Nah, they're nice guys, but not for me. The one decent guy is dancing with somebody else."

"Hey, Lucy's got plenty of talent in her phone book. We'll keep looking. I gotta go find Daddy."

"Okay. Don't worry about me. My prince will come."

I found Daddy and Lucy in Lucy's kitchen, pouring coffee for Trixie. I was going to try and sneak away but Lucy saw me and opened the door.

"Hey! Come on in! You want some coffee?"

"Jesus. Busted." I said, as quietly as I could without hissing. "I didn't know Trixie was here."

"What did you say to her?" Lucy whispered. "She's as mad as a hornet's nest!"

"Don't get involved," I said, knowing that she already was. I stepped inside and decided I'd had enough of Trixie.

"Hi, honey," Daddy said, "great party." *She's toasted!* he mouthed and pointed to Trixie. As if I didn't know.

"Weeellll! Looky who's here!" Trixie said, nearly sliding off her chair.

"O! Kay! That's it! Trixie, you're tight as a tick, okay? And I don't argue with drunks. Being fried in front of your granddaughter is bad enough. But you will no longer come over to my house and leave your venomous droppings wherever you please. I am all done with you. Do you hear me?"

"Ah hear you just fine, *Mrs. Abbot.*"

Trixie's eyes were swimming in her head.

"Anna?" Daddy said. "What hap   "

"Don't worry about it, Daddy." I turned back to Trixie. "Good. Then hear this too. You are a mean, mean person, Trixie Abbot. When you sober up, if you even remember this, call me if you want to apologize. Otherwise, don't ever call me again."

"Jim's gay, you know," she said and began to cry. "He had a gay lover too."

Had she gone off her rocker and the porch too?

"Yes, we know that, Trixie, and we love Jim because he is just about the most wonderful, smart, funny, and generous man in the world. What's the matter with you? Emily and I don't care if Jim's from the freaking planet Mongo, okay?"

"It's so humiliating!" Trixie wailed.

"No, it's not," Lucy said.

"Oh, what do you know, you, you . . ." She looked Lucy up and down. "You tramp!"

"What?" Lucy said.

"I'm going to give you something to calm you down, Trixie," Daddy said. "This is unbecoming for a lady like you to be in this state." He took her elbow and pulled her to her feet.

"I am *not* a tramp!" Lucy said, getting upset.

"Come on, Lucy," I said and started to take her out the door. Something made me stop and throw Trixie one more zinger. "Wake up, Trixie, it's 2002 and by today's standards, Lucy is more of a lady than you ever were!"

Lucy and I hurried down her steps and back to our party.

"She is the meanest, most hateful . . ."

"She's jealous, Lucy."

"What?"

"Honey, she's sweet on Doc."

"I'll claw the bitch's eyes out!"

"The LAY-DY has spoken!"

Lucy and I started to laugh. There wasn't a chance in the world that my daddy would trade a hot thing like Lucy for a prim old stuck-up crone like Trixie.

I looked around the yard. Frannie was slow-dancing with a very nice looking man.

"That's Jake," Lucy said. "He used to do my plumbing."

We looked at each other and started laughing again.

"I'll bet!"

Suddenly the deejay changed the music and all I heard was, *"It's getting hot in here! I wanna take off all my clothes!"* The next thing I knew, Jim grabbed my arm, plopped a straw hat on my head, and we started a conga line that wound all across the dance floor, down through the yard, and back up on the dance floor. Every single person there joined in, except Miss Mavis, who was asleep in a chair, and Miss Angel, who stood beside her, clapping in time with us, head thrown back smiling.

The night was the stuff of carnivals and dreams. When the last car left, it was well past eleven. Emily and David were cleaning up, God love them, but also because I had told them I'd give them a hundred dollars to make everything disappear. Emily had balked at first.

"Come on, Momma! I'm tired! I'm leaving early tomorrow and I wanna spend the time with David!"

"It takes me three days to earn a hundred dollars," David said. "We can do this in an hour, Emily. Let's kick it!"

"Oh, all right," she said, giving in.

Loved the boy. Just loved the boy.

Jim, Frannie, and I were sitting at the table with Daddy and Lucy.

"Great party," Daddy said. "Unfortunately, Trixie is in your guest room, Lucy. Fast asleep."

"Oh, that's okay," Lucy said.

"Too much sauce?" Jim said.

"Just a tad short to fill Lake Champagne," I said.

"Yeah, boy!" Frannie said. "I was up there with my man Jake and here came Trixie shaking her booty!"

"Whoa! I missed that," I said.

"Don't worry," David called out, "I got a picture!"

We chuckled over that and just let it go. All of us were too tired to discuss whether or not Trixie had developed a serious alcohol issue or if tonight had been a one-time thing.

"Come on, old boy," Lucy said, pulling Daddy to his feet, "I'll let you stay over if you tell me I'm the queen of the Isle of Palms!"

"Your Majesty!" Daddy said and bowed to her, then he stood and waved to us. "Good night all!"

He and Lucy climbed the steps together and somehow it seemed right. Lucy was a great girl and Daddy could've done worse.

"Shacking up," Jim said.

"That's more than I can say for any of us!" I said.

"Speak for yourself, lass," Frannie said. "Tomorrow I'm having dinner with Jake and breaking the news to him."

"The news?" I said.

"Yeah," Frannie said, "I'm gonna marry him."

"Try and hold out till the third date, Frannie," Jim said. "Men don't like to know they're being reeled in."

"He told me he was looking for a wife. He wants to get married this year."

"That's entirely different," I said. "No more calls, we have a winner. Maybe."

"I'll help you shop for a nose ring," Jim said. "Come on, girls, let's hit the sack."

Later when I was almost asleep, I felt Emily slip into bed beside me.

"Momma?"

"Hmmm?"

"I don't wanna go back to Washington. I wanna transfer to Carolina."

"In love?"

"Yeah. Cooked. No. Deep-fried."

"We'll talk about it in the morning," I said. "Good night, baby."

"No. I really mean it. I love him, Momma. And he loves me."

"I know, sweetheart. I can see it. We'll talk about it in the morning."

"No, you don't understand. He actually *told* me he loved me, Momma."

"That's wonderful, sweetheart."

"I'm not going back."

"Yes, you are. Now go to sleep."

"You can't make me."

"Yes, I can."

I could feel her pounding the mattress with her fist. "Fine. That's just fine. I hate my life."

"When I was your age, I hated my life too."

She was quiet for a few minutes and then I heard her sniffle and I knew she was crying. Then, in a cracking voice, she spoke again.

"It's just that I don't have any control over anything. You know what I mean? I don't want to leave David, Momma. I'll die without him."

I rolled over and rubbed her back. "Nobody's gonna die, baby. Let's talk about this tomorrow, okay? Late at night is when we all make dumb decisions. Let's try to get some sleep."

My poor child. Even though she probably didn't believe it, I knew exactly how she felt. It had only taken me several decades to get control of my life. I tossed around a little, reliving my encounter with Trixie, dancing with Jack, showing off for Jim, picturing Daddy and Lucy and the entire evening in general. Carla was coming to work for me. What would I tell Lucy? And then I thought about Emily again and all the nights we'd had these tiny talks revealing her heart, before we would fall off to sleep. I would miss those moments. A lot. In fact, I knew I would ache for them.

I got up to get a glass of water and tiptoed by Jim on the sofa. He was already gone to the world, jaw dropped, making noise like a freight train. I smiled down at him, trying to understand why Jim did so many extraordinarily bighearted things for me and Emily. And then I knew why. He wanted us to have good memories of our new home and he wanted to be a part of them. It made sense. I knew then that no matter what life brought our way, we would always keep Jim at the heart of everything.

Thirty-five

Nightmares No More

TUESDAY, September third, started out like any other, except that I was exhausted before the day even began. And, I wasn't very happy that the two people I loved so much were traveling on airplanes the same day. See, I had this theory that my Hail Marys held the planes in the air. I'd need to double up in number and sincerity and hoped I could manage it. And, just as bad, they were leaving and I wouldn't see Jim or Emily for a long time.

I took Emily in my car and we followed Jim in his rental car to the airport at six-thirty.

"You don't have to come, Anna, I can take Emily," Jim had said earlier.

"I know that, but I want to go anyway."

"She thinks I'm going back to school," Emily had said, "but I'm not."

Jim and I assured her that she was indeed going back to school and it was time for her to finish packing. She had been packing reluctantly all week and argued with me about staying and leaving until she had fallen asleep last night.

Jim was flying Continental to Newark on the eight o'clock flight and Emily was flying US Airways to Washington, changing in Charlotte, at eight-thirty.

They checked their luggage, bought magazines, and then we decided to have breakfast. I was in no mood to eat but I ordered a poached egg on a toasted English muffin, Jim ordered an omelet with home fries and biscuits, and Emily couldn't decide.

"I guess I'll have pancakes," she said. "If the plane rocks and rolls, my stomach will do better with pancakes in there."

"Good call," the waitress said and left to get coffee for us.

We talked with Emily about school and in the end we decided that if she and David were still dying for each other by Christmas, we'd consider a transfer for the following semester.

"Oh, don't worry," Emily said, fooling with the various ring tones on her new cell phone Jim had given her as an early birthday present, "David and I are gonna be together for a million years. Do you have this number, Mom?"

"What do *you* think?" I said.

Jim and I smiled at her remark about David. I was thinking that it would be wonderful to find someone you could spend your life with when you were her age, and then I realized I had married Jim at eighteen.

"If the man's brain is only slightly larger than a parakeet's, Emily, he won't let you go," Jim said. "Come on, I gotta get to my gate."

We walked with him to the security check at Terminal B and we all hugged and kissed. In a best-case scenario, we all hated good-byes. It had been a long hot summer, one of significant gains, personal losses, and many twists of our roads. The days and weeks we had spent with each other would sustain us until we could be together again at Thanksgiving. For my money, Thanksgiving couldn't arrive fast enough.

"Love you, Daddy."

"Me too, baby, I love you too."

I could see Jim's eyes tearing up. Since Gary had passed away he had been much more sentimental, but who wouldn't be? Or maybe he felt emotional for another reason. I didn't know.

I reached in my bag and pulled out a tissue for him. "Here. Now, call me when you get to France so I'll know where to find you, okay?"

"God, I'm such an old sap!" Jim said and blew his nose. "You know, I was all set to go and then I looked at both of you and thought, Wow, you are both *so* beautiful and I am so lucky, just *so* lucky that you love me."

I lost it. I burst out into tears and threw my arms around him. "No, sir, we're the lucky ones. Who wouldn't love you?"

"Good grief!" Emily said. "Get a grip, you two! We're in public!"

Then Jim and I regained some self-control and laughed.

"Okay," he said, "okay." He took a deep breath. "I'll call you tomorrow, okay?"

We watched him walk down the concourse until we couldn't see him anymore.

"He's so great," Emily said.

"He sure is."

We walked back to Terminal A together, my arm around her shoulder, and I squeezed her every couple of minutes.

"It was a good summer, wasn't it, baby?"

"The best. And Mom? I really like our little house."

"You do?"

"Yeah, 'cause it's ours, you know?" And then in the next breath she switched gears. "D'ya think Doc is gonna marry Lucy?"

"Who knows?"

"If he does, does that make David my cousin?"

We giggled. "Who cares?" I said.

"Yeah. Hey! Can we paint my room over Thanksgiving?"

"What color?"

"You said it didn't matter what color."

"You're right. I did. You'd better go now." I kissed her on her forehead and looked at her in the eyes. "I love you so much."

"Love you too, Mom. I'll call you when I get there."

I handed her tote bag to her and gave her the final hug.

As I drove back to the Isle of Palms, I was feeling kind of blue. I'd miss them so much. I already did. But, I had plenty to keep myself busy until November.

I swung by my house to dress for work and, true to his threat, Daddy had a team of men from Charles Blanchard Construction Company in my yard measuring for a deck with a cook area, just as we had discussed. Old Ebenezer had changed his heart and the evidence was everywhere. I was getting a deck.

Daddy's car was gone and I spotted Lucy in her yard, picking up the morning paper.

"Hey! I gotta talk to you about something!"

"Some party, huh?"

"Yeah! Listen, remember Carla?"

Surprisingly, when I told Lucy about her, she didn't mind at all.

Lucy said, "Great! Because to tell you the truth, I'd rather concentrate on buying merchandise than answering the phone. We're always running out of stuff! Besides, I was thinking that we ought to have our own label of shampoo and all that? Remember the day Jim had all those little bottles that smelled like fruit? I mean, I can help Carla, you know, show her the ropes? And then maybe I could take some time to go back to aerobics. Frankly, honey, I'm getting a little flabby."

Lucy was going to show Carla the ropes? I hoped she would humor Lucy.

"We'll figure it out," I said, breathing a huge sigh of relief.

Walking back to my house, I saw Trixie's car and remembered how she had behaved. I couldn't believe how hardened my heart had become toward her. My feelings surprised me because I hadn't felt so negative about another woman since my grandmother had dropped dead and gone to hell. At least, I assumed she was in hell.

I arrived at the salon about twenty minutes before nine and opened up. Carla would be there any minute. If she'd work with us, I could relax about a lot of things. She'd have our salon whipped into shape in no time at all. Most importantly, I knew she'd bring a slew of new clients with her. Maybe she could help me find two more stylists. An optimistic vision passed through my head—full chairs, a ringing cash register, a struggle to keep enough merchandise in stock . . . No, I'm sorry, Mrs. Snodgrass, Anna is booked up six weeks in advance . . . Yes, we can fit you in for a manicure with Sonya. Yes, she's new. . . . Ah, Carla. Hurry!

I made myself a cup of coffee and realized I was out of Equal. I went next door to borrow a packet and saw about five people standing around the television, watching.

"What happened?" My first thought was—you guessed it—that some nut was going to commemorate September eleventh for us with a reality demo a week early.

"Nothing. Just news that ain't news," a man said.

"Good," I said, "I like it when the news is boring."

"There's a hurricane down around the Virgin Islands that's a hel-luva lot more interesting," the woman behind the counter said. "Want a muffin? The blueberry ones are still warm."

"I shouldn't, but shoot, why not?" I picked one up and, on feeling the warmth through the plastic wrap, I couldn't wait to get it in my mouth. I gave her a dollar and threw the change in the tip cup by the register. "Thanks."

I left, thinking about the shifts in expectations and how change was subtle. It used to be that you bought something and a salesperson would count your change back to you. Now, you were expected—no, not quite expected, but, it would be *nice* for you to leave your change in the cup for the staff to divvy up at the end of the day. In exchange, you could take a penny from their dish if you needed one. As someone who had counted pennies for years, my first brush with a tip cup was weird. Though the more I thought about it, it seemed okay to me. I mean, the world was cold enough and human touch was being removed from our daily lives at every turn. Etickets. Email. Voice mail. Internet shopping on eBay for anything from your next car to a lock of Matt Lauer's hair from his last haircut. What a world! Well, at least you didn't stick your head in a machine like Jane Jetson and come out with the haircut you had punched into a keypad. I still lived in the world of people and was glad of it.

I unlocked the salon, went back inside, and just stood there for a moment, looking at the place I had started and Jim had trimmed out to a fare-thee-well. The coffee machine, the neon sign, the bamboo—the touches of him that were everywhere—the benches, the robes, the turbans—the bits of his imaginings that led your eye to fantasy, glamour, and humor. Jim wasn't over the top—he had *invented* over the top. He *was* better than a rare bird. He *was* the Bird of Paradise. The Head Banana. No wonder I'd never fallen in love with anyone else. What man could be more or even as much as Jim? He was compassionate, intelligent, and funny. He was gorgeous, elegant, and sophisticated. The litany of his qualities was as long as my leg. Since I was seventeen years old, Jim had held the door to his heart open for me and for Emily. Still, I knew that at some point, I had to open the door of my heart for someone else.

I felt like laughing out loud, wondering then if I would ever stop trying to tempt him. My flirtation with him was ridiculous and I knew it. Maybe we were Francis of Assisi and Saint Clare or Abelard and Heloise or just a modern-day corruption of tradition. Well, I thought, whatever we were not, we were loyal and bound to each other forever. It didn't get much better or more screwy than us.

The phone rang. It was Jack Taylor. *Knock, knock.*

"Hey, how are you doing? Okay?" he said.

"Well, first thing this morning I put Jim and Emily on separate planes. . . ."

"Flying used to be exciting," he said, "now I hate it."

"Yeah, those guys really took all the fun out of it, didn't they?" I looked in the mirror and saw that I had circles under my eyes. It might be a good idea if I put on some makeup, I thought.

"They sure did. Um, about dinner?"

"Oh! Right!"

"Well, tonight's a problem. My mother is eighty-four—she lives out in Monck's Corner—anyway, she's not feeling so great and wants me to come out to see her. I told her I would, provided I could rearrange our plans."

Was he *serious* that he wouldn't go to his mother if he couldn't change our plans? Was there something *wrong* with him, or what? *Stop it,* my inner guidance counselor said. *He's being polite.* After Arthur, I didn't expect consideration and that was yet another reason why I shouldn't have mourned his departure.

"Jack, we can have dinner anytime. Go see your mother. Who knows? Maybe she's really sick?"

"You, ma'am, have a kind heart and I appreciate this. How about if I call you tomorrow?"

"That's fine. Really."

With the tinkle of the front door's bell my business day began. Bettina and Brigitte came in together. No makeup, hair in ponytails.

Bettina was talking a mile a minute about our party the night before. Brigitte was giving her minimal responses, like, *Um-hm, You know it, girl,* and the ever useful *You can say that again,* at which point Bettina would gladly repeat herself. We said hello (which is really *hey!*), made each other coffee, split my muffin all around, and then Lucy arrived.

"Y'all look like y'all been drug by a mule all through the ditches of hell!"

"At least we have a good reason," Brigitte said. "What's worse than looking like hell for nothing? When's my first appointment?"

"Ten," Lucy said. "I'll keep the coffee coming! All of y'all are booked all day."

"I look like death warmed over! Who's got concealer?" I said. "Man. I look bad!"

"I need a spackle knife to fill in my wrinkles today!" Bettina said. "My legs are killing me!"

At nine on the dot, the door swung open and in the morning light stood Carla with two young male stylists from Harriet's House of Hell and a shopping bag. She was smiling from ear to ear.

"All right, you party monsters, Carla's here with reinforcements. This is Raymond and this is Eugene."

"Carla? What . . . ?" I said. What was going on?

"When I told Harriet I was leaving, she got mad, they laughed, and she fired them. If you don't need them today, you'll need them by next week." She opened her bag and pulled out an address wheel. "This is Harriet's Rolodex. Where's the nearest Xerox machine?"

Well, you could hear us laughing all the way to Columbia and maybe even Greenville.

By the end of the day, Eugene and Raymond were part of the family, Harriet's Rolodex had been copied and secretly returned through a friend, Carla had booked enough appointments to keep me solvent for a year, and we all looked forward to bedtime like never before. I kissed them all on the cheek and left at the first available opportunity.

I pulled my car into my yard and got out. The side of my house was measured off with sticks and strings, which I followed around to the backyard, where they were measuring for the deck. But I hadn't said anything about a side porch. At that moment, I didn't care.

Miss Angel was sitting on the bottom step of her house, basket weaving.

"Hey!" she said. "I'm making y'all some more baskets!"

"Hey, Miss Angel! Good! We need them!"

"Okay," she said, "you building a deck or what?"

"Yeah, looks like it, doesn't it?"

"Your chile gone back?"

"Yeah, but not without a fight! Seems she fell in love."

"Ain't nothing like it, Miss Anna. Nothing like love in all the world."

"You're right. That's so true! See you later!"

Somewhere in between two loads of laundry and the looks of intense longing I was giving my bed, the phone rang several times. Emily was safe in her dorm room. Frannie, who was out with Jake, called to say she would not be in that night. I ate a peanut butter sandwich and fell asleep before ten, deciding to fold the sheets another day.

The rest of that week and the next went by in a blur. Frannie returned to Washington, swearing she was going to figure out how to move back to Charleston and marry this fellow she'd known for all of five minutes.

"I'm not kidding, Anna, this Jake is something else."

"Does he make you sweat?"

"Humph! I sweat just thinking about him!"

"Wow," I said, and hoped she would.

On Saturday I worked late and got home around nine o'clock. My lights were on and somebody was in my house. I walked in to find Daddy and Lucy sitting on my couch.

"What's going on?" Wasn't this what happened when somebody died?

"It's Emily," Daddy said, "she's . . ."

Before he could say another word I started screaming. *What?*

"She's home, Anna," Lucy said. "She's fine. She's sleeping like somebody hit her in the head with a hammer."

"What in the world?" I said and sank into a chair.

"She's like you, Anna," Daddy said and smiled, "stubborn as a mule. She called me this morning and I sent her a ticket. She hasn't slept since the eleventh and she's all wrung out. She's quit school and wants to be here with us. And, she transferred to the College of Charleston."

"What did you do? You can't just let her . . ."

"Anna," Lucy said, "before you get all upset, you should listen to what she has to say. It's not just about David. It's not."

I knew that it wasn't just about a boy or a boy she loved or thought she loved, but they were right. I knew I should listen to her side and I would.

"She says that she belongs here, Anna," Daddy said. "You, above all people, should understand that."

"I do."

"She thinks you need her, you know, to help with the salon and all."

"I can always use an extra hand," I said, smiling.

"I let her in with my key," Daddy said, "and Lucy said she thought we should wait here until you got home."

"Yeah, so you wouldn't yank her outta the bed by her ears and kick her butt back to D.C."

"Thanks, I mean it."

"We're gonna go back to my house now. You want to come and have a drink with us?"

"No, thanks. I just want to . . . um, think for a while. Okay?"

Daddy stood up and gave me a kiss on the cheek. "She's a wonderful girl, Anna; try to understand her. She's got a beautiful heart."

"Okay, Daddy. Thanks, I will."

As soon as I closed the door behind Daddy and Lucy, I opened the door to Emily's room. She was sleeping peacefully on her lavender sheets, her blond hair spread out over her pillows. I leaned over her bed and kissed her head.

"Welcome home, baby," I said, in a whisper.

My heart was so full, I decided to take a look at the night before I broke down in tears. A change would do me good, thank you, Sheryl Crow.

The sand was cool under my feet and I walked for a while. I thought about the day and what it meant. I looked up at the stars in the sky and started remembering a flood of things—being a little girl, moving to Mount Pleasant, changing friends and schools, recovering from Everett Fairchild, having Emily, and marrying Jim. I'd dealt with so many things and never believed in myself. Maybe that was what Emily was trying to do—to find a way to control her own life and believe in herself.

Because of Jim and Frannie, Daddy, and even good old Lucy, my life had changed in every single way. And, let us not forget, there was a river of my own sweat involved. Emily needed me to do the same for her. In any case, despite the crazy world out there over the causeway, my life was good.

I thought about Jim. Jim was probably reading wine lists all over France and Emily was hopefully dreaming something sweet. Like Miss Mavis had said to me months ago, *the world has changed around me . . .* screw the outside world.

I walked on toward Sullivan's Island, watching the light from the lighthouse scan around and around, flooding everything in wedges of gold light. I wondered what the future would bring. I decided to sit on an old palmetto log for a few minutes. Sifting cool sand through my fingers, I thought about all I had learned about myself, the people around me, and life in general. Living the life you wanted took a lot of strength, a little bit of vision, and definitely it took some luck. Good humor helped. Love made it worth the trouble.

I got up and stretched and looked up at the sky again. It was so breathtakingly beautiful, and immense, and thrilling right down to the tips of my toes. I began walking home, feeling ready to lie down and knowing I could sleep.

Tomorrow Emily and I would talk and I would find out what had happened to make her leave Washington. I was very inclined to keep her with me. Let's be honest. She was staying with me for as long as she wanted.

When Jim came for Thanksgiving we would talk and finally get the business about her birth behind us, but I would not tell her it was rape. I would just tell her I had done something irresponsible. I realized then that maybe one of the reasons I had never told her the truth was because it was connected with violence. My sweet girl didn't need to go through the rest of her life knowing that an unspeakable act of violence had brought her here. It was an unnecessary detail.

Before I crawled in between my covers, I checked on Emily again. She was sleeping without a sound and the breeze coming through her windows had the identical fragrance of the smell of the breeze from my own childhood.

It was true that I had a small house, a small salon, and only one child. At that very moment, I realized that it was important to know how much was enough.

Thirty-six

Regroup

～～～

EMILY made her case and won. She would immediately begin classes at the College of Charleston instead of Carolina and no one argued with her reasoning.

"Look, Mom, I'm not going back to Washington. I watched all that 9/11 rerun stuff and it drove me nuts. I don't need all that craziness in my face. I can't concentrate. I could go to Carolina but then we'd have to pay for an apartment for me. That's pretty stupid, don't you think? Anyway, this is where I belong. I missed you."

"I missed you too. I mean, the College of Charleston is fine but I think it really depends on what you want to major in, baby."

"Mom? I know you're going to think this is insane, but I want to be a writer and there are truly excellent—"

"A writer? You'll starve!"

"I won't starve. I'll do fine. I'm gonna write sitcoms. And all the courses I need to take are right here. And, they have a new totally excellent literary magazine called the *Crazy Horse* and—"

"If you want anyone to take you seriously, you'd better stop saying *totally* and *excellent*." Sitcoms? I hated sitcoms. Ah well, at least she didn't want to be a doctor.

"Whatever. And they have more creative writing courses than anyone. Besides, you need me to help you anyway. And, I can see David on the weekends."

I called Jim and found him. Jim thought the transfer was fine.

"Well, Anna, maybe this makes me a worrywart, but I feel better just knowing she's out of Washington. I mean, I know she was completely safe there, but still. And, if she can't sleep and can't study, what's the point?"

It was settled. Emily began attending classes, Frannie had Emily's belongings shipped home, and even though there was no reason to ring the national alarm, we all slept a little better. There was just something about having your chickens in your own coop.

Over the next few weeks, I had dinner with Jack Taylor a few times and it looked like we were becoming something of a couple, which is to say I knew we were heading to the bedroom door and I knew I wasn't ready.

I had also discovered that he was years and years older than I was. That didn't mean anything except that—and I know this is going to sound shallow—I wasn't in a hurry to find out what a fifty-something-year-old guy was like in the sack and, much more importantly, my little fling with Arturo had left me feeling slightly used.

Our most recent conversation on the topic of intimacy had taken place at Jack's house the previous week. We'd been to dinner at Cypress—which is heaven on this earth—and went back to his place for a nightcap. We were standing in the living room and one thing led to another and the next thing I knew we were about to violate his Persian rug.

"I don't know, Jack," I said, "I just feel like we might be rushing into something for the wrong reasons."

"I thought you cared about me," he said.

"I do, but, you know, lately I've been thinking. I don't want another relationship with someone that's about what's convenient and not about love. I don't think it's right to just, I don't know, screw."

He sat up and ran his hand through his hair. "It's why Caroline and I didn't last very long."

"What do you mean?"

"Look, I'm a traditional guy. She really didn't want a husband right now. I'd really love having a wife and maybe even another child. But, I guess I'm not like most men."

Okay, this is when you decide I am permanently flawed and beyond rescue. Another child? I was looking at forty! Worse than that, Jack Taylor was a lovely man but without a single mystery left for discovery. Not that it was a crime, it just didn't make for much of a challenge. Not that I wanted a challenge, but I wanted something he hadn't shown me so far.

I didn't go to bed with him that night and after that, he sent flowers twice and called me all the time. Holding out was paying off in some ways because what girl doesn't like all the attention? The problem was that the man giving the attention just wasn't the man of my dreams.

Then it happened. The last week of September, King Arthur and Excalibur returned to Charleston. It was late afternoon and we were walking on the beach and talking. It didn't take long for the sun to set and the dog to howl. After so many evenings with Jack Taylor, he had remained a perfect gentleman. After ten minutes with Arthur, the poor guy could barely concentrate on anything except shaking the bacon. Frankly, I was still completely discombobulated around him and it made me mad that my physical body fought my commitment to avoid making the same mistake again.

As the nuns probably would have said, if they'd been acquainted with having the unholy hots—pheromones are unfamiliar with the boundaries of decorum.

But, Lord! The second he had arrived, I wanted him in the most urgent way. I had it bad for Arthur. Bad, bad, bad. Oooh! But, *but!* I didn't let it show.

"I'm sorry I didn't call you," he said. "I got an offer from Citarella—a restaurant in New York. My old friend from Bouley,

Dominique Simon, had taken a job there to sort of give them a fresh image and he needed a maitre d'fromage. Immediately. I just sort of took off and I apologize."

"You're a snake and you stink."

"You're so feminine."

"Oh, bite me, Arthur. Why'd you come back to Charleston?"

"Because I realized I really was happier here. So, I'll live on a little less money and maybe I'll open a restaurant if I can find investors."

He had not come back because of me. But! He had called me, hadn't he? Didn't that mean something?

"Wait a minute. Are you talking about committing yourself to something? Isn't that against your politics?"

"Yeah, but my politics are evolving. I think I've been a Yankee long enough. Besides, I missed you, Anna. I kept telling myself that I didn't care but at the same time, I couldn't stop thinking about you. I couldn't stop wondering how you were doing."

This was good, very good, and I wasn't about to tell him he'd always be a Yankee.

"Are you staying with Mike again?"

"Yeah, he's really a great friend. You know what else? Today I was thinking that I hadn't seen Mike in a million years and he gave me his house to live in for nothing while he was away. He's been a better friend to me than I've been to you and I *slept* with you. I realized there was something really wrong with that."

"Yeah, it's why you suck, Mr. Introspection."

"Excuse me, Miss Poetry, I'm trying to tell you something that's pretty serious. Look, I want us to start over, okay?"

I looked at him. He wasn't lying. Then the practical side of me took over. He wasn't a doctor like Jack, he didn't wear expensive suits like Jack, he didn't drive an old Mercedes like Jack, and in fact, he didn't even have a car. He used Mike's. He was the Cheese Whiz, for Pete's sake. If I married Jack—which I was pretty sure I could take it that far if I really wanted to—I'd be playing golf (God help me) and leading a perfectly respectable life of predictable everything. And, if I married Arthur, which I wasn't sure would ever happen, I might get my heart trampled and in any case, I'd surely be working for a thousand years. But I'd be working for a thousand years because I loved what I did! And I didn't need a man with money because I could earn my own. Therefore, if I wanted to pick a partner, I didn't have to worry about whether or not he could support me!

"Well? Say something!"

"There's nothing to say . . ."

"Really? Oh, God, come on!"

"Let me finish! There's nothing to say except, *Let's go to Mike's!*"

"He's home."

"Give the man ten dollars and send him to the movies."

Just call me Guinevere.

The return of Arthur brought the demise of my relationship with Jack, which even he knew was lacking something to make it work. It lacked chemistry and there's no substitute for that. I just told him that I was seeing someone I had been in love with long ago and I had to find out where my feelings were.

He said, "Look, Anna, it's all right. Give me a call if it doesn't work out, okay?"

The next surprise was not far around the corner. Frannie called the second week of October and announced that she was moving back to Charleston.

"Fabulous!" I said.

"I'm so in love with Jake I can't see straight."

"Nothing like romance, 'eah?"

"You said it, sister. He's been here three times, we talk on the phone all night—I mean, look, it might never be a marriage or maybe it will but if I don't come back and try, I might be making the biggest mistake of my life."

"What can I do to help?"

"Do you know a broker? I just put my condo on the market and I think I'm taking a job in Joe Riley's office. I just have to negotiate one more piece."

"You took a job in Charleston and I didn't know this?"

"I know I should've called but I actually flew in one morning and flew out the same afternoon. The whole thing happened so fast. I saw the job opening on the web, called them up, I faxed them my résumé, and they said come, so I went. I've had it with this blooming rat race. What are you doing for Thanksgiving?"

"Making dinner for you and Jake?"

"Mashed potatoes?"

"Absolutely! If the Irish Goddess is coming, there will be great dunes of mashed potatoes! And, I'll call Marilyn Davey for you. She just found these two friends of mine, Simon and Susan, a house in Wild Dunes. They're getting married December seventh."

"Oh, yeah! I remember them. She's nice."

"Yeah, I'm invited, doing everyone's hair. You watch. I'll go and sure as anything, I'll run into Caroline on the arm of Jack."

"Take Arthur and wear that navy dress."

"Totally excellent idea. . . ."

"You've been spending too much time with Emily."

"Bump you. Hey, you want to hear the latest on Doc?"

When I told her that Lucy and Daddy were all but living in sin, Frannie and I snickered like crazy.

But it was wonderful to see Daddy so happy. A few weeks later, Daddy and I were sitting on my new deck having a glass of tea, waiting for Lucy so that they could go out to dinner. He had brought me a turkey fryer, and we were going over the details of how to fry a perfect turkey. Apparently, this meant that he had decided that we were having fried turkey for Thanksgiving.

"I don't know, Daddy. I mean, I know fried turkey is delicious, but all that oil? What if the thing turns over? Isn't it dangerous?"

"No! It won't turn over! Look here!" He showed me how it was weighted and then he said, "Oh, forget it! I'll fry the turkey myself!"

"You are one cranky old codger sometimes, do you know that?" I gave him a kiss on the cheek and he smiled.

"Women!" He was quiet for a minute and then he said with a great sigh, "You know, Anna, it was probably a mistake years ago to ever have left the Isle of Palms."

Really?

"It sure is great."

"Just smell this air! I think I might love it almost as much as you do. If you hadn't moved back here, I might never have met Lucy."

"You're really crazy about her, aren't you?"

"She makes me feel alive, Anna. Alive in a way I didn't even know I could. I'll tell you this, but if you repeat it, I'll call you a liar."

"What?"

"She thinks I'm sexy," he whispered.

I spit my tea across the breeze. "Euuuu! Gross! Daddy! Augh!"

"And your Arthur doesn't think you're sexy?"

"Touché."

"Anyway, I'm going to ask her to marry me. Do you think it's too late for an old man like me to find happiness?"

"No, that's wonderful, but, oh, Lord! That will make Lucy my *stepmother!*"

Thanksgiving was in a week and that meant preparations were well under way. I had a theory about that particular holiday. It was open to everyone I knew who didn't have a place to go. Maybe the fact that our family was so small contributed to the fantasy I had about a table filled with people. Probably. But over the years that tradition had fastened together the seams of many new friendships. Whoever was there took part. We all cooked together and it was always a day-long feast of food and football. And now, we would have a beautiful peaceful Thanksgiving on the beach, listening to the ocean.

One day at the end of the previous week, we were in the salon, discussing our plans for the holiday. My guest list was Jim, Emily, David, Frannie, Jake, Daddy, Lucy, Arthur, and, of course, Miss Mavis and Miss Angel. I invited Carla, Brigitte, and Bettina. Brigitte accepted and Bettina had wrestled with it and finally decided to take a week's vacation and see her family in New York. Carla was going to her mother's house.

She said, "Lemme put it this way. My mother, the tireless and effervescent Mrs. Joyce Hahnebach, cooks a thousand different things for Thanksgiving and everybody in the world comes. Especially for her pies. If my husband and I don't show up, I'm a dead duck. Dead and stuffed."

"We'll have no dead ducks. Go to your mother's. And bring us some pie on Friday."

"We're taking the train to New York," Bettina said. "First, Bobby wanted to drive the Yacht. I just gave him the hairy eyeball. Then he wanted to fly but I said, Whaddaya, nuts? It's a zillion dollars! Besides, we can sleep the whole way on the train. Ma's been cooking and baking for a month. I can't wait! All my cousins are coming. It's gonna be some scene, lemme tell ya."

"I wish I could come! Have a ball, take a zillion pictures, and tell every single person there that we love New York too, okay? We'll miss you."

"Yeah, me too. Isn't it funny how we all got thrown together and how great it's all worked out?"

"Yep, it's great. It is."

I had come to care for Bettina and Bobby like they were part of my family. I always worried when someone I knew was flying or traveling but I knew that was my own paranoia. They would be fine.

The morning of Thanksgiving was overcast and humid, but around eleven the sun came out and a wonderful breeze began to roll in from the ocean. Lucy and I were cooking in her kitchen and serving from mine, because she had space, better ovens, and a larger refrigerator. We were going to make some sandwiches to snack on until dinner was ready. Daddy, as you've heard, was in charge of the turkey.

Brigitte arrived at one and I met her at the door. She was carrying a cardboard box. When I peeked in, I saw eighteen hollow oranges filled with whipped sweet potatoes.

"Did you expect anything less?" she said. "Happy Thanksgiving!"

"Thank you, thank you! You are incredible," I said. "No marshmallows?"

"They're in the car. I have another load. You want me to take this over to Lucy's?"

"May as well."

"I made oyster bisque too. And a Lady Baltimore cake."

"Good grief! I haven't had a Lady Baltimore cake since I was a kid!"

"It's all fat-free."

I giggled. "You're such a liar."

"Yeah. True." She headed across the yard to Lucy's and I went back through the house to check on the decorations.

Jim and Arthur had strung all the lights around the deck and moved the stereo outside too. David and Emily had the Macy's parade blasting from the television in the living room. Their official job was to set the tables and clear after dinner.

"Fifty bucks," I said.

"I'm in," said David and Emily groaned.

"Okay, okay," she said.

Classes had ended for them on Tuesday and they still seemed to be getting along splendidly. For the last two days they had been collecting shells and driftwood from the beach. Those treasures, combined with hurricanes, big fat candles, gourds from the grocery store, and pecans laid in nests of Spanish moss, would be spread down two long folding tables (that I finally broke down and bought) covered in cheap cotton paisley bedspreads from India. When I looked at the whole shebang put together, I marveled.

"How did we ever live before Pier One Imports?"

"Good question," Jim said. "Let's go inside for a minute, Anna. I have something I need to talk to you about."

"What, precious? Anything wrong?"

"Ahem!" Arthur said.

I gave him a smacking kiss on his forehead. "Be right back."

I followed Jim into the kitchen.

"Well, it's Trixie. I think something's wrong with her—I mean, we all know there's a lot wrong with her. She's as vicious as a copperhead. But she really doesn't seem like her old copperhead self. She's not acting right."

"She rarely does."

"No, that's not the thing. She's complaining of me not coming to see her often enough. In all my life she's never even asked me when I was coming home. You know her. She hates having to deal with my life."

"Maybe she's just getting older, you know? I mean, look at Daddy. All of a sudden he's over here all the time. I mean, he was so cheap all my life! Suddenly he builds me a deck and a porch and landscapes the whole kit and caboodle! Now, he's even got us a turkey fryer!"

"Maybe. But, she's forgetting things. Like, I called her last week to tell her I was going to be here and then I called her the next day to see if I could bring her something from San Francisco. She usually asks me for sourdough bread or Ghiradelli chocolate. She had completely forgotten that I had called her the day before. That's not like her."

"How old is she?"

"She'd slit my throat if I told but let's just say she qualified for Medicaid a decade ago."

"Wow, she looks good."

"She should. Her plastic surgeon in Atlanta just bought a share in Netjet, this private jet company!"

"Oooh! You so bad!" I wagged my finger at him and we chuckled a little. "Well, when you get older, you start forgetting stuff."

"Yeah, the back nine of life. Anyway, here's the point. Yesterday, I lost my head and rented a little carriage house downtown—"

"What? Ow! Ow! I've got my Jim back!" I grabbed his face and planted noisy kisses on both cheeks and I did a little dance.

"You can't dance worth crap, you know."

"Shut up! I'm the dancing queen, I'll have you know!"

"Forgive me, you're the princess. You can't be queen until I drop dead!"

"You are so wicked! I just love you to pieces!"

"And I love you too! So listen, I'm going to be here a lot more. With fax and FedEx and all that techno equipment that's around for a song, there's no reason that I can't run my business from right here. I mean, obviously, I'll have to be in Napa and Sonoma a good bit, but that's not a big deal. I can fly. Besides, since Gary's been gone and all—well, I miss you and Emily and I realize I'm way out there with no family."

"This is the best news I've had in a million years, Jim."

"Do you think I'm crazy? I mean, the years are just flying by."

"Isn't that the truth? You're anything but crazy. I think you ought to surround yourself with the people who love you. That's what I think. I mean, try it! If it works, fabulous for me, Emily, Frannie, and everybody. Including Trixie."

"Yeah, well, I feel bad for her, you know? And I need to talk to Frannie. I've got two bedrooms and thought she might like to pitch her tent and camp with me, so to speak. Or, if Emily has a night class, she can bunk with me too."

"I think old Frannie is gonna be sharing her tent with Jake."

"Oh, that's right. When is her move date?"

"December first."

"It'll be great to be a fifth wheel with y'all."

"Maybe you'll meet someone. Emily's going to be so happy, Jim. You know what?"

"What?"

"Call the old biddy Trixie and see if she wants to join us."

"I did but I think she's got plans. Anyway, I told her it was your idea and you get points for asking."

"Like I can redeem them?"

"What's going on in here? Inquiring minds want to know," Emily said as she came through the back door. "I still think you should've enlarged this kitchen, Mom."

"Never look a gift horse in the mouth, sweetie."

"Right. I was just telling your momma that I rented a townhouse in Charleston and the kitchen is smaller than this one."

"Oh, ma God!"

"So, naturally, I'm going to have to buy a car and someone's going to have to take care of it for me when I'm away on business. I was thinking about a convertible. . . ."

Their shrieks were too loud for my ears.

I took my clippers from the drawer and went out to the front yard to see if there were any roses to cut. An expensive foreign car was driving by very slowly and then it stopped. I ignored it, thinking it was just someone coming to look at the beach, which happened all the time. I heard the car door close, so I looked up.

I saw Everett Fairchild coming toward me.

Thirty-seven

Mad Dogs

~~~

EVERETT Fairchild was in my yard and carrying the picture I had framed for Joanne, his wife.

"Anna? Anna Lutz?"

"How did you find me?"

"There's an emergency number on the door of your salon. I went through the phone book until I found the address to match it. It said A. ABBOT, but I thought I'd give it a try."

There was a long silence that passed between us. What in the hell was I supposed to do then? Invite him to dinner? I wasn't about to give him the slightest welcome. I hadn't exactly been standing around waiting for him to show up on Thanksgiving Day.

I could see that he was trying to figure out what to say.

"I haven't been sleeping very well. . . ."

"That's too bad," I said. "I didn't sleep too well nineteen years ago either."

"It was a long time ago."

I cannot describe the feelings I was having. If I'd had a gun in my hand I would've shot him dead on the spot. Obviously, it had been a terrible mistake to send that picture along with Joanne because here he was. How was I supposed to deal with this?

"This is probably not the best time for you to be here."

"I don't think there could ever be a good time. Look, I know you think I'm the worst person on the earth. . . ."

"That pretty much covers it," I said, realizing I had never thought about the terrible anger I would feel if I actually saw him again. Suddenly, I wanted to stab him over and over with my clippers. I wanted him to writhe in pain and agony and bleed to death right there in front of me so I could laugh.

"Well, I'm not," he said. "I'm really not." He looked out toward the beach and then took a deep breath. In a voice so low I could barely hear him he said, "She's mine, isn't she."

"No. She's mine." Looking at him for the first time after so many years, I remembered my broken nose and how he had never called, even once, to apologize. My fury became a blinding hatred. I was becoming irrational. Moreover, I didn't care if I made a scene loud and scary enough for the police to come and haul me away in a padded wagon.

"I'd like to see her."

"Really? Well, guess what? If you think that you're going to just show up after all these years and ruin our holiday, you can go to hell."

"Anna, I don't blame you for being furious and I know you hate me and you should. But if I have a daughter, I want to know." All the while he spoke, his voice was calm and carefully modulated as if he had practiced those words, *I want to know*, a hundred thousand times.

"You have no right to be here. Leave! Leave now or I'm calling the police! Leave now and never come back! Ever!"

I could see that Everett Fairchild was not accustomed to being told to get off someone's property or to vanish from people's lives.

My door opened and Jim came out.

"What's the problem here?" Jim took one look at Everett Fairchild and knew exactly what the problem was. Satan had arrived, all dressed up for a friendly visit.

"Well, well. Mr. Fairchild, I believe?"

Jim shook his hand and I was so mad at him for doing it that I wanted to chop his hand off at his wrist.

"Oh, are you gonna be *nice* to this creep, Jim? Are you gonna be *friends* now?"

"Anna, why don't you go over to Lucy's and let me talk to this man for a few minutes."

"Fine, Jim. *Fine!* You handle it!" I zeroed in on Everett's face with the most poisonous expression I could muster. "You bastard," I said and left them to stall-kick their way through the manure.

When I pushed through Lucy's door, she and Brigitte were sitting at her kitchen bar, having a glass of wine, peeling potatoes and dropping them into a huge pot of water. They looked at me and knew immediately that something terrible had happened.

"What? Is Douglas okay? What?" Lucy said and came to my side.

"What's happened?" Brigitte asked.

"Everett Fairchild. He's in my front yard talking to Jim. I think I'm going to explode." I held on to the counter for support.

"Here, honey, come sit," Lucy said and took me to her living room.

Brigitte followed with a glass of water and handed it to me. "How in the world . . . ?"

"Phone book," I said, and the tears started to flow. "Not today! Everybody's here! Oh, God!"

Lucy looked down to my yard. "Now Frannie's out there with Jake and Arthur."

"I told him to get lost and don't ever come back," I said. "I didn't realize how horrible it would be to see him."

Brigitte went to the window and looked down. "He's got some sense of timing, doesn't he? Thanksgiving? What an idiot."

Lucy handed me a box of tissues and I took three, blowing my nose and wiping my eyes. "Y'all? What am I going to do? I can't have this happen today!"

"Too late," Brigitte said. "Who's that pulling up?"

I got up and went to the window.

"Oh, no! It's *Trixie!*"

"I'll go get Douglas to keep her busy," Lucy said and flew out of the house and down the steps.

"I may as well kill myself right now!" I said and began pacing the floor. "How did this happen? Why do these things always happen to me?"

"*Anna! Stop it right now!*"

I turned to see Frannie standing there with her hands on her hips.

"What?" I said. "Just what would you do if you were in my shoes? Don't you *understand?*"

"Here's what I understand. One, he's the bad guy, not you. Two, the only thing you've done that maybe wasn't done early enough was to tell Emily the facts. Three, quit being a victim. You have raised a wonderful daughter and you have nothing to be ashamed of. If I ever hear you say *poor me* again, I'm gonna knock your head off. So, pull yourself together and let's go talk to the mule-headed son of a bitch. He ain't leaving until he sees her. He said that twenty times. You have two choices: You can lie your behind off to Emily and everybody else and make yourself look bad in the long run. Or you can be a woman and deal with it."

"What about Trixie? She's going to make a horrible scene! Emily's going to . . . I don't know, disown all of us!"

"So far, Trixie is having a glass of wine and talking on the deck with Lucy, Douglas, Miss Mavis, and Miss Angel. And if Trixie says one word, I'll slap her silly. There's no reason why you should have all the fun today. What do you think, Brigitte?"

"I think I'm really glad I didn't go to the S&S Cafeteria today. I would've missed this whole thing." Then she turned to me. "Sorry. Listen, Anna, here's what we're gonna do. You're going to calm down. Right now."

"I'm okay. It was just the shock. Now I'm just seriously pissed off. I mean, I never expected him to just show up like *this.*"

"If I'd been you I'd be covered in vomit by now," Brigitte said and shook her head. "Okay, so we're going to go down there together and bring him back up here and have a civilized discussion with him. We'll ask him to come back tomorrow."

Frannie nodded her head in agreement. "Good idea. Blot your mascara and let's go."

"Screw my mascara."

We went down the steps and were halfway across the yard when Emily bolted backward out the front door of our house, nearly knocking Everett over. It was like watching a film in slow motion where the mother's child falls in front of the moving train. *Noooooooooooooo!* Before I could reach her, he had grabbed her by the shoulders so that she didn't fall. I stopped and listened. Neither one of them said a word. They simply stared at each other as though they were looking in a mirror. Jim moved in to make introductions but Emily held up her hand in a motion and Jim stopped. I was no more than five feet away.

"I know who you are," she said, in wonder. "Oh, my God!"

I finally moved and went to Emily's side, putting my arm around her shoulder. "Why don't we all go over to Lucy's where we can talk privately," I said, trying to get us away from Daddy and Trixie. I realized then that Daddy was going to go ballistic when he found out that Everett was there. It might even kill him.

Emily didn't budge.

"You're my birth father, aren't you?" She seemed to be unable to take her eyes away from his face. She started to giggle and then she laughed. "You know, I always hoped I looked like you. This is some amazing holiday. Man! Look at you! I've got your eyes! Wait till I tell David! He's gonna freak! You are staying for dinner, aren't you?"

"I don't think so. I mean, it's Thanksgiving and all and maybe I could just come over tomorrow or something."

"No *way!* Um, excuse me, um, but what's your name anyway?"

"Everett Fairchild," he said. "Call me Rhett. And what do they call you?"

"I'm Emily."

"What a perfectly beautiful name, Emily; it's beautiful, just like you."

"Thanks. Anyway, Rhett old boy, it's Thanksgiving and, good grief, what's Thanksgiving for anyway? Is this weird or what? Wow. Genetics. Man, look at your eyes! I thought I was a freak of nature! Now there's another one!" She started giggling and Everett smiled at the sound of her laughter.

He had never heard her laughter. He was hearing his eighteen-year-old daughter laugh for the first time.

Their exchange all but flattened us—Jim, Arthur, me, Brigitte, and Frannie. We looked at each other and they shrugged their shoulders. My fury was still mushrooming. I didn't want Everett there. But, I had expected hysterics from Emily and I got little more than biological curiosity instead. My thoughts were in a dozen places at once. Daddy. Trixie. What would I tell them?

"Jim?"

"Yeah?"

"What about Trixie?"

"Let the old bitch figure it out for herself and we can watch her twitch."

"Mother McCree! I could probably sell tickets if I had the time," Frannie said.

"This is not one damn bit funny, okay?" I said.

Everyone became quiet.

"Momma? Who the hell cares what Trixie thinks anyway? Come on, we gotta set another place at the table."

"No," I said, "not so fast."

"I hear my potatoes screaming," Frannie said. "Let's go up to Lucy's."

I looked at Everett. "I can't think of a thing you could say that I'd want to hear. And all of you can go up to Lucy's. You too, Emily. Go! All of you!"

How could he just show up? What did he think? Did he think we'd just say, *Everett! So nice to see you again! How're they hanging, bubba?* I knew Frannie's joke about selling tickets was her nervous anxiety. And, obviously it didn't matter what Trixie thought.

I watched them cross the yard and climb the stairs to Lucy's. They let him in the house like he was a normal person. A normal person. There was the man who had drugged and raped me, broken my nose, and left me pregnant, walking up the stairs with my daughter and my dearest friends as though he belonged. He did not belong.

I could already see that Emily could handle this. In fact, everyone could handle it except me. I was going to do something terrible.

I went inside my house, reached under my sink, and took out the hammer. The house was empty. I went back outside to see what was going on. Everyone else was on the terrace or still up at Lucy's. I looked at Everett's shiny black Mercedes-Benz SL600 and wondered how he'd feel if I banged the hell out of it.

I started with a headlight. It smashed and glass fell all over the road. I looked up at Lucy's to see if anyone had heard the sound of it. All quiet. I smashed the second one. I started to perspire like crazy. Then I hit the hood as hard as I could—the passenger door, the roof, the back fender, the trunk a few times. I went around to the driver's door and pounded it about six times before I heard the voices.

Anna! Stop! Jim! Somebody! Make her stop! Anna! Please! Momma! Stop!

I turned around and saw every single person invited there for dinner, all of them, staring at me. The look of horror on Emily's face would follow me to my grave. So would the faces of the others. I started to cry again and dropped the hammer on the road. I felt myself slide down the driver's door. I sat on the ground with my head buried in my arms and from somewhere outside of my own head, I heard my own convulsive sobbing.

In seconds, I felt someone take my elbow to lift me up on one side and then the other. What had I done? I looked up to see who was trying to help me and I saw Jim on one side and Arthur on the other.

"Come on, baby," Arthur said, "it's okay."

"Someone go get a Xanax or something, okay?" Jim said. "Come on, Anna, let's go in the house."

I saw Frannie, Lucy, Trixie, and Brigitte all leave to search for something to calm me down. I looked back at the car. It was ruined. I didn't care. Before I could think of what to say, Everett came up to us and we stopped.

He looked at his car and back at me and said, "I don't blame you one bit. If I had only known about Emily . . . things would've been so different. Forget the car. Are you all right?"

"Fuck you, Everett. I mean it." I looked at him again. "I feel better, I think. I'm not sorry about your car."

"Don't apologize, Anna."

"I didn't."

Then, to our complete and total amazement, Everett Fairchild burst out into tears, then got in his car and locked the doors.

"Mercy!" Trixie said.

Finally, Daddy spoke up loudly. "Would somebody like to tell us just what in the hell is going on here?"

"Come on, sugar, let's hush," Lucy said, taking his arm, "and let's go get my blender." Then she turned to everyone else and said, "Y'all come on over too! Yes, you too, Miss Mavis and Miss Angel! It ain't gonna kill you to come in my house! We'll explain everything."

Off they went, everyone except Emily, Jim, and Arthur, who took me in the house, and Everett, who was hanging on his steering wheel, weeping in his locked car. He could sit there until Christmas for all I cared.

I plopped on my couch and put my legs up, kicking off my shoes. Jim gave me a glass of wine. Arthur got a box of tissues and gave it to me. Emily just stood in shock. She spoke first.

"Momma? Are you crazy? Why . . . ?"

"Be quiet, Emily," Jim said, "your mother did what she had to do."

"Yeah, Everett's lucky as hell she didn't use the hammer on him," Arthur said.

Emily was staring at me and little lights began coming on in her mind. If Everett was the birth father and I had demolished his car, the relationship could not have been a good thing.

"Everett drugged and raped your mother at her prom, Emily," Jim said. "She got pregnant, didn't prosecute, and then I married her. We never heard from him again and we never tried to find him. We never told you because we couldn't figure out *how* to tell you and now here we are. That's the truth. I'm sorry."

"Holy shit, Momma. No wonder you whacked the daylights out of his car!"

Jim had told Emily that it was rape. But it was all out and there were no more secrets to keep. I began to relax a little and sat up to blow my nose.

"Take a sip," Arthur said, and held my goblet out for me.

"No, no, thanks," I said. "I'm okay now. Thanks, y'all."

"Anna," Jim said, "nobody blames you for what you did. We only just wish we could've helped you do it."

"There's more to the story, Anna," Arthur said. "Do you want to tell her or should I?"

"I'll start," Jim said, "and you correct me if I get it wrong."

Everett had told them everything at Lucy's. Bettina had been right. His wife, the evil Joanne, had been having an affair with one of Everett's employees. He caught them at a motel by accidentally spotting their cars.

"He said it was a pretty ugly scene. He knocked on the door and this dumb sumbitch answered it. There was Joanne, naked as a jaybird, sitting up on a water bed with a look of *holy shit* on her face."

"Can you imagine?" Arthur said. "That must've taken some monster-sized balls to knock on the door."

"Probably took King Kong's to come here," Jim said. "Everett said he didn't think twice before he did it. I mean, her car was sitting there for all the world to see with her license plate that said CARPEDIEM. Seize the day. Puh-leez! Go seize yourself a good attorney, girlfriend."

"He said he said to his employee, 'You're fired,' and then he looked at Joanne and said, 'We're all done,'" Arthur said.

"Too bad," I said. "Joanne deserved it."

"Who's Joanne?" Emily said.

"His wife," I said. "I'll tell you everything in a few minutes."

"Yeah, well, anyway," Jim said, "he went home and threw all her clothes in four suitcases and that's how he found the picture in her drawer. After he stared at it for a few minutes, he thought it was you, Anna. But he completely flipped out when he looked at Emily's face. Apparently our Emily is the spitting image of his mother. And the eyes were the final clue. He sent all Joanne's things to the Holiday Inn, drove up here, and that was pretty much that."

"That's some story," I said. The plan had worked, but not as predicted.

"This guy may have been a bum in college," Arthur said, "but he was on drugs too. Did you know that?"

"No. I didn't. I should've figured that out, but I didn't. What else did he say?"

"That he got kicked out of the Citadel, went to jail for distributing, had the hell scared out of him by the boys inside the cooler, and then got his life together. He doesn't drink, smoke, or do drugs of any kind. And, he wants to pay for Emily's college tuition."

"You're kidding."

"Nope. He said to tell you he'd call you over the weekend to discuss it."

"What does he expect in return? Our adoration?"

"It seems he doesn't want a thing," Jim said. "He might need a tow truck, but . . ."

I looked up at him and then to Arthur and to Emily. There were traces of relief and half smiles on everyone's face, including mine.

"Tell him to get his ugly ass out of his ugly-ass car and come in here like a man and talk to me."

They all left to get him and returned in a few minutes.

"Hey, Emily," Arthur said, "how's about you and me moseying over to Lucy's and seeing what the old people are doing?"

"Yeah, good idea. At some point, we gotta eat."

As soon as they were far enough away not to hear us we started talking.

"I just didn't know, Anna," Everett said. "How could I have known?"

"I don't know," I said, "the news killed my grandmother, you know."

"Oh, my God!" Everett said.

"Don't worry. You did me a personal favor. She was unbelievably awful."

I sort of smiled at him then and saw that it didn't pay to be angry anymore. It was time to let it all go. He was dealing with his own serious pain and guilt. Somehow, I'd have to find forgiveness in my heart for him, or at least be open to the possibility that he had changed and was truly sorry for everything.

I looked over at Jim and said, "Oh, fine. Call Lucy's and tell Emily to set another plate on the table."

If I was going to forgive the son of a bitch, I had to forgive the son of a bitch. Forgiving him would surely earn me time off in hell. I washed my face a dozen times and tried to make myself presentable.

Inside of an hour we gathered for the strangest and most stressful Thanksgiving dinner of all times.

Daddy was calm when he spoke to me. "If you can find forgiveness, Anna, so can I. So can I." He hugged me and went to get his bird out of the fryer.

Trixie was smug and I knew as sure as anything that she'd have something to say at the worst possible moment. I was prepared for her.

Frannie, who was licking a mound of whipped potatoes from her finger and feeding Jake at the same time, said, "How is it that the lowly spud can make my heart sing so?"

"It's the butter," Brigitte said. "Everybody take a platter, okay? Let's go."

We were using my table with the umbrella as a buffet. It was loaded all around with every kind of delicious thing we could manage to produce. Daddy had the fried turkey on a huge carving board at one end, where he stood *in charge* like an admiral on a ship. He had on one of those ridiculous aprons. On the chest it had a printed cartoon turkey dressed like a pilgrim, holding a sign that said EAT MORE CHICKEN!

"Where'd you get that apron?" I asked him as I put the stuffing and gravy down.

"I bought it for him," Lucy said. "Isn't he adorable?"

"Adorable." Daddy harrumphed. "I'm a dignified man!"

Lucy and I smiled at each other and, looking around, saw that everyone seemed fine, that the tornado had done its damage and had apparently moved on. They were all talking to each other, gathering around to serve themselves dinner.

Everett was talking to Brigitte a lot and I thought that it would be good if she could keep him occupied. Now, if I could just manage to be sure he wasn't seated facing Trixie. Fate was as deaf as a freaking doornail.

"Let's say grace," Daddy said.

We were all standing around the buffet table. Everyone became quiet and bowed their heads.

"Dear heavenly Father, thank You for this beautiful day, this bounty of food, and for each other. As we look in our hearts to examine our souls, please make us see Your greater will. Please bless us with Your grace and Your love so that we may be of better service to You and to each other. And, Lord? Please send a special grace to those . . ."

"The potatoes are getting cold," Frannie whispered.

"Shush," I said and actually managed to squeak out something like a giggle.

"Thank you, Lord. Amen."

"Amen!" everyone said and began helping themselves.

Miss Mavis was the first to give Everett the once-over. "Let me look at you, young man! Who are your people?"

"My family's from Atlanta, ma'am, but I live in Clearwater, Florida."

"How's that?" she said.

"*Fla-ra-da!*" Miss Angel said loudly enough to scare all the fish in the Atlantic out to the Gulf Stream. "You'll have to speak up, young man, if you want to talk to Mavis."

Everett nodded his head and smiled.

"I went to Florida not long ago," Miss Mavis said. "I was looking at *retirement communities* where I can live *alone!*"

"Humph," Miss Angel said, "she ain't gwine nowhere."

I shot Trixie a look and she looked upset.

"You look very nice, Trixie," I said, "I'm glad you could come."

"Ah'm not so sure if you really meant for me to be here, Anna, but . . ."

Would you believe the old Great White choked up? Just how much crying was going to go on today anyway? I put my hand on her arm, not wanting her to rust. *Go rust at your house*, I thought.

I said, "Come on, Trixie, it's Thanksgiving. Let's try to get along."

"Ah didn't want to be alone today, you know? And when Jim called Ah thought well, gracious me, Ah could certainly make some effort. You're the only family Ah have here."

"Well, today let's try to be cheerful. There's enough misery in the world."

That had gone well enough, until, don't you know, she parked her fat butt right across from Everett and began to stare. Everett was seated next to Emily. I thought Trixie's eyes would surely land in her plate at some point.

Here we go, I thought.

But all through dinner, she didn't say a word. A miracle. A world-class miracle. A world-class miracle of short shelf life, I have to add, because when she left—and thank heavens she left earlier than everybody else—she turned to me and whispered, "Ah knew it."

The old viper just couldn't keep her tongue in her head, could she? I looked at her and said, "So what, Trixie? What does *it* mean?"

She stood by my front door with a smug expression and said, "It means that Emily's not my *bloooood*. Ah knew it all along."

"Well, thank God she's not your blood or she might be like you. There's the door."

I heard her laughing on her way to her car and thought, *Well, I guess that's what it sounds like in hell.*

Daddy, David, and Lucy had taken a pile of dishes back next door. Frannie, Brigitte, Jim, Everett, and Emily were still at the table.

"Y'all ready for dessert?"

"We're ready for everything and anything," Emily said.

"She's a wonderful young woman, Anna," Everett said.

"Thanks. Yeah, she is."

Although I tried as hard as I could, I couldn't wait for him to leave. I wondered if his car would even start. It probably would. I made myself busy and avoided him. He didn't push me.

Later, when everyone had finally either gone home or gone to bed, Arthur and I walked on the beach. It would've been an exhausting day even if Everett had not shown up. But I didn't want everything to end without a walk along the water.

Billions of stars lit up the crisp November sky. It was breathtaking. At first we walked and then Arthur took my hand. The temperature was dropping and I shivered a little in the damp air. He stopped, took off his sweater and gave it to me. I put it on and we walked again, this time with his arm around my shoulder.

"Life's good," he said.

"Yeah. Except for the surprise guest and Trixie's usual truckload of trash. How'd you like Everett showing up like that?"

"Pretty heavy. But you know what? When the flatbed truck showed up to remove the ruins, we shook hands and all that."

I stopped and looked at him as if to say, *Between you and Jim, y'all's hands must be worn out.*

"Okay, look, I mean, at the moment he seemed like a perfectly decent piece of shit to me, so I shook his hand. It's not like I want to be his fishing buddy."

"Well, that's nice to know."

"Man! You've got some understandable but unresolved anger issues, you know that?"

"And you wouldn't?"

"No, you're right, you're right. Anyway, Emily said to him, 'So now what? Will I ever see you again?' And he said, 'Here's my phone number and address. If you ever want to come and visit, bring some friends, whatever, I have a big house in Clearwater and I'd love to get to know you. After all, you're my only child.' I mean, pretty stressful day for the guy, you have to say."

"Forgive me, but I don't give a rat's ass about his stress, okay? I was dealing with my own?"

"Yeah. Definitely. Well, all things considered, that was about the best thing he could've said."

"Oh, hellfire, it was a long time ago and I was pretty stupid too."

"You're not stupid now."

"Really? I destroyed a hundred-thousand-dollar car earlier today."

"That wasn't stupid. It was genius. But remind me to get out of your way when you're in a bad mood, okay? Maybe I'll go to Lowe's with old Douglas and get something to lock up the tools."

"Thanks, I think."

"Besides, he really didn't care that much. He said he expected something would happen."

"He was right. He's lucky he didn't spend twenty years in the cooler."

"Yeah, he got off cheap."

We walked along a little and I thought about Arthur and Daddy at Lowe's looking for lockboxes.

"Hey! Did you hear this? Daddy's gonna ask Lucy to marry him."

"No kidding?"

"Yeah, is that weird or what?"

"No. They love each other, don't they?"

"Yes. A lot."

"Well, when two people love each other, they usually do something like that, don't they?"

"Holy hell, Arthur! Are you asking me to marry you?"

He started coughing and stammering. "What? No! I mean, I don't know! I mean . . ."

"You are such a worm! You don't have a clue what you mean!"

"I know that I love you, though." He cleared his throat, then stopped, and looked me in the face. "How's that for openers?"

"You do?"

Holy hopping hell. He had just told me he loved me.

"Do you love me?"

"What is this? Fifth grade?"

"Well?"

"You put me through the wringer, you know."

"*Well? Spit it out.*"

"I love you, Arthur. You know I do."

"I know. And, as terrifying as that would've been to someone like me three months ago, now I can't live without it."

"Me either."

We walked and listened to the sounds of the beach at night, marveled at the glisten of the water and the smell of salt, saying to each other that we were so lucky, so fabulously rich to have each other.

The random connections in my new life were a fascinating study in synchronicity. Leaving Daddy, finding Lucy, and then David coming into Emily's life. My love of the beach, and the beach having delivered Arthur. Everett had bound me to Jim and Emily forever. Gary's death had brought Jim back to all of us and Frannie had found Jake. Even Miss Mavis and Miss Angel had more company and excitement in their lives. Everything had changed with that first move. There just couldn't be that many coincidences in life.

Maybe my life *was* part of a plan and the choices I made affected the outcome only ever so slightly. I didn't doubt it anymore. The cynic in me had taken some heavy bullets in recent months. And now, I had become practically romantic. I had even faced down my worst enemies and survived to tell the stories.

"Hey, Arthur?"

"Yeah, sweetheart?"

Sweetheart? Excellent.

"Life *is* good. Real good."

"Come on," he said, "it's late. Let's get you home and to sleep. You had a rough workout today."

"Good idea."

I wondered if he could see me smiling in the dark.

I would sleep, all right, like an old Lowcountry girl, just an old Geechee brat who was grateful and finally truly and deeply in love with her life. Momma would probably show up in my dreams and do a little victory dance. Who knew? Maybe she'd do the Charleston. I hoped she would. I'd kick up my heels with her.

Epilogue

"SHE'S a wreck and I don't know why she should be," Maggie said. "She's known Simon since she was just a kid."

Maggie, in a perfect little black dress and pearls, was the matron of honor in the wedding of Susan Hayes (and also her older sister).

"Honey, any woman getting married ought to have the good sense to be nervous. It wouldn't be normal if she wasn't!"

I was trimming Maggie's hair, Eugene was washing Susan's daughter Beth's hair and Susan was under the dryer. The wedding was to take place at five that afternoon, at Stella Maris Church, followed by a reception on the beach in front of her family's home, the Island Gamble. I loved it that so many houses around here had names and I thought to myself that maybe I should name ours something like Blond Ambition, or Wild Life Sanctuary. I liked the last one best. Life was wild and the house was my sanctuary. I'd have to ask Emily what she thought about it. Naming a house would be a great excuse to have a bunch of company come over, have a barbecue, and unveil a sign over our front door.

"I'm dry!" Susan hollered and I went over to check.

Her hair was still damp so I said, "Another fifteen minutes! You want a smoothie?"

"No, thanks! But, good grief! I've been under this thing for a year!"

"You've got a lot of hair!"

She closed her eyes and shook her head in exasperation.

Bettina had given her a manicure and a pedicure and waxed her from stem to stern. She pulled me aside.

"We oughta give her a discount on the waxing 'cause all her hair is on her head. Her legs ain't nothing but duck fuzz."

"She's my favorite client. I ain't charging her a dime. It's a wedding gift."

"That's nice. You know what, Anna?"

"What?"

"It pays to be nice in this world, don't you think?"

"Yeah. I think. Having a heart makes all the difference, Brooklyn, all the difference in the world."

Susan, Beth, and Maggie left looking spectacular. If my Emily had the green eyes, those three had the waters of Bermuda sloshing in their heads.

"She sure looks beautiful," Brigitte said, "God bless her!"

"Amen," Bettina said.

"She *is* beautiful and she's marrying the right man too."

The afternoon flew by and I left the salon at three to go home and change. Arthur, who had finally bought a car, picked me up at four. I wanted to check their hair again before the ceremony.

"You look good enough to eat!" Arthur said and kissed my cheek. "And you smell good enough to drink."

"Don't start with me, boy, I'm still on duty."

"There's always later, my little vine of delight. . . ."

"Vine of delight? As in wrap myself around you? Get in the car! I'm gonna be late!"

Arthur was always saying these dumb things but the truth was that I was thrilled to wrap myself around him. Whoo! Amazing!

We drove down Middle Street to Station Nine and pulled in their yard. The railings on the steps had been festooned with ivory tulle, asparagus ferns, and enormous white lilies, tied at intervals with bows of wide ivory-watermarked, wired French ribbon. And that was just the back steps!

Torches, also decorated, were in place to create a path to the front of the house for the guests, which made sense as I couldn't imagine they wanted people coming to the wedding reception through the kitchen. But I went in the kitchen anyway, which was in a complete frenzy. There were about twelve waiters and two or three chefs barking orders, moving racks of glasses, and garnishing platters of finger food.

Susan was nowhere in sight.

Arthur and I squeezed through the crowd into the dining room.

"Wow," he said.

All chairs had been removed, and the table was draped to the floor in a magnificent white damask cloth. I was struck by two things at once. First, the cake. It had four tiers and at the base of each one were tiny white roses and gardenias made of spun sugar. All around the sides were tiny silver balls worked into a biased lattice pattern. On top were two figures. The bride was reading a book and wearing a big diamond and the groom was wearing a doctor's jacket and a stethoscope. How clever! And, in each corner were two of the biggest floral arrangements I had ever seen. These huge sprays of white roses and fresh gardenias stood on deep red lacquered pedestals, in blue-and-white-patterned vases, and filled the room with perfume.

Susan was still nowhere in sight.

I turned around and saw the porch ahead of me.

"Come on," I said to Arthur, "there's got to be somebody out there."

"Or at least a bar."

We passed the living room on the left and Arthur stopped.

"What?" I said.

"That mirror! I could've sworn that I saw something in it besides us."

ISLE OF PALMS 477

"Yeah, right. Come on, let's go."

Arthur backed up and went back into the living room, staring at the big mirror on the far end. It was a floor-to-ceiling mirror with a gold gilt frame, obviously an antique.

"I *swear*, Anna, I saw an older black woman in there, all dressed up. There was a man next to her. They were both waving at me trying to get my attention. I'm not *lying*! I *saw* it!"

I didn't see a thing in the mirror and thought Arthur had gotten too much sun or something.

"Let's get you a drink and park you somewhere safe while I go find Susan, okay?"

"Yeah, sure. Okay. Man! That was . . . oh, forget it!"

There was a bar on either end of the porch, and the porch, by the way, was festooned everywhere with more monster arrangements on deep red lacquered pedestals. I got Arthur a glass of wine, and one of Susan's brothers—I think he said his name was Henry—said he'd take me to Susan. We went upstairs and left Arthur, who was a little ashen, standing by the railing looking out at the ocean. What was up with him?

"How many people are coming?" I asked Henry.

"I think only about fifty to seventy-five people. This whole she-bang was planned so fast that if I didn't know better, I'd say that devil Simon knocked up my poor sister."

"Not a chance."

His eyes twinkled. "Here we are. I think she's in here."

He opened the door for me and Susan turned to see who was coming in. Well, can I just tell you that it never fails that when I see a bride, I get choked up. Susan was all sort of drenched in afternoon light and looked so beautiful and so happy that I nearly lost it.

"Hey, Anna, thanks for coming early. Can you believe I'm actually doing this?"

"Oh, Susan! You look so incredible I could cry!"

"Don't cry! Help me get this dumb thing on my head!"

Her dress was heavy, pink-hued ivory satin—with cap sleeves and a scooped neck, and it went right to the floor in a slight flare without stopping. The back had a long slit and tiny covered buttons climbed all the way up her back. The "dumb thing" was a small pillbox hat with a long graceful veil attached to it. She wore pearls and pearl studs and I couldn't think of a more elegant wedding outfit, especially for a woman who wasn't exactly a spring chicken.

The door opened again. Maggie and Beth had arrived to do a last-minute check on Susan.

"Oh, Momma! You look so pretty!" Beth kissed her mother on the cheek.

"Yes, You do!" Maggie said and gave her a kiss too. "I think we are almost ready to go, Susan. Do you want to run away to Tahiti? Last call?"

"Are you crazy? I've been waiting to be married to this guy all my life!"

They kept talking, the kind of nervous chatter you would expect, and then I realized Susan was talking to me.

"I'm sorry," I said, "I was lost in thought."

"No problem. I asked if you'd brought Arthur."

"Yeah, and you know what? He's so crazy! He thought he saw something in the mirror in your living room."

Dead silence.

"What?" I said.

"What did he think he saw?" Beth said, choking on a giggle.

"Oh, man. You're gonna think this is crazy if I tell you this."

"No. I can assure you, we won't," Maggie said.

"Okay. He said he saw an older black woman and a man, all dressed up, waving to him. Is that about the craziest thing you ever heard?"

"Livvie. And Nelson," Susan said, her voice cracking, rubbing the goose bumps on her arms.

"Hadda be," Beth said.

"Who's Livvie?" I said.

They looked at each other and then to me and finally Susan said, "Livvie was everything. And she never missed anything. I'll tell you all about her another time."

"I think I hear the chamber musicians tuning up," Maggie said. "I'd better go see if the limo is here yet."

We chatted for a few more minutes and when I was happy with the veil and pillbox I said, "Don't you worry. We can have a hurricane and that thing ain't moving!"

Maggie stuck her head back in the door.

"Time to go! The man of your dreams is waiting!"

Henry came in the room with Susan's bouquet, which was, for the record, an armful of ivory roses and greens tied with ivory ribbon.

"I believe it's time to take my sister to the guillotine? Gee, Susan. You look really good. I mean, considering how you *usually* look and all."

"Thanks, jerk," Susan said, "I love you too."

I left to let them have a minute together and found Arthur outside, waiting in the yard.

"All done! The bride's ready! Let's go."

We drove the short distance to the church and parked our cars. The church was lit with candles and the organ was playing something beautiful. We slipped into a pew and sat down. Arthur took my hand and squeezed it.

"I love weddings," Arthur said.

"You do?" *He did?*

"Yeah. What more hopeful act is there than getting married?"

"Can't think of one," I said, "except maybe having children."

The organ music changed then to something classical and we knew it was time. Everyone stood and turned to the back of the church. Beth came up the aisle first. She carried a big bouquet of simple flowers—Gerber daisies of all colors—tied with ribbons of burgundy, cream, and deep green. Her deep green dress was sleeveless. She looked like a Xerox copy of her mother's youth. Next came Maggie, blond and beautiful. In one hand she held her bouquet and she gave little waves and pinches to everyone she knew as she went up the aisle. And suddenly, on the swell of the organ's music, Susan and her brother appeared at the back of the church.

"I swear," I whispered to Arthur, "you could put Cruella De Vil in a wedding dress and I'd still get choked up."

"Look how happy she is!" he said.

We turned and watched her take Simon's arm and the ceremony began. When Father Michaels got to the part about *Do you take this man to be your lawful wedded husband?* Susan said *yes!* so loudly that everybody giggled. In no time at all, Susan and Simon became man and wife and we were all back at the *Island Gamble.*

Somehow, Arthur and I got separated and then I spotted him in the front yard. He was talking to Jack Taylor and Caroline. I was wearing my dress, the *Dress Formerly Known as Skin.* It had the desired effect on Jack and Arthur at the same time. They gulped and Caroline said, "Hey, Anna! How nice to see you!"

There were even flowers on pedestals in the yard! The strings started to play.

"I don't believe it," Caroline said.

They were playing "How Sweet It Is to Be Loved by You," but it didn't sound like James Taylor to me.

"James Taylor wrote this," I said.

"No, he didn't," Arthur said. "Holland-Dozier-Holland wrote it."

"I knew that," I said. "I was just checking to see if you knew!"

Jack, Caroline, and Arthur all looked at me at the same time.

"That's a joke, y'all! Jeesch!"

"That's our music, young lady!"

Their generation was a bunch of know-it-alls.

Susan and Simon came down from the porch and joined their guests. All of a sudden, Simon kissed her and swooped her up and ran down the beach with her in his arms. Then the chamber ensemble began to play "I Feel Good." People started singing the words along with each other, sort of dancing their way to the dunes to watch

Susan and Simon. Even Father Michaels, who had arrived to wish them well, did a little twist.

"*Good God Almighty! Get down!*" I said. "*Get down! It's James Brown! Come to town!*"

Arthur looked at me and then to Jack and Caroline and finally back to me again.

"What is it about you?" he said. "You are just so, I don't know! What? Different! You're just so happy to be alive!"

"Yes. I know." I felt like I could fly. I gave him a kiss on the cheek. "Must be the Geechee in my blood."

"And every time I'm around you, I want to feel like you feel."

"Honey, if there's one thing we got plenty of to go around, it's good feeling."

We stayed until they cut the cake and then we left. It was a wonderful wedding. They were going to Bangkok on their honeymoon. They were excited like children going to Disney World for the first time. Everyone, to the last person, was thrilled for them.

When we got home Arthur said, "You tired?"

"I should be, but I'm not."

"Wanna come to my place?"

"Yeah, but I shouldn't. It's late. David's here this weekend and Emily's out with him. I should, you know, be here."

"And, I don't guess I could stay either, huh?"

"You know that wouldn't be right. Bad example and all that. Scandalize the neighbors and all."

"Anna?"

"Yeah?"

"I don't want to go on spending every night alone, without you in bed next to me."

"So, what do you suggest?"

"I don't know. What do you think I *should* suggest?"

"Arthur, we're back in the fifth grade again."

"Did you see the way that guy Jack was looking at you?"

"No," I lied.

"Well. We're gonna have to figure this out. Christmas is right around the corner and maybe you can think of something you'd like to have. From me, I mean. You know. Something."

I took his face in my hands and kissed him good and then I stood back and said, "Don't worry so much, okay? I love you. We're fine."

"Okay."

I crawled in my bed and placed a piece of Susan's wedding cake that I had put in a Ziploc bag (bugs, you know) under my pillow for good luck. I was dozing until I could hear David's car door close, meaning Emily was back safely.

I rolled over and thought about Arthur. Anna Fisher? It had a nice ring to it, didn't it? We would see. I heard Emily come in and close the door. And, finally, she closed her bedroom door.

It gave me great comfort that I knew the sounds of my own house, but then there were many places in my life in which I could find something good. I knew that I had worked for them, I was thankful for them, but I wasn't ready to give my independence up quite yet.

My thoughts eventually turned to Momma because I was going to say my prayers for her and there was always that part of me that hoped she was watching. I'd been molded of stronger stuff than she was. I had independence, a little money tucked away, and a most useful hammer under my sink. In spite of the fact that she didn't live long enough to explain herself to me, and I imagine that was the only thing I was missing—to hear it in her own words—she had given me a little bit of free spirit and ambition.

Daddy had given me fortitude. Fortitude wasn't nothing. It was huge. I would've withered and died without it. There was a reality about sticking things out for a better day to dawn that was not a cliché, but honest-to-God good advice that we should all weigh and consider.

Miss Angel and Miss Mavis tiptoed across my mind. Those two. They had made me see things differently and from a kinder and more forgiving point of view. And they reminded me of so many important things—that the past carried value and explanations. If my momma had lived, and she had divorced Daddy, which probably should have happened, would Momma have been like them? Would anyone have cared about her? I think I would have.

Oh! Didn't everyone you loved rub off on you a little, leaving a soapy residue of their best self? They *did*. And through them, you might become somebody with your own residue worth leaving around. Although my life would never change the world like Gandhi or somebody like him, I decided my life still had significance. I was just going to keep working on my tiny piece of the planet.

Time would tell about Arthur. Although, I *was* in love with him. Oh, who was I kidding? I was really as far down the rabbit hole with him as Emily was with David and Daddy was with Lucy. Maybe there was something in the water supply.

What was funny about it was that I wasn't afraid. Too much time in my life had been spent being afraid. Worrying. There was no rush. No. No reason to rush anything.

"I'm home, Momma!"

Emily, her tired voice, calling out to me. She said she was *home*. Our home. That alone was enough to carry my spirits for a long while.

"Good, baby! See you in the morning!"

Emily. My girl. Arthur. Crazy wonderful Arthur. Everyone. All of them.

I pulled my covers up around my shoulders, pounded my pillow for the sake of positioning my tired head, and squeezed my eyes shut. For a moment I wondered what the morning would bring, and then . . . then I decided to just let the spirits of the Lowcountry and the Isle of Palms work their legendary magic. Oh, Lord. If I had ever learned anything, I had learned I could rely on that. Yes. I could definitely rely on that. If people only knew about this place . . . But logistically, it was probably a good thing that they didn't. The Isle of Palms wasn't big enough to hold everyone—maybe the rest of the world would have to change a little. It would be such a good world to live in if everyone could just change a little bit. Oh. It wasn't up to me. It wasn't. I was doing my part.

What? Sorry. I nodded off. I was dreaming that it was tomorrow and that you were back in my chair.

Well, these are some of the things I had wanted so badly to tell you. That there were so many things worth the struggle. And that, eventually, even if taking a risk scared the daylights out of you, life would bring risk to you dressed up so fine you'd accept the invitation, even if you didn't know quite how to get where you were supposed to go. It's all about that first step. First you stand up and then you take that first step. It isn't right to live anybody's life except your own.

I can see it all now. Tomorrow you're gonna show up at the salon, desperate to have us blow out your hair for a holiday party. I'll give you a glass of tea or an espresso or something. You and I will run our mouths about the party you're heading to and what you'll be wearing. We'll rehash our lives since the last time we've seen each other and laugh over this and that. Then, you'll get in my chair, I'll do your hair for you, with pleasure, and you'll look in the mirror. Your hair will look fabulous and you'll be happy. And because you always do, you'll probably take a moment to fret about your color and I'll say, No, darlin'. Your roots aren't showing—mine are.

Author's Note

I AM dee-lighted to report that I am the recipient of a ton of friendly email. Mostly they say something like, "I read your last book in two days! When's the next one?" Ahem. Writing takes so much longer than reading that it's not funny. I wish I could write faster and I'm trying to figure out how to do that, but I don't think there's an easy solution. Anybody out there got a clue? Tell me!

Then there are some other questions people ask me over and over again. Reference to the Gullah culture and its language leaves a lot of people baffled. I am no expert in this field and the linguistic experts would probably argue with me on different spellings. I grew up speaking it from the time I could make my first words, that's all. What do I know? In this book I have used quite a few so I offer this little glossary hoping it will help you understand.

GULLAH

Word	*Meaning*	*As in . . .*
ain'	ain't	She ain' chea.
chea	here	She was righ' chea.
chile	child	That chile got a thick head, 'eah?
chillrun	children	All dem chillrun . . .
'eah (also spelled heah, yea', *and* chea)	here; do you agree; ain' it true; *now!*, listen!	He crazy as a bedbug, 'eah?
debbil	devil	Bad as de debbil!
dem	them	Take dem shoes and go home!
fuh	for	Tha's fuh true!
gawd, Lawd	God, Lord	Oh, Gawd! Oh, Lawd!
geechee	someone from the rice plantation area of the Low-country who doesn't need this explanation	
gwine	going	She done gwine home.
shuh	mild slang denoting frustration	Shuh! Not again!
tha's	that's	Tha's all folks.

Now, having offered this in print . . .

    . . . *I know I gwine catch the debbil from all dem folks tha's down in de weeds, jus' waiting on my own self to mess up dis 'eah t'ing. Humph! Ain' easy, chile, trying to bring Lowcountry fuh all He chillrun to see fuh true, 'eah? Shuh. All I be fuh know is dat I been make a Geechee from Gawd's hand. I gone be waiting fuh you, 'eah?*

Anyway, you get the point. There are any number of good books around that will explain the Gullah culture and language at length. It is not an aberration of English nor is it slang. It is one of six Creole languages still spoken in this country. My usage of it is designed only to heighten awareness of yet another distinct feature of the Lowcountry. Gullah is a language of love, taught to little white barefooted island brats like me by loving women descended from slavery. Please use it accordingly.

READERS GUIDE

FOR

Isle of Palms

Discussion Questions

1. Discuss the role of motherhood in the novel, especially how Anna's loss of her own mother at such a young age may have contributed to her own tempestuous relationship with her daughter Emily.

2. Douglas has many difficult relationships with the women in his life: his late wife, his domineering mother, and his daughter. Who is Douglas really and what changes to bring about the giddy happiness he finds with Lucy?

3. How does the setting play a role in the novel, especially Anna's quest to move back to the Isle of Palms? Though just separated by the span of a bridge from Mt. Pleasant, where she lived for years, what makes the Isle of Palms different?

4. Friendship plays an important role in all of Dorothea Benton Frank's novels. In *Isle of Palms*, old friends play an especially important role. Discuss how Jim and Frannie are essential in Anna's life.

5. One of the ironies of Anna's return to the island is that she moves next door to Miss Mavis and Miss Angel who took care of her when her mother died. Have these ladies changed in the intervening years? What does Anna learn from them?

6. How has moving next door to Lucy changed Anna? And not just her daddy's relationship with Lucy. What qualities does Lucy bring to Anna's business and life that completely shakes them?

7. What is the nature of revenge and the power it holds over us? How does Anna deal with the issue of revenge in her life? Does she actively participate at first or is she swept along by the passion of her friends' feelings?

8. The theme of "women recreating their lives" runs through all of Dorothea Benton Frank's novels. How does Anna go about doing this? By the end of the novel do you think she's succeeded and to what extent?